LISTEN HERE!

A Critical Essay on
Music Depreciation

by VERNON DUKE

Ivan Obolensky, Inc.

New York

LISTEN HERE!

A Critical Essay on
Music Depreciation

CONTENTS

CONTENTS

LISTEN HERE!

A Critical Essay on
Music Depreciation

Preamble

This is a book on music depreciation. I doubt that it will start any new trend—music appreciation, a thriving business, being firmly entrenched in this country. Various manuals, textbooks, guides to opera and concert hall, fictionalized or reasonably accurate biographies, with technical terms carefully explained or safely omitted, all tend to help the amateur listener. I have no quarrel with the intent. But assisting, as we do, at the sad spectacle of the Rape of Euterpe, what is there left to appreciate unless one is content with forever restoring the vanished sounds of yesterday?

The truth is that the Sound of Music (and I don't mean the Rodgers-Hammerstein bonbon of that name) is no longer sweet—soothing the savage breast is a pointless pursuit, few breasts being savage these days. Caressing the ear—oh, come now: music isn't synonymous with sex. Music hath charms, yes, if you are capable of drooling over stereo saccharin or singing along with bearded recording tycoons. Tell a young composer that he writes charming music and he'll be ready to slit your throat from ear to ear, ears being useless anyway: he wants the intelligent listener to listen with his brain. Just think of what would have happened if the obstinately charming Francis Poulenc's name had been Frank Poole! Such an outmoded freak would have been the object of merciless ridicule in this country—no "progressive" publisher or conductor would have touched his stuff. Of the Americans, only Barber and, unwittingly, Bernstein display a measure of spontaneous charm; perhaps that is why greatness is denied them by some—to be great, one must be grim. Why? The habitual answer is that we live in grim times, and the arts, music included, must reflect them, not sugar-coat the impending doom of what passes for our civilization. *Après nous le déluge* very possibly, but we are, miraculously, still afloat. Must we drown in a musical morass *before* the general deluge engulfs us? To go on with our cavalcade of clichés, why not fiddle while Rome burns? Do the screeches and blasts of dodecaphonic or "concrete" music accomplish anything or help matters in any way? Ultimate chaos is probably around the corner; let's not turn the corner before our time.

I will be told that there is a surplus of "entertaining" music all over the place. Want an earful? Twist a knob or two. True enough, but 95 per cent of such entertainment consists of countless re-recordings of proven favorites in every musical field, serious or otherwise; or (if it's novelty you're after) assorted aberrations and inanities relished by the pre- and immediately post-puberty groups. To obtain adult musical fare representative of today, written by living composers, you had better repair to such *recherché* stations as WQXR or WNYC in New York or KPFK in Los Angeles. The big radio guns will have none of it unless a new piece is smuggled in as part of a live symphony concert by a dangerously adventurous conductor, or a "new" (to whom?) opera commissioned by NBC's solemnly conservative policy-makers.

Nothing could be more pitiful or tedious than the penchant demonstrated by formerly avant-garde composers now past fifty (and I am fifty-nine!), gradually pushed into an uncomfortable back seat by the present fashion dictators, for dipping their pens in vitriol and lambasting the production of their enterprising juniors. Spohr, Saint-Saëns, Glazunov, Rimsky-Korsakov, Cui, Rachmaninoff, Medtner—all considered dangerous radicals at their beginnings (a piquant aside: Cui thought Medtner, yes, Medtner, a futurist!)—didn't do their own music any good by crotchety condemnation of "revolutionary upstarts" who protested too much and too eloquently and succeeded in silencing the tired voices of the older men. The opposite is true in my case; I have always rejoiced in anything truly new, truly upsetting, truly *"bouleversant."* I could never share the enthusiasm of dedicated comparisonists for a great performance of a familiar work. Phrases like: "X really made me see Mozart in a new light," or "Isn't it miraculous what Y does to Beethoven?" or, worst of all, "You haven't lived until you've heard Z's Brahms" are incomprehensible to me and, therefore, profoundly irritating. If you know your Mozart, Beethoven, and Brahms, as every music aficionado should, the best you can hope for from X and Y and Z is that they live up to the composer's own concept of his work and execute it beautifully. Thus, the only *real* excitement I know of in listening to music is the spine-tingling discovery of a vital, inevitable, really and unmistakably *new* piece. Its being new, however, is not enough. The piece must have the kind of vitality or inevitability that will make its presence felt instantly. If the listener, after the initial twenty bars, say, wearily asks himself; "Why should it go on *this* way, when the *other* way might have done just as well?"—my advice to him is: Stop listening; the music isn't worth it.

That's precisely what I deplore in the utterances of the would-be *young* generation: the only too readily discernible absence of youth, of daring, the impotent conformism of the puffed-up nonconformist. Note that the reactionaries—Glazunov, Cui, and Medtner—were shocked to the core by the buoyant athletic vigor, the brute force of such upstarts as Prokofiev and Hindemith. Would that my younger contemporaries could shock me! Boulez, Stockhausen & Co. do make a tremendous amount of journalistic noise, but the noises they make in the concert hall are more of a sedative than a stimulant.

And don't soothe me with statistics, with jubilant accounts of increased attendance, more orchestras, more recording companies, greater opportunities for the young; don't placate me with platitudes anent "the organic growth of our music," "communities demanding music," and the like. Music? What we are getting today is a palpable substitute: *ersatz* in the fullest sense of the word, and it is so in every field where this margarine—*almost* as good as the *real* spread—is used. The substitute is overproduced by too many composers, most of whom have no business composing, worthy citizens though they may be. Too many recordings are issued daily of ephemera, the kind whose first performance in the concert hall is also its last. The so-called "serious" stuff written today is in too many instances unlistenable, unpalatable, and also unperformable, because of its absurd and unnecessary difficulty. It is also hopelessly old-fashioned, in spite of the novel tags with which its manufacturers adorn it. In the twelve (tone series) apostles' own confession, they employ the "pointillist" method which, as every art lover knows, was invented by Seurat, the *fin de siècle* impressionist. I will later endeavor to show that the entire post-Webern, Boulez- and Stockhausen-led movement is nothing more than a cunningly camouflaged, escapist return to impressionism; like scared ostriches, our apostles (and Webern was their Christ) bury their heads in the sands of tedium, the better to escape life, which, admittedly, is not as pleasant as it once was. Equally old-fashioned is the utterly unmusical idiom in which the contemporary popular song is written; the awkward wedding of Grandpa's vaudeville shuffle and tap beats to the nasally (not throatily) produced yokels' yodels was let loose on the gullible teen-agers shortly after World War II. The unholy mélange rocked their world—idyllic no longer—by rolling them in the aisles. Rock 'n' Roll was born.

Why insist on real music when so many assembly-line substitutes are available? Go to the movies; the feature will be accompanied by impressive sounds, scary and treacly by turn, borrowed from the Masters in public domain and subtly disguised as the film composer's own. Mr. Dimitri Tiomkin was honest enough to give thanks to the classics, who enabled him to receive the Academy Award in Hollywood. Stay-at-homes, turn on your TV; regale yourself with the "progressive" bleating and blaring that intensifies the horror of gory murder yarns; tune in on a Variety Show featuring "name" singers who shun progress by sticking to "standards," properly embellished and improperly toyed with; or saturate yourself with celestial strains that help sell deodorants. How about a live concert? Not much life there: you have your choice of oldies, or a yawn-provoking "newie" that, with luck, will never be heard again. Would you rather see a musical play? *See* it you will—what you'll *hear* is another story. It's not likely to be music—not the kind that stays with you, moves you, enriches you in any way. Bright, smart, dazzling sounds, yes. Music, no. We will eventually awaken to the fact that the musical tastes of the nation are being dictated by non-musicians: radio and TV bosses, commercial producers, performers, publishers—and the prosperous holders of previously nonexistent offices, who bear the strange titles of "A. & R. men" and "disk jockeys."

In the serious music field, no one has ever dared accuse the concert managers of any excessive preoccupation with musical progress—*names* are what they buy and sell, not *music*. Conductors and virtuosi of renown cannot maintain their box-office strength without sticking to gilt-edged securities. All new material, good and bad, being notoriously insecure, they are leery about investing in it, and who is to blame them? By whose standards is a new piece judged to be worthy of a performance today? Lastly, no matter how great the need, who needs *more* music when the safe, the time-tested, box-office-proven kind has already been written?

This organized chaos may or may not have been caused by the gradual but inevitable decay of European civilization. American civilization is of so recent a vintage that one hopes it will give itself a chance to blossom before rotting away. Thus, while the serial-row stranglehold does mirror the sad decline of the countries where it originated (Austria and Germany) and while France and Italy, having followed suit and adopted the sterile teachings of Webern and his disciples, may be historically justifiable, what are we Americans doing "*dans cette galère?*" Are we, the newcomers, satisfied to find ourselves in the same boat with the drowning elders, without any reason for being there?

Our present troubles were, obviously, hinted at in a prophetic dream that haunted Thomas Weelkes, whose first book of Madrigals was printed in 1597. "For originality of ideas and ingenuity in part-writing, Weelkes, in my opinion, leaves all the other composers of his time far behind," stated learned Thomas Oliphant in his 1837 *Musa Madrigalesca*. Weelkes called music "a sick man's jewel," and admonished:

> "Lads, merry be with music sweet;
> And, *fairies*, trip it with your feet."

Trip it they did. Weelkes further predicted the advent of the Disk Jockey (four centuries ago!) and the boredom of his radio program in one immortal line: "Jockey, thy horn-pipe's dull." The clairvoyant madrigalist can also lay claim to having invented the jazz jargon: the lines, following the one about the jockey, read:

> "Give wind, *man*, at full;
> Fie upon such a sad gull,
> Like an hoody doody
> All too moody.
>   Tootle tootle."

The stuff is in public domain, fellows; help yourselves. The current American greeting, "Hi," has also been invented by Weelkes. "Ty hye, ty hye!" he pipes in a madrigal, while Oliphant elucidates: "A sort of chuckling, ironical exclamation."

That America's musical voice was not really heard until after World War I is factually true; important claims have been made for Billings, the "fuguing" tanner; Gottschalk, the Louisiana Chopin; for Charles Ives, the pioneer-music-making industrialist, and one or two others. The Americanisms of Billings and Gottschalk, touching and gratifying to their compatriots, rather like Grandma Moses's landscapes, were not of the decisive, instantly recognizable stamp that alone can create interest in a new country's product and make it exportable. Ives deserved energetic exploitation, but didn't get it. Scoff if you must, but the first U. S.-made musical article to gain universal exposure was George Gershwin's *Rhapsody in Blue*—and that did not appear until 1924.

American music—serious and light both—has made gigantic strides in the thirty-nine years that have followed the birth of the much maligned or unduly admired *Rhapsody*. We now have a true Voice of America—in music as well as political radio propaganda; will this voice be allowed to grow and strengthen and mellow, or will it be reduced to the tomcatting wails of a cretin with sideburns or the impotent cacklings of a Europe-worshiping eunuch? This is entirely up to us—composers, performers, educators, critics, and plain listeners. America always needed music, and got the best the old country had to offer before finding that she could supply her own, home-grown variety. The question is: Are we to remain smugly content with music being brought to The New World —or are we determined to create a New World in Music?

CHAPTER

I

The Unpromising Beginnings

Should you ask an average civilized European or South American whether he knows and likes U.S. music, he will assure you that he loves jazz—the two being synonymous to him. Apply a little pressure and he may volunteer added approvals of *Porgy and Bess*, Gershwin in general, the immortal *No, No, Nanette*, certainly, and Bernstein's more recent sensation, *West Side Story*, just possibly. "What about our serious music?" you'd persevere. Try as he might, our knowledgeable foreigner is sure to be stumped by this. A shrug will ensue, then a final admission of defeat: We might as well make an admission, too—not a single work by an American, living or dead, Gershwin excepted, has become a staple of concert or opera repertoire abroad.

There is nothing catastrophic about the situation. Music as young as ours cannot be expected to make a sizable imprint on the well-worn yet durable fabric of the musical body of the Old World. Considering our foolish youth, we've done wonderfully well. This country can boast a top-notch symphonist in the person of Walter Piston (with Prokofiev's death, I don't know of anyone writing better symphonies), a superb chamber music craftsman such as Elliott Carter, a magician of the *lied*—the late Theodore Chanler, and several able opera composers—Douglas Moore and Carlisle Floyd, to name two. Though I would hesitate to classify Gian Carlo Menotti as an American composer, he owes both his musical education and his operatic triumphs to this country. Then we have less easily pigeonholeable but no less significant figures such as Copland, Harris, Schuman, and Cowell—crafty jugglers of Americana all; trenchant and stimulating Leonard Bernstein; the late Wallingford Riegger, an uncompromising individualist; Sessions, the purist; and the lyrical and listenable Samuel Barber who, with Bernstein and Menotti, comes nearest to having gained a measure of universal acclaim. Bowles, Diamond, Fine (who died in 1962), Shapero, Mennin, Kirchner, and not a few others have turned out some very good things, and if I leave out composers of foreign birth it's only because I feel that their European background and beginnings make them atypical of current U.S. trends. Such a list, to vary a mildewed bromide, is something to shake even the most hardened conductor's stick at.

Some commentators talked of American Renaissance; "naissance" would be more apt—how can you claim rebirth when you were barely born but yesterday? To me, the thirty years from 1924 to 1954, say, were the good years in American music. The productivity of our better men in that period was truly prodigious, the quality of their product almost uniformly high, the public interest at least encouraging. Before getting down to the present impasse, I would like to trace briefly the story of this country's musical growth that led to the mid-century boom.

"O ecstatic! Rush on, you sons of harmony," exclaimed William Billings (1746–1800), the tanner, erroneously considered by some as the first of the native composers. The sons of harmony were in no rush—and their ecstasy upon hearing Billings's would-be fugues was so moderate that, in the words of Louis C. Elson (*The History of American Music*, New York, 1904), the composer "suffered poverty almost constantly." No wonder the first chapter of the still earlier *Music in America*, by the Alsace-born Dr. F. L. Ritter (New York, 1883) is lugubriously styled "Low State of Musical Culture." Since, in pre-Billings days, "both Pilgrims and Puritans united in a distrust of music" (Elson), we'll leave these respectable but obviously tin-eared parties strictly alone. Billings enthusiasts' claims to his being the first composing pioneer on these shores are not substantiated—the omniscient Benjamin Franklin, born forty years before Billings, was known to write about music, play the guitar and the harp, invent the oddly named Glassychord (a glass harmonica which Mozart later employed in his Quintet for harmonica, flute, oboe, viola, and cello), and do a little composing. I saw a published (Paris, 1946) copy of a quartet for three violins and a cello in five movements, signed Benjamin Franklin, at the Yale Music Library. The music is written for open strings only, and is of the greatest harmonic simplicity, not to say poverty, imaginable. Gilbert Chase, whose *America's Music* (1955) far surpasses all previous histories, although one seldom agrees with Mr. Chase's pronouncements, warns us that: "The manuscript is not in Franklin's hand, nor is there any further evidence to substantiate his authorship of this string quartet, which has been called (By whom? V.D.) a mathematical Tour de Force."

Because of the vagueness surrounding Franklin's composing activities, it would perhaps be more correct to transfer the title of the first U.S. Music Creator to Francis Hopkinson (1737–1791); at any rate, Grove's Dictionary states that his song, "My Days Have Been So Wondrous Free" (1759) was "the first piece of secular music produced in America." Neither Ritter nor Elson had ever heard of Hopkinson, one of the signers of the Declaration of Independence and a member of the Convention that framed the United States Constitution. Evidently, his notoriety as a "son of harmony" prejudiced his unmusical contemporaries and was responsible for the man's speedy oblivion.

As for the humble tanner, he has been quite the fashion for some time now (Hopkinson, too, has his learned partisans) and with good cause. There is a pungent savor to Billings's awkward music; such awkwardness bespeaks the loose-limbed, gangling, sheepishly grinning American. The familiar national characteristics are all present in the tuneful "Chester," the quaintly charming "The Bird," the gnarled, crudely unfugue-like fugues. Does it matter that, to Billings, "a Single Fugue or Imitation is when Parts imitate one another: A Double Fugue is when two or several Points or Fugues fall in, one after the other?" It does. It makes one's heart go out to the self-taught composer.

Billings was a purely local figure, and his technical limitations precluded any lasting impact on the development of American music or any real influence on younger composers. In fact, if you accept Dr. Ritter's testimony, "the opposition to the ludicrous, unsymmetrical 'fuguing' pieces of Billings . . . became so great that the compilers of psalm tune collections went so far as to exclude *all tunes written by American composers.*" Although not in the "genteel tradition," rightly scoffed at by Chase, Billings's hymn tunes, carols, and anthems hardly qualify him as the true "bard of the folk" (Chase); still, he was instinctively closer to folk sources than Lowell Mason or Thomas Hastings, sacred-music specialists, both born at the close of the eighteenth century, both scrupulously genteel. That the real core of American music is in its abundantly fecund and varied folklore cannot be denied; that the folk sources were unexplored or rigorously soft-pedaled throughout the nineteenth century is equally true. Revivalists, Shakers, Negro spirituals' exponents, Ethiopian minstrels, Creole dancers and singers went on lifting their voices in song, their feet in dance, happily oblivious of pedantic Pharisees who affected to ignore their existence.

The honor of fearlessly drawing on the multifarious folk sources of his country fell to a Pennsylvania farmer's son— Stephen Collins Foster (1826-1864). In a letter to E. P. Christy, written when he was twenty-six, Foster confessed his ambition to establish his name "as the best Ethiopian songwriter." He did better than that by becoming America's Minstrel. What is there to be said about Foster? "He touched the hearts of his fellow countrymen as few, or no others, have ever done before" (Richard Aldrich) about sums it up. Some of Foster's songs have been, and probably still are, considered as genuine folk songs. Although his opening gun was a waltz for four flutes, he was first and last a songsmith, not what is generally known as a "legitimate composer" (a horrid and inaccurate term). Legitimate or otherwise, Foster and his antipode, Gottschalk (the only common denominator being their predilection for folk sources), were both miniaturists, having neither the necessary technique (which is especially true of Foster) nor the inclination to essay larger forms. Foster's pet vehicle was the song, Gottschalk's, the *morceau de salon.*

Louis Moreau Gottschalk (1829–1869), the son of an English father and a French mother, born in New Orleans, did write a symphony entitled *La Nuit des Tropiques*, but, judging from the excerpts I saw and heard, this was about as closely related to a full-scale symphony as a Billings fuguing song was to an honest-to-goodness fugue. Gottschalk was an indolent dandy, a dispenser of pianistic aphrodisiacs, an elegant *flâneur*—the consummate man of fashion, in short. When he appeared in New England a local music critic "devoted a whole column to his kid gloves, another to his handsome appearance and French manners." (Gottschalk, *Notes of a Pianist*). His views on music must have seemed as uncomfortably foreign as his dandified airs. "Music is a thing eminently sensuous," said he. "I have a horror of musical Puritans...they must find in music the stiff and the starched gait which they like in themselves. This is the reason of their rage for oratorios. They discover an air of great respectability in this music, which they do not understand, but which they listen to with comic gravity." Exasperated by the local Philistines, he exclaimed, somewhat rhetorically: "The form! O pagans of art! When will the time come, routine fetish worshippers, when you will have the courage or the talent to avow that there is more genius in the pretty waltzes of Strauss than in five hundred pages of schoolwork?" (This was in 1863 —just a hundred years ago, yet it could have been written about certain fetishists of our day.) The outburst comes to a halt with this puzzling statement: "Beethoven and Liszt have contributed to the advent of long hair."

On the other hand, our longhair hater was a self-confessed snob. Appearing at a concert in Stamford, Connecticut, he "perceived on the wall of the artist's salon the ornamental signatures of musical celebrities who have preceded me. Sam Something, 'the best dancer in wooden shoes in the whole world,' Charley Such-a-One, 'a first-rate drummer who can't be beat.' There are anomalies in the credulity of Americans which proceed less from a bad disposition than from candid ignorance."

Gottschalk, the *"beau ideal,"* "our first matinee idol," the "white-gloved *poseur"* (John Tasker Howard, *Our American Music*, 1929), "first made his mark through his arrangement of Creole Melodies" (William Mason). "The Banjo," "Bamboula," and "Le Bananier" still possess a tropic-scented fascination for the listener; but to conjecture that "Gottschalk might have been the Glinka of America's music under more favorable circumstances," as Gilbert Chase does, is going too

far. Although an American patriot (on occasion), the New
Orleans composer did not choose to strengthen or intensify
his Americanism in the course of his career: his two unper-
formed operas, *Charles IX*, and *Isaura de Salerno*, his *Escenas
Campestres Cubanas* were not America-inspired; the countless sentimental trifles, wherein Thalbergian tremolos and
Herzian trills were employed for the sole sake of effect, are
hardly distinguishable from similar *"pièces d'occasion"* supplied by assiduous *"salonards"* of his day, and pay no obeisance
to the country of his origin.

It may be pertinent to point out the striking similarity in
the musical beginnings of the two great countries that today
hold the balance of the world's fate—the United States of
America and Russia. Secular native music was, too, virtually
nonexistent in Russia in the eighteenth century, should one
discount the Bologna-trained Evstigney Fomin (1741 or 1761,
according to Baker's Dictionary—1800), composer of three
popular "operas"—*Miller, Wizard, Cheat and Marriage Broker,
Aniouta,* and . . . *The Americans!* Although ignored by Fétis,
Grove's and Groot (*A Short History of Opera,* 1947), who dismisses all eighteenth-century operatic efforts in Russia as
"amateur affairs of no importance," Fomin had the "unques-
tionable right to the title of Russia's first national composer"
(Karatygin). He was also the first composer who chose an
"American" (American-Indian, to be precise) subject for an
opera—years before native Americans saw fit to experiment
with the possibility.

Just as they did in Russia, native composers began to sprout
in the United States in the first half of the succeeding century.
There was this signal difference: The Russians got off to a
portentous start with full-scale operas (Glinka and Dargomijsky); the Americans made their first mark with hymns,
quasi-folk songs and showy piano pieces (Billings, Foster,

Gottschalk). Glinka's pioneering brought about a rich "*floraison*" of significant and authentically national opera (Moussorgsky, Borodin, Rimsky-Korsakov, Tchaikovsky), just as the older master's orchestral fireworks pointed the way to symphonic production in Balakirev, Borodin, and the more cosmopolitan and eclectic Tchaikovsky. No such splendid and sudden flowering occurred in the States; the wedding of folk-source material and the hallowed traditions of opera and symphony was considered "bad form," shockingly vulgar, therefore unthinkable. It is in vain that the overly eager Chase likens not only Gottschalk but even the obviously mediocre, albeit ambitious and articulate William Henry Fry (1813-1864) to Glinka. Clearly, neither man merited such a comparison. Neither Fry nor his contemporary, George Frederick Bristow (1825–1898), had the right stuff in them, although they tried hard enough.

Bristow wrote four symphonies (one of them revived in New York by Richard Korn recently) and a fleetingly successful opera, *Rip Van Winkle* (1855), which outshone Fry's *Leonora*, produced ten years earlier, thus earning the title of the first American opera. If Fry was no Glinka, Bristow was no Dargomijsky; when excerpts from *Leonora* were given in 1929, Herbert Peyser of the New York *Telegram* said "the music played sedulous ape to Bellini, Donizetti and Auber." *Rip Van Winkle's* last revival was in 1870—and, judging from press comments, it was not overloaded with originality, nor even the mildest Yankee characteristics, either. It's all very well to call for a Declaration of Independence in Art on the part of American composers, as Fry did, when you have something to declare. Alas! All he and Bristow could account for was a tired bag of tricks, smuggled in from Europe.

Fry is the subject of a 1954 monograph by W. T. Upton, who tells us that his *Santa Claus Symphony* (1853) was enormously popular. Fry's brother, Horace, says it was performed by Jullien's orchestra some forty-odd times, both in New York and on tour. But he reveals that it was also "held up to scorn by Willis, Dwight and others"—then proceeds to "align himself with Fry against his critics" while somewhat condoning ("in view of so many really good passages") the too exuberant realism of the sleigh bells and the cracking whip. The two "really good" passages cited in Upton's book suggest Donizetti or Mercadante rather than Santa Claus, American-style. The other two "symphonies" cannot be considered as such, the *Niagara's* score consisting of twelve pages, *Hagar in the Wilderness* of fourteen. Fry also wrote ten string quartets and such scarcely American productions as his second opera, *Notre Dame de Paris*, and a Stabat Mater.

The plain people, as early as in the eighteen thirties, began to weary of the "highbrow" fare, and would settle for home-grown goods any time. When a small theatrical band attempted to play a portion of a Haydn symphony, the "gods" in the gallery cried out: "Stop that noise! Give us 'Washington's March' or 'Yankee Doodle'!" About the same time, Daniel Schlesinger, a Hamburg-born pianist, played Hummel's concerto in New York, and his own *Variations on American National Airs,* the latter received with deafening applause. Ignoring these symptoms, our composers went on "musicking" in the Milan- (opera) or Leipzig- (symphony) approved fashion.

Discounting Bristow's four attempts and Fry's one full-scale effort, the building of symphonies fell into reasonably capable hands. John Knowles Paine (1839–1906) wrote two such— the Second (*Spring*) Symphony given at Boston in 1880, being received with "unprecedented enthusiasm" (Chase). Characteristically, Chase regards this production as an echo of "current clichés of German post-romanticism." The first subject of the *Spring Symphony,* "Winter," is reproduced in Chase's book and, paraphrasing the author, we "may well wonder what all the carping was about." The "Winter" subject, even unharmonized, is uncommonly attractive and makes one want to examine the rest of the "cliché-ridden" score. As a matter of fact, Paine was more than just a dexterous craftsman (his String Quartet is a good sample of his deftness), and lacked only that indefinable something that enables one to break fresh paths, rather than re-explore the well-trodden ones.

In another genre, both *St. Peter* (an oratorio—therefore taboo to contemporary Gottschalks) and the unproduced opera, *Azara*, are laced with melodious lilts that so horrified Rupert Hughes when he caught one in Paine's music for Sophocles's *Oedipus Tyrannus*. They give lie to Chase's assertion that "as our leading academic composer, Paine seldom succumbed to the temptation of writing catchy tunes." Apparently, to Chase, only birds of exotic plumage or folk bards are capable of inventing a melody.

It must, however be admitted that neither Paine nor the better-known Boston sages—Foote and Chadwick—were composers of real importance: Their Americanism, when present —and that, not often—was only skin-deep. As late as 1930, another "routine fetish worshiper," in Gottschalk's phrase, Daniel Gregory Mason, trying to whitewash his own and his spiritual fathers' failure to wave the American flag in their music, declared: "America is . . . made up of endless races, groups, classes, points of view. From such a melting pot it is not easy to distill artistic clarity, and it seems hardly likely that there will ever be an 'American School' in the sense that there is a French School, or a Russian, or an English." The trouble lay not with the melting pot (which is even more many-faceted in Russia) but with the distillers: They simply had no faith in folklore as the basis for a national music, nor enough talent to dispense successfully with the people's song as a prop, and sing out on their own, unshackled and unafraid. Arthur Foote's only hesitant excursion into the native lore was the 1883 *Farewell to Hiawatha.* George Chadwick preferred to pay musical tribute to Thalia, Melpomene, Euterpe, Adonis, Cleopatra, Aphrodite (How un-Bostonian!), lovely Rosabelle and the Lily Nymph, rather than bother with ill-mannered Indians or Ethiopians.

Did Foote and Chadwick reflect the tastes of their country? No, indeed—because, in common with most professors, both were bent on dictating, not reflecting them. Russell Lynes, a shrewd observer, tells us in *The Tastemakers* (Harper & Brothers, 1955) that "after the Civil War . . . The North was full of song and gaiety. Returned American expatriates heard Negro melodies and ballads in the streets. "Minstrel" shows packed nightly crowds into the 'opera houses' and . . . banjo solos, clog dances and Mr. Bones delighted the multitudes. There was singing everywhere." Shutting their windows, the Boston savants went back to their schoolroom exercises.

John F. Porte's 1922 biography of the most acclaimed American composer of the past century—Edward MacDowell— bears two gladsome quotes preceding the title page and used in lieu of epigraphs: "What a musician! He is sincere and personal—What a poet—what exquisite harmonies." The accolade was signed Jules Massenet. Edvard Grieg supplied an even better reference: "I consider MacDowell the ideally endowed composer," said he. The committee, formed to appoint a professor for the newly founded department of music at Columbia, pronounced MacDowell "the greatest musical genius America has produced." A pupil of Joachim Raff, MacDowell in his *lernerjahre* succeeded in impressing the musical *arbiter elegantiarum* of Europe—Franz Liszt. After hearing the youth's first piano concerto, Liszt turned to Eugene d'Albert, his most promising pupil, and warned him: "You must bestir yourself, if you do not wish to be outdone by our young American!" The American's teacher,

Raff, chimed in with: "Your music, Herr MacDowell, will be
played when mine is forgotten."

No American ever garnered such verbal bouquets before
MacDowell; few, if any, garner them today. Europeans are
still persuaded that Americans turn out better automobiles
than concertos. Or, as the director of the Paris Opéra said
to William Henry Fry when the latter approached him about
producing *Leonora*: "In Europe we look upon America as an
industrial country—excellent for electric telegraphs, but not
for art." What was it, then, that interested Liszt in the young
New Yorker's music? One would like to think that, having
been enraptured with the "barbaric" Russianisms of a Borodin
(whom the Master befriended in 1877), Liszt discovered an
equally barbaric New World strain in the American neophyte.
Not so, I'm afraid. MacDowell was firmly against all nationalism in music, as can be seen in this excerpt from his writings:
"So-called Russian, Bohemian, or any other purely national
music has no place in art, for its characteristics may be dupli-
cated by anyone [!] who takes the fancy to do so . . . We have,
here in America, been offered a pattern for an 'American'
national musical costume by the Bohemian Dvořák—though
what the Negro melodies have to do with Americanism in art
still remains a mystery." This would have made an odd preface
to his own Indian Suite, wherein MacDowell strove to express
"the manly and free rudeness of the North American Indian."
Why was the Indian more worthy of musicalizing than the
Negro, one may well ask? "The American Indian has never
been essentially musical," Louis C. Elson testified in *The
National Music of America*. "The Indian themes have no
especial inspiration beyond the music of the rest of the savage
[!] world. Yet Mr. MacDowell has . . . brought forth an Indian
Suite for orchestra," preferring the "not especially inspired"
Indian tunes to the wonderful Negro ones, no doubt. And
he was not even a Southerner! Even the ultra-conservative

Dr. Ritter allowed that "the colored man has a rich store of original, melodic motives and forms that compare favorably with many collections of people's songs among the European races." Hamlin Garland, American novelist and essayist, whom Wallace Stegner thought "forerunner of the many writers who now profess cultural regionalism as a literary creed," and who got a rare accolade from Granville Hicks, who said: "Garland wrote some of the finest fiction we have—direct, comprehensive, moving and savagely honest," met MacDowell in 1888 and had a most interesting discussion with the composer as regards American music. In his *Roadside Meetings*, Garland thus quotes MacDowell; "I don't believe in 'lifting' a Navajo theme, enfurbishing it into some kind of a musical composition. That is not American music. Our problem is not so simple as all that. A national music cannot be found in the songs of Reds or Blacks." He added, however, somewhat lamely; "Some day, when you and I are old, there will be an American School of music as well as of fiction."

Thus, in spite of the weakly hopeful conclusion, MacDowell, too, missed the boat. Lawrence Gilman (*Edward MacDowell, a Study*, 1908) quite accurately opines that "in its general aspect his music is not German, or French, or Italian—its spiritual antecedents are Northern, both Celtic and Scandinavian." Everything Northern, in other words, except North American.

MacDowell's music was successful for a spell; perhaps because of its curiously spineless eclecticism, it was not long for this world. Chase asserts that "to the present generation, MacDowell's name is more familiar than his music"; even forty-one years ago (1922) "the sentimental element, which in every young American ought to be called the MacDowellesque, had been warred on" (Paul Rosenfeld). The piano concertos and sonatas, rewarding in their way, are too full of old-hat fustian; the shorter pieces, those depicting New England, for instance, have the tear-making *sehnsucht* of faded daguerreo-types but very little warmth or freshness; the songs are overly sweet. "MacDowell minces and simpers, maidenly and ruffled. He is nothing if not a Daughter of the American Revolution" (Rosenfeld). There was also a vexing harmonic insecurity in MacDowell's musical language, resulting in clumsy voice-leading and pointless modulations that don't really "modulate"; a convincing example can be found in the third movement of the *Sonata Eroica*, marked "tenderly, longingly, *yet* with passion" (*and* without logic, one is tempted to add). We know that the composer labored arduously in academic Ger-many, but "was badly equipped in polyphonic technique" (Rosenfeld).

Yet MacDowell possessed a real power of communication; and, if he did not qualify as a sorely needed Glinka, he should go down in posterity as the American Anton Rubinstein—the two of them talented epigones, producers of watery concertos, respectable romantics, Leipzig-oriented professors. Rubinstein was overshadowed by the bold entrance of the "Mighty Five" and their equally mighty champion and apologist, Stasov; no such concerted might appeared in the States to dethrone MacDowell, while the critics indulged in what may be called, by stretching a point, un-American activities, scoffing at the dormant riches of folk music and keeping America safe for autocracy—the German kind.

MacDowell found a soul mate in the present century in the coy and capricious person of Mr. Virgil Thomson, of all people. Thomson thought highly of MacDowell as a com-poser. (This was in 1944, and he may have changed his mind.) After listing such "great masters of genre painting in music as Couperin, Mendelssohn, Schumann, Debussy, Grieg, Smet-ana and possibly [?] Albéniz and Villa-Lobos"—the strangest assortment of names I ever beheld—Thomson declares that "MacDowell might well rank with these last if he had access to a body of folklore comparable in extent to theirs," which, of course, is the sheerest nonsense. MacDowell *did* have access to folklore but, as the reader gathered from earlier paragraphs, had no use for it. Nothing daunted, Thomson goes on to inform us that MacDowell "borrowed more from German sources than he would have liked," the meaning of which is unclear to me. While admitting that MacDowell "did not leave his mark on music as a stylist," the critic triumphantly avers: "No other American composer has painted a wild rose or an iceberg, a water lily or a deserted farmhouse so neatly." I am not familiar with this sort of "genre painting" on the part of "other" composers, and I suspect that Thomson's assertion is gratuitous, since no basis for comparison exists: "Other" men had a tougher job on their hands than depicting icebergs or deserted farmhouses.

Thomson praised things other than wild roses and water lilies in MacDowell's music, and justifiably so; but, when he echoes the German-trained professor's views on the *raison d'être* of native music—and as recently as 1948 (in *Music Right and Left*), one can only marvel at Thomson's reputation as our most brilliant, perceptive and—worst of all—influential critic. "There is no such thing as an American style," Thomson pontificates in the same volume. "Nobody becomes an American composer by thinking about America while composing [An iceberg would be healthier thinking, one surmises. V.D.], and any Americanism worth bothering about is everybody's property anyway." Lord help our composers if they are still influenced by MacDowell's and Thomson's practically identical dicta.

Returning to the past century, "what we really needed was some American music to which no European master of composition could sign his name and get away with it. This the Boston classicists were incapable of giving us" (Chase)—even the technically adroit and resourceful Horatio Parker (1863–1919). Our two leading exponents of the America-at-All-Costs musical creed, Rosenfeld and Chase, are in complete disagreement as regards Parker's status. *Hora Novissima,* Parker's best cantata, is "one of the few successors of Beethoven's loftily pitched 'Solemn Mass,'" to Rosenfeld; a "rather disconcerting hodge-podge of influences" to Chase. With disarming candor he admits, in the preface to *America's Music*: "I prefer 'Beale Street Blues' to *Hora Novissima.*" The two commentators' difference of opinion is even more acute when they come to grips with Parker's *Mona,* which won the Metropolitan Opera's $10,000 prize for the best opera written by an American (1912, but essentially a nineteenth-century product). "That it contains some well-written academic music is undeniable, but this does not establish it as a viable dramatic work for the lyric theatre," Chase opines; while to Rosenfeld, "*Mona* ranks with *Salome, Pelléas* [!], *Sette Canzoni* and other notable post-Wagnerian operas . . . certainly the high mark of American music up to the most recent time."

In one respect only do the two writers resort to a similar procedure—that stemming from their determination to bracket any American figure of their choice with Russia's one and only Glinka. Chase, as we saw, had two near-Glinkas up his sleeve—Gottschalk and Fry; Rosenfeld, in all seriousness, added a third—Horatio Parker. "Parker's roots seem to have been half in the Protestant hymnology and half in the classic European music, *just as* [?] Glinka's were half in Russian folk song and half in eighteenth-century opera," said he. Perceive that Protestant hymnology and Russian folk song were horses of the same nationalistic color to Rosenfeld; but the American public and the Met's bosses knew better—and the "high mark of American music" has not been revived to date.

Horatio Parker, a civilized and skilled musician, imparted far higher technical gloss to his product than did MacDowell, yet his music, rooted as it was in a "hodge-podge of influences" from Palestrina to Vincent d'Indy, lacked MacDowell's directness and spontaneity. Parker had a capacity for winning important prizes but did not become a truly popular composer.

No other nineteenth-century luminaries need detain us unduly: Not Charles Martin Loeffler (1861–1935), an agreeable Alsatian impressionist of the second class, whose Americanism was about as authentic as *paté de Strasbourg,* but whom the late Carl Engel proclaimed the greatest of American composers; not such determined cultivators of the Victorian aspidistra and inventors of the deadly "Town Hall Ballad" as Ethelbert Nevin and Charles Wakefield Cadman; not the innocuous and colorless Edgar Stillman Kelley, who delivered himself of a "New England Symphony" complete with bird notes, Indian songs, and Puritan psalm tunes but devoid of music; nor yet the tight-lipped and strait-laced Daniel Gregory Mason, who knew how to swing a mean paragraph, but whose well-tailored pieces were stillborn; not even genuinely poetic and sensitive Sidney Lanier (1842–1881), to whom Gilbert Chase devoted five heartfelt pages.

A sympathetic and touching figure, this poet-flutist-composer, who died at thirty-nine, a victim of tuberculosis, may have been "a stifled genius," but the extreme slimness of his output—practically unobtainable and still unrecorded!—hardly qualifies Lanier for the title of "the most magnificent and tragic failure in the annals of American music" (Chase). Ironically, the poet-musician was better known as other musicians' poet, Chadwick's setting of Lanier's "Ballad of Trees and the Master" "ranking as a classic" (Howard). Sugary Dudley Buck's "Centennial Meditation of Columbus," performed under Theodore Thomas in 1876, also had words by Lanier.

A passion for "firsts" is the conductor's self-inflicted malady —also the music commentator's; each of them has his special candidate for firstness—*the* founder of this or that, *the* first authentic composer, *the* first and greatest failure, and so on. An overly eager exponent of this tiresome method, Alice Fletcher, hastened to honor poor Lanier with two such titles: She declared that the poet-musician "was not only the founder of a school of music, but the *founder of American music*"—the fourth would-be Glinka, in other words. To Edward Mims, "one of Lanier's best biographers," according to Chase, "it is unfortunate that Lanier left no compositions to indicate a musical power sufficient to give him a place in the history of American music." Why the *grand tapage*, then? After a dozen efforts, I finally chanced upon one solitary *morceau* from Lanier's pen: a pleasant enough but distinctly amateurish piece for flute solo. Possibly, the elements of greatness are discovered in his longer works—but I had to give up bothering Lanierites and so must regretfully abstain from passing judgment on music to which I have had no access. The curator of the Lanier collection at Johns Hopkins was on an extended vacation at the time this book went to press.

I will end this joyless chapter on an optimistic note: Charles Ives, the *first* (The malady is contagious, as you see) really original and unmistakably American voice of the nineteenth century, was born in 1874, and one can say with some justification that, looking back on Ives's achievements, "America Was Promises" (to crib from Archibald MacLeish) from the time he began writing music. But this music was kept under wraps; the promises went unfulfilled until well into the present century, and we must happily divorce Ives from the starched-collar ambiance that dulled the musical fortunes of his country and into which he was born.

II

The Promising Yesterday

•—•

I'm not, in any sense of the word, a musicologist, but I do think I know music: old and new, good and bad. I suspect that musicologists as a class know a great deal *about* music, rather than know music—which is not the same thing. Few of them have much use for composers born after the seventeenth century, and that creates an occupational hazard: musicologists see masses of old music, but hear precious little of it. The Middle Ages plainsong, to cite an example, is a worth-while thing, unquestionably, and according to the authoritative Gustave Reese (*Music in the Middle Ages*, 1940), its "rhythmical interpretation . . . has been a subject of intense controversy . . . that still rages today." Apparently, the Accentualists have no use for the monks of Solesmes and are in their turn unacceptable to the Mensuralists, which is fine with me; I'm still in the dark as to whether I should join the Accentualists or the Mensuralists, knowing full well that my pagan past would make me ineligible for the Solesmes school. I cheerfully confess to not knowing the difference between a "diastema" and an "episema" (see Reese), which have unpleasant medical associations to my shallow mind, and if I opened this can of Ambrosian, Mozarabic, and Gregorian beans, it's only because I have a real shocker in store for the entire musicological fraternity.

In the postlude to 1900 *Contemporary American Composers,* versatile Rupert Hughes, novelist, dramatist, biographer, and musical essayist, stated: "In the ninth century Iceland was the musical center of the world; students went there from all Europe as to an artistic Mecca." The spectacle of ninth-century students saving up, pulling strings, applying for grants (Was there a G.I. Bill in those days?) and then swarming all over Iceland in quest of True Music is, I admit, fascinating. Here's the rub, however; try as I would, which involved reading obscure treatises, annoying bona fide musicologists, and even searching for an Icelandic native (the nearest thing I found was my Finnish masseur, but his knowledge of music didn't go further than "Rose Marie, I love you"), no one had the slightest familiarity with the ninth, or any other century, Icelandic song, Plain or Fancy. In despair I feverishly perused Gustave Reese's book and did discover that "neumes had crystallized into the square or quadratic form" . . . and that "this form penetrated without much delay even to Iceland." But this was in the thirteenth century—and so I return the Icelandic squares to Mr. Rupert Hughes and his conscience.

Unable to elaborate on his opening gambit, Hughes went on hastily (same postlude): "Iceland has long lost her musical crown, and Welsh music in its turn has ceased to be *chief on earth.*" Well, what do you know? Frank Kidson, in a lengthy dissertation on Welsh music, in *Grove's Dictionary,* says guardedly: "It is not very clear when Welsh music began to have attention paid to it . . . a great number of tunes . . . have been classed as Welsh upon insufficient grounds." In the John Parry Collection (1842), Welsh tunes . . . "have evidently been taken down from the playing of harpers in North Wales." The collectors "appear to have considered that [the harp] was the sole instrument worthy of attention and that Welsh vocal music was of but little interest." The insecure Welsh chiefs having given up their monopoly of the earth—"Russia is sending up a strong and growing harmony marred with much discord. Some visionaries look to her for the new song," Hughes continued. The man was, patently, a sensation seeker of no mean order. What happened to the "new songs" that have supplanted the Icelandic and Welsh product *before* Russia made her bid for earth chiefdom? To those that came from Rome, Leipzig, Paris, and Vienna, which places attracted a few musical Mecca-seekers following the earth-shaking downfall of Reykjavik and Cardiff?

If "some visionaries" looked to Russia "for the new song," that was the visionaries' business, not ours, nor Mr. Hughes's. For he "did not hesitate to match against the serfs of the steppes the high-hearted, electric-minded free people of our prairies; and to prophesy that in the coming [twentieth] century the musical supremacy and inspiration of the world will rest here overseas, in America."

Let us concede that, although an erratic musicologist, Mr. Hughes proved a near-accurate prophet. I say *near*-accurate because, while we may not have achieved supremacy, the present musical world is certainly more "inspired" by the U.S. than any other country. That jazz is the strongest new musical influence the world over is undeniable—and jazz is American, although it may not be music to some. To pretend, however, that jazz is the cornerstone of authentic American music is just as palpably incorrect as to see in jazz the only possible panacea for the world's musical ills, which naïve contention nullified the importance of Henry Pleasants's *The Agony of Modern Music* (1955), and lessened the impact of the many incontrovertible truths, stated with laudable clarity, with which the book is studded.

To this day, there is no all-embracing definition of "jazz." Whether "jazz" is a corruption of the Elizabethan "*jass,* which had survived in the vernacular of bawdy-houses" (C.E. Smith, *The Jazz Record Book*), or whether "its root is in the French verb *jaser,* meaning to babble or cackle" (Gilbert Chase), or whether one should go along with Lafcadio Hearn, who found the word, "jazz," in the Creole patois of New Orleans and insisted that it meant "speeding things up," is relatively immaterial. What jazz *is,* what was its function in musical America's coming of age, and to what extent must it be reckoned with as an organic stimulus in contemporary music in general, is of such importance that no writer can avoid speculating and pragmatizing on it; no two of them are in agreement.

While Paul Rosenfeld maintains that "American music is not jazz. Jazz is not music," to Pleasants "there is more real creative musical talent in the music of Armstrong and Ellington, in the songs of Gershwin, Rodgers, Kern and Berlin, than in all the serious music composed since 1920."

George Gershwin (in *Revolt in the Arts*) said: "Jazz has contributed an enduring value to America in the sense that it has expressed ourselves," but Henry Cowell ("the persuasive and not altogether convincing advocate of new harshnesses in music," in Isaac Goldberg's estimate) told us that "we" (Who are we? V.D.) "know that jazz is accepted by most Americans as something delectable and to be enjoyed, but that it comes to them just as much as something from the outside as it does to the European, who, it must be pointed out, has also accepted jazz in the same way. The Anglo-Saxon American has no more talent for writing or playing jazz than the European. Both of them are bungling at it." (1922). Two years later, a white man named Gershwin gave birth to a *Rhapsody in Blue,* so maybe it was the rash Mr. Cowell who did the bungling; but then, Gershwin and the *Rhapsody* have no connection with jazz to the purist.

The usually articulate and polished Aaron Copland used jazz (pure or impure, who cares?) with profit in his music, as we shall see later, but his pronouncements on jazz are no more accurate than Cowell's. Copland surmised, in Julia Smith's *Aaron Copland* (without a doubt the most wretchedly written musical biography to date; if you can use a laugh, take a gander at her translations of Nadia Boulanger's letters), that "jazz had its origins on *some* Negro's tomtom in Africa and descended through the spirituals. Ragtime is its closest ancestor . . . the fox trot was the beginning of modern jazz [!!]." John Tynan, West Coast editor of *Down Beat* magazine, wrote me in rebuttal of the above: "To surmise, as did Copland, that 'jazz had its origin on some Negro's tomtom in Africa' is a gross over-simplification of the question. While it is true that the rhythmic pulse of jazz originated with transplanted African Negroes, it is not at all accurate to pin an African label on American jazz as we know it. According to Copland: 'ragtime is its closest ancestor.' This surmise is equally over-simplified. Even at the time when ragtime was being popularized by such as Scott Joplin or Tony Jackson in New Orleans bawdy houses, a raw and primitive form of what we have come to term 'Dixieland' jazz was being performed in the New Orleans streets . . . As to the composer's assertion that 'the fox trot was the beginning of modern jazz'—if true, we are left with the rather alarming conclusion that Vernon and Irene Castle were true jazz pioneers."

One must agree with Gilbert Chase that "in no other field of American music does one have to tread more warily than in that of jazz and its manifold ramifications." To say that, in order to "go American," one has to write jazz—and many still say it—is as silly as to insist that a true Russian stick to the trepak, the gopak, or to what foreigners invariably refer to as the "kasatski" in his music. The Americanists (the apt word is Chase's), those who tried very hard to sound American, can be (roughly) placed in three groups: (1) the folklorists, (2) the urbanists, and (3) the jazzists. Each method had its representative and persuasive adherents—and the most ambitious, like Copland, who "was anxious to write a work that would immediately be recognized as American in character" (Aaron Copland, *Our New Music*), practiced all three and even managed, on occasion, to fuse them into an "All-American" whole.

Charles Ives's music also embodied all three elements, with this signal difference—he was not anxious to be recognizably American; he just went on (many years before the Americanists) writing the genuine article, an article for which there was no exposure and no market. The wonderful *Three Places in New England* was written between 1906 and 1914; *Decoration Day* and *The Fourth of July* in 1912-13; the Fourth Symphony was completed in 1916; and the four violin sonatas were ready a year before. To quote Henry Cowell, who, with his wife Sidney, turned out a masterful *Charles Ives and His Music* (1955): "The first stage in the career of Ives's music came to an end about 1918 when he decided to make no further personal effort to introduce the music to performers who had shown no interest in it." The "career" was resumed with the Pro Musica's concert in January, 1927, at which point the Johnny-come-lately Americanists were on Ives's bandwagon *en masse*. Future historians, please note: In neither the *Musical Portraits* (1922—or four years *after* the "close" of Ives's first "period") nor *An Hour With American Music* (1929)—two years *after* the Pro Musica concert), both by Paul Rosenfeld, is there the slightest mention of Ives, while the "young 'uns"—Copland, Sessions, Roy Harris, Thomson, Leo Ornstein, and Adolph Weiss—are given their just (or unjust) due on dozens of pages in the inimitable Rosenfeldian baroque style. The forgotten Ornstein "made" both volumes— the other five lads, for reasons of youth, only the second one. Yet Lawrence Gilman and Olin Downes, neither noted for excessively "modern" tendencies in their criticism, made "a real attempt to understand Ives's music" (Cowell), in 1927, and found in it "an irresistible veracity and strength—an uncorrupted sincerity" (Gilman), "real vitality, real naïveté and a superb self-respect" (Downes). Rosenfeld did not become an "important friend" of Ives's music until 1931, in Cowell's testimony; perhaps Ives's would-be amateur status as part-time composer (he was a successful business man by profession) caused our "leftist" critic to bypass him in favor of "revolutionaries" of Ornstein's or Rudhyar's stripe?

Let's return to the younger men, who "got there" or were getting there ahead of Ives: folklorists, urbanists, jazzists. Folklorists, those who lean heavily on the people's music, were unfashionable in nineteenth-century America, whose aesthetics were formulated by MacDowell and the learned Bostonians, as we already know. This state of affairs seemed incomprehensible to foreign observers; Vincent d'Indy once remarked that it was too bad that Americans did not "inspire themselves from [sic] their own landscape and legends" (Cowell). "Were I in America," said Massenet, "I should be exalted by the glories of your scenery . . . National surroundings always inspire national music." The two Frenchmen obviously didn't have deserted farmhouses and water lilies in mind—but hinted at the desirability of local music sources to embody the local scene in sound. The honor of starting the nationalistic ball rolling fell to a foreigner—the Czech, Antonin Dvořák.

He had a feeble precursor in another Bohemian, in the curious person of Anton Philipp Heinrich (1781-1861), who came to the States at the age of thirty-seven, after a banking career in Hamburg, Germany. His ambition was to become the first (here we go again!) authentic American composer; with which John R. Parker, the founder of the *Euterpiad*, heartily concurred. "His genius triumphs over everything. He may . . . justly be styled the *Beethoven* of America." (This was *before* Glinka's advent.) Heinrich wrote the grandiosely titled *Dawning of Music in Kentucky or The Pleasures of Harmony in the Solitudes of Nature*, but aware of his technical limitations, journeyed to London (he was forty-six at the time) to . . . study music. The ill-fated *Combat of the Condor* and *The Columbiad, Grand American National Chivalrous Symphony* were the unimpressive outcome of his studies. He then began soliciting subscriptions to his *Jubilee* ("a grand national song of triumph, commemorative of events from the landing of the Pilgrim fathers to the consummation of American liberty"), which he fondly imagined to be his masterpiece, and asked John Hill Hewitt to introduce him to President Tyler, who was to be the dedicatee of Heinrich's song of triumph.

In his *Shadows on the Wall*, Hewitt tells the delicious story of that momentous Washington meeting (cited by John Tasker Howard): "We visited the President's Mansion, and were shown in the presence of Mr. Tyler, who received us with his usual urbanity. I introduced Mr. Heinrich as a professor of exalted talent and extraordinary genius. The President . . . readily consented to the dedication and commended the undertaking. Heinrich was elated to the skies, and immediately proposed to play the grand conception. The composer labored hard to give full effect to his weird production . . . occasionally explaining some incomprehensible passage, representing, as he said, the breaking up of the frozen river Niagara . . . the thunder of our naval war-dogs and the rattle of our army musketry. The inspired composer had got about halfway through his wonderful production when Mr. Tyler arose from his chair, and, placing his hand gently on Heinrich's shoulder, said: 'That may all be very fine, sir, but can't you play us a good old Virginia reel?' "

President Tyler was, obviously, a dedicated folklorist and had no taste for grandiloquent program music. As for poor

Heinrich (who told Hewitt, following the Washington fiasco, that the President "knew no more about music than an oyster"), he had a fine knack for titles and would have made a corking advertising agency executive had he lived in our times, but the "American Beethoven" was "absolutely untouched by any fundamental art culture such as is obtained through the study of theory and musical literature" (J. L. Zvonar, reviewing Heinrich's Prague concert in 1857) and we must regretfully deny him the splendid office to which he so zealously aspired; although I would love to hear the man's *Indian Carnival or The Indian's Festival of Dreams* (with a startingly Freudian subtitle—"Sinfonia Eratico Fantachia"), his *Indian Fanfares*, or (above all) *The Mastodon*, which grand symphony in three parts occupied three volumes.

While we may agree with Howard "that Heinrich was the first to attempt American nationalism in the larger forms of musical composition," the task was a man-sized job and required the services of a composer, not a pathetic buffoon. That Dvorák proved the right man for the job, and that the *New World Symphony* (1895) (his fifth) became "his most celebrated work" (Banes), must have been a blow to the native aspirants. Their dreams of firstness came to nought. Dvorák is said to have declared (as reported by Gilbert Chase), regarding the *New World*, that the program-notes compiler should "omit that nonsense about my having made use of Indian and American motives" because he only "tried to write in the spirit of these national American melodies." There was no gainsaying the plain truth that the enterprising Czech was "pointing to a potential source of inspiration" (Chase), and conveying "a spiritual message" to American musicians. Dvorák, himself, was quoted (in a statement issued before the New York première) in reference to the plantation melodies: "These beautiful and varied themes are the product of the soil. They are American. They are the folk songs of America, and your composers must turn to them." In Chase's well-chosen words—"he [Dvorák] issued a challenge, which was accepted by a small but enthusiastic and determined group of American composers, with significant results for America's music." Only one of these preceded Dvorák (by two years, chronologically speaking) by creating "Variations on a National Hymn" for organ, subsequently published by Mercury; "This is the earliest piece using polytonality," add the Cowells. Two bold strokes, made simultaneously (and prematurely) by a native American — Charles Ives.

Early folklorists, those who heeded Dvorák's advice, were not, in themselves, an especially brilliant group; the best known were Arthur Farwell (who founded the Wa-Wan Press, for the publication of American music, in 1901); Henry F. P. Gilbert, Arthur Shepherd, and John Powell. Although Chase insists that the Wa-Wan men were "not a clique of Indianists and Negrophiles," Indian dances and Negro rhapsodies (one each for Gilbert and Powell) began to sprout all over the place. Whether the first folklorists achieved anything of substance may be open to debate, but they certainly succeeded in dusting off some Leipzig cobwebs; becoming a *Negrophile* was healthier by far than sticking with the New England *Necrophiles* who went on embracing academic corpses with a righteous air.

There were some intermittently good things in the folklorists' output and Powell's *Rhapsodie Nègre* (the French title may have been a mistake.) had "more than fifty New York performances in 1929 alone" (Howard), but this music had no staying powers; the clothes were new, the body was old. In other words, Farwell, Powell, *et al* used fresh material, but the craftsmanship was conservative and impersonal, although the German-school precepts were occasionally abandoned for the sake of the more "modern" (basically, just as traditional) formulae of the Franco-Belgian school — César Franck and Vincent d'Indy. Powell may have striven "to induce his style from the innate character of the material itself" (Howard), but neither he nor his older colleagues knew how to effect the fusion that was to come later — at the hands of more adventurous iconoclasts. Typically, most of the Wa-Wan music is forgotten; you will not find a single item by Farwell, Gilbert, Powell, or Shepherd in Schwann's catalogue — the recording companies' moguls being only too anxious to delete doubtful, because not readily saleable, entries.*

John Culshaw, the English writer on music, stated that "America's folk song . . . is still conspicuously active, though it finds little reflection in the works of contemporary American masters." (*A Century of Music*) This is wholly inaccurate; William Grant Still and, in a lighter genre, Gershwin and Morton Gould, wrote some of their best (and best-known) music under the sturdy aegis of folklore. Aaron Copland, turning to folk sources after a fairly brief flirtation with jazz (the 1926 Piano Concerto is still a fresh and electrifying farrago of jazz devices, technically far smoother than Gershwin's one effort in the genre, melodically less convincing) and a bout with austere abstractions, achieved real popularity with *Billy the Kid, Rodeo, Appalachian Spring,* and *El Salón México,* a snappy salute to our Latin neighbor. As Arthur Berger justly comments in his workmanlike and well-written *Aaron Copland* (Oxford University Press, 1953), "turning to folk music . . . was an aspect of his campaign to achieve a simple style and a content that would engage the interest of a wider audience. But it would be a gross simplification to say that he is no more than a skilled folklorist, a complier of Baedekers for his continent, just as in the twenties it would have been un-

* When I finally managed to locate some John Powell music (the 1912 *At the Fair*—sketches of American fun—and the 1921 *Sonata Noble*), I was agreeably surprised. In addition to the solid workmanship and adroit writing for the instrument (piano), both works had a healthy American ring to them. The sonata's finale is, plainly, a darned good piece.

just to cite him as merely a high-class representative of Tin Pan Alley. [I don't recall his ever having been considered as such. V.D.] For, in the handling of folk patterns, Copland is capable of an exceptional degree of selectivity, transformation and abstraction through which the essence of the material as well as a specific attitude, heightened emotion, ingenuity, and personality are conveyed." Therein lay the main difference between an authentic composer of Copland's caliber, who, having absorbed his country's folk idiom, made it an inexpugnable part of his own musical speech (for a while, at any rate) — in contrast to the Gilberts and the Powells, who used American source material as a peg for their essentially European "fantasia" type productions. It is not true that Copland's music "embraces everything save that indefinable warmth which he possesses but tends to disown," (John Culshaw's contention): *Quiet City*, the *Our Town* film score, and, particularly, the moving children's opera, *Second Hurricane* — all with patent "folksy" overtones — are proof that Copland was capable of "restrained, beatific New England sorrow" (Berger) as well as of the uninhibited and sun-drenched American "good time" spirit of a real down-to-earth hoe-down. If an occasionally obvious "scissors-and-paste" *modus operandi* becomes too apparent,* put it down to the man's determination to achieve his nationalistic goal in a hurry.

Copland's long "folkloristic" period (which Julia Smith chooses to label "third style period, Gebrauchsmusik American Style") began, rather mildly, with "Hear Ye! Hear Ye!"

* "In 1938, Copland readily accepted my offer of fifteen dollars for a 'fanfare,' or, rather, a signature — for the High-Low concerts I founded in New York. He wrote a very good one and it was performed with excellent effect at both concerts. (We only gave two — at the St. Regis Roof. V.D.) Some years later at a performance of Copland's 'Outdoor Overture,' I nearly fell out of my seat on hearing our High-Low signature — in its entirety — as the overture's opening. This was all the more astonishing as our concerts were distinctly an indoor undertaking." (Vernon Duke, *Passport to Paris*, Little, Brown, 1955)

a carryover from the jazz period, staged by Ruth Page in Chicago in 1934, shortly after the first Ivesian "boom," engineered by Henry Cowell and Nicholas Slonimsky (the banker-composer was "discovered" by Henry Bellamann, poet and novelist, and Robert Schmitz, the French pianist, who "went into the office of Ives & Myrick in search of an insurance policy" [Cowell] and found music instead!). We already know that the High Priest of "true" Americanism in music (leaning chiefly toward the "urbanists," about which more later), Paul Rosenfeld, took no notice of Ives's music until 1931; and it is altogether possible — although it has never, to my knowledge, been admitted — that the leading Americanists, then young and floundering, were not Ives-oriented.

There was a good reason for this neglect: Charles Ives, the son of a bandmaster and music teacher, who was fond of daring musical experiments (such as toying with quarter tones) himself, was only a part-time, or "Sunday" composer. After establishing a successful insurance business in 1909, he devoted his leisure time to composition — and thus created a pattern of life which, though usually irksome to most artists, seemed quite satisfactory to Ives. From the point of view of the musical historian, his "undercover" revolutionary activities on behalf of American music and music in general (he wrote polytonal music *before* studying with Parker at Yale, in 1894!) must be a cause for acute discomfort. Upsetting the old academic apple cart *before* the advent of the present century was a heroic feat that had but one flaw; our whimsical Connecticut Yankee did it in private. "Not until 1947, when he was awarded a Pulitzer Prize for his Third Symphony, did Ives approach the status of a well-known figure in American music" (Gilbert Chase) and "had never heard any of his compositions performed by a full orchestra" until he was seventy-one years old.

Our discomfort is intensified by our inability to ascertain the full extent of Ives's influence on budding Americanists in the twenties or early thirties when musical Americana was eagerly embraced by those "higher in the brow." We know that Copland arranged for some songs of Ives's to be sung at Yaddo in 1930 (these were subsequently published by Cos Cob, again thanks to Copland); we also know that indomitable Nicholas Slonimsky persisted in programming Ives (1930-32) and was responsible for the first Ives recording in 1934 — conducting *Three Places in New England,* and the eerily evocative *In the Night.* Slonimsky took his Ives repertoire (including the terrifyingly difficult *Fourth of July*) abroad, with the help of the Pan-American Association of Composers, and caused the European critics to compare the "first truly national American composer" with Walt Whitman, which was pretty smart of them. A sad comment on our own insecurity is to be found in Cowells's wry observation: "It was the respectful and often admiring hearing given Ives's music *by a few critics abroad* that began in the early 1930's to suggest that the music of Ives was perhaps not the joke most musicians in America had at first supposed."

There was no stopping the Ives boom, once it got going. Ives himself was a capable writer and Elliott Carter re-read his 1920 *Essays Before a Sonata* in 1944 and declared that "a man with such ideas *must* be capable of exceptional music. The tone is elevated, the wit brilliant." Funny, no one bothered to investigate just what Ives's capabilities as a composer were for so long a time after the *Essays* were printed! Among other things, Ives said that "a composer who believes in the American ideal cannot fail to be American whether he uses folklore or not"; this was hardly brilliant and it was not borne out by the facts. Foote, Parker, Chadwick, and MacDowell himself were pretty good Americans and dedicated idealists in their own way, which did not make their music any less pseudo-European than the composers themselves intended it to be. What Ives *said* was of no great significance; even less momentous were the writings about his music — "and their number is legion," Carter added (*Modern Music* Magazine, May-June, 1944). It was the man's music that his new champions were "convinced that [if performed] would meet the expectations aroused by his famous [?] ideals," Carter continued, then became cautious. "It probably would," said he, "provided the listener made several allowances." In this he was eminently right.

Ives's music is uneven to an extraordinary degree. The Second Symphony, spectacularly revived by Leonard Bernstein in 1951, is *not* any kind of a masterpiece, although it is often served up as such a one; in my judgment — and I was a more than sympathetic listener on three occasions — it's a longish, dullish work, clumsily harmonized and just as clumsily orchestrated. According to Carter, "it is made up of arrangements of earlier organ works and an older overture," which gave Burrill Phillips an opportunity to invest it with "the style of the parlor organ and the nineteenth-century park bandstand, *not* the European concert hall or opera house." In the finale there are bits of "Camptown Races," "Turkey in the Straw," and "Columbia, the Gem of the Ocean" — and it must be said that these snatches provide the only sadly needed fun in the entire thirty-five minutes of the Symphony's playing time. The work "reveals chromatic influences, Franck, Brahms and Dvo-rák" (Carter) but is hardly a revelation of a powerful personality.

It is difficult to conceive that the wonderful and spanking-fresh Second Violin Sonata, begun only a year (1903!) after the completion of the Second Symphony, was written by the same man. Possibly, the awe-inspiring symphonic idiom proved too much for Ives, who was unable to resist the tackling of *eine grosse Symphonie* and stuck to safe models to make sure he was really writing one. The Second Violin Sonata is a great improvement on the tentative and chaotically discursive First, wherein our "Sunday" composer seemed as yet unsure of the medium; in the shorter Second Sonata we hear sounds, tunes, dance rhythms that could have originated only on these shores. Some are Ives's own, some are of folk origin; why quibble? These sounds, tunes, rhythms add up to a complete victorious *réussite*, to a first-class piece in any language, for any audience; nobody wrote a better one in the genre.

The first and the last movements of the Third Sonata "have a kind of a salon character of the romantic order," opines Lou Harrison in his liner notes for the fine Rafael Druian Mercury recording. Here, also, can be found the "somewhat confusing transcendentalist philosophy of his native New England," a certain murkiness and diffuseness, relieved now and again by sunny melodic intrusions and polyrhythmic clashes. The Third Sonata "contains a gem of ragtime which Ives first wrote for one of the theater orchestras with which he always seems to have been associated (the Globe orchestra of New York played this piece in 1905, three years after its composition)," Harrison reports. Third Stream drumbeaters, please note!

With the Fourth Sonata (*Children's Day at Camp Meeting*), we are back in Ives's folkloric paradise. In it he "recomposes" (the word is Harrison's) "Yes, Jesus Loves Me" and "Shall We Gather at The River" and writes a happy, outgoing romp for a breezy opener. Especially lovely is the peaceful, melodically luscious close of the middle (largo) movement. The sonata ends on a question mark — "Shall we indeed?" — which halts a very short "triple-swinging, almost jazzy setting of a hymn" (Harrison); the unexpected prank could have robbed the work of a "wrap-up" coda, but, somehow, it didn't. It is good Ives, and it "belongs."

The opening of his Third Symphony sounds as though Wagner might have written it, had he been an American. The music becomes freer, as the tempo accelerates, but the symphonic tenets are again an obstacle to Ives; there is too much "soaring strings" type of writing and even misplaced Men-

delssohnian cadences that jibe with typically regional songful-
ness. Compared with the exuberant fiddle sonatas, this is
mighty poor stuff. I doubt that "it sums up in symphonic form
the deep-rooted tradition of American hymnody" (Gilbert
Chase); the hymns were put to better use elsewhere, by Ives
himself, and, as to the form, it is not cogent enough to be
called symphonic. The real, top-drawer Ives is to be found
in the illimitably imaginative *Three Places in New England* —
probably the highest musical achievement by an American —
the Second and Fourth Violin Sonatas, and smaller gems, like
"In the Night," "The Unanswered Question," and several deeply
affecting songs. "One might have thought that Ives, now so
much discussed and publicly admired, would be often heard,"
Elliott Carter ruminated in his "Shop Talk by an American
Composer" (*The Musical Quarterly*, April, 1960). "That a number of his recordings have been discontinued, only a few of
his easiest pieces are heard, while some of his more remarkable works are still unplayed or scarcely known, is surely an
indication of how confused and desperate is the relation between the composer, the profession, publicity, and the musical
public."

II

If it was avant-garde music you were after, there was no
lack of it in New York in 1921, the year I first saw this land,
at the comparatively tender age of seventeen. The more advanced variety was to be had at the International Composers
Guild *soirées*, presided over by that most urbane of all urban-
its — Edgard Varèse, himself. The more "guarded" type of
avant-garde production was provided (two years later) by the
rival League of Composers, run by the able but careful Claire
Reis; two versatile and new-music-minded singers — Eva Gauthier and Greta Torpadie — featured both advanced and
guarded specimens of *dernier cri* local production at their recitals. Quite apart from the urbanists, folklorists, and jazzists —

the last two categories then still unfashionable — there existed
a fourth genre, no longer held in great esteem by the musical
cognoscenti; that was post-post-impressionism, made in U.S.A.
The leading champions of the cult were John Alden Carpenter,
Charles Griffes (about whom more later), Louis Gruenberg,
and Emerson Whithorne. All four, on occasion, permitted
themselves a perilous excursion into the deep jungle of Americana — with French overtones, for safety's sake. Thus, Carpenter composed a *Krazy Kat* ballet, danced by Adolph Bolm and
Ruth Page, and the distinctly urbanistic *Skyscrapers* (indignantly turned down by cruel Diaghilev, to whom the score
was submitted in 1925); Gruenberg wrote things like *Daniel
Jazz* and *Jazz Berries;* and Whithorne made a mild splash with
the unjustly forgotten (Gilbert Chase fails even to list Whithorne in his book!) *New York Days and Nights*, a surprisingly
stimulating piano suite. But their hearts were elsewhere; Carpenter's and Whithorne's songs sounded like an imitation of
Roger Ducasse imitating Debussy, and Paris-perfumed ninths
and various *Pelléasisms* seemed a sound enough guarantee of
correct "modernism." The American Debussyists' music was
rather like that of *La Mer*, if you left out the Debussy and
added plenty of water. Eva Gauthier, otherwise ever ready
to gamble on anything (even rugged Ruggles and violent
Varèse) showed inexplicable predilection for the dangerously
salon-type music of Winter Watts; Watts's songs, nevertheless,
were extremely grateful from a singer's point of view and not
devoid of a tawdry but appealing charm, rather like Poulenc's.

But there were no two ways about it — Urbanism, a musi-
calization of the urbanist poetry of Verhaeren, even a militant
Mayakovsky, was all the rage with the "progressives." The
leader of musical urbanists was French-born Edgard Varèse;
the Number One prophet, Paul Rosenfeld. Listen to what the
prophet had to say about the leader (in *An Hour with American Music*, 1929): "The greatest fullness of power and of

prophecy yet to come to music in America lodges in the orchestral composition of Varèse . . . Following a first hearing of these pieces, the streets are full of jangly echoes. The taxi squeaking to a halt at the crossroad recalls a theme. Timbres and motives are sounded by police whistles, bark and moan of motor horns and fire sirens, mooing of great sea cows steering through harbor and river, chatter of drills in the garishly lit fifty-foot excavations. You walk, ride, fly through a world of steel and glass and concrete, by rasping, blasting, threatening machinery become strangely humanized and fraternal . . . Varèse has done with the auditory sensations of the giant cities and the industrial phantasmagoria, their distillation of strange tones and timbres, much what Picasso has done with the corresponding visual ones . . . His music significantly orientates us to a kind of world to which America is closer than Europe is." Rosenfeld concludes his panegyric thus: "That is the emotional aesthetic man of today no less than the technical scientific one; that is every Columbus directed to every America; that is the spirit of the new Western life."

At that time, 1929, Rosenfeld began to have serious doubts about some of his earlier enthusiasms — especially Russian-born Leo Ornstein, (b. 1895). In 1920 Ornstein, like Varèse, was "a mirror held up to the world of the modern city" to Rosenfeld. Today, it's funny and a little sad to read Rosenfeld, eulogizing Ornstein (now completely forgotten) in almost exactly the same terms he applied to Varèse nine years later. "The first of [Ornstein's] real [?] compositions are like fragments of some cosmopolis of caves and towers of steel, of furious motion and shafts of nitrogen glare become music. They . . . record not only the clangors [Rosenfeld's favorite word. V.D.] but all the violent forms of the city, the beat of the frenetic activity, the intersecting planes of light . . . the electric signs staining the inky night clouds." This kind of rather facile imagery obsessed Rosenfeld from the beginning of his writing career. Ornstein and Varèse were but a pretext for more "grinding and shrieking of loaded trains in the tubes, cranes laboring in the port, flowers that are gray and black blossoming on the ledges of tenement windows," and so on, *ad infinitum*. In 1920, according to the critic's *Musical Portraits*, published in that year, "Ornstein was youth, the spring as it comes up through the pavements, the aching green sap, Lazarus emerging in his grave clothes into the new world"; his music was a "thing germane to all beings born into the age of steel."

I became exposed to the "clangors" of young Lazarus shortly upon my arrival in the U. S. This was at a concert given by Ornstein jointly with militant Ethel Leginska (then also an ardent urbanist), to which I went with Eva Gauthier, one of my first sponsors in this country. I dimly recall a pale and grim-looking young man with tousled hair, clad in a rumpled dark suit and a red tie, and his piano partner — it was a recital of two-piano music — mannishly attired in "grave" clothes somewhat similar to those of Ornstein's—bow tie and a short, no-concert-gown-nonsense type of skirt. The pair plunged into a two-piano sonata of Ornstein's (there is no mention of this piece in either *Baker's* or Claire Reis's useful *Composers in America*, revised ed., 1947*) which was indeed "clangorous," but also unpleasantly hysterical and melodramatic to my ears. I was less impressed with the music, the dissonances of which

---

* Paul Rosenfeld welcomed "the unbreaking gray plinth of sound in the two-piano sonata" as an antidote for "the sweet, sugary ghosts . . . which appeared in the cello sonatas and piano sonatinas composed by Ornstein a few years since." Back again were "raucous cries of suddenly felt steely power . . . the might of machinery" on which the critic thrived. The review (an out-and-out rave) appeared in Rosenfeld's *Musical Chronicle* (N.Y., 1923). Back again was "the fine metallic clangor" of the twin pianos that "howled like beasts in the wilderness when the sap mounts." Ornstein, forgiven for "the sweet sugary ghosts," was "on the verge of becoming a member of the line of composers that moves from Chopin [?] through Scriabin and onward into gray unknown regions." That was a significant slip — for "gray unknown regions" soon became the composer's destination.

were tame enough after a few samples of Varèse' or Ruggles, than with the antics of the two pianists; there was a lot of spectacular head-shaking and athletic byplay on the part of Leginska, a strange, sullen determination characterizing her partner "the only true blue, genuine Futurist composer alive" (James Huneker). Carl Van Vechten met Ornstein in 1915 and they "talked over a table." I feel that some of the young man's pronouncements are worth quoting — if only for the sake of comparing them with the glib sallies of composers who are young today. "I hate cleverness. Art that is merely clever is not art at all," said the True-blue Futurist, clasping and unclasping his hands. "When I feel that the existing enharmonic [?] scale is limiting me I shall write in quarter tones." "Ornstein never rewrites," Van Vechten commented. "If his inspiration does not come the first time it never comes." As you see, it was still good form in 1915 to use words like "inspiration." But to return to direct quotes from the composer: Satie — "not stimulating or interesting"; Schoenberg — "the last of the academics . . . all brain, no spirit. His music is mathematical"; Scriabin "was a great theorist [?] who never achieved his goal." Now for the climax: "Stravinsky is the most stimulating and interesting of all the modern composers. *He feels what he writes.*" No comment; read Stravinsky on the subject. But, as we shall see later, no young American — in 1915 or 1963 — could escape the Stravinsky stranglehold.

Perversely enough, after denouncing Schoenberg's academicism, Ornstein began to lean more and more to the most conventionally academic conception of his art; switched to Tchaikovskian quartets and quintets and even received the first prize in the national anthem contest! That is as often as not the sad case of all *enfants terribles* in music who start out with a bang at an early age and quickly peter out on maturing; the former *enfant terrible* is then reduced to writing music that is either infantile or downright terrible. Two American examples — Leo

Ornstein and George Antheil. We already know about the first-named *"enfant."* His *"enfantillages,"* bruited about at first, were not of the lucrative sort, since he was primarily a composer, unlike the performing *Wunderkinder* Misha, Sasha, Yasha, and Tasha, his compatriots. In his extremely curious *Time Exposures,* an author signing himself simply "Search-Light" (Boni & Liveright, 1926)* included a trenchant, albeit melancholy profile of Leo Ornstein, who was by then dethroned. The following excerpt can still be read with profit: "In the Provinces they did not care for Schoenberg; they adored Liszt. They could not stand Ornstein; they doted on Chopin. The boy had to live: not alone he — his family as well. So Leo Ornstein stepped into the Machine; and the Machine squeezed him. When he was dry like a wrung lemon, he could always be cast off. There's always a fresh crop of geniuses from Russia. This Machine that took him consists of Pullman berths, Statler hotels, press agents, interviews, society ladies of 'forty' with a thirst for 'twenty,' flappers sipping thrills, and programs full of rhapsodies, gimcrack and gymnastics. It is the Machine of virtuosi. It is only dimly related to music. To the Song and the Word of God, it is not related at all. It is far closer in spirit to a stylish motor-works or to a modish tailor's. This is all very well, if you happen to be an Elman or a Moiseiwitsch: a nimble, clever acrobat swinging to other people's music. But if you're the Music, yourself: If you're the sort of creature in whom the subtlest tremors of the air turn into blasts of body-wracking song — well, you'd do better to make your song in a coal mine, in the whir of a sweatshop, than try to keep it living in this cold, cynical, lecherous, sterile, sterilizing world of the American Concert. The frail boy wavered. The usual quota of 'friends' — among them a critic or two who,

---

* It has been ascertained, long after these lines were written, that "Search-Light" was (for the purpose of this one book) the pen name of Waldo David Frank.

properly prompted, had hailed him — prepared to bury him with flowers. And from time to time, the 'music-lovers' grow reminiscent: 'Ornstein? What has become of Ornstein?' They see the old boy in his velvet coat with his wild head hid in a mysterious rapture. (But the new man has muscle, and gets along with his neighbors who are New England farmers.)"

As for Antheil, he stirred up a bit of excitement with the 1926 *Ballet Mécanique,* did less well with Frankfurt-staged *Transatlantic* (Slonimsky), took to writing indifferent film fare, Shostakovich-inspired symphonies, and giving advice to the lovelorn in a syndicated column. European *enfants terribles* were and are legion, one of the strangest cases being that of genuinely gifted Igor Markevitch, powerfully publicized by Diaghilev, Prunières, and Nadia Boulanger; the last told the startled audience at a preview of Markevitch's *Paradise Lost* that, while they were not privileged to assist at the birth of Christ, they were fortunate to attend the unveiling of young Igor's oratorio—his first "frost," by the way. Markevitch did write some quite remarkable things in his youth—*Rebus, Icare,* and the short Cantata to a Cocteau text— then embraced conducting, with great and well-merited success. If he is still writing music, he keeps that fact strictly to himself. The one really accomplished *enfant terrible* whose music retained its youthful freshness to the end, was Serge Prokofiev. Yet Paul Rosenfeld (in 1920), denouncing contemporary critics for permitting Ornstein to "operate in a void," declared that "they [the critics] have either ridiculed him or written cordially about him without saying anything. At present they are *even* [?] classing him with Prokofiev."

Outside of Varèse, the most convincing urbanist music was written by the Mexican Carlos Chavez (*Energia, H.P.*)— seldom by native-born exponents of the Machine Age, such as Antheil. Some of Copland's more strident and "clangorous" pieces (Piano Sonata, Piano Variations) may have "urbanist" overtones, but this composer, as already noted, paid obeisance to jazz and folk sources more readily. As Carl E. Lindstrom remarked (*The Musical Quarterly*, July, 1945): "Our most determined composers have tried to found an American music by taking European tonal cameras and using them to photograph filling stations [Virgil Thomson? V.D.], skyscrapers [J.A. Carpenter? V.D.], and other phenomena of the American scene. All this has been to no avail." The post-post-impressionists didn't contribute anything of lasting significance, either. They dispensed moderately "modern" music of the innocuous and (to some) palatable sort and printed it through the good offices of the Composers' Music Corporation, whose fortunes were guided by Richard Hammond, the inventor's brother; Louis Gruenberg, Emerson Whithorne, Alexander Steinert, the piano merchant's son (His early "Footsteps in the Sand" was a charmingly whimsical song), and Lazare Saminsky, an exceedingly energetic and pompous little man, whose regular uniform was a morning jacket and striped trousers; he wore these regularly, in spite of his unprepossessing physique, earning the nickname of "Ambassador" bestowed upon him by Claire Reis. These men were also League of Composers regulars and had a hand in that organization's policies which were conservatively liberal: according to Mrs. Reis, Olin Downes talked of "unmitigated tonal asperity," "sonorous acerbities"—or was it "acerbic sonorities"?—while some described the League as "a queer little bubble, run by a futurist gang." Both Mrs. Reis and the late critic must have had the International Composers' Guild in mind; asperity (or acerbity) was indeed dispensed in large doses by Varèse and Ruggles. "The League of Composers . . . had more solid financial support and there was a reassuring aura of nice bureaucratic tedium about the goings-on," I reported in *Passport to Paris.* "A lot of middle-of-the-road music was being played and it was as if the sponsors were bent on selling the customers the idea that new music could be conformist and respectable." With the demise of the Guild, the League grew bolder and performed heroic feats in its untiring campaign on behalf of new music.

III

Before we get to the jazzists, let's take up the case of the wistful and isolated Charles Tomlinson Griffes, who died in 1920 at the age of thirty-six. "Isolated" is not necessarily synonymous with "ruggedly individual"—although the two terms *were* synonymous with Charles Ives, who went his own way, uninfluenced and unnoticed by the musical fraternity. Griffes, still esteemed as an outstanding American talent, "was fascinated by the exotic art of the French impressionists, and investigated the potentialities of Oriental scales" (*Baker's*); so did Henry Eichheim, who prettified Orientalism with a Debussy-and-Ravel-patina—and John Alden Carpenter. Although Edward M. Maisel, Griffes's biographer (*Charles T. Griffes, The Life of an American Composer,* 1943), asserted that: "Few American artists in any field enjoy a greater critical prestige than Griffes, and almost no American music is rated higher by the mass of concertgoers than his *Pleasure Dome of Kubla Khan* and *White Peacock*," Griffes was no "Americanist" in any sense of the word, had no affinity with the basic trends of the native music, and exercised little or no influence on younger composers. He was, unquestionably, a sensitive, talented man, whose short and unhappy life didn't give him the chance to desert the impressionist hothouse (there might be a curious parallel with Proust's lot here) and get out in the streets for a breath of crisp, vitamin-laden American air. A Humperdinck pupil, Griffes underwent German, French, and Russian (Scriabin and Moussorgsky) influences before going Oriental, and was understandably classified by Gilbert Chase as an eclectic. The more individual Piano Sonata is, certainly, his best piece. What baffles me is Paul Rosenfeld's, that arch-urbanist's, all-out enthusiasm for an early and, from all accounts, thoroughly derivative "dance drama" by Griffes, titled *The Kairn of Koridwen*. This opus brought out the long-pent-up urge for the juiciest, no-holds-barred baroque writing of the late critic:

> "Swiftly then nocturne-like pages developed from the mournful and glowing phrase for clarinet, the motto of the short prelude took on individuality, carried me away. The priestesses, following the first frenzy of their rite, had consumed their brew, were prostrate, scattered about the altar. Shadowy soft torso after torso aspired toward the riding moon, told its vision, rhythmically sank back again . . . Brusquely into this feminine ferment burst Modred the Gael. The audience tittered: it was a boy in a helmet bearing a sword and shield. Aroused, the corps of druidesses brandished its spears at the intruder on the sacred precinct and fled, leaving a sacrificial Irene Lewisohn crouched by the altar. But the mental question of the male counterweight's age obliterated all."

Music criticism can be a fine and wondrous thing.

By 1924 you couldn't go to a concert without hearing a post-post-impressionist effusion, homemade or imported, complete with resplendent though shopworn ninths, whole-tone-scale glissandi, ethereal flute solos, Ravelian tambours and tambourines, muted shimmering strings and—oh, horrors!—the ever-present, unavoidable celeste or its twin brother, Herr Glockenspiel. Will I ever forget the day I was invited (by a fashionably "leftist," though rich, society matron—naturally) to a symphony concert where Louis Gruenberg's *Enchanted Isle* was being premièred? *"Enchanted Isle?"* I asked tremulously over the telephone. "That sounds like more glockenspiel and celeste."

"And what's wrong with that, pray?" was the lady's cool rejoinder.

"Nothing, except that I've been exposed to so much of that celestial tinkling, I've grown allergic to it. Tell you what," I raced on, "I'll be happy to come if you'll permit me to leave your box at the first entrance of either glockenspiel or celeste."

My hostess giggled good-naturedly. "Very well, that's a bargain. Do come."

That evening at the concert, I listened patiently to the usual classical fare that precedes untried novelties. A pause, a hush, the conductor returns to the podium. He had barely lifted his stick when a fruity celeste (or glockenspiel) solo rang out; I stuck to our bargain and fled in relief.

It seemed as though, after the turgid, Teutonic-style music-making of the preceding century, we were sunk in a sticky, Gallic marsh. Griffes did not "participate in the self-consciously American movements that resorted to Indian, Negro, mountaineer, and cowboy music for their Americanism." (Maisel) He and his confrères leaned toward self-conscious Gallicisms and the exotic Russo-Oriental palette. The credo of these men, which was also Griffes's, was expressed in print by John Alden Carpenter, a sybaritic, gentleman-gourmet type of composer, thus: "It has become the fashion with many of our musical observers and critics during the past half-dozen years to wring their hands and demand, for the future at least if it is impossible for the present, a more unmistakably 'American' quality in American music. Such a demand must inevitably result, for the composer who allows himself to be influenced by it, in a self-consciousness which is death to the real creative impulse . . . You may lead your creative impulse to our very best American folk-music material, but you can't make it drink . . . [The American composer] *must be writing what he feels like writing.*" This could be construed as a musical Declaration of Independence No. 3, after similarly emphatic pronouncements by William Fry and Edward Mac-Dowell; let us for our part emphasize once again that it's all very well to resort to Declarations when you have something to declare. We already know that Fry's "declared goods" were borrowed from Donizetti and Mercadante, MacDowell's would-be Celtic and Nordic goodies were Leipzig-flavored; as for Griffes, Carpenter, *et al,* they led their creative impulses to the muddy waters of French post-impressionism (successfully warred on for some time by Les Six in Paris and Cocteau, their able apologist) and drank their fill. Since Urbanism simply "didn't take," and the post-Wa-Wan folklorists were yet to make their appearance, American music seemed to be reaching another dead end.

Help came from the most unexpected and undesirable quarter. It was the jazzists who came to the rescue, and the undesirability of such help wasn't difficult to grasp; jazz—or what passed for it at the time—was hardly more than a vulgar musical joke to the 1924 diehards. Back in 1909, Max Fiedler, then conductor of the Boston Symphony, "had hesitated to perform Henry F. Gilbert's *Comedy-Overture* because he was afraid of the effect of the opening theme, which was more than a little suggestive of ragtime."* There was no perceptible change in this attitude toward "jazz" intrusions in the concert hall for many years to come, in spite of Carpenter's vaguely syncopated *Krazy Kat* (1922) and Gruenberg's *Daniel Jazz* (1923), which never really caught on in this country, and whose idiom had even less authenticity than the more renowned *La Création du Monde* by Darius Milhaud, written in the same year; typically, both pieces produced a far greater effect abroad.

On the afternoon of Lincoln's Birthday, 1924, American

---

* Claire McGlinchee, "American Literature in American Music," *The Musical Quarterly,* January, 1945.

music came to life—although it would be foolish to claim, as some do, that it came of age. I do subscribe to Isaac Goldberg's summing up (in his *George Gershwin, A Study in American Music*, 1931); "That was a birthday, too, for American music—even an Emancipation Proclamation, in which slavery to European formalism was signed away by the ascending glissandi of the *Rhapsody*." Paul Whiteman, who commissioned the work for his Aeolian Hall concert, told Leonard Liebling: "I desire to show the musical world that jazz, as we arrange and perform it, is no longer merely a dance medium, but feels ready to make a bid as an art, an American musical art, characteristic of our country, and expressed in a tonal language which our people can understand." It was lucky for Whiteman to have the *Rhapsody* for his concert's plum; the rest of the program consisted of four feeble serenades by Victor Herbert, "semi-symphonic arrangements" of popular melodies, samples of "legitimate scoring vs. jazzing," and four snappy piano solos by Zez Confrey (which included the successful and still listenable *Kitten on the Keys*), tricky player-piano-roll stuff, but hardly concert-hall material; these were to the audience's liking, however, and served as a suitable "warm-up" for the *Rhapsody*, placed in the coveted "next to closing" spot by canny Paul. The "concert" ended with—Elgar's *Pomp and Circumstance*.

"It was a strange audience out in front," Whiteman recorded (in his *Jazz*, by Paul Whiteman and Mary Margaret McBride, N. Y., 1926). "Vaudevillians, concert managers come to have a look at the novelty, Tin Pan Alleyites, composers, symphony and opera stars, flappers, cake-eaters, all mixed up higgledy-piggledy." Gershwin and I had been inseparable since 1922, and frantic work on the *Rhapsody* caused him to entrust me with preparing the piano copies of his George White 1924 *Scandals* songs; I knew the *Rhapsody's* themes, but had never heard them pieced together and competently

orchestrated by Ferde Grofé. There I sat, amid the flappers
and cake-eaters, very nervous and rather apprehensive, after
too much "Mama Loves Papa," "Whispering," and "flavoring
a selection with borrowed themes," as the program worded
it (the borrowed theme being the "Volga Boat Song"!).

I needn't have worried, because the *Rhapsody* had an immediate, electrifying success—the kind of success that rocked
even the happy composer, already used to bull's-eye hits. The
first-string critics were present (bully for them) and, with
the sole exception of crotchety Lawrence Gilman, rejoiced in
print—without the patronizing bosh that usually greets the
wayward Cinderellas of the concert hall. Eric Larabee, writing in the July, 1962 issue of *Harper's* magazine, found some
thirty versions of the ever-green *Blue Rhapsody* in Schwann's
catalogue. "The *Rhapsody*, in fact, long ago established itself
as the foremost 'jazz' item in the symphonic repertory," said
he. "As we can now appreciate, nothing about the *Rhapsody
in Blue* is right. It is a pseudo-Lisztian pastiche, with a
Tchaikovsky-like major theme, which borrows from those few
blue notes and dance rhythms necessary to make it seem fresh
and keep it moving. As proper jazz, it is nonexistent. As a
'serious' classical composition it is, to quote the New York
Times's Olin Downes on its first performance, 'at times vulgar,
cheap, in poor taste, but elsewhere of irresistible swing and
insouciance and recklessness and life.' It will outlive anything
you or I say of it."

So lowbrow a triumph brought considerable gloom to the
"legitimate" composers, understandably irked by a successful
Broadwayite's invasion of their sacrosanct territory. Gershwin
was accorded little more than a page by Rosenfeld (to Ornstein's ten, Rudhyar's seven, Sessions's thirteen, and Copland's
fifteen) in *An Hour with American Music*, and what a page!
After blasting (rightly) Krenek's *Johnny* and dismissing Milhaud's jazz efforts with "soft and timid," Paul went after

George with venomous relish." (V.D., *Passport to Paris.*) "The American parallels of these jazz experiments are equally indifferent," said Rosenfeld. "Gershwin's *Rhapsody, Piano Concerto,* and *An American in Paris* have found a good deal of popular favor: and Gershwin, himself is assuredly a gifted composer of the *lower, unpretentious order;* yet there is some question whether his vision permits him *an association with the artists*" (Italics are mine. V.D.). I'm not sure that George was any too anxious to "associate with the artists"—the Rosenfeld-endorsed kind, especially. He just went on his merry way, delighted with life, with his carefree, sunny music, with tennis, golf, and baseball. The "artists," with whom an association was too good for George in Paul's opinion, did a bit of grumbling, pointing to technical inadequacy (Grofé being called in to orchestrate the *Rhapsody*), pseudo-Lisztian piano writing in between hunks of neatly laundered jazz, etc. and, gritting their teeth, muttered about the desirability of Gershwin's speedy return to Broadway—and good riddance, too. Other artists—the noncompetitive interpreters—began seeking Gershwin's services as "guest star accompanist" to spike their Aeolian and Town Hall recitals with longhair versions of his theater hits; George was eager to oblige—and his enthusiastic, unashamedly extroverted collaboration in "Swanee," "Do It Again," "I'll Build a Stairway to Paradise" brought fresh laurels to both Eva Gauthier and Marguerite D'Alvarez.

Typically, "Many of the critics severely reproved the artist for presuming to introduce into a concert of classical songs, the type of music which, they pointed out 'simply did not belong,'" Claire Reis recorded in her *Composers, Conductors and Critics.* "Disciplinary action followed: ... Eva Gauthier was booked to give a repeat concert in Boston and it was canceled. The 'Hub' let Gauthier know that it would have none of her frivolous ideas; the place for jazz was Broadway, not the concert hall." Yet Boston's own Professor Edward

Burlingame Hill, then head of the music department at Harvard, a polished post-post-impressionist and avid Francophile, accepted Mrs. Reis's invitation to take part in a program (League-sponsored) to discuss "Jazz in the Music of Today"; significantly, this was in the year of *Rhapsody's* birth—1924.

Gilbert Seldes, the other lecturer, and Hill "treated the occasion with the greatest respect" (Mrs. Reis). But who do you suppose were the exponents of jazz for the momentous occasion? *Vincent Lopez* and "some members of his jazz [?] orchestra"; to add to the confusion, ultra-conservative Deems Taylor wrote a piece on "Respectabilizing Jazz"—he was all for it. Jazz purists of Rudi Blesh's stripe may be permitted a hearty guffaw at this point.

It was unfortunate that Gershwin's "big fat tunes" as well as technical shortcomings were superficially imitated by a string of "jazzists" to whom the silly term "semi-classical" could be applied for want of a more exact one. Publishers exercised pressure on their "contract writers" to turn out hastily contrived "take-offs" of the Gershwin idiom, bristling with "swingy" rhythm, oily melodies that would later appear as thirty-two-bar choruses, commmercially lyricized, octave runs, glib arpeggios, and grandiose codas à la *Rhapsody*. All such material was eagerly accepted by school orchestras, bands, and "Pop" concert program-makers; it sold phenomenally well, but had no value whatever as music. Of the earlier, post-Gershwin jazzists, only Morton Gould and, upon occasion, Ferde Grofé and Raymond Scott made inroads upon the "respectable" concert hall. We have already spoken of the jazz influence in Copland's music; of other early jazzists with a sound classical background, Robert McBride's (b. 1911) name comes to mind. McBride's language was terse and sharp, with no "love theme" sugar-coating, or pianistic bric-a-brac ("Workout" and "Swing Stuff" written in the thirties), but his scope was not large and he is seldom heard from these days.

Gershwin continued his new "serious" career with dogged determination and, on the whole, with success—although not one of his subsequent productions brought about the electric shock of the immature, yet potent *Rhapsody.* The Piano Concerto (to which George always referred rather grandly as the *Concerto in F,* though he wrote no other concerti), *An American in Paris,* the three piano preludes, and his best achievement—*Porgy and Bess*—can be listed as successes and have proven to possess staying powers. The *Second Rhapsody*—more adroitly constructed than the first but marred by a trite first subject, *Cuban Overture,* and the witty variations on "I Got Rhythm" didn't quite ring the bell. George's technique improved steadily, as did his orchestrating ability: every piece following the Grofé-scored *Rhapsody* was orchestrated by the composer, who also made a point of arranging "at least two numbers" (as he asserted to me) in each of his musical shows. This technical development, obvious to every honest listener, was ridiculed by that Master of the Mot Injuste, Virgil Thomson. Commenting on the Concerto and *An American in Paris* (*Modern Music,* November-December, 1935), Thomson wrote: "Just why the execution was not so competent as in the *Rhapsody* was never quite clear. I used to think that perhaps it was all voluntary, that he [Gershwin] was cultivating a certain amateurishness because he had been promised that if he was a good little boy and didn't upset any apple carts, he might, maybe, when he grew up, be president of American music, just like Daniel Gregory Mason or somebody."

Honest-to-goodness Americanists shrugged off *le cas Gershwin* as a freakish phenomenon they had to live with but affected not to notice, and began discovering—better late than never—native folklore and its box-office potential.

"The principal concern of music in the twenties was the idea of a national or 'typically American' school or style and, eventually, a tradition which would draw to a focus the musi-

cal energies of our country which, as Rosenfeld once said to
Aaron Copland and the author, would 'affirm America,'" Roger
Sessions summed up in his *Reflections on the Music Life in the
U.S.* (N.Y., 1956). The astute Sessions, never an "Americanist" in the narrowly nationalistic sense, went on cautiously:
"The most pointedly American manifestations were sought,
not always in the most discriminating spirit or with the most
penetrating insight as to value; and the effort was made to
call forth hidden qualities from sources hitherto regarded with
contempt." Sessions than attempted to minimize the worth
of native folklore as a point of departure for a truly American
music: "Though these songs [of Old West, the Civil War, the
slaves-in-the-South origin. V. D.] are in no sense lacking in
character, they fail to embody a clear style; and it is difficult
to see how, with their origins in a relatively sophisticated [?]
musical vocabulary, they could conceivably form the basis
of a 'national' style."

Well, the folklore-inspired U.S.A. music might have been
"difficult to see," but it was easy enough to hear. It flourished
in the late twenties and the early thirties, and the stuff was
gratifyingly listenable in spite of Sessions's carping about its
"relatively superficial level, not so much for lack of attraction,
but for lack of the elements necessary for expansion into a
genuine style or at least into a 'manner.'" He does make an
exception for "the extraordinary figure of Charles Ives ... certainly one of the significant men in American music," but one
finds it hard to agree with Sessions's forced and arbitrary conclusion unsupported by evidence: "... among the various
elements of which his [Ives's] music consists—music which
sometimes reaches almost a level of genius, but which, at
other times, is banal and amateurish—*the folklorist is the most
problematic, the least characteristic.*" The worth of this statement can be easily measured when one realizes that Ives's
Three Places in New England, The Concord Sonata (piano),

the Second and Fourth Violin Sonatas, and some songs, the peak of the man's sonorous output, all have their roots in the American folklore and even quote folk songs.

Sessions and the greatly gifted, though never properly appreciated Wallingford Riegger (1885-1961), antipodes in many ways, were fanatical individualists, not to say isolationists, which did not impair the quality of their work. Although Riegger produced an obscure *American Polonaise* in 1923, the rest of his catalogue shows no sign of any nationalistic leanings. Sessions's first and, oddly, most lasting success, *The Black Maskers*, appeared in the same year and, while Riegger's was a Polish-American mixture, Sessions's far better-known piece culled its inspiration from the utterly outmoded would-be symbolist, Leonid Andreyev—a Russian! Neither *Turn O Libertad* (after Walt Whitman, 1945) nor the opera *Montezuma* (1947), the only entries with an American theme or text, had sufficient exposure to modify one's impression of Sessions, he having adopted "an austere style of composition, akin to that of Stravinsky's later works." (*Baker's*) By "later works" Slonimsky obviously means those written *prior* to Stravinsky's conversion to dodecaphony.

Whether one terms it "style" or "manner" is immaterial—Americanist music of good quality did emerge, giving the lie to Sessions's assertion that its folk-song origin "failed to embody a clear style." There was style aplenty in Copland's *Billy the Kid, Rodeo,* and *Appalachian Spring,* the beginnings of one in Roy Harris's first efforts, *Impressions of a Rainy Day* (1926) and *American Portraits* (1929), while the self-consciously "academic" Americanism of Howard Hanson remained "on a relatively superficial level" (Sessions) in its bombastic attempt to make a Yankee out of Sibelius.

Next to Ives and Copland, Roy Harris was—and is—perhaps the most indefatigable and tenacious Americanist; his stick-to-itivness—with variable results—is far more determined than that of the other two composers, who (Copland particularly so) explored other, less confining idioms. Harris's self-adulation and delusions of grandeur (well known to the musical fraternity and gleefully publicized) are not uncommon with the "genus composer" and need not prejudice an impartial listener; yet it must be admitted that while both Ives's and Copland's work is certainly uneven in quality, Harris's catalogue consists of a few real "ups" (the Third and Fourth [folk-song] Symphonies) and a great number of uncomfortable "downs." This may be due in part, to Harris's yeasty technique (he was twenty-four when he "decided that he wanted to be a composer" (Chase), unfortunately frequent lapses of taste, and a shaky sense of proportion, which often caused him to overwrite. "You either like or you don't like Roy Harris. I do," Moses Smith stated in *Modern Music* (May-June, 1944). "I keep hoping that Harris will some day escape from the kind of intellectual and emotional frustration that I detect in his music. Thus each piece, whatever its merits, is a disappointment. The second part of the Sixth (*Gettysburg Address*) Symphony, the movement called "Conflict," is quite naïve. Anyhow, it reminded me of an accompaniment for an Indian War Dance in an old-fashioned Western." Four years earlier, Charles Seeger asked (in the same magazine): "Does Harris not hold himself back by this hankering ever to try on once more the giant's robe?" Seeger also deplored "an amorphous kind of *durchführung* which he seems to think he has to write in order to be a great composer. Harris is not a brilliant orchestrator, even for string quintet." Lou Harrison (*Modern Music,* November-December, 1943) on reviewing Harris's *Ode to Truth,* commented wryly: "Harris seems to have perennial coda trouble; much go, no stop."

Yet "there is ample evidence," in Gilbert Chase's words, "that Harris considers himself to be one of those stanch individuals who are creating an authentic and characteristic musi-

cal expression of American culture," and, further, that Harris's
"honest appreciation of the beauties of his own work is refreshing" (Walter Piston). Notwithstanding such good- or ill-
natured gibes, it must be said that the man's Third Symphony
(premièred by Koussevitzky and the Boston Symphony in
1939) was more than "honestly appreciated" by the overflowing audience, not just the habitually narcissistic composer—
it scored "a resounding triumph. Its success was sensational"
(Chase). What's more, after innumerable performances (both
here and abroad) it "achieved wide acclaim and had an unprecedented acceptance," thus "marking the beginning of a
new era in American symphonic music" (same writer). Harris's
muse is "rough-hewn, sinewy, and directly outspoken" (Harris
on Harris). The man's immense energy and resourcefulness
deserve admiration and sympathy. He may yet come through
with a piece "wonderful beyond *our* wildest hopes"; which is
what the composer said (to Slonimsky) about his own Fifth
Symphony (1942) substituting "my" for "our."

William Schuman, able administrator and representative
composer, is very much a man of today, and if his name is
included in this chapter, it's because both he and Roy Harris,
his teacher, had their first innings in the thirties. The pupil
is a better craftsman than the Oklahoman who taught him
composition, but it should be added that Schuman also studied
at the Mozarteum Academy in Salzburg. Lenny Bernstein,
then only twenty-four, said of Schuman's *American Festival
Overture*, a thoroughly enjoyable piece, that it had ". . . vigor
of propulsion which seizes the listener by the hair . . . This in-
volves a buoyance and a lust-for-life which I find (at the risk
of being called old-fashioned and artificially nationalistic)
wholly American. Young America exists, acts, and speaks in
this music" (*Modern Music* January - February, 1942.) According to Gilbert Chase, Schuman also wrote "some of the grim-
mest music of our times," which, luckily, I have not heard;
most of the stuff turned out nowadays is grim enough.

Schuman, like Henry Cowell many years later, paid homage to Billings in his *William Billings Overture* (1943), using three themes from the New England tanner's choral works; there is a soaring spontaneity about Schuman's short choral pieces that makes them a welcome addition to the often peculiarly austere music in that idiom. To borrow a term from the Brill Building jargon, the composer is at his best in the "up tempo" mood. He tends to be long-winded on occasion (*Symphony for Strings*) and was given to certain harmonic mannerisms that seemed arbitrary—Schuman became more selective in that respect as he matured. He orchestrates superlatively well; the shrewdly organized and executed Sixth Symphony (1949) is evidence of his sureness of touch, although the symphony is less persuasive to some than his *oeuvres de jeunesse;* the long, perhaps overlong, melodic line may be the reason for this. The frankly "tonal" ending to an otherwise outspokenly atonal work (in one movement) was daring, indeed, even in 1949, and, I fear, would be considered monstrous today—just as atonal endings, beloved by a Schoenberg, or even a Scriabin, were rated as monstrosities before World War I.

Mississippi-born (1895) William Grant Still belongs to the Americanists, although calling him an Afro-Americanist would be more apt. Still started as a musical handyman, and had to do a variety of musical jobs for a living; after a Little Rock, Arkansas, upbringing, he studied composition at Oberlin and, on settling in New York, arranged blues and pop songs for W. C. Handy while continuing his serious studies with—Edgard Varèse! His *Darkest America*, the first of a series of symphonic works, was born in 1924, the year of Gershwin's *Rhapsody's* emergence and was followed by *From the Black Belt* (1926), *Africa* (1930), and *Afro-American Symphony* (1931). These and the (1937) *Song of the New Race* (Second Symphony) were admittedly the utterances of "the American Colored Man of today." So was the brutally realistic, yet lyrical *And They Lynched Him on a Tree* (1940), a species of short cantata. Still recreates Negro spirituals in his music with power and skill, but leans toward French impressionism in his harmonic language, and the wedding is not always a happy one.

The two younger Negro composers, Howard Swanson and Ulysses Kay, musicians of talent and originality, both, do not belong with "Yesterday's promises," having really started to function in the early fifties. The same remark applies to versatile and always provocative Henry Cowell, who delayed his adventures in Americana to explore the possibilities of piano-clusters, collaborating with Leon Theremin on something called the "rhythmicon," "designed to produce all kinds of rhythms and cross-rhythms," says Claire Reis. (What happened to the rhythmicon and, come to think of it, the theremin?) Irish reels, Gaelic symphonies, and Celtic sets occupied Cowell's time in the thirties and early forties; the era of hymns and fuguing tunes was not as yet upon him. Randall Thompson (b. 1899) showed "a remarkable feeling for the idioms of American folk and popular music within the framework of academic traditionalism," in Gilbert Chase's estimate; agreed. Among other academic Americanists can be listed Leo Sowerby (b. 1895); among those who attempted a merger of folklore and jazz, the already noted Morton Gould (*Swing Symphonetta, Interplay, Fall River Legend*—all effective in their way) and the even lighter Don Gillis. Ernst Bacon (b. 1898) and Elie Siegmeister (b. 1909) can be bracketed together, if only because of their tireless exploitation of the rural American scene; both excel in vocal music, while Sowerby's forte is the organ.

In the field of theatrical and film music, four Americanists made their mark in the late twenties and early thirties. The senior member of this group is Douglas Moore (b. 1893), whose opera *The Devil and Daniel Webster* (1938) is unquestionably one of the best homemade essays in that form. Here we find clearly etched, theatrically grateful, and melodically appealing music, a rare and enviable combination of opera "musts." Moore "Americanized" in the symphonic field as well, gaining early recognition for his *Pageant of P. T. Barnum* (1924), also *Moby Dick* (1928), and an *Overture on an American Tune* (1931), both still in manuscript. Marc Blitzstein (b. 1905), a Scalero and Nadia Boulanger pupil, taught at the New School for Social Research, and wrote vehement, socially significant music; some of it was musically significant, as well. His 1928 *Triple Sec* was a cheeky opera-farce; in it, Blitzstein displayed a definite flair for the theater, which was also present in the League of Composers-commissioned *The Harpies* (one-act opera 1931), the angrily convincing *The Cradle Will Rock*, (1937), and especially *Regina* (1949), his most durable work to date. The overly shrill *No for an Answer* (1941) is less memorable. Bernard Herrmann (b. 1911), a rough-and-ready type of uncompromising music maker, produced another *Moby Dick* (1937), an uneven, but often potent dramatic cantata, and a charming *Currier and Ives Suite* (1935), which deserves more frequent performance. His main strength lies in such thoroughly un-Hollywoodian film scores as *Citizen Kane* (1940), a minor masterpiece in the idiom; *The Magnificent Ambersons*, and *The Devil and Daniel Webster* (both in 1941); he and Moore seem to have the same literary predilections. Jerome Moross (b. 1913), the Benjamin of the group, made a specialty of ballets; *American Pattern* (1936), *Frankie and Johnnie* (1938), *Susanna and the Elders* (1940), and several others, wherein folk material is spiked with jazz overtones. He is also capable of producing a really first-rate show song ("Lazy Afternoon" in the *Golden Apple* to John Latouche's wonderful words) and is a practiced hand with film scoring.

While the Urbanists boasted a few exciting "high spots," their efforts soon showed (Paul Rosenfeld's championship notwithstanding) that American music would not, could not develop in that direction. The jazzists and the folklorists were jointly responsible for the emergence of a recognizable national school. With so formidable a "nationalistic" backlog accumulated in record time (speed having always been a stellar American virtue)—from 1924 to World War II—our country's composers were enabled to enjoy the new freedom of creating their own, not necessarily jazzist or folklore-saturated, music. At long last, our Declaration of Independence was an accomplished and recognizable fact, not merely an ill-considered and premature gesture.

IV

This extraordinary Birth of a Musical Nation occurred at the height of America's economic boom; the infant grew by prodigious leaps and bounds, and not even the 1929 Wall Street disaster and subsequent depression (no chicken in any pot, but Hoover apples on every corner) could impede its healthy progress. "All of this activity built to an explosion of creative energy in the thirties. Several forces joined to sustain a great upsurge of musical creativity and experimentation. The financial depression created the WPA concerts, which used large quantities of American music, much of it newly composed," attested Nathan Broder in his essay, "The Evolution of the American Composer" (*in One Hundred Years of Music in America*, G. Schirmer, 1961). "Progressive ideas that had percolated in Europe during the twenties began now to boil over into America; Schoenberg himself settled here in 1933." I'd like to point out, however, that Schoenberg was in no way typical of Europe in the twenties—the era of Les Six, and insouciant "Musiquette," neo-diatonicism, and jazzist concoctions: *La Création du Monde, Jonny Spielt Auf,* Walton's *Façade,* and Lambert's *Rio Grande,* with its transparent borrowings from Gershwin. Our first dodecaphonist, the unpredictable, stubbornly nonconformist Wallingford Riegger, was composing furiously, but didn't get the acclaim, long overdue, until 1948, in which year his stark and virile Third Symphony was the choice of the New York Music Critics Circle. That music in any idiom—even the freedom-strangling dodecaphonic one—can be of real interest and value was clearly demonstrated by Riegger in the *Study in Sonority* (1927) and the fascinating *Dichotomy* (1932). Poor Wallingford! Dichotomy, indeed, became his *nom de guerre,* and brought about a succession of *noms de plume* (Gerald Wilfring Gore and John H. McCurdy were two of the more ludicrous ones), and not from choice; he had to make a living and even resorted to copying music to add to his meager income.

Other talented nonconformists sprang into being at that difficult, but feverishly productive time. Theodore Chanler (b. 1902), who, to Gilbert Chase's everlasting shame, did not rate a mention in his *America's Music,* was (he died in 1961) our greatest and most fastidiously articulate composer in smaller forms, especially in the now regrettably unfashionable *lieder* form. Such cycles as the poignant *Epitaphs* (1937) and the more recent *The Children,* the (1950) *Mass* for two female voices and organ, and the beautifully written piano pieces deserve the widest acceptance, which, so far, has been denied them. A just appraisal of Chanler's modest yet intensely personal art, unblemished by box-office and publicity ballyhoo, was made by Robert Tangeman in *Modern Music* (May-June, 1945): "Chanler has developed an integrated, mature style quietly and thoughtfully. He displays complete sincerity and lack of pretentiousness. In him, matter and manner reach an organic synthesis more typical of an older culture than of an artistically youthful nation. [This may be the clue to the general lack of interest in Chanler's music. V.D.] His songs are the expression of a personality whose strength and tenderness bring wisdom and a new beauty into American music." Amen to that; old culture and new beauty need not be incompatible.

Two younger men, whose music and whose fortunes were

(and are) strikingly dissimilar, yet who moved in the same circles and were both commissioned ballet scores by Lincoln Kirstein in the thirties, were Elliott Carter (b. 1908), now recognized as one of our best composers, and Paul Bowles (b. 1910), who, after an exciting start, turned to literature, gaining substantial recognition with his novel, *The Sheltering Sky* (1949) and, in *Baker's* summing up, "became known as primarily a writer." Bowles's early ballet was *Yankee Clipper* (1937), Carter's was titled *Pocahontas* (1939), but, in spite of local themes, neither composer was a U. S.-type Americanist —Bowles leaning toward Mexican and Latin-American rhythms and colors, Carter developing into a virtuoso abstractionist. Bowles's forte appeared to be subtle and evocative background music for the theater (several Saroyan plays); Carter's realm is the concert hall.

It was in the money-poor but music-rich thirties that the voice of America's best symphonist was first heard; the voice had unmistakable authority, for its owner was Walter Piston (b. 1894). His grandfather's name was Pistone, and there is rich Italian blood in the Rockland, Maine, composer's veins. Although his Italian antecedents might induce some foolhardy Latin patriot to bracket Piston with our Italo-American composers' colony, consisting of Paul Creston (Joseph Guttoveggio), Vittorio Giannini, Norman Dello Joio, Peter Mennin (Mennini), and that on-again, off-again American, Gian Carlo Menotti (still an Italian citizen, although this country is his gravity center), such a "patriot" would be dead wrong, for no more introspective, carefully weighed, sensation-disdaining, *non-Latin* music than Piston's has ever been written; this, in a lesser degree, is also true of the much younger Mennin (b. 1923). Piston's composing had the quiet assurance of a master, fully armed with the best weapons of his craft from the beginning but, since his language had real music for its base, not empty mathematical substitutes, the result was never dry.

Piston's work manages to "come off" in performance, however fascinating it may appear on paper. Elliott Carter's succinct estimate of the composer's position (*The Musical Quarterly,* July, 1946) is worth quoting: "... through the early thirties when a new wave of nationalism and populism started many into thinking that the concert hall with its museum atmosphere was finished as a place for living new music ... Piston went his own way. He stood firmly on his own chosen ground, building up a style that is a synthesis of most of the important characteristics of contemporary music and assimilating into his own manner the various changes as they came along. As a result of this tireless concentration combined with rich native musical gifts, his works have a uniform excellence that seems destined to give them an important position in musical repertory."

Although Aaron Copland argued that "there is nothing especially American in his [Piston's] work," he had to admit that Piston's music "if considered *only* [!] from a technical viewpoint, constitutes a challenge to every other American composer. It sets a level of craftsmanship that is absolutely first-rate in itself and provides a standard of reference by which every other American's work may be judged." (*Our New Music,* 1941) As for the supposed (by Copland) lack of dyed-in-the wool Americanism, Piston's "American quality is apparent ... in the sonority and texture of his music, which are quite distinct from those of any of the schools of Europe" (Carter). Also, "It should be observed that Piston's allusions to jazz and other popular idioms of American music became a fundamental feature of his style ... this is spendidly illustrated in the first movement of the Second Symphony, where syncopated rhythms actually impel one's feet to dance" (Gilbert Chase). This doesn't prevent Mr. Chase from calling Piston "our leading academic traditionalist."

A man who was undeniably shackled by academic tradition

until but recently is the popular and gifted, although hardly
"eminent" (the adjective bestowed upon him by *Baker's
Dictionary*), Samuel Barber (b. 1910). Barber's music, until
the late forties, was conservative in the extreme, both as
regards subject matter and technique; this, probably, due to
his Curtis Institute training and traditionally "respectable"
environment (his aunt was the famous singer, Louise Homer).
The young composer — no mean concert singer, himself — had
an appealing melodic gift and a predilection for a brooding,
sehnsucht-laden lyricism; his orchestration was somewhat
gray and overcharged (this was noticeable even in the 1946
Cello Concerto), but, academically speaking "respectable."
Suffice it to say that young Barber collected several important
prizes while still in his twenties, received a Pulitzer Traveling
Scholarship (1935), and got performances from such men
as Molinari and Toscanini — the latter known for his un-
relenting hostility to new music. Gradually, Barber's careful
and somewhat costive craftsmanship extended to healthy
experimenting and general "loosening up." This was gratifyingly noticeable in the *Second Essay for Orchestra* (1942);
the abundantly songful, if unadventurous, *Adagio for Strings*
(Barber's most widely performed piece) was an earlier effort.
The *Second Essay* was followed by the fanciful *Capricorn
Concerto* (1944) and the delectable *Excursions* (1945).
Barber's songs — even those written in his youth — are more
rewarding than his initial tries in the symphonic field, and,
being written by a singer, were welcomed by recitalists everywhere.

To this already impressive list of native composers who
made their debuts before World War II can be added:
symphonists Bernard Rogers (b. 1893) (*Soliloquy for Flute
and Strings*, 1922) and Herbert Elwell (b. 1898), composer
of *The Happy Hypocrite* (1925), the better-known and more
prolific David Diamond (b. 1915), an omnifarious eclectic,

not always discriminating in his choice of tools and materials, but capable of such things as the enchanting background score for Shakespeare's *Tempest* and the oft-performed *Rounds for strings*. His symphonies — the third one, for example — display a tendency to bombast and "modernistic" clichés. Diamond is a product of the Eastman School in Rochester (where he was born) and, whatever one may think of Howard Hanson's own music, he deserves the nation's gratitude for teaching, performing, and often popularizing the productions of the many able, Eastman-trained men. To their number, aside from Rogers and Diamond, belong Hunter Johnson, Burrill Phillips, Gardner Read, Robert Palmer, Robert E. Ward, the already named Ulysses Kay, and Peter Mennin, considered by some as the "American Hindemith"; in reality, a facile and resourceful technician with an excellent grasp of the cycle form, who needs only weightier and more communicable subject matter to become a first-rate composer.

The same observations could apply to versatile Norman Dello Joio (b. 1913), whose music is articulate and pointed, whose vocabulary is rich, and who seems to be equally at ease in every existing genre; somehow, all these sterling qualities, as well as the always useful gift for spare and lucid orchestration, do not make up for the general shallowness of Dello Joio's world of sound.

Among our better chamber-music composers, Quincy Porter and Ross Lee Finney rate more than a passing mention. Arthur Berger (b. 1912), Irving Fine (1914-1962), and Harold Shapero (b. 1920), all Harvard men, were enamored of Stravinskian neoclassicism for quite a spell; with their spiritual master's conversion to serial techniques, the first two followed suit, while the younger, Shapero, "already applied the dodecaphonic method in some of his early compositions." (Slonimsky, who was Shapero's teacher before the composer turned to Piston, Hindemith, and Nadia Boulanger, so testified in

Baker's; Shapero switched to neoclassical precepts in after years.) Having been one jump ahead of the great Igor, and then (as though seeing the error of his ways) adopting the Russian's apparently unexchangeable neoclassical garb, he tempts one to ask: "What method will he apply to his new music?"

Gilbert Chase lists Cowell, Ruggles, and the "characteristically bold" John J. Becker (b. 1886), as "experimentalists," adding the Canadian-American trio of Colin McPhee (b. 1901), Gerald Strang (b. 1908), and Henry Brant (b. 1913). McPhee experimented with the musical lore of Bali and Java; Strang explored the world of percussion (he was not alone in this); while erratic and, perhaps, too determinedly eccentric Henry Brant toyed with anything that took his fancy—hand him a Spanish ox bell, double ocarina, or twenty tin whistles, and a new concerto is born. All three are men of talent and imagination, but it serves no purpose to dump them in the same heap with Cowell and Ruggles, as Chase does.

It would be incorrect to claim that the high-gear productivity of so many authentically promising composers resulted in their getting their just deserts in the thirties or the beginning of the next decade, for that matter. Of course, with the musical market suddenly flooded with worth-while native material, some results were obtained, especially in Boston, where Serge Koussevitzky stood ready to lend his experienced ear to anything made in the U.S.A.—preferably on the advice of trusted "Arosha" (the conductor's affectionate nickname for the composer) Copland.

In the main, jobs were scarce, and—cruel paradox—performances came high, because, as all insiders are well aware, it *costs* a lot of money to write, copy, photostat, and mail one's symphonic productions to conductors; the performance fee is still infinitesimally small compared with the composer's expenditures. "The non-performing, non-teaching composer is

to this day—in spite of all the optimistic propaganda—a penniless lunatic in the richest country in the world." (V.D. *Passport
to Paris*) I wrote this in 1955, at which point commissions,
grants, fellowships, and prizes were within every native composer's reach; there was mighty little of that sort of thing in
the Gloomy Thirties. "The composers were sad, somber fellows
in quest of jobs and performances, distrustful not only of me,
a European pretender, but particularly of one another," I
reported (same book). "There was much talent among them
and also much genuine suffering. Every composer I met
boasted a long record of inhuman trials and tribulations, of
sums spent and none earned, of eternal promises by publishers, performers, and conductors, never fulfilled."

Still, the "boys" (some of whom were past fifty) went on
writing music—the kind they wanted to write, intent on having
their say. What they wrote was American music, whether (to
borrow from Paul Rosenfeld again) it be the kind turned out
by the "uncompromisingly and idealistically lofty Copland,
the rhapsode of the American migrations and pioneer exist-
ences," or the wrong (to Rosenfeld) kind provided by that
well-heeled Cinderella of U.S. music—George Gershwin, the
rhapsode of "splendiferous hotel foyers crowded with important people and gorgeous women." Gershwin, according
to Rosenfeld, couldn't even "qualify as a *vulgar* composer."

Since my own Second Symphony was accepted for performance (thanks entirely to Prokofiev's efforts), I described
at length, in my autobiography, how "Europe got the opportunity to acquaint itself with American fashions in music."
(Not that my obviously Russian work was, in any sense, a
sample. V.D.) The Rosenfeld party was to be represented by
Sessions's Piano Sonata, the Van Vechten party by Gershwin's
American in Paris, both works chosen for performance at the
ninth meeting of the I.S.C.M. in Oxford and London in July,
1931. Ever fair and impartial H. T. Parker reported on the

American contributions and stated typically in the Boston
Transcript: "It is good to find so distinguished a body giving
ear to the side of American music that Mr. Gershwin represents." Alas! There was another, certainly less distinguished,
but uncomfortably weighty body the Americans didn't reckon
with, the English press: "No one can be more savagely abusive
than an English critic when aroused." (*Passport*) The traditionally impeccable manners of a Briton desert him utterly
when he puts pen to paper. The critics said little of Sessions's
Piano Sonata, the other American entry, but they rolled up
their neatly tailored sleeves and went to work on Gershwin:
"Innocent, but tiresome babble . . . the banal and silly piece
drove me from the hall . . . pretty bad; not clever enough
for the occasion," and so on. George (not present) could
well afford to brush such small annoyances aside—he was
basking in the glory of the revived *Strike Up the Band,* and
getting ready for rehearsals of its successor—the unforgettable
and (in its difficult genre unequaled) musico-political satire,
Of Thee I Sing.

The time for American music—other than jazz—to entrench
itself firmly on European shores is yet to come; prior to World
War II our "serious" music was virtually unknown, and certainly unwanted. To our composers' credit, they went right
on turning out yards of music, copying it themselves, when
finances were low, sending it (that costs money, too) to the
shoulder-shrugging conductors, and plaguing the cynical
and weary publishers. By 1940, there was such a hue and
cry about native music's neglect, that the performing fraternity
began "giving in" resignedly; conditions did improve, bringing some of the more tireless composers a modicum of prestige
and (upon occasion) a few microscopic royalties. ". . . In a
number of ways the American composer fares better today
than he did ten or even five years ago," Douglas Moore wrote
in *Modern Music* (November-December, 1943.) "Scholarships

and fellowships, not to mention prizes and commissions, are so plentiful that new talents are fairly pounced upon by the official distributors of benevolence, and once the first hurdles are taken, it is possible to go on for years without the distraction of earning a living . . . opportunities for performance, so vital to the nourishment of the artist, are greater . . . American music seems to be gradually winning its way into the symphonic repertory!"

At the tail end of the thirties—in June, 1939, to be precise—a young New Englander named Leonard Bernstein (b. 1918) was graduated from Harvard *cum laude* in music. The swarthy, handsome, restlessly self-seeking, grandiosely ambitious youth had no Bostonian traits whatever—except, perhaps, a great capacity for learning all there was to learn about his chosen profession, or, rather, three professions: those of composer, conductor, and pianist. Two years at the Curtis Institute followed the Harvard graduation, with helpful advice from Mitropoulos, Fritz Reiner, and Copland on the side. Then came the Tanglewood fairy tale—two summers at the Berkshire Music Center, studying conducting with Koussevitzky, fruitful talks with Paul Hindemith and, again, the ubiquitous Copland. His additional studies completed, Bernstein was ready for a spectacular triple career in music, but encountered a series of vexing setbacks. Came Pearl Harbor: Bernstein "tried to enlist in the army and was summarily turned down because of his congenital asthma" (David Ewen, *Leonard Bernstein*, 1960). More musical tribulations and disappointments followed: the colorful and moving *Jeremiah Symphony,* completed at record speed by the end of 1942 to meet the deadline of a New England Conservatory contest for a symphonic work, failed to win the prize, also failing to please Koussevitzky.

In the fall of 1943, Bernstein became assistant conductor of the New York Philharmonic-Symphony, at the age of twenty-

five, and the furious pace at which he traveled the path of
success has not abated since. The American army's loss proved
to be American music's gain—for Bernstein embodies most
of the qualities of a Gershwin (except George's downright
Mozartean melodic gift) with, in addition, an unusually
variegated and flexible composing technique; if only he had
more time for composing! In addition to his conducting and
piano-playing activities, Bernstein scored a triple-header (in
one year—1944) by way of a debut: the seemingly ill-fated
Jeremiah Symphony, which clicked in Pittsburgh, was picked
up by the initially skeptical Koussevitzky, then conducted by
Bernstein, himself, with the Philharmonic in New York; it
represented his painless conquest of the concert hall. *Fancy
Free* triumphed as a ballet (choreographed by Jerome Robbins, designed by Oliver Smith), while *On the Town,* a musical comedy which opened at the Adelphi in December of
that fateful year (1944), caught on at once and became a hit
of smash proportions.

Those who, unlike Lenny Bernstein, were drafted into the
armed forces, did not fare badly either. Of course, "the sub-
stitution of the military for the highly specialized profession
of music was, to say the least, drastic," Douglas Moore
observed. "However, musicians have shown that they can
make the transition with as much agility as anyone else." "The
Army Musical School (at Fort Myer, outside of Washington)
graduated more than 450 students who are now serving all
over the world as band leaders with the rank of warrant
officer, junior grade." (William Strickland, *Modern Music,*
January-February, 1944.) Among them were conductors John
Barnett and Thor Johnson, composers Robert Ward and Ellis
Kohs. Gifted Gail Kubik (b. 1914), then a corporal, managed
to get a Guggenheim postwar fellowship while in uniform.
He wrote cheerful and informative letters from England,
where he was stationed, to Minna Lederman (*Modern Music's*

editor), which were duly printed on that magazine's pages. Kubik talked of the "hypoed renaissance of English musical life," in his letter of April, 1944. "Almost anything sells . . . The English are ready, with a great deal of interest and support, for new music. Even American scores, if sent over here, might make money!" In the next breath, Corporal Kubik had to admit, however reluctantly, that some native scores presumably having arrived in England, "American works had not fared too well . . . the average English musician still is inclined to think of Gershwin, and perhaps MacDowell [!] as the chief representatives of contemporary America. The Boosey and Hawkes American Music Concert of March 26th provided a departure with the Copland *Outdoor Overture,* Bloch's Violin Concerto, Sessions's First Symphony, Piston's *Incredible Flutist* and . . . the inevitable Gershwin *Rhapsody in Blue.*"

So inclusive a musical invasion of our ally's territory was bolstered by Marc Blitzstein's (Kubik's fellow GI) *Freedom Song,* performed in Albert Hall and vigorously applauded. On the other hand "the critics were not too impressed" with Copland's Piano Sonata; while the audience's reaction was "cordial, though not demonstrative." Blitzstein's *Airborne Symphony,* dedicated to the U.S. Army Negro troops, was performed by the Army Negro Chorus, led by the composer, then the director of music of the American broadcasting station in Europe; a successful première also took place at London's Albert Hall. Lehman Engel (b. 1910), one of our most knowing all-round musicians, equally at home in the region of madrigals and the musical comedy orchestra pit, brought good music to the U.S. Navy.

Tireless Henry Cowell helped with a "clear-cut policy for the use of music in the Radio Program Bureau of the OWI (Office of War Information)." (Cowell in *Modern Music,* May-June, 1945.) "It is not too much to say that music's very precise exploitation has frequently been the deciding factor in our ability to reach hundreds of millions of foreign peoples with the Allied news and American views . . . At about this time [1943] I was asked by Macklin Marrow, then music chief, to advise on serious works, American pieces . . . We found that pieces by modern Americans *whose style is not too complex* [Italics are mine. V.D.] were well received." No one can blame Cowell, a "serious" composer, for going easy on commercial pop music, which was included in the broadcasts "whenever it was needed, though we did not want even the people who request and like it to form the opinion that this is the only music in America." Cowell's "wrap-up" of the article is significant: ". . . while accomplishing the primary objective of gaining world-wide audiences on our radio programs . . . we have succeeded in introducing American music to many people who had never heard it before. They will inevitably now give serious consideration to our place in the international field of art."

Stay-at-home composers, many of them beyond draft age, did their share in contributing to the war effort by supplying musical tools for what was known as "psychological warfare." Charles Ives turned out a "War Long March," Walter Piston a "Fugue on a Victory Theme," Douglas Moore contributed a "Destroyer Song," J. A. Carpenter, "The Anxious Bugler," while Roger Sessions settled for a "Dirge." Short orchestra *Fanfares* (something of a misnomer in this instance) were composed by native musicians, young and old, and sandwiched between weightier symphonic pieces by (for once) obliging conductors. Lucky Barber, who joined the Army Air Forces in 1942, was actually commissioned (see *Baker's,* p. 84) to write a symphony (his second) by that august military body; he also wrote a "Commando March" for band. There was plenty of good non-military music written and eagerly performed on these shores in wartime. "The effect of this enlarged opportunity [for performance] has been to encourage the American composers to write more abundantly and more confidently than ever before" (Douglas Moore). Seemingly, all that the music boys had to do was to come home unscathed, get into civvies and back to "business as usual"—or, rather, to vastly improved business. Also, there was the comforting thought that there would be thousands of noncomposing GI's who, through exposure to honest-to-goodness "classical" music, would form a young, new audience after the victory, eager to sample the fruit of their compatriots' labors, those compatriots, at any rate, "whose style is not too complex," in Cowell's realistic observation.

Robert Ward, whose *Crucible* (1961) is one of the most deserving and enduring operas written by an American, was bandleader of the Seventh Infantry Division Band in the Pacific Theater. On being "mustered out," he went back to Juilliard in 1946, first to complete his studies, interrupted by the war, then to teach. Ward's earnest and deeply impressive bit of advice to Post-War Musical America (given in 1943, while he was at Fort Ord, and printed in the March-April issue of *Modern Music*) should have been accepted as the only workable blueprint by his composing colleagues: "If the ends of this war are worth our lives, then certainly they are worth the best our talents can produce. There is also a very simple satisfaction in contributing to our comrades' happiness by playing the music they deeply wish to hear, even when that music is not what would give us the greatest personal satisfaction. This is something for artists to think about in relation to Post-War America . . . a little realistic forethought along these lines might not be wasted, particularly on the part of the composers *who must create what all may understand* [Italics mine. V.D.] . . . All of which should mean an American music more by, for and of the people, and more interested people."

Did our composers heed Ward's advice? Do they *go on* heeding it, or was it interpreted as a request for a musical "pat on the back" to celebrate the boys' homecoming—then back to the lab, task accomplished and charitable largess dispensed? The answer may—or may not—be found in the next chapter.

III

Here We Are, Or Are We?

▶—•—•—•—•—•—•—•—•—•—•—•—•—•—•—•—•—•—◀

On October 24, 1915, in the thick of World War I, Claude Debussy wrote Stravinsky: "In these last years, when I smelled 'Austro-Boche' miasma in art, I wished for more authority to shout my worries, warn of the dangers we so credulously approached. Did no one suspect these people of plotting the destruction of our art as they had prepared the destruction of our countries?" (*Conversations with Igor Stravinsky*, N. Y. 1959.) Debussy died in 1918—while the Germans were bombing Paris—but he retained his sense of smell to the end; not only his country, but also his art, was in danger. Luckily, the "Austro-Boches" did not conquer France or her allies in 1918; luckily for us, they failed again—in their second attempt, with the fate of the whole world at stake—in 1945. The Allies won the second war, then let the "Austro-Boches" take over music; no one with enough authority was around to "shout his worries" or warn of the impending dangers—what do generals and politicians know about music, anyway? As for the musicians themselves, their nostrils were not sensitive enough, their fear of missing the boat (even the enemy's) proving stronger than their patriotism.

"Austro-Boche" is not a pretty term, although prettier by far than "Nazi." I don't know what "Austro-Boches" Debussy had in mind—probably Richard Strauss and Max Reger (who

were still among the living in 1915)—but there was no cleavage
between the Kaiser and Germany's music dictators. Reger,
for one, held the position of *Hofkapellmeister* at the time of
his sudden death in 1916. The men whose influence is responsible for the present state of music, Schoenberg and von
Webern, were strictly *verboten* in Hitler's Germany, their music
rigorously excluded from all Nazi-sanctioned concerts and
opera performances. Schoenberg fled to the U.S.A. in 1933,
while Webern was accidentally killed by an American police-
man in Germany, in 1945. Both were born in Vienna (as was
Alban Berg, a far greater composer than either), while the
present standard bearer of the Schoenberg-von Webern creed,
1928-born Karlheinz von Stockhausen, is a native of Modrath,
Germany. "Formalist degenerates" to Hitler and Stalin, the
two late Viennese (as would have been the postwar addition, young Stockhausen) are "Austro-Boches" to the French;
but Debussy is no longer among the living to "shout his
worries," and if he were and did shout at the top of his lungs,
I fear the world-weary French would shrug it off with the
Gallic equivalent of "So what?"

Younger French musicians did some shouting themselves
once the Germans were defeated and order restored. *La Revue
Musicale*, France's most authoritative music magazine, resumed publication in February, 1946, after six years of silence.
To it, André Jolivet (b. 1905), a "progressive" composing in
an atonal (yet not in dodecaphonic) idiom, contributed a
significant semi-manifesto, semi-accounting of music's status
after the war. "Above all, let us note that the movement aim-
ing at reintegrating music in terms of *humanism reborn* [Italics
mine. V.D.] was foreseen before the war by those among us
who were especially attentive; this movement is affirming
itself at present, thanks to the support of the young ... Great
works that met with success between the two wars are
successful once more, but for a different reason. Such works

(at the time of their appearance) may have impressed the listener with their showy facade: rhythmic power, sonorous innovations, instrumental virtuosity. Today they retain their place by the music's expressive quality and its lyricism." Jolivet cited three French works which became repertoire staples because of their capacity to reach the audience: Albert Roussel's Fourth Symphony, *Jeanne au Bucher*, by Honegger, Ravel's Piano Concerto (for the left hand alone)—and "even that composer's *Bolero*." In the second rank, Jolivet placed "those productions that had no merit other than representing a sacrifice to the exigencies of fashion"; period pieces, in other words. Third and *last* came "*laboratory essays*, tentatives of musical pyrotechnics that flourished [between the two wars]."

Jolivet then proceeded to advise the tyro composer by suggesting that on "entering the Temple [of music?]—or one of its chapels—he will hear singing of the Heroes' glory; the Heroes being Stravinsky, Bartók, Falla, Schoenberg. All four are spiritual heirs of Claude Debussy, the great liberator." (No doubt, the Austro-Boches gritted their teeth on reading this.) After enumerating the various changes in new Occidental music, such as: dispensing with tonality, utilizing dodecaphonic procedure, re-employing modes—the medieval eight and also the Polynesian (?) variety—Jolivet goes to the core of the matter: *le discours*, in this instance *musical speech*, "Speech that must be efficacious and *accessible to the listener*—essentially melodic, that is . . . the sum of our past experiences will be at the service of human expression in the abundant production of the new classical era. *Thus the divorce between the creator and his public will be annulled*." Fine, brave words that echo the aspirations of Robert Ward, cited in the previous chapter.

In the following month's issue of *La Revue Musicale* (April, 1946), two of Jolivet's *Jeune France* fellow organizers and composers, Yves Baudrier (b. 1906) and Daniel Lesur (b.

1908) published a curious dialogue titled, *Towards New Romanticism?* The two Frenchmen made light of the (already, then) stale neoclassical conception of music: "To 'take off' the musical styles of the past will always remain a game, a pastime," said Lesur. "To exclude emotion is to drain the very sources of music." After some groping to determine the exact meaning of "romanticism," as opposed to "classicism," Baudrier made the following pronouncement: "Our contemporary romanticism is, certainly, destined to utilize both emotion and good sense, but it cannot lean on any sort of classicism, on any existing structural precepts. It must create its own new, efficacious language."

Lesur: "Do you really believe in the possibility of musicians' rallying to a sort of a communal conception of aesthetics?"

Baudrier: "It would, indeed, appear audacious to imagine such a thing. But let us understand one another. We are not to insist on conventions or procedures, analogous, for example, with those of the sixteenth century, but only on a new, serious devotion to human interests; an approach to aesthetic problems not from an individual angle, but on the social plane."

Lesur: "Beware of the dangers of *directed* art. Even the worst kind of anarchy is better."

This sudden note of warning was, in view of subsequent events, more than timely; but well-meaning and perceptive Lesur did not have the authority of a Debussy, even though his sense of smell was just as acute. Meanwhile, other forces were at work to rally musicians to a "communal conception of aesthetics" that excluded the humanist element entirely.

Warsaw-born René Leibowitz (b. 1913)—his family settled in Paris in 1926—spent three years in Berlin and Vienna (1930-1933) studying "serial techniques" with Schoenberg and von Webern. One year after the publication of Jolivet's, Baudrier's and Lesur's "humanist" credos, on which young French music was, hopefully, to be based, our Frenchified Pole aimed his

Middle-European darts at any and all music (except that written by his mentors and idols, the dodecaphonists), in *Schoenberg et son École* (Paris, 1947)—one of the most ferociously fanatical books ever written. For those unfamiliar with Paris musical salons and "chapels" of the avant-garde, it must be noted that their habitués are scared stiff of being caught napping; anything remotely revolutionary and upsetting, especially when supported by someone fascinatingly *new*, someone articulate and possessed of publicity-getting talents, is worthy of serious consideration. The Paris *salonard*, tired of Regency armchairs, will gladly jump on a barricade if his personal safety is not at stake.

Neither Schoenberg nor the intermittently atonal Berg cut much of a figure in musical Paris prior to Leibowitz's angry screaming in print; von Webern was little more than a name, a fairly obscure one. At an undisclosed time, between the two wars, "Milhaud and Poulenc went to Vienna to see the man who had reversed the time-honored tonal principle and had dissolved its concept with all its implications."[*] The trip "remained without consequence. None of the French composers was really tempted to impose upon himself the discipline of Schoenberg... Suddenly, in the forties, the 'twelve-tone fire' was rekindled by a number of young composers who took their first steps into the musical world. They were mainly products of Olivier Messiaen's class at the Conservatoire." Messiaen, a member of the Jolivet-Lesur-Baudrier *Jeune France* "humanist" headquarters, was not a party to the "sudden" Austro-Boche invasion. "Strangely enough," Claude Rostand continued, "the rigid dogmatism of the method did not seem to embarrass the young French twelve-tone composers, notwithstanding the fact that the French opponents had shown an antagonistic attitude, including a no less systematic rejection." Unfortunately, the French opponents—

---

[*] Claude Rostand, *French Music Today*, translated by Henry Marx, N.Y.

conservatives, *amuseurs*, and humanists—spoke fluently and entertainingly, but produced little of genuine significance or originality. The young were waiting to be led. As early as 1945, most of them "deserted Messiaen's class to attach themselves to the St. John the Baptist of Schoenberg's 'religion', namely René Leibowitz" (Rostand). Messiaen, to Pierre Boulez's horror, allowed himself to flirt with hateful tonality: "Certain effusions in F sharp major in his *Talas* were not to my taste," stated the disciple haughtily (Goléa). "I observed a complacency in Messiaen's uses of tonality that, at the time, revolted me profoundly. I told him so—and, naturally, an estrangement was the result."

Thus, the Paris youths abandoned *la Jeune France* in the person of its most colorful member—the Avignon-born Olivier Messiaen—to submit to yet another occupation, that of Middle European dodecaphony, brought to France by René Leibowitz, a naturalized Frenchman. In a startling parallel with the Soviet method of invading, then annexing more and more territory, ultimately calling the process "liberation," the ardent champion of serialism in France, Antoine Goléa (*Recontres avec Pierre Boulez,* Paris, 1958) had his own Soviet-type white-washing of the new invasion ready: "The liberation of France (and of Europe) from the Nazi boot, which occurred in the last months of 1944 and the beginning of 1945, coincided most naturally [!] with the liberation of music from its oppressor's yoke, in Germany since 1933, in Austria since 1938, in France and other occupied countries since 1940." The jubilant Goléa failed to admit that another type of yoke—the dodecaphonic one—was to replace the Nazi tyranny in the very year of Free Democracy's victory, 1945.

He had to note—with simulated joy—that a concert dedicated exclusively to Prokofiev's music, another to Hindemith's, and *seven* concerts to the complete works of Stravinsky, were given by the Orchestre National (France's best symphonic body) and conducted by Roger Desormière and Manuel Rosenthal only three months after the liberation of Paris. Goléa also had to record that the young followers of *St. John Leibowitz the Baptist* were not happy over quantities of music they despised—music "dishonored by Nazism" received ecstatically by the huge audience, the members of which felt as though they were facing friends long supposed dead or banished to musical concentration camps. Poker-faced, he (Goléa) describes how, during the fourth or fifth concert of "this unforgettable series," while Stravinsky's innocuous *Four Norwegian Moods* was being played, "all at once, from the top of the theater's gallery [Théâtre des Champs Elysées, where the concert was held. V.D.], came loud yells and hoots." At the next concert the "very young people, not numerous, but exceedingly energetic" reacted in similar fashion to Stravinsky's *Danses Concertantes,* another mild *morceau.*

"Who are these youths and why these manifestations?" Goléa's narrative goes on. "Everywhere, at musical gatherings, people made inquiries, astonished and disturbed. Soon, the turbulent listeners became known as the 'Messiaeniques'—the origin of this strange word being 'Messiaen,' not 'Messiah'; and the energetic hooters were readily identified as members [or rather, deserters. V.D.] of Olivier Messiaen's harmony class." Thirteen years later, conscientious Goléa asked Boulez whether he had been among the anti-Stravinsky demonstrators. "Smiling and very proud, he answered: 'Of course!' (Relatively modest [!], Boulez did not admit that it was he, himself, who initiated the yells and the hoots.) "Why did you make so much noise?" Goléa persisted. "Naturally, I asked the question solely to have the pleasure of hearing Boulez make exactly the kind of answer I expected from him: 'To protest against Stravinsky's neoclassicism.'"

Pierre Boulez (b. 1925) an aggressive, bull-like character, showed extraordinary gifts as a mathematician, "spending his

studious youth in a small-town Catholic college." He was a
native of Montbrison, in the Loire district. His predilection
for mathematics caused his detractors (as Goléa tells it) to
exclaim: "You can readily see that Boulez is no musician—
merely a calculator!" I cannot go along with that; Borodin's
eminence as a brilliant professor of chemistry did not sully
his musical reputation, well earned and universally recognized.
Boulez is unquestionably a man of many talents—but I would
hesitate to say that composing is one of them. Novelist
Katherine Anne Porter (*Ship of Fools*), in an interview with
a New York *Herald Tribune* critic,* thus dispatched France's
Jean Paul Sartre :"I despise him—first, because of his attempt
to Germanize French thought, and, second, because he doesn't
seem to know anything about human beings." This diatribe is
equally applicable to Pierre Boulez. As for "calculating,"
there is, I hope, no denying that every dodecaphonist calculates
—which does not prevent Luigi Dallapiccola, certainly the
best of the "serial technique" users, from writing music of
genuine worth and even warmth.

As was to be expected, Dallapiccola is sneered upon by
"purists" of Goléa's ilk "He is, with Alban Berg, the only
'serial' composer who finds grace with the reactionaries, a composer of whom it is said that his 'Italian lyricism' makes up
for him musical dialectics . . . At a 'Musical Youth' concert
Dallapiccola 'proved' to his young audience the *inanity of
serial music* by dedicating a séance to Serge Nigg, erstwhile
a colleague of Boulez at Messiaen's class, an immensely gifted
composer, but lacking in character; Nigg turned his back on
dodecaphony, after cultivating it with success [?] for several
years, to plunge into the healing water of musical 'progress,'
dictated by cultural politics of Moscow and its acolytes"
(Goléa).

I fully expect to be accused of siding with the Soviets in

---

* As reported by *Time*, April 13, 1962.

their ruthless onslaught (in the Stalin-Zhdanov era) on "formalism," and their insistence on good, safe "all-Russian" models, these being Glinka, Tchaikovsky, and the "Mighty Five." Anyone remotely familiar with my musical activities will have to forswear so easy a line of counterattack; what's more, my own music (strictly formalist to the Soviets) stemming from my notoriously "white" antecedents, is taboo in my native land. But, red or white, formalist or folksy, human beings— absurd, misguided creatures—do require warmth and (for a change of pace) humor in the music they hear; both are conspicuously absent from the atonal and the serial-row product. The often needlessly rancorous Constant Lambert thus aptly diagnosed the atonalists' total humorlessness: "Although atonalism has produced complicated and objective fugal structures, subjective and neurasthenic operas, it has produced nothing that we can set beside Chabrier and Offenbach, let alone the comic operas of Mozart. The dance movements in the *Serenade* and *Op. 25 Piano Suite*, which are Schoenberg's nearest approach to this genre, are sufficient proof of the essential solemnity of atonalism. An atonal comic opera is a chimerical thought" (Lambert, *Music Ho!* 1934). Warmth? As early as 1922, Erwin Stein (in the *Chesterian*) asserted that "the works of Anton von Webern are suffused with an extraordinarily tender and intimate feeling." He must have had Carl Maria von Weber, not von Webern, in mind.

As for Boulez, his greatest talent lies in his violence; in savage, yet beautifully timed, verbal onslaughts on the existing order—or, if you will, *dis*order—of things, the art of effective entrances and exits and, especially, in heaping articulate abuse (he writes well) on those who happen to disagree with him and the conception of art he so frantically espouses. Dan Morgenstern's comment on Gunther Schuller, the Third Streamer, would apply more readily to Boulez: "I only wish," said Morgenstern in *FM Listener's Guide*, (May, 1962) "that his [Schuller's] music had half the conviction of his polemical prose." The enraptured Goléa was struck by: "this head [Boulez's] with its broad forehead, belying an exceptional hardness, an unusual stubbornness, and an inflexible will; there is a somber, a rather angry ardor about his looks." But stubbornness, hardness, and the most inflexible will do not necessarily characterize a first-rate composer. They do characterize a leader, though—and that is what Pierre Boulez became, from the time he quit saintly Messiaen to join forces with scrappy Leibowitz.

"It is with difficulty that one imagines today the great clap of thunder that Leibowitz's two books [*Schoenberg et son Ecole* and *Introduction à la Musique de Douze Tons*, Paris, 1946] produced in the blue sky of French musical life," Goléa noted, rather too imaginatively. "For the first time, a musicologist as well as a technician presented, in France, a picture, coherent and of remarkable clarity, of the essential current of contemporary musical thought—*serial* music." On Boulez, Leibowitz's thunderclap effect was especially staggering: "It was, for me, a revelation," said he. "While still in Messiaen's [harmony] class, I formed a group, with several fellow students, and we asked Leibowitz to give us 'initiation lessons.'" The "relatively modest" leader, who initiated the anti-Stravinsky demonstrations, was at it again: he led former "Young France" adherents, who basked in the "blue sky" and sunshine of their country's musical "humanism," to the thunder-machine importer's den. Their sojourn in Leibowitz's camp did not last long; "I soon understood," Boulez admitted, "that there were other things in serial music than the manipulation of a series of sonorous 'highs' [*hauteurs sonores*]—a manipulation, of which the mechanical aspect was underlined by Leibowitz. This irritated and displeased me."*

---

*"I owe a lot to Leibowitz," said Hans Werner Henze, the young (b. 1926) and prodigiously gifted German composer of four operas and five symphonies. "However, I soon abandoned the orthodox dodecaphonic methods Leibowitz

The tone of chronic irritation, not to say rage, is extremely typical of the twelve-tone apostles. Oh, where are the snobs of yesteryear? Denis de Rougemont, a cultivated writer and a well-informed "nonprofessional" musician, (president of the Executive Committee of the 1952 Fleischmann-Nabokov "L'Oeuvre du XXe Siècle" Paris festival) contributed an article titled "There Is No Modern Music" to the Paris *Preuves* (July, 1954), which is lucid and objective in that it's neither "pro" nor "anti," but presents the views of an impartial observer. In it he said: "One finds them [the dodecaphonists] much more affected by the resistance that they foresee than by the joy of discovery. They make their discoveries against [Shouldn't it be, in spite of? V.D.] the others, whom they readily treat as imbeciles . . . They have a habit of 'placing' and evaluating themselves in the perspective of history, and talk a lot about the 'needs of the epoch,' of being integrated in a 'necessary' evolution . . . yet it has in no sense been proven that the work of nondodecaphonic composers is, in Boulez's words, 'unnecessary . . . and placed beyond the needs of this era.'" The so-called "new needs of music are those aimed at the ears and the intelligence of a very small group of people, well versed in the entire history of musical techniques."

The present book is for the layman, as well as the professional musician, and I do not intend to cram it full of highly

---

preached . . . I found that the serial system became a bombardment by all musical phenomena used *simultaneously*: rhythms, sounds, intervals. To my way of thinking, if one wishes to obtain a degree of receptivity on the part of the auditor, one should bring about certain phenomena, one or two at a time but not all of them used all at once. If you do so, the bewildered auditor will be unable to distinguish, to follow, to understand, to recall. I abandoned the avant-garde clan at the time when I had the best chance of a grand success, because it (the clan) was all the rage in Germany; since I mistrust fashion—especially in Germany—I turned my back on it and went to Italy to live." (As quoted in *Les Nouvelles Litteraires*, October 11, 1962.) Significantly, the Frenchman Boulez, who still considers himself *the* arbiter of Musical Fashion, abandoned his native land, wherein dodecaphonism didn't "take," and went to live in Germany.

specialized terminology or "inside" shop talk; however, since constant references to twelve-note, serial-row, and dodeca-phonic music may confuse the average reader, I'll attempt a short and, I hope, sufficiently lucid explanation.

Tonality in its strict form, having begun disintegrating at the end of the nineteenth century (with the advent of Debussy, Schoenberg, and Charles Ives), the "old keys" were declared "dead" for modern composition. "Step by step, the development of harmony during the last century has robbed them [the old keys] of their purpose," declares Erwin Stein (*Orpheus in New Guises*, London, 1953). "The continuous inbreeding of all chords and keys obliterated the differences in relationship, and instead of twenty-four keys, the twelve notes of the chromatic scale have remained . . . Harmonically, this development means, first of all, an immense enrichment." Stein then triumphantly enumerates fifty-five "constitutionally different" three-note chords, 165 four-note chords, 330 five-note chords, 462 six-note ditto, and so on. "All this opens a vista of new, highly differentiated harmonic effects," he assures us; but here's the vexing rub—the "method of composing with twelve notes which are related only with one another" (Schoenberg's own definition), provides for poly-phonic part-writing (putting it plainly, horizontal), but is of no help with vertical, *simultaneous sound,* chordal (har-monic) structures which are instantly grasped by the ear, not the eye alone. Stein admits that, in spite of the splendid vista of "differentiated harmonic effects" made possible by destroying tonality (*or* tonal centers, which is *not* the same thing; you'll find the latter in the music of Berg and Hinde-mith,) "an organizing principle has not yet been found; nor is it likely to emanate from the theory of harmony, but rather from counterpoint *and* [?] from practical experience [??]," whatever this absurd alibi may mean. In short—having de-stroyed the tonal order, the dodecaphonists plumb forgot to organize an atonal one, harmonically speaking. Stein's admission was made in 1953—now, ten years later, we are still at a loss as to what *did* replace good old J. S. Bach's chordal organization, for *his* polyphony had a sound harmonic base at all times.

The Western man, after several centuries of contact with music, is conditioned to seek out and recognize three elements that to him constitute, or add up to, enjoyable listening. The three elements: (A) MELODY—to be followed by the ear as a line of musical speech, i.e. *horizontally*; (B) HARMONY—the simultaneous sound of a given number of notes, produced *vertically* and (C) RHYTHM—or time organization, which also serves to punctuate and underline said musical speech. None of the three elements are recognizable to the Western man—or layman—who is old-fashioned or ignorant enough to listen *with his ears*, not with other organs prescribed by the musically aware. Thus, Mr. Milton Babbitt's "Twelve-Tone Invariants as Compositional Determinants" (which is the euphonious title of his *Musical Quarterly* article) may deal with a system that "cedes nothing to any musical system of the past or present" but *that* is also what it does to the average musical ear: *nothing.*

Pleasants (in *The Agony of Modern Music*) accurately observes that "the serious music audience is *harmonically* conditioned. The music in which it finds pleasure is harmonically conceived." But when he declares: "As long as the contemporary composer continues [?] to give primacy to harmony, either tonal or atonal, contemporary music will not matter," he falls flat on his face. The contemporary composer is handed rigid rules concerning a prearranged order of his twelve notes and a strict warning not to repeat any of them, but, harmonically speaking, is left in a vacuum, nothing being said about a new system replacing antiquated tonality. In the next chapter, "The Crisis of Rhythm," Pleasants is in even deeper waters,

regrettably mistaking rhythm for "beat," which is the feature
of jazz and its various outgrowths. The "pulsation of the
music itself" (independently of the conductor or leader) is
not synonymous with a steady 4/4 or 2/4, which is the only
meter employed in contemporary dance music—even waltzes
are converted into it in order to be played or recorded by a
jazz group. "Faced with his own predilection for the . . .
concept of rhythm and his audience's prejudice against the
obvious, he has come up with a compromise . . . to emphasize
rhythm, but in a sophisticated way. The composer rejects the
four-beats-to-the-measure . . . he chooses, instead, to regard
this symmetry as the 'tyranny of the bar line' and to defy it
accordingly."

To say that to do so "deprives music of rhythmic intelligi-
bility" or does away with "pulsation" and the resulting im-
mediacy of impact on an average audience is deliberately to
overlook strong evidence to the contrary. I was one of the
four pianists in the London première (1927) and subsequent
performances of Stravinsky's *Les Noces* (the others were the
late Poulenc, Auric, and Rieti; the late Eugene Goossens conducted) and I can vouch for the spontaneous effect the work
produced on the auditor—although the only critic (self-
appointed at that) who strongly championed that amazing
score and derided the hostile "official" commentators was . . .
H. G. Wells. Now, the "breaking of the bar line," as everyone
knows, is the salient feature of *Les Noces;* and, although it
is true that we four plus the accomplished Goossens labored
arduously and anxiously to keep things going, that in no way
diminished the immediate communicative power of the piece
over the listener. We may have been "preoccupied almost
exclusively with the problem of marking time and giving
entrances" (Pleasants), but Stravinsky's music came across
with the utmost clarity, and always does (in *Les Noces*)
when adequately performed; I cannot think of a better or a

more convincing example of *rhythm* triumphing over mere *beat*. Equally convincing—to this writer, at least—is the fact that no composition strictly adhering to serial precepts makes its point by rhythmic "pulsation," all the protestations to the contrary notwithstanding.

How does a dodecaphonic composer set about his job? Once liberated from tonality, how does he use his new "organized freedom"? Gilbert Chase tells us that he (the composer) ". . . begins by arranging the twelve tones [of the chromatic scale] in a series or row. Once arranged in a special order, *with no tones repeated* [To avoid tonal implications, I'm told. V.D.], this tone-row provides the material, both melodically and harmonically, out of which the entire composition is made." It may be said, therefore, in the words of René Leibowitz, that "every twelve-tone piece is nothing but a series of variations on the original row." Nothing but a series of variations is right; good old, hopelessly dated tonality gave the composer far more leeway. The non-dodecaphonic musician—lucky dog!—could repeat any tones he liked, to begin with.

I turned to Leonard Rosenman, one of the few really gifted composers who embrace the dodecaphonic canon (He manages to get away with using serial techniques in his Hollywood-produced film scores.) for a plainly worded statement on the principles of dodecaphonic composition. He furnished me (1962) with the following: "A strict *adherence to precomposed ordering of the components of music,* such as: pitch-relations, density and rhythm, music written in a serial order corresponds to a set of parametric rules, dictated by the composer in his initial selection of musical components." One surmises that the widely heralded 1945 musical "liberation" meant a "strict adherence" to a new set of rules—those supplied by Arnold Schoenberg to replace the outdated J.S. Bach ones.

Pierre Boulez, who, with a group of kindred souls, deserted Messiaen for Leibowitz, soon discovered that the "liberator,"

while possessed of "great merit," was "essentially lacking in
natural gifts" (Goléa). "To exchange Messiaen for Leibowitz
was to exchange creative spontaneity against a total lack of
inspiration [The hateful word isn't mine, but Goléa's. V.D.]
and the menace of . . . *academic sclerosis.*" What, in the Lord's
name, became of the "remarkable clarity" with which Leibowitz's great thunderclap admittedly shook the very foundation of sclerotic academicism, rampant in 1946? Has Leibowitz become infected with the disease of conservatoire official-
dom, has *St. John the Baptist* turned into *Judas*? Not at all;
the poor man stuck to the job for quite a while, and some of
the Boulez-led youths stuck to their new mentor. Trust Goléa
to dismiss them as "fatally the least talented, the least curious,
the least mistrustful [*méfiants*]" of the lot. Indeed, "those who
remained faithful produced insignificant work and contributed,
by the stiffness they applied to their adaptation of the serial
techniques, to the discredit of the new procedure." Further,
Liebowitz was a poor and ineffectual conductor, unable to
grasp new music's "inner significance;" what was the ardent,
ever impatient, Boulez to do? Quick as a flash, he "liberated"
himself from Leibowitz.

Boulez's explanation of his action is characteristically callous:
"Leibowitz's academicism was the worst kind, far more dangerous for the future of serial music than was official academicism for the status of the tonal kind. If Leibowitz created an
illusion that was fairly durable, it was simply because of the
ignorance, in France, of the entire evolution of serial music
during the last thirty years" (cited by Goléa). The Number
One ignoramus, lucky Pierre, was obviously yourself—for it
was Leibowitz, by your own admission, who provided a surefire "revelation," and who initiated you in the mysteries of
dodecaphonic craft *at your own request.* That initiation must
have been a fearful bore (I'm with you there.) Even for a
dedicated dodecaphonist, judging from this sad confession

by your one-time master: "Truly, the reading or performance of a musical work, whatever it may be—and I have read and listened to thousands—was never for me an object of pleasure or distraction." (René Leibowitz, *Schoenberg et son École*) The uninitiated may well wonder about the relevance of this tragicomic tale in a story of America's career in music. Having successfully issued a bona fide Declaration of Musical Independence before the war we helped win, have we again fallen into the cunningly laid European (and *again*, Middle-European) trap? *Le cas Boulez,* although seemingly unconnected with America's musical destiny, will help trace our present involvement in the "interdependent" imbroglio; unwittingly, it was an American who helped dodecaphony to infiltrate the musical world on a practically global scale—the Soviet bloc excepted.

II

The American was Minneapolis-born (1913) Everett Helm, Vaughan Williams-Malipiero-and-Milhaud-trained, now Dr. Helm, editor of *Musical America,* composer and (in wartime) theater and music officer under our military government in Germany (1948-50), stationed in Wiesbaden. Liberated from Messiaen and Leibowitz, Paris residents both, Boulez chose the obvious course—to go to West Germany, where the musical climate was more congenial and the chances of quick recognition more realistic. The new Mecca for music-hungry young Germans was Darmstadt, the town "created for the young illiterates" (Goléa) who haven't heard a note of good-quality modern music since the advent of Hitler. The Darmstadt Institute of Contemporary Music was the brain child of one Wolfgang Steinecke,, a young and unknown musicologist, who—although Darmstadt was almost entirely wiped out by repeated bombings—became convinced (in 1945), just a few weeks after the cessation of hostilities, that the moment had

come to reveal "the true spirit of the Germans, numbed by
twelve years of Hitlerism," and that Darmstadt, "with its
great artistic tradition [?] was the logical home of living
music."

After some wrangling with the town's harassed mayor, more
concerned with finding lodgings for abandoned children and
their bombed-out parents than with the proposed Living
Music Home, Steinecke was directed to Everett Helm's office
in the neighboring town of Wiesbaden, miraculously untouched by the allied bombers. Helm, described by Goléa
as "understanding, generous, and under forty," was easily
swayed by Steinecke, and, thanks to Helm's, or rather his
country's, dollars, the Institute of Contemporary Music was
lodged in the old Kranichstein Castle. Helm, himself, soon
realized that the Darmstadt enterprise America (in his person) helped launch, was veering rapidly in "serial" and even
"ultraserial" direction; Goléa magnanimously suggests that
our composer in uniform became a patron and a benefactor to
an art to which "at that time, he was thoroughly hostile."
Helm, even "thought, in those days, that serial techniques had
something tyrannical, as well as mechanical about them, but
silenced his own doubts before the mounting pressures of the
young [of Germany and other countries], to whom the mysteries of new music were at last revealed; and so continued
to act in favor of Steinecke's more and more audacious plans."

Steinecke was a crafty operator and, dreading too violent a
shock on the sensitive pupils, hired Wolfgang Fortner, a mild
Regerian ("not as yet seduced by the charms of dodecaphony,"
said Goléa), as professor of composition. Then, in 1947, Paul
Hindemith, himself, "the great Window-smasher before Eter-
nity in 1923, also during the years that followed his shattering
debut at the Donaueschingen Festival," agreed to preside over
the Institute's fortunes; but Hindemith, Goléa hastens to add,

"was, *after being domiciled in the States,* leaning towards a rather disheartening neoclassicism . . . faced with atonality, nay, serialism, Hindemith, like so many others, got frightened. He deliberately attached himself to tonal discipline, which he re-arranged to his taste, very systematically, indeed; because this enemy of the 'serial system' felt the necessity of rigid order in music-writing procedures . . . the charm [of Hindemith's adages?] being terrifyingly intoxicating to the unlucky former inmates of spiritual concentration camps, Steinecke felt the danger of the Hindemith cult and the accompanying realization that the young began confusing Hindemithism with the *ne plus ultra* of modernism; that is why Steinecke had to produce the first of his 'grand coups' (in 1948)—by sending for . . . René Leibowitz."

Perversely, Mr. Goléa has no criticism to offer insofar as the selection of the hapless man, victim of "academic sclerosis," denounced by ardent Pierre Boulez, is concerned. Leibowitz's "least talented, least curious" pupils, previously scoffed at, moved to Darmstadt in a body (1949); in the next year, these were joined by Bruno Maderna and Luigi Nono, then utter nonentities—for the final coup. *Le Soleil des Eaux,* by Boulez, deserter of the Messiaen and Leibowitz camps, was performed in Darmstadt (1950). From the Institute also emerged the not even "relatively" modest Karlheinz von Stockhausen; a mere pupil then, he joined his brethren—Nono of Italy and Boulez of France—as a full professor in 1956. The proposed "global" conquest of music by the technically defeated Austro-Germans was effectively and solidly launched.

III

There were no immediate repercussions in the U.S. Outside of Schoenberg, the slightly outmoded *chef d'école,* there were other Austro-German expatriates who practiced serial techniques without creating any particular stir many years prior to the emergence of Leibowitz, Boulez, and Stockhausen. Ernst Krenek (b. 1900 in Vienna) embraced dodecaphony in the thirties after his self-confessed "meandering through styles." The Berlin-born, American-settled Stefan Volpe (b. 1902) also "assimilated many styles and experimented with many techniques before turning to the twelve-tone method" (Gilbert Chase). Neither had any sizable influence on young Americans.

A part-time dodecaphonist of native origin was the already named Wallingford Riegger, who started by writing "the kind of conservative music that was most generally acceptable" (Chase). With his fascinating *Dichotomy* (1931-32), Riegger began experimenting with precomposed tone-rows, one of eleven tones, the other of thirteen. This was typical of the freedom-loving composer; you wouldn't catch *him* turning out countless themes with variations, whatever the Schoenberg-Webern dicta. Thus, in the Third Symphony—probably the high spot of his entire catalogue—"traditional and tone-row procedures are combined and the sense of tonality is not abandoned" (Chase). Riegger's abhorrence of uncompromising dogmatism saved him from Austro-German handcuffs; he was too much of an individualist to align himself with the power-grabbing disciplinarians of the Darmstadt persuasion.

A dangerous aspect of musical America's growing pains has always been a fear of provincialism, of regional backwardness; we have already seen how sadly music was marred by the blind adherence to German academic precepts during the entire nineteenth century. These precepts were the "correct party line" at the time, and any deviations seemed the sheerest heresy; the first twenty years of the present century were marked by an almost equally slavish "follow the leader" pre-occupation with ill-digested French impressionism. Came the "promising yesterday" and America began giving voice in accents unashamedly autonomous. Our country's musical growth was swift, perhaps too swift; the popularity of a few homemade pieces was not to the purists' taste, the composer bent on finding the audience, whether he be a "humanist" or a mere crowd-pleaser—even less so. "Music human, logical, intelligible? Well, you know that batch of clichés," sneered Boulez. (Goléa, p. 38) "Music must be written with the idea of someone listening," said Walter Piston. Oh, yeah? Fred Goldbeck, Paris musicologist and "progressive" commentator, observed that: "The composer has no other company than his fellow composers; he is bound to be a specialist among specialists, a highbrow and a snob *malgrè lui* . . . In the general listener's household, contemporary music is only a minor commodity. Something like pepper." (Goldbeck in his address "Music Today," delivered at the International Conference of Contemporary Music, April 7, 1954).

"What of an American style?" asked Nathan Broder in the *Evolution of the American Composer* (1961). "There have been American pieces—that is, pieces entirely built from the characteristic qualities of native folk music—from Gottschalk's *Bamboula* to Copland's *Hoe-Down,* and in the last three decades certain elements appeared in our music that could coalesce into an indigenous style . . . But any possibility that such traits would be fused into an American idiom is being swept away in the swift current that bears contemporary music along today." In other words, following those hopeful three decades, "certain elements" appeared in our music, making it quite undistinguishable from any determinedly "contemporary" music, composed (or is it "precomposed"?) by anyone, anywhere. "On the whole, young American composers today are writing in an eclectic, cosmopolitan style," Harold C. Schonberg stated in the New York *Times* (January 19, 1962). "Much of it is anonymous-sounding and very little has vitality or personality behind it."

Lastly: "The young composers today are not overtly inter-ested in Americana. They are interested in avant-garde music but are bewildered as to what to do" (Piston). The young GI's back from the "big" war *and* the Korean one, even those who began acquiring a taste for "not too complex" serious music, knew *exactly* what to do; they gave the bewildered would-be avant-gardists the heave-ho, and went back to jitterbugging and rock-and-rolling. It was the *marriage*, not the "divorce between the creator and the public" (Jolivet) that was annulled.

Nancy Mitford caused a stir with her U versus non-U varie-ties of English speech. You may recall that U (for upper-class) English was, according to Miss Mitford, the unmistakable stamp of a gentleman, of one who "belongs," while the un-fortunate non-U's were those outside the pale—vulgar and unacceptable in polite society. A similar distinction appears to exist in the world of music, or rather that of music creators; for non-upperclassmen, we have the box-office composers, who eat, while the impeccable U's are represented by the soapbox boys, who often starve, but pretend that they are not hungry.

Let me elucidate. The vulgar box-office characters write music for which there is a popular demand—and are so busy making money that they have no time for proclamations and high-brow articles in arty magazines. The soapbox geniuses disdain "commercial" appeal, scoff at music for the masses, and, when not putting together epics for the élite, are extol-ling those "in," denouncing those "out," and reaffirming their own allegiance to the party in power—a practice only too familiar to those living under a dictatorship.

Successful practitioners of the composing trade usually leave the business of pamphleteering to the less gifted, and less busy soapbox prophets. Those who support themselves by their music are palpably non-U: it is terribly unchic to be commercial, especially if you write for Broadway or Hollywood, which automatically makes you an *untouchable*. Paul Carpenter, in his useful though little known book *Music, an Art and a Business* (University of Oklahoma, 1950), summed up the situation thus: "While the Music Business lives in a palace, the Musical Art lives on a dole." Does that necessarily mean that the plutocratic music purveyor deals in trash, while the starving artist creates masterworks as the hoary cliché would have it? I question it. Carpenter, who belongs to the Art versus Business school of thought, stated emphatically that "very few American composers of serious music are today earning a living directly or entirely from the music which they wrote." Can a contemporary composer really support himself by his serious, or noncommercial output? I'm afraid the answer is "no."

Let's take a look at the "dedicated" U-type of composer's finances; since our government has not as yet provided state support for the arts—only for a few exports—how does the man expect to get paid? By whom and for what? ASCAP, being a collecting agency, distributes its income on a performance basis—and it's easy to see why a "standard" song may get 10,000 performances a year, while a symphony, however meritorious, is lucky to achieve two. ASCAP's rival, BMI, not really a collecting agency at all, does sponsor a good many "name" composers of standing and makes quite a fuss over nurturing native music for propaganda purposes, but this is a speculative operation; I doubt that any composer can depend on a yearly revenue *for life*, for something that does not pay off. On the other hand, not a few composers are helped (at least temporarily) by prizes, grants, commissions and such, which are doubtless good for the composer's sagging morale as well as his pocket. The recipients of Ford, Fromm, or Guggenheim fellowships, the Pulitzer Prize-winners, those who receive a nod from the Koussevitzky Fund committee, or a *laissez-passer* from Louisville, get a momentary feeling of security, which soon proves a fleeting illusion. That "something" is always being done for the poor but deserving composer is in itself indicative of the fact we might as well face—there is no healthy market for the man's merchandise. The glib answer to this, on the part of "new" music's apologists, is, of course, the old chestnut about artists being ahead of their time, the lot of misunderstood genius through the ages, bad faith on the part of the general listener, and so on. However invalid one may judge Henry Pleasants's conclusions in his *Agony of Modern Music,* one must admit the sturdiness of his documentation, the irrefutable logic of some of his deductions: "The most devastating single inhibiting factor standing in the way of spontaneous and honest judgment of modern music is the general acceptance . . . of the fable that new serious music is never 'understood' and appreciated in its own time." Pleasants stated in the chapter on "Success and Failure": "This is the result of decades of popularized history and hack program-note writing, both of which have consistently indulged in the sentimental dramatization of great composers' initial difficulties, subsequent economic and social setbacks, and occasional musical failures . . . Usually omitted in the accounts of these failures [*The Barber of Seville, La Traviata, Carmen, Madame Butterfly, Le Sacre du Printemps,* and the Franck Symphony—Pleasants's partial list] is the fact that every one of them became a great success within a few months of the unsuccessful première . . . the truth is that every great composer, without exception, has been appreciated, admired, applauded, and loved in his own time." (Pleasants, p. 63)

Now let's assume, dear reader, that you are an ambitious composer combining youth, gall, know-how with a little talent. What do you do to get played, O Smart Alec-in-Wonderland? Simple; write in the U-endorsed manner and you'll get by, though your stomach be empty. Only a few years ago, three Wonderlands were open to you: (1) The neoclassical land of

Stravinsky, whose next-to-last period exercised a tremendous influence on our young, if not on the young of Europe; (2) The dodecaphonic Land of Sweet Opportunity, embracing respectability; and (3) Copland, then chief spokesman and arbiter of native music. Now that Stravinsky has at last abandoned his pseudo-classical pose (1920-1956) and gone over to the twelve-tone camp, (whose "techniques reached into virtually every corner of contemporary composition, finally enwrapping such recalcitrants as Stravinsky *and* Copland")* there is today only *one* correct approach; it will be interesting to see where the Stravinskyites and the Coplandsmen will land. They seem to have but one choice, the sad little Johnny one-notes— follow the leader and go dodecaphonic with a vengeance; most of them have already done so. It is still safe enough to put all your eggs in the dodecaphonic basket, unless you go "way out" and embrace "concrete" music or get very cagey—beg pardon, *John* Cagey—and dedicate yourself to performing *silence.* "Serial" composers practically grow on trees today— some are converts, deserting suspect (because outmoded) other "isms" in droves; few, very few, are hardy pioneers who, like Riegger, took up the "serial row" while still in their twenties. Most interesting of these, a man worthy of genuine respect, is Ottawa-born George Tremblay (b. 1911), a Schoenberg pupil, who eventually settled in Los Angeles and wrote his first major work, a string quartet, rigidly adhering to the serial techniques, in 1935. In a letter to this writer, Tremblay stated that it was in 1933 that he "discovered the twelve-tone system of musical composition. This is not startling except that I did not know at the time that Arnold Schoenberg had already invented it. I was working on a piece from a suite for piano when I noticed that the principal theme, which was a kind of *cantus firmus* for the whole work, contained eleven different independent notes. Why show partiality, I thought;

---

* Harold C. Schonberg in the *New York Times*, January 19, 1962.

include the missing C sharp and you will have a complete melodic row of all the twelve chromatic tones. This was a great moment for me, because it gave a me a certain sense of security to realize that I had gained control in an organized manner of all the tones at my disposal. I have always regarded this event as proof of the validity of this system. This was not the whim or brain child of a personality or a mere musical stylist. On the contrary, it was one more of those great natural steps in the evolution of musical science. Now that it has become a tradition throughout the civilized world, I would like to describe some of my personal findings on the subject. It is agreed that it is desirable to have laws to govern all things. This is especially true where abstract values are concerned. Now it is a popular pastime to compare non-objective art, painting, sculpture, etc. with serial music. This is a fallacy, since the comparison begins and ends nowhere. Now that abstract expressionistic painting has become the plaything and the anti-barbiturate of actors and actresses of the cinematographic profession, serial composition on the other hand has become a sort of bipartisan coffee break for the laboratorist. Must we all become Astronauts?

"I undertook recently, on a wager, to teach a friend of mine, a painter (I must admit in all fairness to my argument, a very intelligent painter.), how to compose a piece in the serial technique à la Webern in one lesson," Tremblay continued. "Needless to say, I won the bet. But, as I said, he is a very intelligent painter. Of course, this does not imply that all painters or all composers, for that matter, would automatically fare as well as my friend did. But there is a lesson to be learned here nevertheless. And that is that where at one time musical composition was the natural consequence of talent, it has now to some extent been relegated to the mental processes of mathematicians. Having two composers at work simultaneously on the same composition in a musical laboratory is like having an assistant in the bridal chamber on one's wedding night. The Moon is Earth's only natural satellite, yet man with his ingenuity has changed all that with fabrications of his own. Perhaps an assistant in the wedding bed might forestall a lot of future psychological complications at that."

Of the other active dodecaphonists of the earlier vintage, we will name: Adolph Weiss (b. 1891), also a Schoenberg pupil and an alumnus of the militant International Composers' Guild, who joined the ranks of twelve-tone explorers as early as 1928 (Chamber Symphony), after a tentatively impressionistic start; the "strict and uncompromising" (Chase) Milton Babbitt (b. 1916), who "feels that he has made a sacrifice in renouncing tonality" but "believes in cerebral music"; Ben Weber (b. 1916), obviously less cerebral, possessing, in his own admission, a romantic temperament (It must have taken real guts to confess to such a thing—Chase hastens to add, however, that Weber's impassioned lyricism is "always under firm technical control"); Ross Lee Finney (b. 1906), a pupil of Alban Berg, who originally resented the stark "functionalism" of the twelve-tone technique, then stumbled upon it (in his Sixth String Quartet), amazed, like Tremblay, to find it the most natural thing in the world; lastly, a typical in-and-outer, Harrison Kerr (b. 1897), considered a stanch dodecaphonist by outsiders, marked as an outsider by the official preachers of the twelve-tone cult. All five, whatever the worth of their highly complicated and rigorously "precomposed" structures, at least possess the virtue of operating with recognizably musical materials. Cautiously, one furtive eye on the all-powerful policy dictators of Darmstadt and Donaueschingen, Ernst Krenek, managed to blurt out: ". . . there is no reason to assume that the nature of serial music excludes the possibility of interpreting it as a medium of *some* sort of communication." Let us be thankful for small mercies.*

On the other hand, our "experimentalists" (Gilbert Chase's appellation) will go to any lengths to add external, seemingly most unsuitable, elements and devices to provide their music with an effective shot-in-the-arm, unmindful of the resulting possibility of someone in the audience shooting the pianist, the composer, or the conductor, as the case may be. The big daddy of the experimentalists is, of course, Edgard Varèse, who has come into his own (at last!) in his native France, in the fifties, and who is regarded with awe and grudging respect even by those wholesale haters, the dodecaphonists, as well he should be. I have already spoken of Antheil and Cowell; the one claim the former had to experimentalism was his single sortie into the mechanical jungle, *Ballet Mécanique,* wherein an airplane propeller and several typewriters were employed with dubious effect. Cowell's tone clusters and the vanished rhythmicon were, historically speaking, sins of youth; his musical profile is an amiably American one, of which his subsequent production is ample and welcome proof.

Lou Harrison (b. 1917) employed iron pipes and packing boxes (a cadenza for a quartet of these would undeniably be fascinating) in his *Canticle III,* the sounds of which were thought "charming and well-organized" by Richard Franko Goldman. He joined the twelve-toners' ranks subsequently and

* Lack of space prevents me from listing nondodecaphonic young and youngish hopefuls, but at least four deserve more than an honorable mention: Brooklyn-born Leon Kirchner (b. 1919) fuses atonalism with supercharged, emotion-packed romanticism laced with rhythmic intensity; Ned Rorem (b. 1923, Richmond, Ind.) is an outspokenly lyrical musician capable of writing a good tune and, consequently, is at his best when serving the human voice; Grant Fletcher (b. 1913, Hartsburg, Ill.) is a diamond in the rough, in that he lacks the slickness of his better-known contemporaries but owns a distinctive—and pronouncedly American—profile instead; and lastly, the splendidly gifted Benjamin Lees (b. 1924, Harbin, China), who may not have made the Slonimsky editions of Baker's Dictionary (why?) but who makes some of the most exhilarating music (his Second Symphony being a good sample) heard nowadays.

dispensed with charm. Harry Partch (b. 1901) has his quota of sincere admirers; he is, obviously, a man of imagination. Calling dance music an *Afro-Chinese Minuet* or *Cuban Fandango* bespeaks a certain freshness of approach. Partch is an inventor of "microtonal instruments" such as the Kithara, the Harmonic Canon, the Chromelodeon, and—best of all—the Cloud-Chamber Bowl (employing a carboy, which is "a large glass bottle used for corrosive acids"). Whether the delectable racket produced by these outlandish noisemakers can be construed as music is a moot point.

Somewhere in between eclecticism and experimentalism lies the path of indefatigably industrious Lukas Foss (or Fuchs—b. 1922 in Berlin), a composer determined to draw attention to himself at all costs. His Coplandesque *Prairie* (1944) constituted a promising start, and while he didn't "make it" in ballet (*Gift of the Magi*, 1945) and opera (*Griffelkin*, 1955), Foss displayed a dramatic sense in the solo cantata *Song of Songs* (1947) and, increasingly so, in the 1953 *A Parable of Death*—effective music of no pronounced individuality. Foss then attracted some attention with the "improvisation" gimmick applied to preconceived symphonic and chamber-music structures, and called by some, "classical jam sessions." The future of this notion is highly problematical; we hear so much music that appears disorganized to the naked ear that adding hit-or-miss "organized improvisation" only deepens the confusion.

Of the increasingly absurd activities of John Cage (b. 1912) no illusions need be entertained. Dr. Calvin Darlington Linton, dean of liberal arts and professor of English literature at the George Washington University, Washington, D. C., in "What Happened to Common Sense?" an article that should become a classic (*Saturday Evening Post*, April 28, 1962), didn't mince words: "Blind faith in authority in the realm of the arts is even easier [Linton dealt with the scientist's authority

in the first half of his article. V.D.] to illustrate. Here is a
single sentence from a piece of authoritative art criticism
which appeared in *Art News* and was quoted in *The New
Yorker*: 'He [the artist] pictures the stultified intricacy of
tension at the plasmic level; his prototypical zygotes and
somnolent somatomes inhabit a primordial lagoon where
impulse is an omni-directional drift and isolation is the consequence of an inexplicable exogamy.' For all its own desperate
problems, ignorance permits a healthy disbelief in such sem-
antic idiocy; excessive sophistication, on the other hand,
compels acceptance—on faith. The author, after all, must be
an authority or he could not write that way."

That is precisely what the various musical quacks are also
counting on; masters of mass hypnosis, they can sell the
masochistic authority-worshipers of the average "highbrow"
audience, anxious to preserve their U status, any worthless
product, so long as it's touted as the peak of avant-gardism.
"In such an atmosphere, fraud is easy to perpetrate," Linton
continues. "In October, 1960, composer John Cage, assisted
by pianist David Tudor, put on a concert at Venice's International Festival of Contemporary Music. The performance
consisted chiefly of plucking a single string of the piano at
twenty-second intervals and, later, of thumping the piano stool
with a rock and *attacking the insides of the piano* itself with
knives and pieces of tin. The result was solemnly written up
by the critics." Were I the owner of the long-suffering piano,
I would go after Mr. Cage's insides with my own knife, which
could result in less solemn write-ups for the two of us.

Cage started with *Constructions in Metal* and the more
widely known tinkering with the prepared piano for unpre-
pared audiences (1939). The music sounded like hopelessly
inebriated Scarlatti, but the sounds emanating from the
mangled instrument were far from disagreeable. As a creator,
Cage always suffered from shortness of breath and soon began

to repeat himself; all his pieces sounded alike and the trick wore dangerously thin. "The preparation entailed placing on the piano strings various objects, such as screws, copper coins, rubber bands, and the like" (*Baker's Dictionary*), but Cage was kindness personified to the piano, compared with the murderous assault on the defenseless box which he committed in 1960. His career is a long series of unfunny jokes that are clearly perpetrated in a desperate attempt to "stay on top" publicity-wise (as they say on Madison Avenue); he conducted (?) an *Imaginary Landscape* scored for twelve radios (1951), "dialed according to prescribed wave lengths by the partici-pants, resulting in assorted noises and also silences when no program happened to be broadcast over a particular dial num-ber." This was termed "random composition." The second bid for immortality involved "a method of composing with a set of Chinese dice, each throw indicating the pitch, note value, etc. according to a prearranged system of indices." That was Cage's second step in "eliminating the subjective element in composition"; it became quite obvious that having squandered whatever "subjective element" he possessed on the "prepared" piano, the man was now bent on getting even with the art he could not master legitimately. Step three was "the ultimate negation of the creative principle"; Cage programmed the "première" of his *Four Minutes and Thirty-Three Seconds* (1954)—the performance of which involved a tail-coated young man, who sat at the piano, a watch by his side, *without playing a note* for—you guessed it—exactly the time indi-cated in the "piece's" title. A dues-paying Musicians Union member, I confess to not knowing what the scale is for *un-played* music. Following the gory knife attack on the piano (1960) already described, Cage, probably realizing that the idea of composing with murderous weapons, in public, had no future, other than a highly probable night in the clink, began surrounding himself with ready-and-willing sympa-

thizers, writing an article, or a book or two (not overly stimulating, these), and trying to achieve a modicum of respectability. Morton Feldman, "whose work is known and studied
around the world" (Whose world? V.D.) as *Variety* had it
(February 21, 1962), got his "music" published, along with
Cage, by C. F. Peters, one of the oldest publishing firms in
Europe. "He [Feldman] finds it somewhat amusing to see a
copy of Cage's music side by side with the works of Handel,
Bach & Co." I doubt that Handel, Bach & Co., would have
shared Mr. Feldman's amusement, were they alive; I know
they would applaud Arthur Berger's lecture in Rome (1961)
on "Cross-Currents in American and European Music Today"—
especially his dry observation that "today, *for the first time
in musical history*, it is possible to be a composer without
technical training, even without special talent" (Robert Sabin
in *Musical America*, September, 1961). Cage, Feldman, and
others went even further: they proved that you can be a *composer without composing!*

The astute BBC startled England (in 1961) with a performance of Piotr Zak's *Mobile for Tape and Percussion;* the
young Pole's "cacophonous creation" (*Time* magazine, April
13, 1962) was, in reality, "the handiwork of two pranksters
who banged away haphazardly at all the instruments they
could find in an effort to discover just how much the public
would endure." The station received not a single complaint.
Composer Cage, a real person as Zak was not, works in much
the same way. Before his *Music Walk with Dancers* began (an
"electronic nightmare" inflicted upon a "shell-shocked" New
York audience at the Kaufmann Concert Hall), Cage had no
idea how it would sound, had determined only that it would
last ten minutes, involve certain props and three performers
doing more or less as they pleased. It was a prime sample of
what students of avant-garde call "indeterminate" music, i.e.,
music that is based on almost pure chance. According to

Time, such music is "all the rage" in Europe. Where?—one is
tempted to ask, hoping against hope that the rage would be
limited to Rupert Hughes's Iceland and the polar bears. "Some
composers refer to it . . . as 'aleatory' (music), from the Latin
word 'alea' (a game of dice), once thought to be derived from
the word knucklebone, out of which primitive dice were made."
Unlucky Cage went "aleatory" back in 1951 (with the *Imaginary Landscape Number Four* for twelve radios), but it is
only now that the "uncomposed" music is "performed with
enthusiasm on the West Coast of these United States is
stadt, naturally. That it is *not* performed, or listened to with
enthusiasm on the West Coast of these United States, is
equally true. "They've gone about as far as they can go in
Kansas City," sang one of the hit tunes in *Oklahoma!*—the
Oscar Hammerstein lines quoted by Albert Goldberg in his
L. A. *Times* review of a Monday evening concert at Plummer
Park, Los Angeles (March 7, 1962). "Music Hits New Low
at Monday Concert," ran the headline, while dozens of auditors ran from the hall before the intermission. "It was like
a cesspool-dredging operation," said Goldberg. "Just when
you have decided contemporary music has reached the lowest
depths, someone always digs deeper and comes up with a new
kind of insanity. This time it was compositions—though that
is not the precise word—by Christian Wolff and John Cage.
The first Wolff piece is called *For Six or Seven Players* (What's
one player more or less between friends?)" According to Mr.
Wolff, "There is also in each part a section which requires
no cue, and so can be played to begin with or *at any time*
that a player *misses or fails to hear a cue.*"

I learned from the program notes that Mr. Wolff (b. 1934,
in Nice, France) began writing music at the age of fifteen,
"without benefit of teachers." Life was kind to him, for in the
following year he met John Cage, David Tudor, and Morton
Feldman, "and the music-making of all three has been the

determining force in the development of his own talents."
To coin a word, those *ham*-sessions by the happy quartet must
have been jolly. The solo hamming by Cage was something
to see, too—but his antics palled very rapidly, as Mr. Goldberg
faithfully reported, "Mr. Cage stood up and beat seconds in
groups of five; later he just made semaphore signals in slow
motion, while the players came in here and there with isolated
single tones. Sometimes he beat time to dead silence for as
long as two minutes; that was the best part of it. This went
on for a full half hour, while the audience snickered, called
out 'Good!' when David Tudor whacked the keyboard with
his flat forearm, and carried on private conversations, although
a few brave souls walked out." It didn't take much bravery
for this soul to take a walk, too.

This sort of outrage is not "pre-composition" or "re-compo-
sition" any longer, fellow sufferers—the name for the dreary
process, of which Messrs. Stockhausen, Cage, Feldman, Wolff,
etc. are the perpetrators, is *DE-composition of music*, plain and
simple; and if you are morbid enough to revel in the spectacle
of poor Music's corpse being dragged through concert halls
and pay admission to do so, don't let me stop you. The man
who helped Pandora open her box and then watched all the
evils incident to music pour out to his ever-increasing horror
was none other than the self-same Antoine Goléa, the high
priest of Dodecaphony; finally (1961) realizing that opening
Pandora's can of beans was, perhaps, a dangerous feat, Goléa
felt compelled to cry wolf in his usual ambiguous fashion.
Obviously panic-stricken, our high priest began invoking the
Humanist doctrine—the doctrine so gently (*too* gently, alas)
expounded by Lesur, Baudrier, and Jolivet in 1946, even earlier
by our own Robert Ward. "Serial composition, as we shall
see, [contains the germ] of *dangerous* freedom, generator of
a new tyranny," scribbled Goléa in *L'Aventure de la Musique
au XXe Siècle* (1961). "It must be said that [the system] con-

ducted serial composers of the young generation toward excesses that rendered their music unperformable, even inaudible. Messiaen...went on creating according to the inspiration [!!] of his genius, *without locking himself up in the prison of total freedom.*" Has greater nonsense ever been written? Goléa then hastens to assure his readers that Messiaen was back on the "royal path toward a reconquered intimacy between Music and the Essence of Man and the universe he inhabits," while the "prisoners of total freedom," the young composers who began functioning after 1945, kept on "despising it [The renewed fusion between Man and Music. V.D.] cruelly." Playing safe, Goléa adds in a hurry, "The *greatest* of these, Boulez and Nono, never really deserted it [the humanist conception]." Oh? And what about Boulez's 1956 gibes at "human, logical, intelligible" music, when he poohpoohed the return to such antiquated slush of which he, himself, was accused? But let the resourceful Goléa explain: "Both [Boulez and Nono] did make a sacrifice to the Demon of Figures temporarily; but they *always* [??] drew themselves away to compose *essentially expressive* music, wherein the means of the newly discovered techniques were placed at the service of an *Authentic Human Message,* rather than sclerotize [*scléroser*] and destroy it." Weren't we told that "music should be nothing but an autonomous order of sound progressions, ruled by the logic of construction, for *music cannot express anything but itself?*" (Paul Henry Lang's report in his editorial on "Problems in Modern Music," April, 1960, *Musical Quarterly* special issue). Such time-honored concepts, revived with relish by Stravinsky, are no longer valid, Goléa endeavers to prove: "[Boulez's and Nono's] great vocal works, especially, while employing total serial combinations very freely [Would that be "the Prison of Total Freedom"? V.D.] reach beyond them constantly by creative originality which does not take stock of anything, whether they [the composers] admit it or not,

other than the *profound cry of the soul*." Victor Hugo could
not have put it better.

Goléa then directs his guns toward ... Stockhausen (whose
Gesang der Jünglinge he considered the masterpiece of "electronic" music in 1958) and the inventor of "concrete music,"
Pierre Schaeffer, whose "famous" high-spot in the genre,
Symphony for Man Alone, was termed "a sort of a classic"
by the chameleonic commentator. It took only three years for
Goléa to make a sprightly about-face. "Those, especially followers in Stockhausen's footsteps, who went so far astray in
the confusion of technical formulae, had an irresistible aspira-
tion towards liberty, the *real* kind, not simply a choice of a
thousand tyrannical devices, and were seized with a desire to
destroy music herself." Schaeffer began his first "concrete"
experiments in Paris in 1948, while, two years later, Stockhausen joined a certain Herbert Eimert for similar research
purposes in Cologne, Germany. Soon enough the two Germans
showed utter contempt for Schaeffer's work, deeming it "amateurish"! Amateurish or not, German or French, electronic
music "wanted no part of an interpreter, of human invention."
Goléa elucidated. "Thus, young practitioners of *integral* serialism have avidly taken possession of these superb and useful
technical toys to permit the realization of the most complicated musical structures, *normally unplayable*, with the cer-
tainty that the 'machines' would reproduce them to perfection."
Inevitable squabbles and skirmishes ensued—and it was Goléa
himself who hastened to compose a timely (if, I fear, premature) epitaph to the robots' demise: "They thought themselves capable of anything, but all they did, in fact, was to
turn around in a circle by producing works ... that brought
about, more and more inevitably, the *supreme death of music*—
(in other words) monotony—generating boredom."

France and Germany are not alone in fostering the robot
approach to music—for their Stockhausens and Schaeffers, we

have our Luenings and Ussachevskys. Otto Luening (b. 1900), a Busoni pupil, wrote music of conservative nature until quite recently, while the younger Vladimir Ussachevsky (b. 1911 in Manchuria, of Russian parents) was relatively unknown prior to his discovery of electronic delights. The two turned out *A Poem of Cycles and Bells* for tape recorder and orchestra (1954), which is not unpleasant to hear and bears a certain resemblance to music, but, as quoted by Paul Henry Lang, "Ussachevsky tells us how he composes for the tape recorder, a bright, versatile, obedient, but *soulless* instrument. The process is very involved and bears as little resemblance as possible to what one innocently supposes to be the course of musical composition, whether tonal or serial." Lang further informs us that "the Pythagoreans held that the mathematical ratios between tones are identical with the basic conditions of music; that the Pythagorean doctrine is debatable, was already recognized by Aristotle and Aristoxenus, who granted the musician what Ernst Krenek denied him: the right of *aisthesis*, that is, the right to his own feelings and interpretations as opposed to the calculations of the Pythagoreans. Today, the scientist and engineer no longer presumes to dictate to the artist, he and his machines take over the artist's role and métier, lock, stock, and barrel, and ramrod." And, further, "Our friends of the electronic tube . . . have the temerity to dismiss the Stradivari violin as useless because it produces 'impurities' on account of the fallibility of the human finger and the scraping of the bow. It is precisely in these human frailties, in this expressive impurity, that life and humanity are revealed. A totally aseptic tone produced by machines will be a dreadful thing,"—not to mention the resulting total unemployment of trained humans who may, however anachronistically, still depend on the performer's art they mastered for a living; that will be more than dreadful—it will eventually mean a total abandonment of the music trade by us mortals and our replacement by robots. To that end we have the outspokenly sadistic scheme of Messrs. Barbaud and Blanchard who—as reported by the ever-watchful *Time* magazine—have conspired to make the "genus composer" obsolete. The conspirators "have worked long and hard," says the *Time* researcher, "to create a composing machine as versatile as the one that swamped the masses with mollifying melodies in Orwell's *1984*." There is a sad disappointment in store for the enterprising B. & B.; their ages being forty-three and fifty, respectively, they are, in all probability, angry at having been obsolete themselves until "dreaming up the electronic brain of an Orwellian monster otherwise known as Binary Digital Computer Gamma Three." Their scheme is far from novel, emerging, as it did, from the fertile brain of the late Joseph Schillinger, who turned Gershwin into a respectable craftsman for the purposes of *Porgy and Bess.* "What we've done," claim B. & B., "is simply carry the old discovery that music is an arithmetic process to its logical limit. Machines could replace every popular tune composer immediately and plenty of serious composers." A similar claim had already been made by Schillinger. "As long ago as 1918, he published an article entitled 'Electrification of Music,' in which he expounded his ideas on the inadequacy of the customary musical instruments and on the necessity of developing new ones, in which sound could be generated and controlled electrically" (V. D. "Gershwin, Schillinger and Dukelsky, Some Reminiscenses," *Musical Quarterly*, January, 1947). The term "musical mechanic" was coined by none other than Robert Schumann *Music and Musicians*), who spoke contemptuously of "untalented folk with musical leanings who, on learning quite a lot, become *musical mechanics.*" Schillinger (in 1935) claimed that there was no such thing as a *talented* composer. "Show me any reasonably smart and not totally tin-eared creature and I guarantee to turn him into another Beethoven within five years," he told me, without a hint of a smile; nonetheless,

I was skeptical of his "genius factory." "My point is easily proven," said Schillinger. "Here is a private recording of a quartet written by one of my pupils, who didn't even know musical grammar three years ago." He handed me a score of the quartet and bade me look and listen. This I did, marveling at the "scientifically organized" sounds; they were cannily invented, with logic and even wit in abundance—everything was there, except *music*. The mechanically produced piece resembled Hans Christian Andersen's tale in reverse—priceless jewels, splendid array, a golden crown—all the royal paraphernalia were present; the one thing missing was the *king*.

Here is what Hindemith has to say on mass-produced composers (Paul Hindemith, *A Composer's World*): "The most conspicuous misconception in our educational method is that composers can be fabricated by training ... We produce composers the democratic way, as we produce congressmen ... It cannot be done. Elbow power and persistence are in this field no proof of your superiority, and seats in highest assemblies signify neither quality nor knowledge on the part of a composer ... composing cannot be taught the democratic way ... artistic creation is aristocratic because it is the privilege of a very restricted number of people. If it could be democratized, it would lose its quality as an art, become reduced to a craft, and end as an industry." That is precisely what music "creation" has become—an industry; for we live in an era of elbow-power-drunk composers, straight off the assembly line. And if you, dear reader, should have composing ambitions, quit worrying about whether talent is among your qualifications; on becoming dodecaphonic, concrete, or aleatory, you will learn how to camouflage its absence.

To return to Messrs. Barbaud and Blanchard and the *Time* findings: "The only catch, of course, is that if Gamma Three and other computers were turned loose to compose to the electronic limit, the frenzied output would need someone to judge it—someone to decide which compositions were worth keeping and which were pure junk." Thus *nous revenons à nos moutons* and their shepherd Schillinger; with no qualified and impartial judges to evaluate the production of live composers—who is to judge the robots? Or can qualified critics be turned out on an assembly line, too? Perhaps the enterprising Frenchmen would consider a Binary Digital Computer Gamma *Four*—this being a critical machine. To go yet another step further, how about a Gamma *Five*—a machine-produced audience, complete with applause, cheers, whistles, and boos; this would be a great boon to aspiring virtuosi, budding conductors, and other prima donnas—but stay . . . won't the performers be robots as well? Who will do the aspiring and the budding? Let's give up the whole thing.

All is not lost: contrary to the incessant drum-beating on behalf of what passes for "contemporary" music, the reports of its triumphs are most incorrectly, not to say dishonestly, slanted, for which we can blame only the soapbox U-boys, overzealous champions of the movement. With the exception of their Paris stronghold—the *Domaine Musical* concerts and those German festivals that are sponsored and subsidized by the dodecaphonists' and experimentalists' publishers—the serial-row and "concrete" brands of music are flopping everywhere with a dismal thud.

Pierre Boulez, whom I took to dinner in Paris in 1953, and whom I nearly caused to choke with my irreverent questions, first appeared in Los Angeles four years ago to conduct his *Le Marteau Sans le Maître*—a work that took some eighty-five hours to rehearse; this was at one of the Monday Evening Concerts, attended by the West Coast U's and their sympathizers. I was present, and can testify that Boulez's reception was perfunctorily polite and no more.* Back home the

---

* Goléa reported (p. 179 of his *Rencontres*) that *Le Marteau* was "triumphantly received" in Vienna, Zurich, Munich, London, New York, *and* Los Angeles.

Boulezites made it appear like a travesty on our land's beginnings: the discovery of Pierre-Christopher Columbus by grateful, but oh, so backward, America. As to "taped" music, I must report a mirthful episode that took place at the same concert. Prior to the unveiling of a Karlheinz Stockhausen potpourri, one of the avant-garde spokesmen stepped gingerly onto the podium and cleared his throat. The audience, keenly expecting an enlightened *avant-propos*, craned their collective necks. "Ladies and gentlemen," said the man, bespectacled, tense, and unsmiling, these being the earmarks of a true U-musician, "will the person who owns a green Dodge sedan kindly remove it from the driveway to enable the performers to park their cars?" A few titters ensued, while a short, squat citizen hastened out to correct matters. The Stockhausen opus was then allowed to go on. It consisted mainly of rude noises, generally associated with the bathroom, a series of uncomfortable squeaks and screams and a few ear-splitting hisses. This went on for a while, shocking no one and boring quite a few. The performance over, a grizzly, aging cowboy-type customer got up lazily and cackled over the thin applause: "They'll never start *that* Dodge!"

The third member of the "avant-garde axis spearheaded in Germany by Karlheinz Stockhausen and in France by Pierre Boulez" (Albert Goldberg in the Los Angeles *Times*), Luigi Nono of Italy, had the American première of his *Cori di Didone* at yet another Monday Evening Concert in January, 1959. The text of this essay in "serial technique in its most advanced form" consists of six stanzas by Ungaretti, a contemporary Italian poet. Thirty-two human voices, along with eight suspended cymbals, four tam-tams and a set of chimes manned by six players, are employed. "Since entire words are never pronounced," Goldberg continued, "the separate syllables being distributed here and there among the thirty-two solo voices, complete linguistic unintelligibility is achieved." What did poor Ungaretti think of the resulting "double gibberish," one wonders? Or what about Boulez's willful distortion of René Char's poems, already distorted and made gratifyingly unintelligible by the poet himself?

Boulez's own defense of the "double gibberish" method is priceless: "When one sets a poem to music... a series of questions relative to declamation, to prosody, presents itself. Is the poem to be sung, 'recited,' spoken?... Singing it implies carrying forward the sonority of the poem on intervals and a rhythmic pattern *fundamentally diverted* from the sound and rhythm of the original verse; that does not mean exaggerated diction, but transmutation and, let's admit it, quartering (*écartément*) of the poem. Let us ask quite pointedly: is the 'impossibility to understand' the words, assuming that the interpretation is perfection itself, an absolute, unconditional sign, that the setting is devoid of merit?... If you want to 'understand' the text, read it! or make someone recite it for you; there is no better solution. The far more subtle next step that you are asked to take implies a *previously acquired knowledge of the poem*: All arguments in favor of the 'natural' are nothing more than silliness, 'Natural' things being out of the question (*in all civilizations*), the moment one considers setting words to music" (quoted by Goléa). Be of good cheer, ye stars and starlets of the opera and concert hall; from now on, do not trouble to enunciate the words that go with the music you are called upon to sing. Don't even bother to memorize them—it isn't civilized; feel free to substitute any lines that come into your head—your favorite nursery rhyme will do handsomely. Since the audience will have read your lines before you open your mouth, they won't feel cheated. The new procedure also has the advantage of letting the orchestra drown you out, if you're not in good voice. But stay—what happens to the "natural silliness" of a Mozart, a Schubert, a Moussorgsky, or a Debussy, who were uncivilized enough to make their texts intelligible at all times? I fear that an up-to-date transmutation may be of the essence; why not apply to the dodecaphonic headquarters, wherever that may be—in Darmstadt or Donaueschingen? They are sure to give you the business, although it may not be the kind you're seeking.

Since other characteristics of the "only true music of today" are complete lack of rhythmic drive, no aurally discernible melodic line, and unbelievable, crushing monotony, the human ear, once attuned to musical crawling ants, which process takes, roughly, two minutes, soon wearies. There is absolutely no shock impact, no invigorating tonal clashes, or sweeping momentum, all of which were present in the works written more than a quarter-century ago—those of Edgard Varèse or Carl Ruggles, in Stravinsky's *Les Noces, Villa-Lobos's Choros,* and, every so often, in the really prophetic music of Charles Ives, who preceded them all. Sunk in the dodecaphonic or "concrete" morass, the unhappy listener finds himself actively longing for the good old days, when vigorous cacophony caused irate dowagers to hit each other over the head with umbrellas and shout uninhibited obscenities at the perpetrators of such outrage. No one shouts any more, one just falls asleep.

IV

Dare we hope that the beginning of the end is in sight? At any rate, I am told by those who use the "in" and "out" system, which has replaced the U and non-U terminology of Miss Mitford, that the "concrete" boys are "definitely in" while the senile "serialists" are "out, out, out." Were "concrete" and similar experiments confined to the university music lab, where they belong, something worth-while might conceivably evolve eventually; but Stockhausen, Schaeffer and their disciples are persuaded that no other music has any *raison d'être* today;

their apologists insist that Boulez's crawling ants and Stock-hausen's vivid sound-reproductions of internal disorders have mass appeal. In the testimony of K. Werner, an uncomfortably impartial commentator (impartial enough to be translated into Russian and given three pages in *Soviet Music,* the official Communist magazine), Stockhausen "dreams of perpetual music programs, changed periodically, counts on the public attending such concerts with the same regularity with which they go to picture galleries or the movies. The clash between such a sociological conception and 'space music,' hitherto created, is certainly, more than obvious." At any rate, the ruinously costly 1958 experiments at Donaueschingen, em-ploying three orchestras (109 players), three separate con-ductors, dozens of outsize loud-speakers, specially built elec-tronic equipment, etc., presided over by Boulez, Stockhausen, and Rosbaud, resulted in a fiasco fully as colossal as the organizers' nerve. Such experiments, thank heaven, are an impossibility in the States: where would the pontifying pioneers find the money—*or* three conductors, agreeing to share the podium *and* the credits?

Hélène Jourdan-Morhange, a most lenient commentator habitually, got pretty restless on the pages of *Lettres Françaises* (February 26, 1959). She reviewed the first spring concert of the *Domaine Musical,* adding her own sour note to the sour notes with which the occasion was generously supplied: "It's not this last concert that will convert many to dodecaphony. What boredom! What monotony in this 'novelty' which con-geals itself faster still than the 'conformism' it would purport to battle. *Everything sounds alike.*"

Returning to our Smart Alec-in-Wonderland, anxious for both self-support and U-type self-respect, we come to the formidable paradox: The farther away from the audience the composer gets, the more ruthlessly he complicates and dis-torts his musical speech; the less playable and listenable his music becomes, the louder he complains of abuses and neglect. Does he ever stop to think that it is *he* himself, with the egregious disdain so typical of his kind, who abuses and neglects his audience? Yes, *abuses* it by foisting turbid experiments on it, experiments for which the proper place is his own ivory tower or a privately endowed laboratory, hardly the concert hall: *neglects* it by refusing to supply the kind of music that would *move* the listener, excite his senses, or, at the very least, his interest.

Of many atonal accomplishments, Berg's *Wozzeck*, Schoenberg's *Ode to Napoleon*, Varèse's *Amériques*, Hindemith's new *Octet* are engrossing and stimulating, whether you are or are not familiar with the idiom; Glazunov's symphonies, Pfitzner's operas, Reger's chamber music, Elgar's oratorios are fully as dull as *Marteaux, Didones, Agons,* and *Threnis*—although the first four are "tonal" and the last four "dodecaphonic." It's still the *music* that counts, not the style it's written in. Audiences do crave musical nourishment—but they need something more sustaining than Karlheinz's canned foods.

A composer myself, I've been an indefatigable composer's champion for some twenty-six years. It was I, aided by Carlos Chavez, who activated the Composer's Manifesto in 1933—a stillborn collective credo dedicated to "reinstating the composer to his rightful place in the world of music." The manifesto's objectives contained a plea to enable composers ("penniless lunatics in the richest country in the world") to gain a livelihood from their work. It was signed by twenty-nine composers, ranging from Joseph Achron to Bernard Wagenaar, of whom only one made big money writing music—George Gershwin. I also spearheaded the equally abortive Westchester Festival, for which Koussevitzky was ready to abandon his lucrative Boston job, but which failed to materialize when the conductor realized, to his horror, that it would be run by composers. It was I who gave birth (with much help from Paul

Bowles) to the so-called High-Low concerts, whose programs combined "highbrow" fare with "lowbrow" fun; there were two of them—both sold out and enthusiastically reviewed—but the series was abandoned, because I had to go back to self-support and my associates to their self-esteem.

On removing to California in 1951 and becoming a box-office composer again—this time for Warner Brothers—I had to revise my views on my colleagues' plight rather drastically: I no longer shed tears for them. If modern music in America is not solidly on the map, insofar as popular acceptance goes, the fault probably lies in the ineffectual role played by the living composer. Determined to baffle or antagonize the auditor, rather than woo him, our note-scribbler, perhaps fearing physical mayhem, prefers to remain unseen and unheard as his own interpreter; the composer-virtuoso is now practically extinct. Yet nearly every concert artist of the late eighteenth and the whole of the nineteenth century was a composer first and an interpreter second. Most of the soloists and conductors engaged by the leading music societies of European capitals of that period were expected to furnish their own compositions. Starting with the end of the nineteenth century, the increasingly "nonappearing" composer began to be superseded by the "noncomposing" interpreter. With the exception of prodigious Leonard Bernstein, one is unable to name a single American composer who is also a truly sought-after virtuoso or conductor.

Contrary to the fancy theories expounded by the purists, music—to the paying public at least—is primarily entertainment. A concertgoer attends a concert largely because of the "personal" attraction it offers, whether it be a favorite conductor or a much-lauded soloist. Small wonder then that the retiring composer's absence from the concert hall tends only to increase the audience's apathy and unwillingness to become excited about the work of someone whom they cannot see or hear.

The "social" composer, the lion of the salons, is also a thing of the past, as is the salon—in this country, especially. Chopin and Liszt, habitual *salonards,* owed their careers to the *haut monde* and frankly reveled in the adulation bestowed on them by musician-conscious men and women of rank. Such people are still about, although titles and money seldom go hand-in-hand these days; France has its Polignacs, Noailles, and Rothschilds, while we can point to our Fords, Rockefellers and Huntington Hartford, who contribute generously to arts and sciences. I've never been to a Ford or Rockefeller salon, but were I a young hopeful, I'd brush up on my manners, take piano lessons (Stravinsky did—late in life and with profit), and get busy with *services mondains,* as Henri Sauguet used to say, where it can help the most. Of the contemporary men, I cannot name a single devoted *salonard;* Bernstein, Barber, Bowles, and Menotti do not disdain drawing rooms but, Bernstein excepted, I've never heard them perform in such surroundings. Great pity, too: music takes on an added glow in a festive décor provided by the rich. Stravinsky's *Renard,* de Falla's *El Retablo,* or Poulenc's *sorties* with Bernac contributed to the éclat of a Polignac gathering and put many a well-lined purse at a composer's disposal. What astute hostess would expose her guests to Boulez's "double distortion," Nono's "double gibberish," or Stockhausen's gastric gavottes?

To the above, add the music creators' well-known dislike of each other and you get the picture: the composer is an unbending misanthrope who shies away from people, then accuses them of shying away from him.

Is there a solution, other than a grant or a commission? Is there any future in being a composer, and if so, what's the recipe? Well, here's mine: Do not be ashamed to deliver an honest job in whatever you tackle—from a TV commercial to an oratorio. Do not write an unplayable and interminable symphony, employing obsolete instruments and requiring endless rehearsals, then cry about being unable to obtain a hearing. Above all, try to get on wax: your music, once recorded, will be performed again and again on the radio and you won't have to spend the rest of your life chasing conductors.

Two more ways of combining composition with three meals a day: teach your craft (be sure, however, to *learn* it first) and marry rich, which has also been suggested by Virgil Thomson, a dedicated bachelor. Most composers do teach. Regarding marriage, one bit of well-meant advice: When you woo your heiress, and she gushes: "I just love music," don't upbraid her for being pitifully non-U. Don't advise her to digest music, rather than love it, to listen to it with her brain, rather than her ears; don't sing scatological serenades to her in the approved Stockhausen manner; don't subject her to a musicalized tapeworm extraction, however beautifully taped. Perversely, vulgarians still believe that "music hath charms" and that "a musician that maketh an excellent air in musick, must do it by a kind of felicity and not by rule" (Bacon). Free yourself of rules and shackles imposed on you by smug dictators, and remember—if your music does nothing for the people, don't expect the people to do something for your music.

IV

Composers on Themselves

• — • — • — • — • — • — • — • — • — • — • — • — • — • — • — •

Felix Valloton (1865-1925), a somewhat reticent symbolist and "synthetist" painter, was taken to the Salon des Independents by one of his friends, a noted "fauve." The "fauve" showed Valloton his newest painting, fresh from the easel. "Well? . . . These distortions . . . aren't they interesting? They say nothing to you?" he queried anxiously. "Of course they do," Valloton replied. "I let 'em talk—I don't answer them."

Similarly, it may be wisest to keep one's silence when exposed to musical distortions: fearful of displaying their backwardness and lack of up-to-date know-how, most auditors—and paid commentators, too—do that anyway. American music critics have become so conditioned to the serial techniques and other modish "musts" that, whenever exposed to work credited to what Leonard Rosenman calls a "white-key composer," one who does not altogether eschew tonality, they dismiss it patronizingly as a sample of archaic "lush romanticism"; saturated with increasingly bolder "isms," the critic is obviously on the spot.

It occurred to me that presenting only my own findings, whether for or against, is unfair. The man most qualified to appraise the current trends is the practicing composer, one who is faced with the uneasy job of creating in this era

129

of organized unrest—and who, let us hope, knows what he is
doing. The French, the first, as we saw, to revive the Viennese
dogma and impose it on the musical world, were also the
initiators of the first all-inclusive musical *enquête*, a practice
of which they are especially fond. Again, it was our "humanist"
friend Daniel Lesur who, in collaboration with Bernard
Gavoty, took the job of musical census-taking upon himself
with *Pour ou Contre la Musique Moderne?* (Paris, 1957)
and made some valuable discoveries. "Many divorces are born
of a misunderstanding," Henry Barraud, head of the music
section of Radiodiffusion Française and an eminent composer,
wrote in his preface. "The divorce between modern music
and the public may well be one of those . . . what *is* modern
music, when one witnesses the co-existence of Hindemith,
Poulenc, Menotti and Boulez? . . . Let us get the meaning
of words clear. There is no such thing as a 'public'; there are
a hundred-odd 'publics'—their tastes and reactions varying
in accordance with their cultural status. There is no *one*
Modern music; only musicians with varying degrees of ability."
Barraud then points out that the sport of *épater les
bourgeois* is a thing of the past, that the audience of today
is not easily startled, having digested Picasso, Le Corbusier,
and Bartók "without undue stomach distress. It [the public]
will absorb many others . . . it no longer needs elbow room
at the concert hall, since the music is furnished today by the
means of a sonorous or luminous box reposing on a piece of
furniture in a man's living room, his bedroom or, even, his
kitchen. The purpose of the 'For or Against Modern Music'
broadcasts, conducted by Gavoty and Lesur, . . . is to create
a bond between the composer and the auditor, clarify ideas,
dissipate misunderstandings, underline the seriousness, the
sincerity of creative effort." The broadcasts took place between January, 1954, and July, 1955; every week a composer,
critic, conductor, or musicologist was invited to submit to a

series of questions, relating to the state of New music. Thus, ninety-eight specialists made their pronouncements—those unable to be present sent in their answers by mail—Stravinsky, Hindemith, and Shostakovich abstaining for a variety of reasons. "Every epoch has had its art. All art was judged by its contemporaries," stated the editors. "Were they always as severe as they are in our time? Because—and it is a fact—contemporary music does poorly at the box office. The large majority of listeners *follow* it, rather than *desire* it. Few are those who are really interested." Lesur and Gavoty then assert that, while "clubs" composed of avant-garde music cultists have their fanatical adherents, the "large" public—or "Sunday melomanes" as they are known in France—shy away from programs composed of new works exclusively and even from those wherein a modern piece is slipped in between tried-and-true favorites. There follows a glossary, with modal, polymodal, tonal, polytonal, atonal, dodecaphonic, concrete and "electro-acoustical" varieties patiently defined in clear and simple terms. The editors further tell us that they received hundreds of letters from the radio listeners, but print only two of these—both of considerable interest.

The first ("short and ironical") quotes Plato: "A noise is not a musical sound," on one side of a postcard. On the reverse is a drawing representing a *"concert à quatre"* given by a small child pounding on the piano, a howling dog, a rat manipulating a big drum, and a monkey blowing into a trombone, from which a white kitten emerges. The editors express hope that the reading of their volume will induce a "sounder examination of the problem" on the part of the musical amateur. The second epistle deemed worthy of publication by Lesur and Gavoty was more representative of "melomanes of good will," puzzled by certain manifestations of contemporary art: rather like Barraud, the second melomane begs leave to tell the editors that Modern music does not exist. What does exist is "living musicians who write music on a technical or aesthetic base which *they* consider valid; this is perfectly legitimate and no one has the right to reproach them for it . . . As for me, give me *good* music; it is no concern of mine whether it is 'modern' or not."

The same commentator (Julien Martel by name) has, in common with our Henry Pleasants, little use for unrecognized precursors, or the "judgment of posterity," the comfortable mirage so dear to every would-be precursor's heart. "For those who lived in the Middle Ages, Virgil was a prophet who announced the advent of Christ," he opined. "By what yardstick do we measure the Greek of Euripides or Caesar's Latin? Posterity's judgment is both disconcerting and prejudiced." The writer expresses the hope that the *enquête* will merely "characterize the creative effort of our time and the contemporaries' reaction to same." Mr. Julien Martel is nothing if not way down to earth when he talks of the man in the street who had no taste for *Pelléas and Mélisande.* "Today he is unable to remember a single note of *Wozzeck* or *The Rake's Progress.* So he goes elsewhere." "Elsewhere" is, obviously, the domain of the popular song—*la rengaine*, as it is affectionately tagged by a Frenchman. "That explains the small audiences available to our (advanced) musicians," Martel goes on. "I'm not speaking of the ignoramuses, or the cultivated listeners who follow the new trends. There is, however, an *intermediate* audience, in no way hostile to novelty, in no way rebellious to the idea of adapting itself and striving to understand, in no way influenced by scholastic dogmatism . . . Could such a public be shocked by the use of new and unfamiliar techniques? I don't believe it for a moment. A man of sixty-six has seen and heard so much: from *Mignon* to *Parsifal;* from *Le Petit Duc* to *L'Après-midi d'un Faune;* lastly, from tonal music to '*musique concrète!*' He's gotten used to so many unusual procedures that he became "unshockable.' This apathy, when placed face-to-face with the unexplored is a bad sign; the absence of reaction is, in effect, very close to indifference. One listens to these pieces with the same polite interest one accords a scientific lecture . . . no intimacy is established. Jazz . . . never leaves one indifferent; on the contrary, 'grand' music of today produces the effect of a boring task, certainly meritorious, which could perhaps interest us if we had a lot of time on our hands. This is about as captivating, after all, as Chinese scrawls or supersonic airplanes. Stuff for the initiated. The amateur couldn't care less. Contemporary art—painting and poetry—appears to be an *art of concepts, not of images;* a sort of difficult and dexterous algebra, fit to engage one's intelligence, but saying nothing to one's sensibility or imagination. If art is no more than a concept, *it amounts to but little.* Every time I listen to new music, I know I'm in the presence of very intricate mechanics, comparable to a watch's insides—but neither my senses nor my heart are in any way engaged . . . Beckmesser replaced Walter; thus Eva no longer recognizes her lover. Modern art cannot survive unless it leaves the lab for a public meeting place."

This long quote from an obscure source sums up the average intelligent listener's attitude with such purely Gallic clarity that I found it worth reproducing *before* letting the composers speak. Most auditors "applaud with resignation" when served an avant-garde dish (note Lesur and Gavoty), having been told time and time again: "See what your fathers and grandfathers did: They passed up the masterpieces and covered themselves with ridicule . . ." Marc Pincherle, the noted critic and lecturer, witnessed, at Aix-en-Provence, in the course of an afternoon devoted to new music, the enthusiasm of a young girl, who declared ingenuously: "I'm applauding like mad, for fear that, if I don't, I'll be taken for an idiot." The editors remark wisely: "There is nothing wrong in rejecting a new piece *after* examining it, but condemning all modern production, without being well acquainted with it, is unfair." Now for a little guesswork: Who uttered the following? "The new rules that obtain today and the new fashions that follow them make modern music disagreeable to hear." An anti-Boulezite? A Cage-hater who ardently wishes his pet musical aversion would go back to exploring mushrooms?* An escapee from another cage—the "prison of total freedom"? Wrong with all three guesses: It was Canon Gian-Maria Artusi, the Bolognese composer and critic, who greeted the publication of Monteverdi's madrigals with these bitter words . . . in 1600.

The young girl who applauded vigorously to prove that she was no idiot, may have been one of the luckless melomanes virtually unable to stumble through a contemporary piece at the piano, even though they be facile readers. Lesur and Gavoty illustrate this spiritedly: "A young Lady of Fashion in 1884 was capable, after a few years of study, to decipher correctly Massenet's *Manon*; in 1925 you had to be a phenomenally good reader to wrestle with *Wozzeck* 'reduced' for voice and piano; *no* amateur, in 1957, can tackle a dodecaphonic *morceau*." Such a state of affairs is hardly calculated to swell the ranks of serial-music champions.

Mr. Martel, the young girl who applauded for reasons of self-defense, the sixty-six-year-old melomane who'd seen and heard it all and was ready to give up, would hardly be welcome in avant-garde circles. "Can one offer serious arguments in an effort to convince such people?" Lesur and Gavoty inquire at the end of their preface, "Will the composers be gracious enough to answer the auditors? Assuredly," they conclude, "the accusers having had their say, the defense will now take the stand."

II

Although the principal interest of the French *enquête* lay in the divorce between the composer and his audience, the

---

* Cage's hobby.

causes thereof and the possible remedies, Lesur and Gavoty weakened their case by the method they adapted. The "chatty interview" format of their broadcasts was, in fact, so chatty that the interviewers and their guests continually got away from the main issues, often covering up by the means of breezy persiflage, so dear to Gallic *causeurs*. Even with this regrettable handicap, the conclusions are clear—uncomfortably so to those defending the most *outré* New Waves in music: Of ninety-eight composers and musicians interviewed, fifty were against serialism, *musique concrète*, and such; forty-two either evaded the main point or went off in other directions; six were emphatically "for" what is now taken to mean "modern music."

There was (presumably) a seventh "aye"-voter in the person of the puissant spokesman for dodecaphonism. His answer, which did not help the cause one whit, was—unprintable. "To our letter which observed the strictest rules of courtesy," wrote the editors, "Pierre Boulez replied [on October 16, 1959] in the following terms, "For or against modern music—*que voulez-vous que ça me foute?*" (Better left untranslated. V. D.) This opener was "followed by a few insults: for that is Mr. Boulez's attitude *vis-à-vis* anyone who does not admire him blindly. Such college-boy vulgarity sheds a new light on the marvelous 'purity' of the young master," Lesur and Gavoty observed drily. They contented themselves with a few quotes from the "young master," quotes culled from various publications he graced with his "pure" pen. Of these, one or two will suffice as samples of the man's style: "To answer the adversaries whose ambitions are those of a burglar or a prostitute [!], wouldn't it be our objective to play the role of an engineer? ... Facing reality, there is but one attitude to adopt: Let's not be bothered by the sick and the deaf who will always treat honesty with disrespect, courage with overweening, independence with vanity ... We are always exposed to the whorelike [!] screams of horrible degenerates unconscious of their own filth."

Before talking about a divorce between the composer and the listener, Jean Absil (b. 1893, Belgium) wanted to know whether works like *Le Sacre du Printemps*, a Prokofiev symphony, Bartók's Concerto for Orchestra should be considered as modern music. "The truth is that these productions possess, undisputably, the potential of human sensibility—the basic reason for all art; they are further enhanced by perfect workmanship, the latter being placed in the service of said sensibility. That is what the public demands of music: *human expression.*" Ernest Ansermet, who has done more for new music than any other living conductor, contributed this frank statement: "Debussy created his own technique *spontaneously,* making his music his own (special) language and never explained the reason for it; this technique, to begin with, *does not adhere to any preconceived rules or systems.* In contrast with Debussy, who *produced his technique by making music first,* composers of today, generally speaking, are seeking to produce *music* by practicing a certain technique and—since compositional techniques do not provide music with a 'reason of being,' the 'sense' of what such composers do remains *conjectural* . . . In spite of such conditions, I do have the good luck, on occasion, to find a new piece in which I recognize—what joy!—*Music.* I then do everything in my power to give it a hearing—and the results are infallible; the auditors 'understand.' "

When asked to compare the activities of Les Six with those of the avant-garde "schools" of today, Georges Auric replied: "Our group, founded on friendship, was the exact opposite of a school. We never dreamed of dragging our young friends into our circle and imposing a doctrine or two on them. The only doctrine we recognized then was the right and the duty to preserve the most complete freedom.

Today, the puniest scholar is encouraged, by a series of curious manipulations and with all dispatch, to assume the rank of a 'master.' As for serial music, while I agree that certain pages of Schoenberg, Berg, and Webern occupy an important place (in music production) this in no way proves that I am impressed by serial 'revelations.' I studied with, I think, all honesty the problems posed by them; and I greatly regret to have to confess my total skepticism insofar as the 'solutions' that system pretends to bring us are concerned."

"The creative part played by the public is one of my manias. *No work of art exists without an audience,*" said Henry Barraud who, as head of the Music Section of RDF, has his finger on the people's pulse.

To a shrewd question posed by the interrogators: "Don't you think that attaching oneself to the language, rather than to the ideas it is called upon to express, is like putting the cart before the horse?" Yves Baudrier—erstwhile of *Jeune France*—replied: "The language problem is a tragedy of our time . . . the serial musicians propose, with a complacency subtly directed towards themselves, a universal panacea for our uneasiness and our empiricism. Through their services, our art attains a degree of the narrowest specialization which they justify in the name of History." Robert Bernard, who took over the direction of *La Revue Musicale* after the war, refused to disdain all contemporary production other than that of dodecaphonist or "concrete" origin, and recognized that the "music of today, with some rare exceptions, is inaccesible to amateurs, not from the point of view of comprehension, but because of being undecipherable." Bernard warned of "grave consequences" for music's evolution due to this fact alone. Gaston Brenda, a Belgian composer (b. 1902), made the encouraging observation that "serial discipline appears to be more or less abandoned hereabouts"—in Belgium, that is. Benjamin Britten, one of England's top composers, does not believe

that the "public at large is uniformly hostile to new music."
Britten, of course, is lucky in that his music, while certainly
new, is never inaccessible.

Jacques Chailley (b. 1910, French) volunteered: "... one
does not build one's aesthetics on a formula, and the serial
principle is nothing but a formula: Schoenberg himself never
presented it in any other light ... If they [the serial com-
posers] don't see in music anything but a means to align
sounds and intervals in an order more or less satisfactory to
the eye and the mind, the composers will estrange themselves
from their audience, which is not concerned with consulting a
cookbook, but would rather have an appetizing meal. That's
like the noodles recipe of Pierre Dac's; three pages of detailed
and complicated instructions and, when it's all done, you throw
the dish out the window, because it isn't any good!" Another
Belgian, Michel Ciry, adds: "We suffer from an odious sec-
tarianism which prohibits, rejects, stigmatizes and executes
mercilessly. A sure sign of disorder and weakness." Our own
Aaron Copland who, too, has been "dodecaphonizing" for the
last few years (Piano Quartet, Fantasy for the piano alone),
confined himself to a few typically guarded remarks: he
evoked nostalgically the decade 1920-1930, when "The opposition to new music was very robust, and seemed all the
stronger, because it was so healthy. New pieces were played,
the newspapers attacked them regularly, the public was
shocked—but everything was discussed passionately. Because
of these contacts and exchanges, contemporary music was
becoming an intensely living art. The great difference between
those times and our day is in that very few people discuss
new music with any amount of passion. The proportion of
such music in our concerts is so infinitesimal that, soon, one
would have only the vaguest conception of the art one
opposes." Luigi Dallapiccola contributed a long, somewhat
rambling pronouncement on the present musical "divorce,"

stating with satisfaction that "on the elimination of Nazism in Germany, works, that only fifteen years ago were supposedly 'rejected' by the public, are listened to today with attention and—upon occasion—warmly applauded." His conclusions will hardly give any comfort to the dodecafanatics: "The only time-defying quality in art is *authenticity*. [Italics Dallapiccola's. V. D.] It matters little whether the composer attaches himself to Guillaume de Machaut or to 'concrete' music. As for myself, personally, I continue to believe that the Man, with his joys and sorrows, still stands for something."

Young Jean-Michel Damase (b. 1928), one of France's best ballet composers, when asked whether he was a "passéist" or an "avant-gardist" replied: "I hope I am neither, but I prefer sincerity to forced 'newness,' because every really valid 'find' should be sincere above all; such a 'find' must be of *vital* necessity to the composer." To the next question: "Were you ever solicited—or tempted—to join certain avant-garde 'doctrinaire' groups?" Damase's brief answer was: "Never solicited and even less tempted!" Prolific Marcel Delannoy (1898-1962) refused to "render himself interesting by grimacing laboriously." He claimed to be "evolving towards a certain simplicity, *not* complexity"—preceded in this aim by such "retarded neo-classicists" as Honegger, Hindemith, and Milhaud. He had warm words for Olivier Messiaen, whose *Turangalîlia Symphony* (1948) he thought "overflowing with sonorous joy and sensuality"; in it he detected "shadows of Massenet [!!], Strauss and Gershwin [?]." This sample of "early dodecaphonism" was considered by Delannoy, somewhat startlingly, "an exhibitionistic and magisterial work." As for the newer samples of serial music, the composer found "more boredom, than aggressiveness" in them. René Dumesnil, one of France's oldest (b. 1886) and most respected critics, pleaded for simplicity and sincerity. The celebrated organist Marcel Dupré (also b. 1886) said that "people went to concerts to listen to music, not noise. They are not, in themselves, hostile to novelty, but they demand that such novelty should interest or touch them. That is why, in my opinion, the only divorce that exists is the one between *BAD* music and the people."

Maurice Duruflé (b. 1902), whose *Requiem* (1947) made quite a stir in his country, confessed to being "terribly bored by atonality set up as an absolute system." One of France's better new symphonists, Henri Dutilleux (b. 1916), said that serial techniques did not suit his temperament. "To me it appears natural to write atonally *by instinct*, but to do so *by control* would be monstrous." Even better-known Jean Françaix (b. 1912), like Damase, "never solicited" to enter into the sacred spheres of Serialism, was warned that "if he rejected such and such doctrines, he himself would be rejected and *deprived of all publicity* [Italics mine. V. D.]. That's what I call liberty!" was Françaix's parting shot.

The late Arthur Honegger, author of the remarkable and tragic *Je Suis Compositeur* (1951), declared emphatically: "I am entirely skeptical about dodecaphony. It's a *very old story*, whose birth I witnessed; it [serialism] then died a beautiful death until an attempt to revive it was made. It is not a matter of aesthetics, but merely a *procedure*. The Schoenberg school is bankrupt, never having found an audience, and without an audience there is no art. Schoenberg's tragedy was in his use of atonality, not because of an artistic need, but because of his hatred for the tonal order—in other words because of impotence. Rigorous application of his method led to the serial system, to the dreadful production of a series of complicated, puerile and boring little bits and pieces. It is not art, but a recipe; dangerous, because everyone believes himself capable of employing it. A young musician, celebrated in those circles ... admitted to me recently that, in spite of an excellent ear and a profound knowledge of writing procedures, he was absolutely incapable of *hearing*, mentally, the stuff he wrote. 'If so, then what good is it?' I asked him, laughing. He responded by a glance of such sadness that I understood . . . Don't let's make a mistake; the means used to force us to admire serial music mirror exactly those utilized by Marxism in its experiments with nations it controls. It is historic determinism—no more, no less . . . If I had anything to add it would be this: 'Music is an art that touches the heart by the route of intelligence, the intelligence by the route of the heart.' "

The late Jacques Ibert, one of the most meticulous post-Ravel craftsmen, told of his meeting with Dallapiccola, to whom he said: "You are a dodecaphonist at any cost, but you didn't manage to eliminate the tonal pivot from your music." "And was he mad!" Ibert added good-naturedly. André Jolivet saw no cause to change his position from that of 1946; "The rebirth [of music]," said he, "is not in an imposed discipline, but in the increasingly more profound, increasingly more true knowledge of the human being."

The editors painted an amusing portrait of "athletic and self-assured" Maurice LeRoux (b. 1927), a dedicated dodeca-phonist: "While he is impressionable, LeRoux believes only in intelligence. A hypersensitive man, he considers himself an engineer of sounds. A man of culture, he would like to be considered as a barbarian. A skeptic, he is fond of affirming himself as a conductor, lecturer, writer, composer. His small vice is to astonish people . . . In reality, he is passionately enamoured of his art." The amorous LeRoux achieved some notoriety by pointing his guns at Fauré (in this he became an unwilling ally of Poulenc, a Fauré-hater of long standing) and . . . Stravinsky! To the militant young man "Fauré repre-sents exactly what one shouldn't do in music. Outside of a few admirable details (some bars of the *Requiem* and *La Bonne Chanson*) Fauré's music gives me goose flesh [!] because of its inane and outmoded sentimentality: in that genre, I prefer certain syrupy passages of symphonic jazz!... [in short] Fauré's music is stupid [!!]. As for Stravinsky, that's another story: a case of uprooting and cowardice. It would seem that his genius and puissance became soiled when he arrived in America."

LeRoux's estimate of Schoenberg is another minor bombshell: he considers the master's music "often heavy, badly orchestrated, even *ugly*." Webern is LeRoux's idol, having "organized spaces and silences." Intent on "astonishing," whatever the cost, our athletic rebel insisted that "conventional forms—three-movement sonatas, well-constructed symphonies, fugues, chorales—don't mean a thing today. What would a *menuet* be doing in 1957, when we have *danses* that are infinitely more "sexy"? ("Sexy" in the original French. V.D.) The connection of the *menuet* (replaced well over a hundred years in cyclic works by Beethoven and others by the scherzo) with sonatas, symphonies and other "conventional" forms is unclear; but LeRoux stumbled on an interesting point, obviously unaware of committing a self-damaging faux pas. We *do* have "infinitely more sexy" *danses* than the priggish *menuet*, but their music is never supplied by the serial technicians. Perish the thought—sex, together with emotion and humor, are strictly *verboten* in dodecaphonic circles. Another mistake in LeRoux's small talk, to my way of thinking, was his dismissal of harmony as an important ingredient of all music (see Chapter III). "To search for new harmonies is an error. Harmony is in no way essential to constituting a (musical) language: It is a recent [?] development, to which serial music attaches an entirely different significance." *No* significance would be more exact.

The Portuguese Fernando Lopes Graça (b. 1906) did not astonish anyone when he asserted that "furiously orthodox dodecaphony succeeded only in forging a new academism, just as systematic as the old kind." Jean-Étienne Marie (b.

1917), a native of Normandy, would apparently try anything once—"prepared" piano, "concrete" music, etc.—and apply such innovations to theater, film music—*and* the church service as well! I fear that a "tape-recorded" hymn, complete with the sounds of a "prepared" organ, may turn many a churchgoer into an abject atheist. When asked "how he happened to become attracted by serial music," Marie answered with unexpected humility: "In our very difficult times, hedonist or chatty music . . . is a sign of egoism. My instinct guided me towards another kind of music, the kind wherein *economy of means* [??] is pushed to its extreme limit: serial music, that is."

The views of Frank Martin (b. Geneva, 1890), one of the world's outstanding composers, were voiced in the following: "Integral atonality is more than a revolutionary doctrine—it represents complete anarchy. All the notes being placed on the same level, without hierarchical preferences, there is no light or darkness any longer—no possible nuances: What we have is an obligatory grayness—and the resulting indifference. *Beware of art that withdraws from all humanity.* Abstract art is an art without a future — and, for me, without a present, Shun also the artists who work for 'fifty years hence.' They are not merely pretentious, they are sick. Schizophrenics are all over the place! Art has a much better chance of really enriching your life, *if you don't take it too seriously.* Ridiculous discussions—the favorite pastime of our 'young masters' in public places [The same old U-boys on the soapbox. V.D.] are the result of their seriousness, approaching naïveté. No one took art seriously in the XVIIIth century and thus a great service was performed on behalf of the artists. Art is a game— the noblest of all: don't let's turn it into a religion or an imposing task!"

The late Bohuslav Martinu (b. 1890 in Czechoslovakia), who had a fairly long and productive American career, said little, but what he said was to the point: "[a composer] writing for tomorrow, expects to be showered with praise today. When an artist isolates himself, the public isolates itself also. God alone will be able to recognize his own." Gian Carlo Menotti, in a long statement, worded it differently but the meaning is the same: "Art must be essentially an act of love, not a masturbator's pleasure . . . That does not mean that the composer should endeavor to *please* the people, but [he must] convince and move them. We must have the modesty of realizing that our experience is not a purely personal one and that our aspirations express a sort of a great universal desire, capable of being shared by a large number of humans. Unfortunately, too many contemporary composers address themselves to fashion and snobbery, not to what is noble and elevated in a man. While secretly disdaining their special little public, they are afraid of their verdict and become ready to sacrifice the rest of the world in order to impress and startle these few 'sophisticated' amateurs. Later, embittered by the very sterility of their success, such composers console themselves by saying that theirs is the 'music of the future.' Is that necessarily a guarantee of quality? . . . All artificial invention, all arbitrary ideology are bound to share the fate of Fashion." Regrettably, the seven questions asked of Olivier Messiaen had no bearing on the main point of the inquiry; the interrogators missed a great opportunity to get at the real credo of a remarkable musician, former teacher of the French dodecaphonists, who has been known to utilize serial devices (in this he is akin to Dallapiccola), bending them to his own ends and discarding them at will. All that emerged from the Messiaen interview was the disclosure of his not being a Mystic, only a Believer—in the religious sense, which shed no light on his musical beliefs. Milhaud was asked to name his likes and dislikes in the music of the past: we already knew that he didn't care for Wagner and Brahms, but added to this intelligence was Milhaud's aside: "a most natural reaction of a Latin heart!" Equally natural—if a shade too narrowly patriotic—was the list of his "predilections"; Rameau, Couperin, Bizet, Chabrier, Berlioz, Satie, and Fauré—how Latin can you get? There was also a disappointing comeback to the one "loaded" question: "Why is there so much anguish and ennui in so many 'serial' works?"—"Young musicians have on occasion lost the sense of modulation [There is no modulation in music employing serial techniques. V.D.] and they are afraid of charm, which is a fact. Luckily, we have *Latin* dodecaphony capable of expressing emotions other than sadness." The name of the happy Latin dodecaphonist was, unhappily, omitted.

Of special interest was the Serge Nigg interview. We already know that this young rebel deserted the twelve-tone camp to become an "anti-formalist." "The demon of doubt and the passion for truth explain away Serge Nigg's career," stated Lesur & Gavoty. This "open-faced young man" proceeded by "successive explosions, taking contradictory stands, unconditional adherences—all justified by a thirst for the absolute [?], prompted by . . . intellectual honesty." The Messiaen influence gave way to "historical determinism," to "integral dodecaphony"—then came the total break; Nigg joined the ambiguously named Association Française des Musiciens Progressistes . . . "whose doctrine was that of the Prague Manifesto." Unfamiliar with the Prague Manifesto, we can readily surmise that its "humanism" was of the Soviet stripe. After joining the "serialists" in 1947, Nigg plumb forgot "that music was meant to touch the man's heart . . . that music is brought into being . . . to respond to this or that aspect of human life, and not resort to mere jugglery . . . Francis Poulenc called Webern's *Piano Variations* 'pebble-stone soup,'—today he talks of it as though it were a most succulent venison *paté*. The fear of passing for a retrograde transforms even hermits into devils!" When asked the reasons for which be broke with the serial doctrine, Nigg admitted that "it often takes a very long time to discover one's true artistic nature . . . a prisoner, for many years, of artificial conceptions, contrived, unhealthy, I did not dare to write a simple chord, nor a free and airy melody . . . The greatest reproach one can make to dodecaphony is that its expressive possibilities are extremely limited. I defy any musician, of whatever power and strength, to convey, with dodecaphonic means, sentiments of joy, enthusiasm, optimism or Dionisian intoxication. By contrast, hysteria, sadness, worry, pessimism, fear and boredom all find fertile ground in serialist music. I'm thinking of Hölderlin's phrase, quoted by Leibowitz as the epigraph to a chapter dedicated to Alban Berg: 'To live is to defend a form.' For me living is not defending a form, but only *what is inside that form.*" In common with Darius Milhaud, Nigg rather unexpectedly rallied to the "spirit of the French nation." "Don't you run the risk of falling into the chauvinist trap?" queried the editors, taken aback by the new Prague associate. "I don't adhere to nationalism in music. I say simply that a French musician should express himself in French." Nigg ended his interview with an outspokenly patriotic fanfare: "Long live *L'Arlésienne,* la *Cevenole,* vive le *Requiem* de Fauré!"

The distinguished Italian Goffredo Petrassi (b. 1904), an on-and-off serialist, disclosed that he thought the "imposition of uniform religion on music perfectly ridiculous. Everyone should do as he pleases and let the music go whichever way she chooses. *Long live expressive music*—Stravinsky notwithstanding; I admire him, but he volunteered the curious notion that music is not the proper means of expressing anything at all."* The talk with Poulenc was the most comical of all. The obstinately tonal charmer, who died early in 1963, wanted

---

* Similar statements on art and music have been made since time immemorial by Victor Cousin, Béranger, Théophile Gautier, Saint-Saëns, and Hanslick.

the young to be violent. "If I were twenty years old, I would probably become a dodecaphonist and certainly go on a 'serial' adventure: I would essay it French style, just as Dallapiccola and Petrassi have attempted it *'à l'Italienne'* If my generation was not attracted by Schoenberg, it was because of Stravinsky's sun [!] that dazzled us all," said the last of the *"salonards."* To the vague query, "How to listen to a new work?" Poulenc responded crisply: "With the ears. Music is made for the ears in the same way that painting is created for the eyes." Nadia Boulanger's pupil Léo Preger (b. 1907), sensitive writer of vocal music, does not believe in a tonal system, only in the existence of *tonal necessities.* "I also think that there are *laws* in music, analogous with those of *gravity in space,* that should not be confused with *rules.* Every well planned composition, in my estimate, develops from a *germ,* not a *skeleton.* The systems, those too frequently conceived nowadays, resemble skeletons that one tries to cover up with skin—an artificial procedure."

Henri Sauguet (b. 1901), a "lyrical hedonist" if there ever was one, long admired by Milhaud for his melodic gift and noted for the simplicity and directness of his music, thus spoke up on behalf of his art: "It isn't easy to be simple, while using a complicated language. Let us heed the advice of Rameau, who spoke of 'hiding art with the art itself' and believe with Stendhal that only vain and cold souls mistake the 'difficult' and the 'complicated' for beauty."

So great a similarity in the views expressed by musicians of varying ages, social strata, and allegiances may strike the reader as being a shade too pat: in actual fact, they spoke their minds without any preliminary briefing and what they said was seldom the expected thing. (Dallapiccola's, Petrassi's, and Poulenc's answers certainly had the charm of the unexpected.) I felt a little sorry for the Messiah of "concrete" music, Pierre Schaeffer, who, like Oscar Wilde, must have felt like a lion in a den of Daniels. When reminded by [Daniel] Lesur that "The dictionary generally defines music as an art of producing sounds agreeable to the ear," the cornered and wounded lion Schaeffer snarled: *"Musicians have no ear!* [Italics mine. V.D.] They do have an *abstract* ear [?] and this trait causes them to reduce musical phenomena to notations they reconstruct automatically in their musical memory— *which prevents them from hearing* [!!]"

That should have clinched the case for the prosecutor, it would seem. Lesur and Gavoty treat us to a seventeen-page "Conclusion" of a largely conciliatory, all-forgiving nature. But we know better than that; the only conclusion, so admirably pinpointed by Schaeffer, is that *new music, composed by earless musicians is aimed at an earless auditor—* which would automatically exclude those still equipped with organs of hearing. Isn't that a relief? Roland-Manuel claimed that "most contemporary auditors listen to music with their grandfathers' ears"—but even an antique, wrinkled, and shriveled-up pair of ears is better than the "abstract," nonexistent variety. If what the deaf musician needs is a deaf audience, it becomes a matter of new-fangled therapy, wherein the doctor and the patient are both incurably sick—and common courtesy as well as an instinct for self-preservation would preclude the still healthy concertgoer from attending such gatherings.

The Deification of Stravinsky

"The natural tendency in discussing the composer of such dehumanized music is to forget the personal element completely. Yet Stravinsky is by no means a Martian. There are plenty of Americans who remember his first visit to our shores in 1925, when he seemed like a herald angel, like the harbinger of a new dispensation in art. Despite his unpoetical resemblance on the podium to a trained seal, one was tempted to say of the composer of *Petrouchka* and *Le Sacre*, 'I, too, have seen the Shelley plain.' He still comes to America from time to time—a little, hurried man, awkward in his gestures and looking myopically from behind horn-rimmed spectacles. Alas, alas! We should have seen it on his first visit: Stravinsky looks like a businessman, and nothing else. It is difficult to think of him as the composer of two or three indubitable masterpieces, ever more difficult to think of him as holding the future of music in his (much photographed) hands. And when he takes up the baton, and begins to conduct another of his recent compositions, we can be sure that the future of music belongs to other, younger men."

These lines were written by Wallace Brockway and Herbert Weinstock in their *Men of Music* (Simon & Schuster, New York) in 1939. Stravinsky, born in 1882 in Russia, became a French citizen in 1934; five years later, in the year of the

Brockway and Weinstock book's appearance, he left France
to settle in the U. S., making Hollywood his home. By the
end of 1945, the composer became a citizen of this, the
second country of his adoption. It is to Europe that he goes
"from time to time" now, having found the States more receptive to his increasingly "dehumanized" music than the
Old World, the scene of well-deserved early triumphs.

Ever the astute business man (although "and nothing else,"
quoted above, was certainly gratuitous), Stravinsky succeeded
handsomely in this country, whose "hard cash" is usually
hard to get for a musician—especially a composer.

Bartók, Schoenberg, and Ernest Bloch, scarcely less eminent
than the enterprising Russian, also settled on this soil late in
life, eking out a living at best (Bartók's lot was neglect and,
actually, poverty) and going relatively unappreciated and un-
rewarded. Stravinsky's musical brilliance is fully matched by
his talent for self-promotion; every new piece coming from
his pen is generally prefaced, annotated in advance, loudly
trumpeted—to put it bluntly, ballyhooed by either the composer himself or his agile acolytes. The publicity accorded
Stravinsky continues unabated; thus, while the Stravinskian
sounds themselves and the ensuing comments may be sour, the
monetary dividends are very sweet, indeed. Like so many
other successful music men (I believe Liberace started the
gag), Stravinsky used to shrug off the bad notices on his way
to the bank; he has now changed his ways.

Always adept at culling commissions, the Master has been
graciously receptive to those singling him out for such honors;
starting with Diaghilev, Ida Rubinstein, Princess de Polignac,
and Lincoln Kirstein, he showed himself equally pliable in the
service of John Ringling North ("Polka" for the Circus Elephants), Billy Rose (ballet for *Seven Lively Arts,* a revue),
Paul Whiteman (*Scherzo à la Russe*), Woody Herman
(*Ebony Concerto*) and, recently, Mr. Breck the Shampoo King

(*Noah and the Flood* for TV). His eightieth birthday has been celebrated almost every week of the year 1962—which meant, of course, increased performances, personal appearances, and other profitable fanfares and festivities. Good for him, I say: to be able to turn "serious" and difficult music to profit is a neat trick that could and should be copied by our younger aspirants to musical fame *and* fortune. The trick was unknown to Bartók, Schoenberg, and Bloch—and more's the pity: Their birthdays were of a far shorter duration than that of Stravinsky's and went practically unobserved by the musical fraternity and the paying public.

Stravinsky's exalted status as the No. 1 music personality in this country is one of the most amazing—and, in a sense, enigmatic—phenomena in the history of our art. Composer of four (not "two or three," which is Brockway and Weinstock's count) "indubitable masterpieces"—*Petrouchka, Le Sacre du Printemps, Les Noces*, and *Symphony of the Psalms*—Stravinsky was also responsible for *Pulcinella*, a tasty pastiche based on Pergolesi's music, and the uneven and highly eclectic early showpiece, *The Firebird*, of which the orchestral garb is so dazzling that it still makes for delectable listening. To a much lesser degree, *Le Rossignol*, another bag of artful tricks, and perhaps *Apollon Musagète* and *Oedipus Rex*, high spots of the composer's "neoclassical" period (1920-1955), also belong on the meager list of his "standards." The deafening drumbeating on behalf of Stravinsky's other entries cannot disguise the sad truth—not a single work of his after the superb *Symphony of Psalms* (1930) could by any stretch of anyone's imagination (not even Stravinsky's or Mr. Robert Craft's) be called a lasting success. Such ballets as *Jeu de Cartes* (1937), *Danses Concertantes* (1942) (originally written for concert use), and the hollow and pretentious *Orpheus* (1948) received their measure of acclaim, thanks to the ever-resourceful choreography by Stravinsky's No. 1 fan, George

Balanchine; but, viewed purely as *music*, nothing from the composer's pen created an effect comparable with those memorable early victories. For the past thirty-two years—1931-1963—Stravinsky's music brought him fat dividends and meager applause. Everett Helm, now Dr. Helm and respected editor-in-chief of *Musical America*, asks us to "consider what was being written at that time [1917]" in the June, 1962, issue of his magazine. "In 1917, when Stravinsky was working on *L'Histoire du Soldat*, Pfitzner's lush, neoromantic *Palestrina* was first produced." Other "lush" pieces of the period Helm lists are Strauss's "monster-opera" *Die Frau ohne Schatten* (1919) and Sibelius's Seventh Symphony (1924). "It would be a mistake to consider Stravinsky as the 'inventor' of neoclassicism ... Stravinsky sensed it earlier and more keenly than most." How now, Dr. Helm? Have you forgotten—or are you deliberately omitting—the far "earlier" neoclassicist and a far more genuine one, Serge Prokofiev? To use your own comparisonist method, it can be said that while Stravinsky was painting his own "lush" canvases—such as *Petrouchka* and *Le Sacre*—Prokofiev gave neoclassicism its first real innings—with the First Piano Concerto (1911), Second Piano Sonata (1912), the *Toccata* (1912), and those extraordinarily new (for the period), because stripped of all extraneous lushness, Ten Piano Pieces, Op. 12 (1908-1913).

Always the leader and the revered arbiter of musical attitudes, Stravinsky leads no longer, having turned dodecaphonic in his old age; he was understandably tired of rewriting the same piece for the last thirty years. After publicly confessing his admiration for Boulez—a curious feat for a man who has little use for his contemporaries, young or old—Stravinsky "is now writing *under* his newly assumed Webern-Schoenberg mantle ... It is curious that California should be spawning so much of this spirit, with late Schoenberg, Krenek and now Stravinsky dodecaphonizing *beneath* the smog." (Oliver

Daniel.) Dodecaphonizing *under* a mantle and *beneath* the smog must be taxing, but the Master manages to come out on top—in this country, where, seemingly, he can do no wrong.

Stravinsky's *Threni* (1958), loudly heralded as a smash at its première in Venice by his retinue, was a complete bust in Paris—with both the audience and the critics. Typically, such busts are always hushed up by the U-soapbox fraternity, and so the impression is created that dodecaphonic music, including that of the eminent new convert, Stravinsky, has conquered the world. The previously pro-Stravinsky Paris critic Clarendon (Gavoty's pen name) has this to say about *Threni*: "The musical substance of the work seemed to me of *tragic poverty*. No true harmony or melody, no rhythm, no accents of any kind, but a monotonous recitation of a Latin text, culled from Jeremiah. The serial system giving preference to disjointed intervals, one gets tired quickly of these incessant leaps, as uncomfortable for the singers as they are for the listener's ears." He then asks: "Why so many sacrifices, so much austerity when the subject chosen doesn't seem to justify it? In the name of *what* does Stravinsky, in his old age, submit to so arbitrary a set of rules? I can easily see what the youths, who surround him, gain by his 'conversion'; the presence of the great man reassures the audience. But I can see with even greater clarity that Stravinsky *himself* is the loser." While it's true that *Agon* in its ballet form has its admirers, it is equally true that it laid a monumental egg, wherever played "straight" —that is, minus choreographic embellishments. Of particular interest was an article by Émile Vuillermoz, published in 1959, in which the old and usually unpredictable French critic went to work on both the twelve-tone dogma and the new convert Stravinsky, freely quoting from Ansermet, formerly a faithful devotee of the composer: "What especially impressed the young [the occasion was a public meeting and concert of the *Jeunesses Musicales de France*. V.D.] was the loyalty, independence and courage with which that legendary champion of all avant-gardes (Ansermet) judged the bad shepherds and the snobs who lead music to an 'impasse' and expose it to the dangers of cerebralism. He denounced the impoverishment which the serial technique inflicts upon us. And, with the crushing authority of one who played so great a role in defending Stravinsky's past masterpieces, he (Ansermet) did not hide his sadness at seeing this man of genius disown his past and dig deep in fruitless furrows [*des sillons sans issue* in the original. V.D.] under the pretext that 'music cannot and should not express anything.' "

It would be foolish to pretend that Stravinsky's latest "conversion" brought him fresh laurels—even in his new home, where Clarendons and Ansermets are ineffectual, because untranslated; there was nowhere to go, but down, after the Master's final neoclassical splash, *The Rake's Progress*, failed to catch on and, on revival, proved a dud at the Met's box office. "The dodecaphonists remind me of galley slaves who, having thrown off their chains, voluntarily hang two-hundred pound balls on their feet in order to run faster," wrote Honegger in *Je Suis Compositeur*. Thus, Stravinsky courageously freed himself of neoclassical chains to enter the Prison of Total Freedom—serialism, which, so far, has succeeded in causing his public to run faster in the opposite direction. Yet, so great is the man's influence on our "advanced" composers, that the dodecaphonic headquarters, hitherto fairly inactive, suddenly became swamped with orders for two-hundred-pound balls. "It is not necessary to study in detail the reactions of Stravinsky's followers, who, with touching unanimity, mimic his different movements and changes of style. They are like the confidante in *The Critic*, who imitated her mistress even to the point of coming in mad, dressed in white satin" (Constant Lambert, *Music Ho!*). Alexis Haieff (b. 1914), Stravinsky's Russo-American follower, composer of attractively neodiatonic music in the Master's earlier manner, rushed into print to proclaim that his idol "writes the best twelve-tone music today." Yet, even the stanchly pro-Stravinskian Roman Vlad (b. 1919 in Rumania) was taken aback by so abrupt a metamorphosis: "Stravinsky's Volte-face after *The Rake's Progress* was all the more disconcerting in that just previously he had given the impression that he was moving in a totally different direction ... it might confidently have been expected that ... the trend of Stravinsky's composition would be towards a more and more marked simplification of expression." (Vlad. *Stravinsky*, London, 1960, translated by Frederick and Ann Fuller.) Instead, he "edged closer and closer to the opposite extreme of contemporary musical sensibility of which he was for so long the antithesis." (Massimo Mila in *L'Espresso*, Rome, 1956.) Drastic departures of this sort would have brought wrath and ridicule on the heads of lesser fry, but up to the *Noah and the Flood* disaster, Stravinsky could and did get away with murder. As Sir William Walton said: "Stravinsky is Stravinsky, in all probability the greatest composer of this century, and a complete law unto himself." Emily Coleman, the able music-and-ballet commentator for *Newsweek* (May 21, 1962), quoted Walton as well as St. John Perse, France's Nobel Prize-winning poet and diplomat, in a featured article: "Stravinsky at 80: Some say the greatest." Said Perse: "We have been taking Stravinsky for granted for a long, long time. He is a giant. A great keystone, and a great far-reaching influence."

The extent of this influence in the U.S. is such that each successive failure from the composer's pen is accepted as gospel by his disciples. The mystery grows as we examine Stravinsky's activities, other than composing music. Did I say disciples? Stravinsky does not teach, just surrounds himself with idolaters, who eventually come through with a book or an article, adding fuel to the ever-burning Stravinsky fire. He mastered enough piano in his middle years to acquit himself adequately as occasional soloist in neoclassical showpieces from his own pen, but no one ever went into ecstasies over his infrequent performances. As a conductor, a charitable appraiser would call him plodding and painstaking and let it go at that. As a writer, Stravinsky succeeded in making even his own spectacular and exciting life appear a masterpiece of dullness: *Chronicle of My Life* (1935) is a thoroughly unimaginative autobiography. *Poetics of Music* (The Charles Eliot Norton Lectures at Harvard University. English edition, 1948) are even less readable. The three volumes written in collaboration with Robert Craft (1959, 1960, 1962) are grimly fascinating—but atypical of the composer's literary style, consisting of lengthy answers to Craft's "leading" questions: answers obviously Englished by Stravinsky's helpmate, the Master's own knowledge of the English language being notoriously poor. "He is still dictating his extraordinary memoirs to Robert Craft," said *Vogue* (May, 1962) "—a fourth volume *Dialogues and a Diary* is on the way. He [Stravinsky] is still conducting, still pursuing perfection, still upset by critics, still fighting them. He is, as he prefers to be called, *Le Maître.*" Italians have another name for him (as reported by Miss Coleman in *Newsweek*): "Stravinsky's fondness for money is legendary. Venice is his favorite Italian city, and many of his premières have been presented there. Because he wants to be paid in advance—and paid more than anybody else—he has earned the name of 'The Merchant of Venice' . . . When offered the gold medal of the Royal Philharmonic Society [in England], he is supposed to have asked 'How many carats?' Another tidbit tells of a friend who suggested that such a great man ought to have a proper monogram. Stravinsky at once put pen to paper and came up with an I over an S, making a $." Love of money, as well as the most passionate self-love, were always part of Stravinsky's make-up. Misia Sert, one of the last true *"mecènes"* of music, and Diaghilev's devoted helper, wrote in her posthumous memoirs (*Misia*, Gallimard, 1952. Paris; most of the Stravinsky material was carefully excised from the Moura Boudberg 1953 English translation, published in New York): "Stravinsky, whose pride justifiably grew very rapidly, was soon to forget all he owed the founder of the Russian Ballet [Diaghilev]." "*Our* success went to his head," Diaghilev wrote Misia around 1918. "Where would he be without us, without Bakst and myself? . . ." "With success," she goes on, "a taste for money was born in Stravinsky . . . he remained perfectly indifferent to the Machiavellian difficulties Diaghilev was undergoing in order to finance his immense enterprise, and never stopped harassing his mentor with recriminations of pecuniary nature. While I was compelled to execute veritable *tours de force* annually to help Serge accomplish the miracle of balancing his budget, I also had to lend an ear to the increasingly strident lamentations on Igor's part, who forgot himself so much as to call his benefactor a pig and a thief . . . Stravinsky's animosity toward Diaghilev continued to grow . . . he began to think more and more of America and its financial possibilities." In 1919 Misia received a long, vitriolic letter from *Le Maître* in which, after a long harangue regarding Otto Kahn, he accused "one Russian of stealing from another, declaring that he [Stravinsky] was defenseless abroad. Isn't it a real scandal?" Following this letter, the relations between the two men became unbearable. Stravinsky soon declaring that his "religious convictions" did not permit him to employ his art on "something as low as the ballet," wrote to unfortunate Serge that the "ballet brought Christ's anathema upon him." On which Diaghilev's terse comment was: "I learned that Stravinsky, my first son [Diaghilev always called Stravinsky his first, Prokofiev his second son. V.D.], has dedicated himself to the double worship of God and money." Consequently, Ballet was no longer "low," provided the fee was high, and Stravinsky, religious convictions put aside, went to work for Ida Rubinstein, who offered "more lucrative perspectives." Misia then expresses her sadness, caused by "perusing the correspondence of the greatest living composer," and adds that "between poverty and the get-rich-quick anxiety there is, fortunately, a world—precisely the world where one would wish to find the living artist." The conclusion of this, the eighteenth chapter, is noteworthy also: "America did the rest, by placing the ocean between us [Stravinsky and herself. V.D.]. But I know full well that the *real* ocean which separates us is the one between Stravinsky of the *Sacre* era and the one of today."

II

Stravinsky's American success is based on two factors: (1) his awesome reputation as World's Composer Number One, and (2) the inspired salesmanship and unfailing business acumen with which the Master made use of our land's "financial possibilities." There was also the spiritual comfort of becoming a god all over again: The youth of Europe no longer deified Stravinsky and, for the most part, shrugged off each succeeding production from his pen as another tame exercise in moribund neoclassicism. While Stravinsky's messages to the press lacked wit and finesse, the readers were more than compensated, and actually cowed, by the ring of arrogant authority of his every published dictate. Here, at last, is the Leader—thought our young composers, flattered beyond words by Mr. Music himself taking up residence in their midst; they were oblivious of his, by then, shaky position in Europe. The young soon became aware of Stravinsky's dedication to one cause alone—The Stravinsky Cause—and his total lack of real interest in their own progress (I am yet to hear of a single personal effort on Stravinsky's part to help promote any composer except himself), but things worked out surprisingly well for the worshipers. Being part of the great man's entour-

age gave them a new and rather elegant *cachet*; as long
as they contented themselves with singling out this or that
facet of their idol's music, the young men were rewarded by
quotes in newspapers and periodicals, even articles and books
—which were welcomed by the editors so long as Stravinsky
was the subject. Thus, some of the Master's glory rubbed off
on his retinue—without the slightest effort on his part—and
when the music machine needed oiling, the oilers were right on
the spot, happy to be of assistance and profiting by it in one
way or another.

Martin Mayer, in an objective and unprejudiced article
published in the New York *Times* (June 10, 1962), tells us
that Stravinsky, after *The Rake's Progress,* "a satisfactory cul-
mination of a great career . . . quite abruptly turned to new
'historic facts'; he looked to the young, and took his cue from
them, both in silliness (his books are full of silliness) and in
substance. Specifically, he looked to a pale, slim, nervous yet
strong young man named Robert Craft." Originally a trom-
bonist in a high-school band, Craft, after "a good deal of
studying" in New York, had the bright idea of putting on the
1921 *Mavra,* an agreeable Glinkaesque pastiche in one-act
opera form, and "wrote Stravinsky for advice; and Stravinsky
not only gave advice, he came to New York for the occasion."
That letter must have been a masterpiece of craftiness, Stravinsky not given to displacing himself, unless the fee is right.
"Perhaps," as Martin Mayer shrewdly surmises, "he saw in
Craft some of the *monstrous intensity* of his own youth. Whatever his reasons, he made Craft his assistant in preparing
orchestras for him to conduct, his companion on travels and
eventually a resident in the Stravinsky household, his collaborator on his series of autobiographical books, and his
cicerone through the post-World War II avant-garde." Craft's
"monstrous intensity" certainly paid off. An able "collaborator"
and cicerone, Craft is a dry and ineffectual "finger" conductor

—so known to people in the trade, because of his preference for using his fingers, rather than his arms, while on the podium.

Craft was invaluable to Stravinsky as writer, scholar, editor and general guide in the production of the three slim volumes begun as *Conversations with Igor Stravinsky* in 1959. An idea of the Master's own knowledge of English can be gathered from the words with which he addressed the TV audience immediately preceding the performance of *Noah and the Flood*: "I don't vant to speak you any more—I vant to play you more." The style of the Craft-Stravinsky prose is meticulously correct, if stuffy and pretentious—archaisms and fancy adjectives, encountered only in the fattest and most obscure dictionaries, abound; but I don't propose to bother with style or technique here—although to Stravinsky "Technique is the whole man." (*Conversations*) He adds: "At present it [technique] has come to mean the opposite of 'heart,' though, of course 'heart' is technique too." I have no doubt that this is true of Stravinsky's own heart—as it is true of his charm, which he knows how to turn on upon occasion, although Diaghilev insisted that "*Stravinsky est le seul musicien slave qui n'a pas du charme slave.*" (*Passport*, page 120). In the article from which I have already quoted, Martin Mayer says that "people who have actually *worked* [Italics Mayer's. V.D.] with Stravinsky in his music—performers, managers, recording directors—often feel for the old man an affection so deep it demands the word "love"; together with the fierce independence comes, at moments when there is no threat, a great sweetness of temperament . . . At a time when grown people were terrified of him, children followed him like the Pied Piper." So did composers, whose childish awe of the Master was such that they never really grew up to see him in the proper light—and, in all probability, never will.

Second to critics, the genus "composer" is, generally, regarded with either contempt or hostility by Stravinsky. There

are exceptions, of course: he spoke well, almost warmly, of
Mahler, Varèse, Krenek, and our own Elliott Carter, especially
of his Double Concerto, which, while generally regarded as
a masterwork, is, to me, at least, a disappointing concession
to dodecaphonic pointillism. Of fellow Russians, such minor
men as Arensky, Liadov, and Withol received a magnanimous
accolade, while the great teacher, contrapuntist, and Russia's
best chamber-music composer, Sergei Taneiev, got a coolish
pat on the back. Stravinsky's verbal treatment of Rimsky-
Korsakov, his teacher, is a model of catty ambiguity: "There
was nothing profound either in Rimsky's nature or in his
music," "The librettos of his operas . . . are, on the whole,
embarrassingly bad." "The stale [!] naturalism and amateur-
ism[??] of the 'Five' (Borodin, Rimsky-Korsakov, Cui, Balakirev, and Moussorgsky)." These cracks are glossed over with
"I hope I am not unjust to Rimsky" . . . "[he was] deeply
sympathetic, deeply and unshowingly generous" while "sometimes shockingly shallow in his artistic aims." "I adored
Rimsky but did not like his 'mentality.'" The bulk of six and
a half pages on the "stale naturalist and amateur" (Rimsky was
an impeccable technician, as the whole world, including Stravinsky, knows) consists of an analysis of Rimsky's "feelings"
about his pupil's (Stravinsky's) music and a few digs at the
teacher's family, including a positively horrifying (and, I hope,
distorted) quote from his widow on page 46 of the *Conversations.*

Somebody, other than Craft, should have done a careful
job of editing and checking all these volumes; laughable
errors and misstatements abound in them, such as the one
where Stravinsky declares that he couldn't "take César Cui's
orientalism seriously." *What* orientalism? Of the five "stale
naturalists and amateurs," Cui was the only composer who—
with the exception of *one* tiny salon piece—shunned orientalism like a plague.

This slip was minor compared to the really colossal *triple* blunder committed by the memoirist on page 42 of *Memories and Commentaries* (1960). Here, Stravinsky lists dancers and choreographers he worked with and says this regarding Balanchine: "I had met him in April 1923, in Nice, just as I was finishing *Noces*; in fact, Balanchine had come from Russia with his wife Danilova expressly to attend the première of *Noces*." If it's "facts" Stravinsky is after, here they are: (A) Balanchine, having arrived in Europe in 1924, was not in Nice in 1923, (B) he did *not* flee to Europe "expressly" to attend *Les Noces* and (C) his wife (at the time) was Tamara Gevergeva, *not* Alexandra Danilova. I direct the reader to the very thorough *The New York City Ballet* by Anatole Chujoy (Knopf, New York, 1953), to which Mr. Craft, a pretty thorough researcher himself, should certainly have directed his careless interviewee. The passage from Chujoy, which corroborates *my* facts, runs as follows: "[After Lenin's death] it looked as if everyone in the professions, in the arts, everyone who was not a member of the Stalinist faction of the Communist party . . . wanted to get out of the country. Only a few thousand succeeded in stealing across the border; still fewer risked the dangers of applying for a passport under some pretext and getting out legitimately. It took a brave, shrewd man to talk the suspicious Soviet government into issuing a foreign passport. Vladimir Dimitriev (a singer of the Theater of Musical Drama and the Maryinsky Opera) was such a man. He assembled a group of dancers of the Maryinsky, including his friend Gheorghi Balanchivadze [now George Balanchine. V.D.], Alexandra Danilova, Tamara Gevergeva (known to the U.S. audiences as Tamara Geva), Nicholas Efimoff and two other people who have since returned to Russia. The little troupe assumed the name Soviet State Dancers; Balanchine choreographed a repertoire for them, and Dimitriev set out on the Sisyphian task of selling the authorities the idea of issuing foreign passports to the members of the group so that they could go into Germany and France to propagandize Soviet ballet . . . the little band left Leningrad aboard a small German steamship bound for Stettin, a port in East Prussia . . ." They next went to Berlin and "settled in a cheap hotel. Dimitriev . . . succeeded in arranging a tour through summer resorts along the Rhine . . . In early autumn they moved to Paris" and auditioned for Diaghilev, who accepted four of the group into the company. "The third candidate, Balanchine, was more obviously gifted, as he had shown by some dances he had already composed, which had been performed by *his wife,* Tamara Gevergeva (Geva)," adds S.L. Grigoriev, Diaghilev's regisseur and trusted collaborator in *The Diaghilev Ballet 1909-1929* (Constable, London, 1953).

So blinding is the "Stravinsky Sun" (Poulenc), so leery are his admirers and occasional co-workers of stepping on the Master's toes, that Stravinsky's absurd and unnecessary fabrication went uncontradicted to date—neither Balanchine, nor Danilova, nor Geva, the principals in the mix-up, giving voice to correct the story. Not content with presenting Balanchine with a wife to whom he was not married at the time (George did marry her later, but the marriage did not last), Stravinsky manages a backhanded slap at the man to whom he owes almost as much as he did to Diaghilev: "Poor Bronislava's (Nijinska's) sex, looks, and name were against her," says he in *Memories and Commentaries.* "I regretted this because, except for her and Fokine, the choreographers of my ballets were not so much dance composers as dance performers. They had been elevated to the position of choreographers not by education or experience but through being Diaghilev's *eromenoi.*" That would mean that George Balanchine, five times married, belonged to their number! Fokine did not, but, according to Stravinsky, "was easily the most

disagreeable man I have ever worked with. In fact, with
Glazunov [who had no love for young Stravinsky's music.
V.D.] he was the most disagreeable man *I have ever met.*"

The mention of Glazunov brings us back to composer-
baiting, Stravinsky's agreeable little game, of which he is so
fond. *Rachmaninov*: "I remember [his] earliest compositions.
They were 'watercolors,' songs and piano pieces freshly influenced by Tchaikovsky. Then at twenty-five he turned to
'oils' and became a very old composer indeed. Do not expect
me to spit on him for that, however. He was, as I have said,
an awesome man, and besides, *there are too many others to
be spat upon before him.* [Italics mine. V.D.]" *Max Reger*:
"He and his music repulsed me in about equal measure."
Maurice Ravel: "When I think of him, for example, in relation to Satie, he appears quite ordinary." *Richard Strauss*: "I
would like to admit all Strauss operas to whichever purgatory
punishes triumphant banality. Their musical substance is
cheap and poor; it cannot interest a musician today . . .
Ariadne makes me want to scream." Yet, "There is between
Stravinsky's career and that of Richard Strauss a parallel so
tragically close that one wonders whether a twentieth-century
composer can live fully in the world, and yet come to the
fullest fruition," say Brockway and Weinstock. "They both
started out tepidly with Brahmsian echoes. ["Rimskyan" would
have been more correct in Stravinsky's case. V.D.] Strauss, as
the better-taught man, produced his academic symphony at
an earlier age than Stravinsky. Both quickly spouted revolutionary works, threw off fireworks for a couple of decades,
and then fizzled out, though in different ways. Strauss's creative
energy dried up. Stravinsky, always an experimentalist, continued to experiment. But for a number of reasons, his later
experiments have failed." This was written twenty-four years
ago; the picture remains unchanged. When asked by Craft
whether he was "interested in the current revival of

eighteenth-century Italian masters," Stravinsky replied: "Not very. Vivaldi is greatly overrated—a dull fellow . . . Galuppi and Marcello . . . are poor composers . . . Pergolesi? *Pulcinella* [Stravinsky's ballet reworking of Pergolesi's material. V.D.] is the only work of 'his' I like." *Scriabin*: ". . . he was personally so maladroit, and his way of treating me and Rimsky's other pupils '*von oben nach unten*' was so detestable, that I never wished to cultivate his company . . . Scriabin was an arrogant-looking man with thick blond hair and a blonde *barbiche*. Although his death was tragic and premature, I have wondered at the kind of music such a man would have written had he survived into the 1920's." Even the Schoenberg "or, as it is now called, the dodecaphonic school" (Stravinsky obviously overlooked his own allegiance to it) comes in for a few barbs, of which one contains a reference "to the most turgid and graceless Brahms." Charles Ives is "an inventive and original man" to Stravinsky, who "wanted to like his music" but found it "badly uneven in quality, as well as ill-proportioned and lacking strength of style."

The peak of cattiness was reached in the Master's appraisal of Prokofiev; the late composer (he died at sixty-two, at the height of his career), Stravinsky's junior by nine years, had everything that his illustrious compatriot had-and-has not. Prokofiev was a great, spontaneous melodist—in line with Mozart and Schubert, a composer "by the grace of God," who did not need elucidations, forewords, glossaries, and other such extraneous paraphernalia to propagandize his music. No one was ever *ordered* to like his music or warned that lack of understanding of it would immediately stamp a man as an incurable idiot (a word for which both Stravinsky and Boulez, his mentor, have a peculiar liking: in *Conversations*, Stravinsky refers to Chaliapin as "That idiot from every nonvocal point of view, and from some of these"); one just cannot *help* liking Prokofiev's music, because in common with all good music, it has the power of immediate communication. Stravinsky had every reason to be "bugged" by the younger Russian, whose concerti began to "catch on" in the Paris days (compare the popularity of Prokofiev's 3rd or the recently "rediscovered" 2nd piano concerti with the lukewarm reception accorded Stravinsky's works in that form, or the "repertory" status of both violin concerti by Prokofiev with the seldom-played Stravinsky one), and who was a phenomenally gifted and technically peerless pianist to boot. The two composers—surface friends at best—shared a common failing: They were both wretched conductors. In the ballet field Stravinsky (of the first manner) is unquestionably superior— *Petrouchka, Le Sacre,* and *Les Noces* towering over Prokofiev's many indifferent ballet scores, of which only one is of the first rank, *The Prodigal Son,* although there are some good things in the earlier *Chout* and *Le Pas d'Acier.* In the field of opera, however, compare the fresh inventiveness and delightful humor of *Love for the Three Oranges* (Prokofiev) with the labored stylization of *Mavra* or *Rake's Progress.* Best of all, read the statistics: in a survey of 1962's "America's Symphonic Diet" by Thomas F. Johnson (*Musical America,* July, 1962), Prokofiev led the "Foreign Moderns" with 105 performances of 17 works, while Stravinsky was second with 83 performances of 15 works. The BMI survey placed Stravinsky *third,* the "quite ordinary" Ravel second, with Prokofiev again in the lead. Mr. Johnson noted, that, in spite of "a comparatively generous 83 performances [of Stravinsky's music], slightly under half of them (40) were devoted to two pieces, *Firebird* (1910) and *Petrouchka* (1911) . . . *Agon, Threni* and *Canticum Sacrum* were absent from the bill of fare—in fact the 49-second-long *Greeting Prelude* was the sole representative from the composer's serial works."

Here is Prokofiev's portrait, as painted by Stravinsky: "Diaghilev wanted him to mix, to exchange ideas with other artists, but the attempt failed, as it always did thereafter, because Prokofiev was 'full of splinters,' as he says about his music in a letter to me, with people who were *more cultivated than he was—and a good many were that.* [Italics mine. V.D.] . . . Prokofiev was the contrary of a musical thinker. He was, in fact, *startlingly naïve* in matters of musical construction. He had *some*[!] technique and he could do certain things very well. His musical judgments were usually commonplace, however, and often wrong. . . . [his return to Russia] was a sacrifice to the bitch goddess, and nothing else. He had had no success in the United States or Europe for several seasons." (A wicked and deliberate distortion of the facts: Prokofiev's appearances with the Boston Symphony in 1937 belonged among that organization's outstanding triumphs. *Prodigal Son* (1929) was the high spot of Diaghilev's last ballet season; the Second Violin Concerto (1935) caught on rapidly and was widely performed here and abroad.) But let us continue with Stravinsky's "appreciation" of his departed colleague:

"Diaghilev had believed at first that Prokofiev would develop into a great composer, and he held to this belief for several years. Then, finally[!?] he confided to me that he was beginning to think him 'stupid.'" Stravinsky then quotes from a Diaghilev letter written in 1915, in support of the above; it is lucky for us that Mme. Sert published the letter in which Diaghilev, without mincing words, told her what he thought of *Stravinsky*. The latter would not dream, of course, of quoting from letters Diaghilev wrote his contemporaries about Prokofiev's *Prodigal Son* (1929) which would have given the lie to Stravinsky's report of Diaghilev's "final" estimate of Prokofiev—made in 1915! I happened to have arrived on the Russian Ballet scene in 1924, when Diaghilev and Prokofiev were not speaking: However, Diaghilev, ever on the alert for important new music, became increasingly conscious of

Prokofiev's rapidly growing fame and his long list of new successes in the concert field. I well remember the tremendous impression that Prokofiev's 3rd Piano Concerto made on Sergei Pavlovitch and the incessant efforts on the part of shrewd little Walter Nouvel, Diaghilev's assistant and valued friend of many years' standing, to bring Ballet's czar and Music's favorite son together. What estranged them was the semi-failure of *Chout* (1920), the choreography of which was entrusted to Larionov . . . a painter! Nouvel insisted that the sprightly and good-natured productions of Poulenc, Auric, Sauguet, Rieti, et al were nothing other than "little music"—"musiquette" was the term then fashionable—and that more substantial fare was urgently needed. Diaghilev finally fell in with Nouvel's persuasive propaganda—a meeting was arranged (at which I was present), and *Le Pas d'Acier* (1927), with Massine's choreography and Yakouloff's *mise en scène* was the impressive result of the renewed Diaghilev-Prokofiev collaboration, followed two years later by the profoundly moving, soaringly lyrical *Prodigal Son.*

Before reproducing one of Prokofiev's "very affectionate" letters to him, Stravinsky magnanimously allows that he "does not wish to criticize Prokofiev: I should be silent if I could say nothing good about such a man." I can just see Prokofiev's face were he alive and able to read the "good things" his "musical friend" (Stravinsky's phrase) printed about him in *Memories and Commentaries.* Since Stravinsky professes not to know whether Prokofiev liked *his* music "beyond the Russian pieces," I can straighten him out on that point; Sergei Sergeivitch thought Igor Fedorovitch's pseudo-classical piano music "puerile in the extreme" and often cited the first movement of Stravinsky's piano "Serenade" as a prime sample of pretentious poverty. I also remember Prokofiev being angry with me for liking *Apollon Musagète*—I still like it, come to think of it.

Stravinsky's digs at his younger rival may be petty and unfair, but at least, Prokofiev is pretty thoroughly discussed on
the four pages allotted to him in *Expositions and Developments*. Stravinsky and Craft are otherwise careful not even to
name the object of their hate and ridicule: "I cannot go about
immortalizing such people by naming them," says Stravinsky
in the appendix to the third book of the series; thus, "little"
Igor (Markevitch—it was Prokofiev who jokingly referred to
the two composing Igors as "big" and "little"), virtuoso performer of *Le Sacre* and other Stravinsky stand-bys, received
this *one* sentence for his pains—he, together with the critics
"big" Igor castigated, is also sentenced to oblivion, not being
named. "[Diaghilev] was eager for me to acclaim the genius
of his newest prodigy, which I couldn't do, for the reason
that the newest prodigy didn't have any genius." For another "anonymous" knife-thrust we have a dilly on the late
Bruno Walter, one of the most universally beloved music
personalities.

As for Diaghilev, quoting the older prodigy's numerous
stabs and half stabs at his discoverer would serve no purpose
in this, a book about music; but I feel compelled to defend
Sergei Pavlovitch's good name against the many barbed
references to his image as a practicing invert. Diaghilev was
an "idealistic" homosexual of the Hellenic, male-beauty-wor-
shiping persuasion; but a strutting or mincing *tante* he most
emphatically was not. He actually forbade any association
with the more exhibitionistic members of the International
Fairyland by his male dancers, had them under surveillance
by trustworthy henchmen and their occasional slips reported;
the sight of a typically urning-dominated ballet audience
featuring bleached hair, ornate beards, and tight Edwardian-
via-Greenwich Village trousers would have filled him with
horror and apprehension. As an example of his attitude, I
need only recall his original hostility to the late Constant

Lambert, who used to waylay him in the corridors of the
Hotel Savoy (London, 1925) in order to force a hearing of
his ballet *Adam and Eve,* which subsequently became *Romeo
and Juliet* at Diaghilev's insistence; Sergei Pavlovitch used
to tell Boris Kochno and myself to "get rid of that dreadful
Chelsea *tapette.*" The reason for so erroneous an estimate of
poor Kid Lambert's sexual make-up stemmed from the young
composer's brazenly orange-colored shirt, which he wore as
a badge of bohemianism and artistic defiance of British
conventions. True, Diaghilev did suggest to me, on hearing
of my "normal" tendencies, that it would perhaps be smarter
to "pose as a sodomite," to use the wording of Queensberry's
nosegay to Wilde, in order to get ahead in composers' circles:
he never tired of amusedly considering that "Tchaikovsky
thought of committing suicide for fear of being discovered
as a homosexual, but, today, if you are a composer and *not*
homosexual, you might as well put a bullet through your
head." But to anyone who really knew Diaghilev and stayed
close to him for any length of time, Stravinsky's snide references to "fificuses" (?), "Nouvel's sensibilities being similar
to Diaghilev's" ("I like Italians," Nouvel is reported to have
said. "They recognize one right away: everyone in Italy
always says 'Grazie tante' to me")—are as unwarranted as
they are unattractive. Stravinsky should take a good look at
the "boys" who applaud the loudest when his newest music
is played.

Although interlaced with passages of foxy humility, the
three Stravinsky-Craft volumes, reflecting as they do the
Master's "nervous and acid hates," are a formidable chamber
of horrors, Stravinsky emerging as possibly the most hor-
ripilating (the collaborator's juicy adjective) of them all.
"The English have a habit of regarding all Octogenarians as
automatically lovable," Jeremy Noble wrote in a summing-up
of *Expositions and Developments* (in *Music and Musicians,*

London. June, 1962). "Stravinsky, as he chooses to reveal himself in this volume, is *not*—or at least, not with the too-easy lovableness of the Grand Old Man." Clearly, he is not the Grand but the Angry Old Man of Music: a passionately angry old man, at that, who "spits" on fellow composers—dead and living ones both—composers whose music also makes him want to vomit or scream. The spitting, vomiting, screaming angry old man ("Some say the greatest." Emily Coleman) "frightened many of the people who met him, from his first eruption into Paris," reported Martin Mayer. "There was something disconcertingly fierce about the slight Russian . . . Stravinsky could be remarkably cruel and contemptuous. A famous story from the Paris days tells of a young composer coming up to him in a public place and requesting an appointment to ask the Master's advice on some scores. Stravinsky pulled out a pocket diary and thoughtfully turned the pages. "Not Monday, not Tuesday, not Wednesday . . . *never.*" Frenchmen report that shortly after he was granted the honor of French citizenship (in 1934, when White Russians did not receive such favors), he demanded that he be paid in pounds or dollars rather than francs for an appearance in Paris.

But why should the Angry Old Man of Music be angry or cruel or fierce? Doesn't he get $7,500 for an appearance as a conductor (Martin Mayer) these days? "May he who insists that music is incapable of expressing anything not well appear to future centuries as the spokesman and highest musical expression of the first six decades of this present century?" (Everett Helm) When Stravinsky is through spitting or screaming, doesn't his "still small voice speak to us in *Threni, Canticum Sacrum, Agon,* etc." (Helm again) to those of us, at any rate, who have the patience to remain in our seats after the first ten minutes? "Stravinsky, in his last works, has achieved the final triumph of fashion, he has created a fashion for boredom." (Constant Lambert) The answer to these questions is quite simple, really: Stravinsky is basically insecure, having traveled for many years with the slimmest musical baggage on the grandest scale but with the falsest possible pretenses. As early as 1924, Cecil Gray, the cantankerous, yet often brilliantly perceptive English writer on music, saw through it all and thus ended his piece on Stravinsky in *A Survey of Contemporary Music*: "No composer is less capable than he of writing music which can stand on its own legs, unsupported by the complicated paraphernalia of stage scenery, costumes and dancing. That he of all people should claim to be regarded as a writer of pure music is one of the most remarkable examples of insolence and charlatanism in the history of art; that he should be accepted as one is only another instance of the melancholy stupidity and gullibility of the musical public." That he is deified by the composing youth of America should cause us even more melancholy reflections on the future of this country's music.

III

For the first five months of 1962 everything was sunshine and roses for the happy octogenarian; every bar from his pen was immediately paid for, authoritatively performed, faultlessly recorded by Goddard Lieberson for Columbia and attractively packaged for the incomprehending but ever worshipful American public. The stage was set for mammoth birthday celebrations in every nook and cranny of this and practically every other land of the globe; then came the Dawn—or, rather, the Flood. Barnum himself couldn't have done a better job on what was to be the biggest and rarest musical event of the decade: Stravinsky's conquest of that unwieldy beast—Television. "Beyond any doubt, the most important television production of this (or any) season is the world première of Stravinsky's dance drama *Noah and the Flood*, which takes the air tonight," Cecil Smith announced breathlessly in the Los Angeles *Times* on June 14, 1962. After listing the illustrious collaborators—Balanchine, Rouben Ter-Arutunian (sets and costumes), Kirk Browning, director, and Robert Craft, conductor, Mr. Smith opined that "this then must necessarily be one of the major events in the musical world, and it is representative of the growing TV maturity that it was conceived, designed and executed strictly for the little home screen. It is being presented as part of the world-wide celebration of Stravinsky's 80th birthday . . . Perhaps to make this long-hair work more palatable, several top-name actors are in the cast, including Laurence Harvey as narrator, Sebastian Cabot as Noah and Elsa Lanchester as Mrs. Noah . . . Cabot said he and other performers were so eager to participate in the program they foreswore their usual hefty salaries to appear for union scale." The modest Mr. Cabot confessed to knowing nothing about music. "I did a little Dixieland," said he. "But really about music, I'm a bloody idiot." He was—and with good cause——"rather terrified to meet Stravinsky. Gad, he's a fantastic little old man. He comes out all bent over with age, you think he can hardly get to the podium. Then suddenly, he faces the orchestra and straightens up—straight as an arrow." Cabot thought it "particularly significant that the voice of God is two voices in the play (those of John Reardon and Robert Oliver) . . . as if," he said, "one voice were not big enough for God." Two lesser deities were brought in to help matters along—Mr. Breck, the Shampoo god, who spoke eloquently on behalf of his product, and Stravinsky, the deified composer, whose eloquence was somewhat impaired by his accent and grammar.

For weeks, the Angry Old Man's face peered at you from countless covers of glossy magazines, mesmerizing the viewer with the intensity of its ferocious scowl: "On your knees,

ignoramuses!" it seemed to command. The kneeling ignoramuses, bowing reverently, awaited the hour when they
would be permitted to sit down facing their TV sets to view
and hear the musical truth, nothing but the truth, so help
them Stravinsky. Among the mesmerized was volcanic Melissa
Hayden, one of Balanchine's best dancers, who did some
ecstatic breast-beating on the pages of the *Saturday Review
of Literature*: "I was a weak woman carried along by the
fates," she confessed. The divine Message soon changed all
that. "I felt I was receiving a new recognition from Balanchine
and Stravinsky. They were accepting me as a creator along
with them." Thus, through *Orpheus* and *Agon,* the fellow-
creators moved on steadily to the ultimate truth of *Noah and
the Flood.*

The ultimate truth, according to Albert Goldberg and
practically every other newspaper commentator in the land,
was contained in capsule form in the Los Angeles *Times* headline on the morning of June 16, 1962. It read: "Igor and Noah
sink in the Flood": "Seldom has a television show or anything
else been glorified with such frantic advance ballyhoo as the
world première of Stravinsky's dance-drama *Noah and the
Flood.* Lyrical columns of publicity had predicted an earth-
shaking event, but what transpired was an inglorious flop—
an all-time dud. The program lasted the full hour, but the
pièce de résistance occupied barely 20 minutes. The major
portion of the time was devoted to pretentious oratory, taste-
less commercials on what to do with 'the natural beauty of
your hair,' a photographic resumé of Stravinsky's career larded
with snippets of his compositions, Balanchine teaching his
dancers, and ending with the composer rehearsing the piece
that had just been performed . . . The inevitable interview with
the composer's Boswell, Robert Craft . . . ran on the usual line.
Question: 'So you are ahead of the public?' Answer: 'I am not
guilty.' " For once the statement was accurate: it was the *pub-*

lic that was *ahead* of the composer. After catching on to the general tenor of the proceedings on the screen, a staggering number of the TV viewers quickly turned the knob and went back to the always safe Westerns, murder yarns, Bob Hope and Jack Benny.

Noah and the Flood was the only TV show within memory, wherein the commercials provided a welcome and soothing relief. "Breck commercials, with sponsor's pretty shampoo models, were almost eagerly awaited," *Variety* chimed in. "Without doubt and without dissension, this program, presented as a Breck 'Golden Showcase' special with costs in the vicinity of $200,000, proved to be a potpourri, a hodge-podge, a mish-mash, a sort of artistic chop suey," stated *Dance Magazine* (August) in Arthur Todd's long, tellingly illustrated article titled "What Went Wrong?" "Apparently stung by the charge that TV is a vast wasteland, CBS-TV presented an expensive hour titled *Noah and the Flood* ... a vast waste-basket of talent ... There has been more 'art' in some parts of 'Gunsmoke,' in some programs by Jackie Gleason, Sid Caesar and Milton Berle, than in this kind of empty and foolish nonsense," was the *Hollywood Reporter's* summing-up. The 22½-minute-long work "proved to be as emptily pretentious as the shenanigans which surrounded it," Goldberg wrote. "The text, arranged by Mr. Craft ... is a jumble of discontinuity ... the music is in Stravinsky's latest 'serial' manner, which must have been a surprise to the millions hearing it for the first time, but which is an old story to followers of avant-garde trends ... the ballet consisted mainly of swirling, half naked men and girls in drapes [probably called "ecdysiasts" by Craft and Stravinsky, this being their word for "strippers." V.D.], with massed groupings to portray the building of the Ark and the Flood." None of it had any special distinction unless one calls pertly balletic Maypole-type ring-around-the-rosie conception of the Building of the Ark distinguished.

To go back to Mr. Todd's unbiased report in *Dance Maga-zine*: "Rumor has it that the morning after the broadcast a noted dancer-teacher posted a notice on her studio bulletin board that said: 'Breck does not use dancers well, hereafter no dancers in this studio will use Breck.' But Breck did put up the money. Where, or where, did things go wrong?" It could never have occurred to the "noted dancer-teacher" that Stravinsky, not Mr. Breck, might have been to blame. I attended the circus rehearsals in Sarasota, Florida (1941), when the otherwise astonishingly musical elephants balked at the irregular beats of the Master's polka in a ballet staged by Balanchine. While humans are (on occasion) even more musi-cal than Ringling Brothers' animals, they, too, may have been stumped by *Noah's* unwieldy music; Stravinsky was not dodecaphonically minded in those early circus days, which was lucky for the elephants.

"As a result of an enormous amount of pre-broadcast bally-hoo, the great American public was led to believe that because Balanchine and 27 members of the New York City Ballet were participating, it could happily anticipate a great ballet experi-ence." Mr. Todd went on, "However, this was never Mr. Balanchine's idea." The choreographer hastened to assure his questioners that *Noah* is a "miracle play more than a masque ... a church play or a choreographed oratorio. Most impor-tantly, it's *not* a ballet." Then he pulled a rabbit out of the hat: "Actually it's about *Stravinsky himself*, as a composer." Clearly then, this being a church play, Stravinsky, the music god, was being deified. Mr. Todd interpreted the mass genuflections thus: "... these dedicated artists were toiling *solely* to produce a birthday garland for Stravinsky in gratitude for all of his great ballet scores." The Great American public, not having been cognizant of Stravinsky's greatness through the medium of TV, was thus left holding the bag—a great big windbag, that is.

"On May 8th, the Honorable Edward P. Boland (Democrat of Mass.) read a long insertion into the Congressional Record, citing John H. Breck, Inc., the sponsor, for his cultural high-mindedness," Mr. Todd continued. Yet, "the sequence of the full hour was planned so ineptly that it literally asked viewers to turn it off." The viewers obliged only too willingly: "The Nielsen Average Audience rating shows that 4,361,000 homes viewed some part of this program that was seen by an estimated seven million viewers. The rating for each quarter of an hour was: 9.9; 8.9; 9.1 and 7.7. Thus, it can be seen that almost a half-million dropped out by the last quarter . . . Either CBS or Sextant, Inc., or both, made the cardinal mistake of underestimating its audience. When you play down and try to be all things to all people you alienate everyone . . . Trying to make it lowbrow, or so it appeared, the program failed . . . Many feel that this program did a disservice and dishonor to Stravinsky and Balanchine and to dance and music as well. At this writing, neither Stravinsky nor Balanchine has made any comment on the show." The critics did—in a body; and their findings were that Stravinsky (and, to a lesser extent, Balanchine) performed a disservice and dishonor to the program, the TV medium, and to the public, led to expect a miracle of epic proportions.

In our time two distinguished figures made quite a splash of belaboring music critics: Harry S. Truman and Igor F. Stravinsky—the ex-President took exception to a Washington music critic's lack of enthusiasm for his daughter's singing, while the composer took three (so far) nationally known commentators to task for failing to eulogize properly the outpourings of his muse. Truman at least castigated his victim openly and addressed him by name, whereas Stravinsky, persuaded that a single mention of his detractors over his signature will immortalize them, prefers to disguise such unworthy people's identity or not to name them at all. The 8½-page appendix to

Expositions and Developments (No. 3 of the Stravinsky-Craft series) is devoted to a vicious attack on Messrs. H. P. Langweilich and S. D. Deaf—who, as the whole musical world knows, are Paul Henry Lang of the New York *Herald Tribune* and Winthrop Sargeant of the *New Yorker*. The "appendix" is subtitled "Slightly More of a Plague on One of Their Houses," which is a fairish sample of Stravinsky's "Christian convictions"; if calling critics Langweilich and Deaf is a sample of the Master's "murderous wit" (so referred to by various commentators), I'll take Phil Silvers.

Stravinsky prefaces his counterattack with a lengthy epigraph which is an excerpt from one of Ionesco's plays: The epigraph is on a far higher literary level than what follows, but its relevance is open to question. After a sneer at the "Brother Criticus," Stravinsky expresses a desire that a composer, not a lowly critic, should review his work. That in itself is understandable: fellow composers have been known to turn out a book or two—of the eulogistic kind, of course—which didn't do the Master any harm. Roman Vlad and Alexandre Tansman—composers both—wrote one apiece; "If non-composer critics prove indispensable to such an enterprise," Stravinsky suggests, "I can even recommend some of those: Lawrence Morton and Joseph Kerman." I am not familiar with Mr. Kerman's work, but Mr. Morton is the mastermind behind the Los Angeles Monday Evening Concerts—a U-boy stronghold; Mr. Morton is also the author of a forthcoming monograph on Stravinsky, which, the rumor has it, is a eulogy to end all eulogies.

Stravinsky's dream, or so it would appear, is a "composer's review" of the "professional"—i.e. non-critical variety. "God forbid that anyone should found a publication dedicated strictly to American music," the Master blurts out, which was perhaps politically unwise from a man who owes so much to the second country of his adoption. Stravinsky's "positive suggestion" is that "each issue should print the translation of some theoretical writing not theretofore in English—the essays of Schenker for example, or Simon Sechter, and of Friedrich Waismann on linguistic analysis." So lively a periodical would, indeed, spell the doom of the wretched *New Yorker,* or the vulgar New York *Times.*

Stravinsky then assails Mr. Sargeant for a slip he made regarding the twelve-tone scale, which is negligible by comparison with countless slips, misrepresentations, and deliberate omissions with which the Master's own volumes are stuffed (plus samples of his surprisingly bad French on pages 98 and 109 of the *Conversations*). There is then a dig at "those really unlucky people whom Deaf commends": the *New Yorker* critic's "giants" being Giannini, Jello Doio, Gian-Carlo, etc., another "murderously witty" verbal prank. Why not fall in line with this kind of wit and call the authors of such literature Straw and Craftinsky?

One of the two (or both) much prefers Deaf-Sargeant to Langweilich-Lang. Deaf is "at least readable, and he can be amusing," while Langweilich writes "atrociously," which will be a surprise to the many admirers of P. H. Lang's crisp and lucid style, totally devoid of glossolalias, ecdysiasts and other pearls of the Straw-Craftinsky prose, which is euphuistic to a degree. The Russo-American collaborators' picking at Lang's straws is tiresome and inconsequential with occasional flashes of old-maidish viciousness, such as dismissing the critic's reference to a 30-second "new chef d'oeuvre" with "characteristically reptilian" or, that calling the Master "a little limited . . . a little superficial" was an "obloquy even more pusillanimous in tone." After a posy graciously rewarding the "intelligent younger generation" of the English [?] musical press—serial, aleatory, U-boyish and (from all accounts) U-girlish—Stravinsky and Craft, to return them to their proper identities, conclude the impotently huffy and puffy "Appen-

dix" with the elegant grandeur characteristic of their manner:
"New York must clean its journalistic house first. It must rid
itself of the cult of the commonplace, which is presently
fostered there, and which gathers to people such as those
here described as *dirt gathers to vacuum cleaners.*" (Italics
mine. V.D.)

The Vienna, Darmstadt and Donaueschingen-oriented composer may be at home with Sechter, Schenker, and Waismann
but, having given up his French citizenship and residence, he
has forgotten his Beaumarchais, who said: *"Il n'y a que les
petits hommes qui se fachent des petits ecrits."* The Angry
Old Man of Music gets progressively angrier with age—not
for him the calm wisdom, the benign dignity of those who
grow old gracefully. To Deaf and Langweilich was soon added
Albert Goldberg, whom Stravinsky did not choose to demolish
by calling him Mr. Dumb—rather conservatively the composer's letter of protest was addressed to the music editor
of the Los Angeles *Times.* The letter was similar in tone to the
already noted "Appendix"—Mr. Goldberg's review was labeled
"ignorant, errant and smug," his unwillingness to go into
raptures over *The Rake's Progress* (the object of the critic's
article) presented as proof of "inability to hear harmony and
melody," of the man's "incompetence to write meaningfully
about music of any kind." Obviously, disapproval of *The
Rake's Progress* was an unthinkable sacrilege to the Master,
who "had thought for a moment that some of my colleagues
might protest, especially the younger ones who profess to
admire my work (and who have helped themselves to pieces
of it)." How about the once youthful Stravinsky who "helped
himself to pieces of" Pergolesi, Tchaikovsky, Schubert (in the
Elephantine polka), Grieg (*Four Norwegian Moods*), and
countless other elders?

The comments on the Goldberg-Stravinsky controversy were
considerably more amusing than the critic's workmanlike and

honest appraisal of the opera, or the composer's petty rant-
ings. A good many letters from both Stravinskyites and Goldberg supporters were printed: While a Mr. Georgie Cooper
gave "three thousand cheers for Igor Stravinsky, a grand
human," Mrs. Audrey Peterson was appalled by the pettiness
of the "grand human's" mind. A Mr. (or Miss) Carol Schultz
was in "full agreement" with Stravinsky and wanted "to see
concrete reasons why you [Goldberg] should be the music
critic for one of the largest newspapers on the West Coast,"
while Mrs. Eve Solomon thought *The Rake's Progress* a dreadful bore, so much so that she left during intermission, and
another matron, Mrs. Sigmund S. Theil, thought Stravinsky's
letter "vitriolic, virulent and most unbecoming to the stature
of a great composer." "It was a boomerang hitting back at
Mr. Stravinsky's character," added Arno B. Davidson; Don
Alpert doubted that the Master would compose "any Goldberg
Variations" after his run-in with the critic. Walter Ducloux,
who conducted and staged the USC production of *The Rake's
Progress*, had the last word: "I find certain aspects of Stravinsky's letter disturbing, not to say downright offensive to
those involved in an exhaustive, if, to us, rewarding labor of
love. President Topping of USC invited the composer to
attend either of the last two performances. Mr. Stravinsky
did not accept, to our sincere regret. From his remarks to you
I must conclude that he considered a production by the USC
Opera Theater ("sung by So-and-So") not worthwhile . . . His
snide remark that your own praise was 'the worst possible
recommendation' regarding the quality of the production
merits no comment. The facts still stand as follows: approximately 150 people, including a large chorus and orchestra,
put forth an enormous effort, over a period of months, to do
his work justice. The fact that their names do not appear in
the headlines does not imply that they are unworthy of a
composer's politeness."

As a matter of record, *Rake's Progress* has its admirers and, notwithstanding its hardly brilliant career at the Met, has been reappearing now and again at Glyndebourne, San Francisco, and just lately in New York—with the American Opera Society and minus scenic trappings. The always outspoken Harold C. Schonberg may yet come in for his share of Craft-Stravinsky verbal venom as a result of his appraisal of that event, which took place on November 20, 1962, at Carnegie Hall: ". . . after some study of the score, and after exposure to the recording, I have learned to loathe it . . . Basically the music sounds formula-ridden and mechanical. Much has been made of the set numbers and ensembles. They are ever-present, of course. But they do not say much, nor do the deliberate melismatic archaisms help. It is all very chic, very sophisticated, and *au fond*, very, very, boring."

The Stravinsky-Goldberg altercation was child's play compared with the telegram calculated to destroy the composer's old nemesis—Paul Henry Lang, who dared to add his voice to the chorus of protests that greeted *Noah and the Flood*. "While aversion to critics is an attitude which most composers have in common, there are those who think that Stravinsky carries this warfare a bit too far," wrote Emily Coleman. This time the Master not only went a bit too far, he stooped lower than any critic-baiter within memory.

There was really nothing overly provocative in Lang's appraisal of *Noah*, except for a reference to Mr. Craft, which was doubtless resented by both the composer's *"auxiliare musical"* (as he styled himself in *Dix Années avec Stravinsky*, published in Monaco) and his patron. Lang said that *Noah* called "on the full resources of a large opera company. CBS assembled its equivalent, placing it under the direction of the venerable maestro himself and his amanuensis, librettist and *valet de chambre*, Robert Craft." The critic found a "junior high school quality" about the prologue, and thought *Noah*, in general, "far from a major, or even a significant work." Mr. Lang went on: "In his patriarchal age Mr. Stravinsky's once flaming temperament expunges all emotional violence and almost all uninhibited movement from his music and softens even his solemnity into a mood that, in the vocal pieces, I suppose, represents a Christian musing . . . Like Monteverdi, who, after a long rest from theater music, bestirred himself in his old age and returned to the stage, Mr. Stravinsky also returns to the theater. Unfortunately, the comparison ends here, for while some of the old theatrical wizardry can again be felt, the 'fluid intermixture of music, dance, mime, narrative, song and legend,' promised in the release was not compellingly realized."

This coolish, but, on the whole, decidedly mild criticism resulted in a telegram addressed to and published in the New York *Herald Tribune* on June 24, 1962, the text of which read: "Of hundreds of reviews of my New York work, most of them, like every opus since 1905, were gratifyingly unfavorable. I found only yours entirely stupid and suppurating with gratuitous malice. The only blight on my eightieth birthday is the realization my age will probably keep me from celebrating the funeral of your senile [Paul Henry Lang is Stravinsky's junior by nineteen years. V.D.] music columnist. Igor Stravinsky." I submit that the ghoulish, inhuman ugliness of this frightening document is unique in the annals of musical —or any other—art.

IV

The usually accurate and conscientious Leonard Lyons, of the New York *Post*, one of our more readable and reliable columnists, reported an interesting luncheon conversation with Stravinsky on December 13, 1960: "Stravinsky, ranked by many as the greatest living composer, mentioned Russia's odd puritanism, and listed some French and English words for which there are no Russian equivalents. And then he discussed the Soviet composers. I told him I'd met Shostakovich, and Stravinsky waved his hand in angry dismissal. Kabalevsky? "A horror," said Stravinsky. And Khatchaturian? "Not even a horror," said Stravinsky. According to Lyons, the Master was "in good spirits"; if he had not been, he would likely have used some stronger words "for which there are no Russian equivalents." Shostakovich, Kabalevsky, and Khatchaturian were "good, as composers," Stravinsky admitted, but as Soviet citizens they were symbols he detested. He frowned and said: "They cannot afford the luxury of integrity." Now for a sample of the Master's own integrity, the luxury of which he, an American citizen, can well afford.

"As an emigré, Stravinsky was the object of even more vituperation (in the Soviet Union) than other celebrated composers such as Schoenberg and Hindemith. Now, however, the Soviet musicians are playing his music and have invited him to revisit his native land. What is even more remarkable is that he accepted," wrote Emily Coleman in *Newsweek*. "The idea of going to the Soviet Union was first brought up last June, when a delegation of Soviet composers visited the U.S. . . ." Following the "warm and heartfelt" invitation, which was extended to the Master in Los Angeles, "he literally paced the floor at night, trying to make up his mind and then decided to go."

The invitation came from ". . . the all-powerful right arm of the odious Politburo in music, the odious musical gendarme, perhaps the most sinister figure in Russian musical history"— Tikhon Khrennikov (U. Elagin, *The Taming of the Arts*, New York, 1952). Comrade Khrennikov deserves a few excitement-packed paragraphs. Following the USSR Central Committee's Decree on Music published on February 10, 1948, the four "greats" of Soviet music, Prokofiev, Shostakovich, Miaskovsky, and Khatchaturian, were denounced as "bourgeois formalists," their music temporarily removed from all concert programs.

If Zhdanov was Ivan the Terrible, Soviet-style, "Tishka" Khrennikov was his Lord Executioner. Following the four top composers' disgrace (with a few minor figures thrown in—actually thrown *out*—for good measure), he became the Secretary-General of the Composers' Union. His first act was to denounce the dethroned masters for their "cosmopolitanism, abstract atonalism, bourgeois neuroticism." A mediocre composer himself, Khrennikov went about his job with hyena-like relish: to quote the well-informed British journalist Alexander Werth (*Musical Uproar in Moscow*, Turnstile Press, London, 1949), Khrennikov ". . . in his 'historical' addresses, went out of his way to make Prokofiev out to be an alien influence in Russian music. Having enumerated at length the foreign modernist, decadent, pathological, erotic, cacophonous, religious or [!] sexually perverted monsters—including Messiaen, Jolivet, Hindemith, Alban Berg, Menotti and Britten—Khrennikov proceeded to tell Prokofiev how wicked and Western *he* was" . . . And further, Khrennikov "identified Prokofiev with Stravinsky and Diaghilev—alleging that, in presenting an exotic, Petrushka-like version of Russia to the West, all three lampooned their own country in front of foreign audiences . . . it all ended in Monte Carlo, where the Diaghilev Ballet found its right mission at last—to cater to an audience of gamblers, profiteers and prostitutes." Lastly, the Lord Executioner "with characteristic meanness, made capital out of the fact that Prokofiev was really an emigré—*though, unlike Stravinsky*, he had had the sense to return to Russia in 1934." Werth's conclusion, on the last page of his book, is especially noteworthy. He records that "in Warsaw recently" a Polish Communist remarked to him. "Glory to the Soviet Union, and glory to the Red Army that tore the guts out of the German army, as your Mr. Churchill said, but thank God we haven't got a Lysenko, a Fadeyev *or a Khrennikov* dictatorship yet."

Admittedly, things have changed for the better, musically

speaking, in Comrade Khrushchev's Russia. The "religious or sexually perverted monsters'" music is being performed freely, and discussed impartially, often enthusiastically, on the pages of *Soviet Music*, the Party-sponsored magazine. Soviet dictators come and go, but Khrennikov, a better diplomat than composer obviously, goes on forever. In the course of the 1961 International Music Festival, in Los Angeles, he headed the Soviet delegation and was represented, as a composer, by a blatantly banal and noisy Second Symphony and an even more banal Violin Concerto. Both Khrennikov and the equally nondescript Kara Karaev, who tagged along with tricky Tikhon, cribbed liberally from Ravel's *Bolero*, a pathologically decadent concoction, assuredly. In the back of the house, Igor Stravinsky applauded magnanimously, and with good cause. It was at Khrennikov's "cordial" insistence that the Master condescended to visit his native land.

Soviet Music (September, 1961 issue) arranged for its correspondent to interview Khrennikov concerning his encounter with Stravinsky. "This encounter was one of the brightest impressions of our American trip. It took place in a most friendly atmosphere and testified to the old composer's sincere interest in the representatives of his motherland. A few days before the concert in which the 'Psalm Symphony' and the Violin Concerto were programmed, we [the Soviet delegation. V.D.] were approached by a Los Angeles musician, one of Stravinsky's close friends, and asked whether we intended to visit the Master following the concert. We replied that we would be happy to meet him." Khrennikov then admitted that "several episodes in Stravinsky's works as conducted by the author made a powerful impression on us. The audience greeted the venerable composer ecstatically; he was so tired, that no one was admitted to see him after the concert except ourselves. He saw us, smiled, extended his hands: 'My dear ones, we meet at last! I know you from your portraits[?]. You are—Khrennikov, you—Karaev, and you [must be] Yarustovsky [critic and musicologist. V.D.]. We told I.F. of the Soviet listeners' love for such works as *The Firebird* and *Le Sacre du Printemps*, of the [several] productions of *Petrouchka* in our theaters, etc. Stravinsky appeared to be profoundly touched by all this."

Followed a visit to the composer's "Hollywood villa"; Stravinsky and his wife showed themselves to be exemplary hosts. In the course of the "unaffectedly warm" conversation "we couldn't hide our sorrow at the unfriendly statements by Stravinsky [in the past] as regards Soviet musical culture and its exponents. Igor Fedorovitch categorically stated, *that he never uttered a single bad word* [Italics mine. V.D.] concerning Soviet music and Soviet musicians. Such statements, he emphasized, were attributed to him by *untrustworthy interviewers,* and he had neither enough strength, nor enough time to refute them."

In the light of what we know of Stravinsky's treatment of his enemies in the press, the above explanation is an interesting example of the composer's logic, which he invariably twists at will when in a spot. Stravinsky "collects his notices with the avidity of a budding prima donna" in Emily Coleman's no-nonsense testimony. "He underlines the remarks that interest or infuriate him, and makes notes in the margin. The reviews are then pasted in a book for future reference, for instance, when preparing such fusillades as the appendix to his 'Expositions and Developments' in which he roasts P. H. Lang and W. Sargeant." I don't recall any "fusillades" greeting the bad words (re his Soviet colleagues) "attributed to him" by one of the "untrustworthy interviewers"—Leonard Lyons. Obviously, Stravinsky found enough strength and time to execute Lang, Sargeant, and Goldberg; refuting "untrustworthy" Lyons appeared to be a physical impossibility. Also, every man, including Stravinsky, should be accorded the privilege of changing his mind: in 1959 (*Conversations*) the Master stated: "I am often asked if I would consent to conduct in the Soviet Union. For purely musical reasons I could not. Their orchestras do not perform the music of *the three Viennese and myself* [Italics mine. V.D.], and they would be, I am sure, unable to cope with the simplest problems of rhythmic execution that we introduced to music fifty years ago. The style of my music would also be alien to them. These difficulties are not to be overcome in a few rehearsals; They require a twenty- or thirty-year tradition." Since Stravinsky is scheduled to visit Russia in the nearest future,* it would appear that his obliging former compatriots have been ordered to "overcome these difficulties"—tradition be damned —and get ready to cope with "the simplest problems of rhythmic execution" as part of a three-year plan dedicated to welcoming Russia's prodigal son.

The over-all likeness of Stravinsky that emerges from the above is not a pretty one; neither are the pen portraits of his contemporaries, as painted by the Master in his (and Mr. Craft's) books. What should be of vital concern to young Americans is that such a man continues as the greatest single influence, as a dictator whose word is still law to the majority of our composers, as a musical Father Divine, who succeeded in selling his own brand of musical religion to the gullible multitudes. They have not the courage and independence of Samuel Pepys, who wrote of one Pelham Humphrey (1647-1674) in the November 16, 1667, entry in his diary: "There got into the theatre-room: and there heard both the vocall and instrumentall musick; where the little fellow stood keeping time; but for my part, I see no great matter, but quite the contrary in both sorts of musick." The sorts of musick

---

* Two weeks after these lines were written, Stravinsky departed for Russia.

now provided by the little fellow who is the subject of this chapter could be forgotten and forgiven were he to give us one really worth-while piece, equal in quality to the *Symphony of Psalms*, say; and I sincerely hope he lives to be a hundred, and that his hundredth birthday will be celebrated by wholesale performances of such a piece, rather than sink in yet another Flood.

VI

Conductors' Conduct

●—●

I

It is hardly necessary to stress again that America provides fewer opportunities for a "respectable" composer than any other place in the world. Our young men of music, fed up with the uphill struggle on this continent, invariably go to Europe and fare better there. The Forgotten Man of Music in the U. S. becomes a *maître* in Paris, a *maestro compositore* in Milan. He may not be paid, but he can get played—and without going into hock, as might happen to him in his native land. Moreover, quite outside of monetary considerations, the musical "climate" in Europe is far more beneficial.

Skipping lightly over the usual plaints about prima-donna worship, performing millionaires and composing paupers, money-loving and music-hating concert managers, etc., let's take up the scarcely fresher subject of conductors. "There's nothing worse than a 'titan of the podium,'" Diaghilev told me in 1924, when the subject first came up and a relatively unknown conductor (Marc-César Scotto) was entrusted with the score of my first ballet, *Zephyr and Flora*. "If it weren't for the composer who puts little black notes on white paper, the Titan couldn't wave his stick, strike leonine poses, thrill women and earn lots of money. The only conductor for me is the kind that does what he is told by the composer, and never talks back."

A conductor functioning in the U. S. may be the same gent we once knew abroad, but now he has become a god. He browbeats his orchestra, hires and fires men at will, tells soloists what he expects them to play and even threatens the trustees. "The conductor of the orchestra becomes thus the key personality, the unelected mayor, of the American musical community," Ernst Bacon observed in *Words on Music* (1960). "Heading the only quasi-public-supported musical institution, he should certainly be looked upon as a public servant." By and large, the "renowned" conductor looks upon the public as *his* servant—and literally demands adoration, adulation, and blind faith not only in his art but also in his choice of performable material. The late Cecil Smith, no conductor-hater by a long shot, wrote in *Worlds of Music* (1952): "Boston's orchestra is very much Boston's own in the minds of its patrons; if Charles Munch conducts a second-class performance of a Beethoven symphony he can be forgiven, for he is Boston's choice to lead Boston's orchestra, and the patrons will wait with equanimity until he gives a first-class performance of something else the following week. If the conductor of a small-city orchestra never conducts a first-class performance of anything at all, his audience nevertheless supports him loyally until or unless the board decides to dispose of him and get someone else to lead the orchestra. If the particular works played by the orchestra in Boston or the small city are not just what everyone would have liked best, the audience willingly accepts the works that are played, for it is better to support anything the orchestra does than to have no orchestra at all." Together with Ernst Bacon, the civic-minded audience gladly subscribes to Napoleon's maxim: "Better an army of lambs led by one lion than an army of lions led by one lamb," not realizing that this maxim could apply to themselves as well as to the orchestra musicians. Thus the lambs of Democratic America eagerly pay through the nose to be led (or misled, who cares?) by the lion on the podium.

Variety, that ever-observant and refreshingly fearless magazine, ran a well-written and uncommonly outspoken article titled "The Cult of Symphony Conductor Worship" in its 55th anniversary issue (January 4, 1961), probably authorized by an indignant composer, who chose to remain anonymous. "Although there may be some naïve members of the citizenry who are inclined to regard the portrayal of the orchestra batoneer in Harry Kurnitz's comedy (1960), *Once More With Feeling*, as an exaggerated lampoon, those most knowledgeable on the subject still consider the Kurnitz characterization as being well on the conservative side," was the inflammatory opening. "Qualified observers agree with striking unanimity that one of the chief causes of the frequent dissension which seems endemic in American orchestral societies is the phenomenon which has come to be widely known as the Cult of Conductor Worship. The frenetic and intransigent attitudes which characterize the practitioners of this cult have constituted the shoals upon which the ships of countless symphonic groups have foundered." The author then tells of the "time when a new conductor is sought and ultimately engaged. He is likely to turn out to be a foreigner—perhaps a middle European—with a nebulous and never fully defined background of musical experience in various foreign centers. A legend usually precedes his advent, bathing him in a roseate glow of alleged musical achievement . . . Comes the day, he moves in with his wife—and sometimes his children. Immediately there is a fanfare of inspired publicity sending the musical community into a tizzy of titillation." There follows an amusing description of the "Potentate's arrival" and his "initial presentations, hailed with paeans of praise and adulation." Then come the "interim" peregrinations—"special tours and appearances across the country, to Europe, Asia and even Down Under" depending on the conductor's "inside connections with the musical groups which he conducts abroad." Just how these "invitations" come about is "omitted or unknown," only favorable notices are reported, adverse reviews being "brushed off impatiently." "When the Maestro returns to the home base, he is feted and lionized by his supporters, especially by the women's auxiliaries which make a fetish of this or any other sort of social obeisance."

Where does the composer, the chap who "puts little black notes on white paper" which enable the Potentate to convert them into big, fat bank notes, fit in? Judging from my own experiences, and those of most of my composing colleagues, young and old, Americans and foreigners, we are regarded as infernal nuisances, unwelcome intruders—to be dealt with summarily by the Potentates' assistants and secretaries. Conductors should not always be blamed for so untenable and illogical a situation; what with the home-base job and the "triumphs" abroad, plus the taxing social game, how does a batoneer find time for perusing new scores or interviewing "promising" composers? And yet the composer has no other choice but to remain at the conductor's mercy in his attempt to be heard. Such attempts usually verge on the desperate, being extremely hazardous. Sending music by mail is a grave risk, as it may never be returned; writing for an appointment is wasting a postage stamp, for few conductors bother to reply. Attempting to see the conductor in person may be humiliating: often the composer must stand in line and wait his turn to see the Great Man, who has just perspired freely through an acrobatic evening and is in no mood for irksome requests, but seeks only ecstatic comments on his performance. Furthermore, the ever-watchful members of the "inner circle" (and believe me, no "name" conductor could go through the after-concert ordeal without their help) see to it that their benefactor's sanctum

is free of undesirables, unless they are certified members of
the clan.

The conductor having absolute reign over his orchestra, "the
audience forgets who is the author of a symphony in its frenzied admiration for the Maestro" (Ernst Bacon). Too, the
Maestro has other problems, more pressing than giving the
composer a fair shake: since most orchestras end up in the
red at the season's close, he must seek to avoid this constant
problem and try to prevent losses. Playing a new piece, even
an exciting and effective one, won't help balance the budget;
so the busy Potentate settles for a minimum quota of "acceptable" novelties—a "me too" gesture to the sophisticates—and
leans heavily on the meat-and-potatoes "classical" diet his
patrons crave. As Harold C. Schonberg, the New York *Times*
music critic, justly remarked, "No orchestra in America can
afford to run entirely counter to the tastes of the audience,
which pays the bill. Even in world cosmopolitan centers audiences are conservative and resist change ... For the most part,
audiences are content to sit and let the old masterpieces bathe
them." As to unfamiliar music, "There is an enormous amount
that can be rewarding, if the listener will only approach without the feeling that the music will bite." I can readily sympa-
thize with the listener who would rather be bathed than bitten.
But how can anyone expect one man to give his listeners a fair
picture of what goes on in contemporary music without unprejudiced and un-clannish help? With the few novelties given
in the course of a year's concert series, how do we know that
these are the most representative of today's tendencies? As
often as not, the new works are those of the members of the
aforementioned "inner circle." Are we, then, to judge the
contemporary music scene by the labors of a chosen few—
chosen, that is, by a man, who because of a busy schedule has
no time for impartial research?

In Europe, a regularly employed conductor, especially on

the radio, which supplies the European listener with the largest quota of new music, is seldom more than an obedient interpreter of the *true maître*—the composer. On the French and Belgian radio the choice of novelties is in the hands of composers and musicologists, who act as music directors and coordinators—people like Henry Barraud in Paris and Paul Collaer in Brussels.

Wearied of peddling my own Third Symphony (originally commissioned, then rejected by Koussevitzky) in the States, I took it to Europe in 1947 and was advised to send it to Paul Collaer, an admirable musician and writer on new music. In less than a week I received a courteous and cordial letter from him telling me of his admiration for my piece and supplying me with a list of nine first-rate conductors, from which I was to choose one to interpret my symphony! Preposterous, isn't it, fellow Americans? And we no longer boast a radio symphony orchestra. (The Radiodiffusion Française alone employed *seven* in 1947.) If we did have one, can you see Bill Paley offering a composer such a list? So extraordinary a procedure is not without drawbacks. Europe's U-boys, inhumanly energetic ones (see Chapter III) now rule some state-owned radio stations, which results in a veto on all musical manifestations of a nonconformist order. But I'd take fighting it out with colleagues any day, rather than coming to grips with conductors of the traditional prima-donna type—those residing in the States, especially. The tradition still obtains with most of them, although the new, postwar crop would seem to indicate that the pompous *poseur* is on the way out, and the era of honest and competent music-making is upon us. Yes, the new conductor, worthy of acceptance by a truly democratic (not provincially snobbish) society, is determined to *make music*, rather than use music to make *him*. To this post-war honor roll belong such men as Paul Kletzki (now in Dallas), Poland-born, one of Europe's most esteemed maestri; Stanislaw Skrowaczewski, the young new chief of the Minneapolis forces, another Pole, who is also a first-rate composer; Zubin Mehta, the extraordinarily gifted leader of the Los Angeles Philharmonic, a Parsee still in his twenties; young, courageous Thomas Schippers, who spoke for most of the audience when he hailed de Falla's posthumous *L'Atlantide* following its première at Milan's La Scala (Summer, 1962) as "the triumph of real music over washboard twelve-tone" (*Time*, June 29, 1962); and, most assuredly, the controversial but always stimulating Leonard Bernstein, a native-born American. There are others who will make their beneficial influence felt before long.

The Potentate of the *vieille souche* is unwell, I fear, suffering, as he does, from "premièritis"—the conductor's occupational disease. "Premièritis," or première mania, if you prefer Paul Creston's 1944 term, is easily diagnosed but practically incurable. The first symptoms of the disease consist of an unnatural flush on the sick man's face, accompanied by violent head-shaking and strident vocal outbursts, when offered a previously performed work—especially if premièred by the conductor's rival. "Time, place, significance, or worth, are of no importance to him [the conductor]," Creston assured us on the pages of the *Music Journal* eighteen years ago. "He worships only Firstness."

Disappointed composers have been a familiar feature of the international music scene, and the reader may surmise that this unflattering analysis of the conductor problem is due to my own disappointments. Not so: up to 1950 (when I returned from a third European trip following my discharge from the U. S. Coast Guard) I was uncommonly lucky as a performance-getter. I have no intention of stuffing this volume with autobiographical data, or in any way blowing my own horn—but it may be best to illustrate the composer vs. conductor friction with my own experiences in the field. Every composer has—and will go on having—his brushes with the batoneers—that's par for the course: I could cite some pretty harrowing incidents, reported to me by fellow sufferers, but some of this data may be construed as hearsay or malicious gossip by my colleagues—and naming names may hurt their chances of getting played, and result in understandable protests on their part. I think it safest, therefore, to stick to my own facts in this instance—because I've long given up hope of getting performances from the old guard *chefs*; they do not program my music, anyway, and revelations concerning my contacts with them in the past can in no way harm me—or them—in the future, simply because we have no future together.

Serge Koussevitzsky, my sponsor and benefactor for over twenty years (1925-1946), was also my publisher. His publishing house, Editions Russes de Musique, had a Paris headquarters and printed Russian conservatives—Rachmaninov and Medtner; Russian "modernists"—Stravinsky and Prokofiev, and Russian "young and hopefuls," emigrés all—Berezovsky, Lopatnikov, Nabokov and myself. Our music didn't sell, but it was beautifully printed; there was a cachet to being "recognized" by Koussevitzky and included in his impressive catalogs, shoulder-to-shoulder with our renowned seniors. As a conductor, Koussevitzky combined the best and the worst characteristics of prima-donna baton-wielders with a childishly naïve curiosity about the "last word" in new music—Russian and foreign: that these "last words" were uttered almost weekly, not to say daily, by a whole battalion of composers, talented and mediocre, famous and infamous, did not bother Sergei Alexandrovitch in the least. Very often such "last words" also proved to be "last gasps," the "new" piece, after achieving one performance and failing miserably, never being played again; its composer, disenchanted and abruptly dismissed, would vanish for a spell, then start paying court to another, lesser, Potentate with varying degrees of luck. The appearance of the dismissed composer's name on a rival's program would bring

forth deep resentment on Koussevitzky's part, especially if the
newest piece hit the jackpot (which was very seldom the case);
in this respect Koussevitzky resembled Diaghilev.

And yet—from the composer's point of view—Sergei Alexandrovitch was the best of all possible conductors, because his
interest in new music was genuine and contagious; because his
search for young creative talent was indefatigable and unceasing; and, lastly, because the doors of his many hospitable
residences, both in Paris and, later, in Boston, were wide open
to composers, whose company was more desirable to Koussevitzky than that of gushing society matrons (barely tolerated
by Natalya Konstantinovna, his second wife), sycophants and
hangers-on and celebrated performers, who appeared as
soloists with his orchestra. That alone brought renewed hope
to the grimly toiling scribbler "of black notes on white paper"
and spurred him on to creative deeds, of which no one believed him capable. Koussevitzky's sundry eccentricities and
mirth-provoking *faux pas* were, in view of his all-round gen-
erosity and *bienveillance,* rather endearing and, actually, more
expected than resented. "Did you hear of the latest stunt
Koussy pulled?" composers would ask one another, then tell
the story breathlessly; the story, however absurd, would be
greeted with good-natured laughter, never with acrimony.

One of the Koussevitzky stories (possibly apocryphal) had
to do with the solemn request he made *a viva voce,* in the
course of a trustees' meeting, that a monument to him be
erected in Tanglewood, Massachusetts, commemorating his
services to American music during his lifetime. Another concerned irate mothers of music-school pupils (male) who were
told of homosexuality being practiced along with the loftier
art in a Koussevitzky-sponsored seat of learning; the prim
New England matrons demanded an immediate investigation.
S. A. summoned the pedagogues and asked them whether
it was true that they were "slightly pederastical." He beamed

on hearing the answer, which was an indignant and unanimous "No," then picked up the telephone and assured the women that there was absolutely no foundation for the scandalous rumors.

My two European sponsors and "protectors" having been the two Serges—Diaghilev and Prokofiev—the third Serge (Koussevitzky) took me on enthusiastically and signed me to a "life" contract—which proved an illusion, eventually, with the Editions Russes de Musique. My "serious" music, signed Vladimir Dukelsky, came off the press slowly, but surely, while the orchestral works were readily programmed by Koussevitzky in Paris and Boston, two of them even receiving the coveted honor of a New York performance. The Bostonians gave only a limited number of New York concerts and only the pick of Koussevitzky's novelties appeared on their Manhattan and—even more rarely—Brooklyn Academy of Music programs. Two of my symphonic pieces were performed in Boston prior to my return to the U.S. in 1929 (Ballet Suite and First Symphony); five more were added—a short choral work, the Second Symphony and three concerti for piano, violin, and cello, respectively, and orchestra. The Cello Concerto was commissioned by Gregor Piatigorsky (1945), who also played in New York under Koussevitzky and in Montreal under Golschmann. The Violin Concerto, introduced by Ruth Posselt (in 1945) and conducted by Richard Burgin, her husband and Boston Symphony's concertmaster, also reached New York, being picked up by Artur Rodzinski, then conductor of the New York Philharmonic (a most unusual break, in my experience at least), while the earlier piano piece, subtitled *Dedicaces* (1938) and employing the services of a soprano soloist for its epigraph and epilogue, was brought to Manhattan by Koussevitzky himself.

hibits" were immature and uneven, the choral piece flopping

I now realize that at least three of my seven Boston "ex-

dismally; but Koussevitzky had faith in me and insisted that each succeeding work marked great progress on my part. The three concerti were definite successes in Boston (much less so in New York), and it was after the second Boston performance of the cello work that Koussevitzky reminded me of the Third Symphony I was to write to "Natasha's (his wife's) memory." Although the symphony was S. A.'s idea (see *Passport*, p. 431), I, upon its completion in 1946, wrote the conductor to ascertain the work's "commissioned" status with the Koussevitzky Music Foundation. "It's rather difficult to answer your letter," the conductor replied, "as the basic principle of the Foundation is, obviously, not clear to you. This fund was formed on a purely artistic basis, not on family- or friendly considerations, to encourage beginners and young composers in need of moral and material support, also to bestow prizes on *recognized masters* and *composers of renown* [Italics mine. V.D.]. Decisions are made at special meetings by our five directors; a commission to this or that composer is arrived at by mutual agreement. Your dedication of the symphony to Natalya Konstantinovna's memory was very touching—but it was *your own* initiative and the expression of your own personal feeling; our Fund did *not* commission your piece and, consequently, it is not on our list. From that list you can judge, that the majority of the composers did not know N. K." In going over the foundation's list, I found that the first four men given grants were Samuel Barber, Nicolai Berezovsky, Benjamin Britten, and Bohuslav Martinu; the first two were hardly in need of "material" support, and none, with the possible exception of Martinu, could exactly qualify as "recognized masters" in 1942, when the awards were made. To the growing list of "commissioned" composers six former Russian nationals were gradually added: Stravinsky, Lopatnikoff, Haieff, Nabokov, Lourié and Tcherepnin—one "recognized Master," four men older than myself, and one "beginner," Haieff. No further elucidations were necessary; my unwanted symphony was turned down by the man who had asked me to write it. Although my newer works did seem to indicate some progress, at least insofar as the public acceptance was concerned, Koussevitzky's new "entourage" was inimical to me, and that may have arrested said progress in the conductor's eyes. Prokofiev never returned to the U. S. after his 1938 visit, Natalya Konstantinovna died in 1942; their successors in the conductor's artistic as well as domestic regime emphasized the "native American" policy with increasing effect. Koussevitzky's cold shower came in the wake of my Roland Petit ballet's success: *Le Bal des Blanchisseuses,* which was produced in Paris at Christmas, 1946 and was an immediate hit—to the consternation of my detractors. "Home is where the hit is" is a good, practical variation of the old saying and I, wearying of my U. S. disappointments, took off for Europe to "cash in" on my unexpected success there; the ballet was produced in my absence. The unwanted symphony was promptly launched in Brussels (Dann Sternefeld), then in Paris, under Roger Desormière, who gave it two performances; it received an excellent press, Henri Sauguet calling it: "A strong work, a work of lyrical beauty, of remarkable quality." Two years later, it was "reprised" in Paris by Dean Dixon, the gifted Negro conductor, again with critical and audience approval.

The great war brought great changes in the musical world —not always for the better. That a piece of music, solidly "registering" in Europe, would be eagerly imported for home consumption, was thought an axiom; it proved anything but an axiom in my case. Having always been assured of a performance at Koussevitzky's expressive hands in this country, I had no more than a nodding acquaintance with other conductors who regarded me as "one of Koussy's boys" and, suffering from "premièritis," showed no inclination to accord me the—to them—pointless honor of a second performance. I now found myself at their mercy: confident that European acceptance of my symphony would bring about significant repercussions on this side, I dictated a dozen letters to the leaders of our big city orchestras. Alas—the response was distinctly discouraging: none of the answers were signed by the conductor approached; all bore the secretary's signature. The contents of their communications were the usual polite brush-offs; secretary X would claim that his patron's programs for the season were already made up; secretary Y informed me that the boss was on vacation, but that my letter would be shown him on his return; while secretary Z suggested that I send a tape recording, which I didn't have, European radio stations forbidding any private use of material they broadcast. Mitropoulos and Ormandy never acknowledged my letters; the first, from all accounts, preferred more "radical" fare than my music, the second was notoriously conservative. At any rate, I hold the proud record of never having been "noticed" by either conductor—although there was no want of trying on my part.

Before tackling Messrs. Munch, Stokowski, and Reiner, who seemed more approachable because I was on cordial "social" terms with all three and found them quite easy to talk to, I decided on a more direct method of communication. This involved making a piano-duet arrangement of the work, handing the conductor the orchestral score and letting him hear and read the piece simultaneously. The "method" was borrowed from Koussevitzky, for whom I often performed similar tasks in the past on behalf of other composers' music; my partners on those occasions were Prokofiev and Jesus Maria Sanroma, the brilliant Puerto Rican pianist. The scheme worked: at any rate, Munch, Stokowski, and Reiner agreed to receive me "and partner" and lend an ear and an eye to my Third Symphony. The audition over, the first two declared themselves more than favorably impressed with the work, going so far as to promise a performance in the course of the coming season. Stokowski's promises were somewhat nebulous, as I knew from the past, and never to be taken for granted. Prior to the piano-duet rendition of that innocent martyr, my symphony, he wrote me a "series of courteous and encouraging letters (ten of them) concerning both works [the Symphony and the Bernstein-premièred *Ode to the Milky Way*. V.D.] and his plans for their performance," I narrated in *Passport to Paris*. "As early as October 1948, Dr. Stokowski began looking for a good "place for my symphony" on his programs and wanted to know the playing time of the symphony . . . "Things are looking up"—I hummed the Gershwin song of that name to myself. But in August of the same year Dr. S., although admitting that he "enjoyed studying the symphony very much," confessed his utter inability to find the coveted "good place" for it, not realizing that I would have been happy with a not-so-good one . . . . In June, 1950, I was startled to receive another letter, wherein the industrious Dr. Stokowski informed me of resuming his search for a . . . "good place on one of his programs" for the symphony. "In case we broadcast it, is the duration twenty-two minutes or twenty-six?" he wished to know. I told him. In July the conductor (again) expressed a desire for a record of the symphony made by the French Radio. Request refused for already stated reasons. In August he wrote offering to study the work by the piano-duet arrangement. The get-together took place in September and Dr. Stokowski wrote to tell me of his enjoyment of what he heard, adding that he would send me Apel's *Harvard Dictionary of Music*, which he thought "absolutely first-class of its kind." Thus our lengthy correspondence produced a beautifully inscribed copy of the dictionary (which, unlike Becky Sharp, I did *not* throw away), but no performance of the symphony.

The treatment I received at the hands of Charles Munch, an affable and easy-going man, was even more singular. My piano partner was Lukas Foss, a former protégé of Koussevitzky's, excellent pianist as well as conductor and composer. Following our energetic reading of the symphony, Munch was even more emphatically "sold" on it than was Stokowski. He told me quite simply that he would program the symphony and even held a *sotto voce* conversation with his assistant—a lady who occupied a similar post in the Koussevitzky ménage. Ah! That's what I should have realized from the outset—the affable Alsatian did not inherit Koussevitzky's beloved orchestra *alone,* he also inherited the Koussevitzky ménage "in toto"— assistants and advisors, male and female both. I was not included in their plans for that or any other season of the Boston Symphony Orchestra. Soon enough came a letter, signed by the lady assistant on Mr. Munch's behalf, to the effect that owing to some kind of anniversary celebrations that were to take place in Boston during the coming season, only *commissioned* new works would be performed; that my work, *not* having been commissioned, no room could be made for it on Boston Symphony's programs, so with deep regrets, etc., etc. Where have I heard that before? A year later I wrote again, asking Mr. Munch whether he could *now,* that the celebrations were over, see his way clear to performing my piece: A letter, again the work of the conductor's amanuensis, stated with utmost clarity that my symphony would *not* be played in the course of the new season nor for *several* seasons to come—no explanations were given. I gave up the recalcitrant Alsatian and, on settling in Los Angeles (1952), thought of telephoning Alfred Wallenstein, for whom I once wrote an ephemeral serenade for strings at his request. A gracious but distant-sounding lady assistant told me in measured tones that Mr. Wallenstein "did not encourage interviews with composers" and that his programs were already made up, anyway.

In a feverish outburst of renewed activity I began bombarding Messrs. Kubelik, Monteux, Steinberg *e tutti quanti* with inducements, including quotes from Paris and Brussels critics, determined to vindicate my unwanted magnum opus and get it a hearing; my letters were either left unanswered or perfunctorily acknowledged, with the exception of the late Rodzinski, who asked to see the score (by then published by Carl Fischer, Inc.)—that's as far as it went. Then came the break —the *one* break, so far; I bumped into Walter Hendl in Santa Barbara, we had a few beers and talked music, agreeing on most points. I showed him my symphony, to which he took an immediate liking and . . . offered to perform it at Chautauqua, New York, the next summer! "Well, it's not the Boston Symphony, but beggars can't be choosers," I mused, my heart brimful with gratitude. My piece was, indeed, played at Chautauqua and played well; it achieved a substantial success and the (one) local critic wrote an approving notice. Hendl appeared genuinely pleased and I thought it opportune to tackle him about a possible performance in Dallas, whose excellent orchestra he was then conducting. There was a sudden chill in the air; after some deliberation, Hendl told me that while my symphony did "go over" in Chautauqua and would, undoubtedly, fare even better in New York, it would lay an egg in Dallas. "Great heavens, why at Dallas?" I exclaimed, completely taken aback. More deliberation, then: "I'll have to think it over—I just know it will. Tell you what I'll do— I'll write you a letter about it." The letter, explaining the egg-laying propensity of my symphony, never materialized; a few seasons later Dallas and Hendl came to a parting of the ways and Walter joined Fritz Reiner as Associate Conductor in Chicago. "Why not Reiner?" was my next brain storm. He had a summer home at Westport, Connecticut, where another piano-duet partner of mine, an extremely versatile lady musician, lived. Through her good offices, I obtained a hearing at Dr. Reiner's home—this time armed with a tape of Hendl's performance—and was told with disarming directness: "A fine symphony, but I must be frank with you. It's been played and I'm interested in first performances only. Why don't you write me a good 'closing' piece?" This stymied me. "Forgive me—but what is a closing piece?" Dr. Reiner smiled tolerantly. "Oh, come on . . . Surely you know that music designed to bring a concert to an effective close is hard to come by." He enumerated a few "safe" closing numbers and repeated that a new one, lasting say twelve to fifteen minutes, would be welcomed by him. "That's fine," I agreed, "but—if other conductors insist on 'firsts' too—who will play such a closing piece except yourself?" "Write new ones for them!" Dr. Reiner suggested with a contagious laugh.

Two younger conductors—with out-of-the-way home bases—became interested in my symphony when a possible recording of it began to loom large on my horizon. They expressed great willingness to program the work, should a recording be *guaranteed;* when the recording plans failed to take shape, their interest waned with lightning rapidity. At Nicolas Slonimsky's suggestion I sent the score to Robert Whitney, Musical Director of the Louisville Philharmonic Society and that Society's Recording Project. There was a new wrinkle to Mr. Whitney's reaction—he declared himself "genuinely impressed" with my symphony and was returning it to the publishers. I wrote back, wanting to know what he did with symphonies he was *not* "genuinely impressed" with? In 1961 (eleven years after the initial try!) it dawned on me that it wouldn't hurt to make yet another stab at Charles Munch; only this time I was going to be smart and entrust a *personal* letter to a *personal* friend who offered to hand it to Dr. Munch, whom he knew *personally.* Somehow my friend couldn't manage an eye-to-eye meeting with the conductor and slipped my letter into the mailbox. The rest is not difficult to guess; intercepted by the ever-watchful lady assistant, my "personal" missive was acknowledged by an *exact* copy of two previous turndowns, spelling out tersely—*Lasciate Ogni Speranza.* End of Symphony Saga. Unconcerned with the sound-weaver's plight, the power-happy batoneer devotes his valuable time to perfecting the sound of his orchestra; if there is any sound-weaving to be done, he'll attend to it—composers are a dime a dozen, anyway, but top-flight conductors are worth their weight in gold—good, sound U.S. gold at that. People like Stokowski, Ormandy, and a few others have been known to dress up J. S. Bach and make him utterly delectable to the "tradition-minded metropolis that has won the title of 'The City of Brotherly Love'" (Robert L. Sammons in *Town and Country* on "Ormandy's Orchestra," October, 1961). This peculiarly Philadelphian occupation caused Albert Jay Nock to note in *Journal of Forgotten Days* (December 31, 1934): "I listened to some gramophone records of Bach 'arranged' by Stokowski; good enough Stokowski, probably, but mighty poor Bach. I detest these miserable collaborations—Bach-d'Albert, Bach-Lizst, etc.—having never heard one yet that I could listen to without aggravation and impatience. For me, Bach is plenty good enough 'as is,' and if I have to hear him bowdlerized or tinkered, I prefer not to hear him at all." Dear Mr. Nock was probably unacquainted with Ormandy's tinkering: the Hungarian's seven and a half years as a movie-house conductor (the New York Capitol) turned him into both an expert bowdlerizer and a top-notch sound expert.

"Nothing brings a smile to the lips of the orchestra's amiable conductor more quickly than a reference to the 'Philadelphia Sound'; but Ormandy insists, with becoming and justifiable immodesty, that it is not the 'Philadelphia Sound,' but the *Ormandy Sound,*" Mr. Sammons rhapsodized. Clearly, the "justifiably immodest" Mr. Ormandy cares little about *what* his orchestra plays, only about *how* it plays. This is not good enough for observant Ernst Bacon, who said: "When people tell me Philadelphia, or any other city, has the best orchestra, I ask, 'Has it the best music?'" Tradition-minded Philadel-

phians are unaware of "best music" not being synonymous
with "best sound"—and it's downright touching to read in Mr.
Sammons's article about "the bond of deep affection between
the vibrant musical group and the people of Philadelphia"
which is almost "unbelievable"; so is Mr. Ormandy's claim that
"he can take any trained orchestra in the world and have it
sounding like the Philadelphia Orchestra in *only fifteen minutes*
[Italics mine. V.D.]—provided, of course, the musicians are
willing to co-operate." Ah, but can the miracle-working conductor make a symphonic work sound the way its composer
intended it to sound? Trust the ecstatic Mr. Sammons to refrain from asking embarrassing questions.

One may cavil with Stokowski's Hollywood-film-star-type
of shenanigans,* but he was "a fiery champion of new music"
(Sammons). Ormandy, while enamored of the orchestra's "new
[Ormandy] sound . . . slowed down the production of new
works . . . freely admitting that he prefers Mozart, Bach and
Beethoven." Back in 1943, David Ewen reported (in *Dictators
of the Baton*) that, "in addition to ping-pong, tennis, and pho-
tography, Ormandy's greatest pleasure comes from poring over
the pages of a new, interesting score." He must have gone back
to ping-pong. While, according to Mr. Sammons, "Ormandy
introduces into the repertoire an impressive list of significant
compositions, in doing so, he is admittedly cautious and follows a middle-of-the-road course in selecting new works."
Even with so conservative an approach, Ormandy "finds that

---

* Hollywood conductors are fond of a typically Hollywoodian conception
of publicity commensurate with their star status, as opposed to the lowlier
species—such as composers or soloists. Thus, Johnny Green (the only baton-
wielder, to my knowledge, still doggedly adhering to the Jasha, Sasha, Misha,
Tosha tradition of using an affectionate diminutive rather than one's given
name) is billed in letters *twice* as large as those accorded Messrs. Adams
and Strouse, authors of the score, in advertisements for the film version of
Bye Bye Birdie; in letters considerably larger than those heralding Lorin Hol-
lander's appearance as piano soloist under Mr. Green's baton at a Promenade
Concert of the Los Angeles Philharmonic in March, 1963.

when he programs a contemporary work, there are still a few traditionalists who have early trains to catch." My guess is that the amount of brotherly love lavished on the Philadelphia conductor by untraditional composers is not excessive.

I would be the last to deny that virtuosi of Ormandy's caliber are excellently suited to their jobs and, with the precarious economic status of our symphony orchestras, must be veritable godsends to municipal bigwigs. If only such men would stick to conducting, about which they know a great deal, and refrain from programming (of new music especially), in which intricate art they are either arbitrary or amateurish—or both! There is a simple solution—which, like all simple solutions, will be indignantly rejected at once; every symphony organization should employ a committee of, say, twelve qualified persons— critics, musicologists, *and* composers—whose job would be screening new scores and making concerted recommendations to the orchestra's conductor. That would relieve the man of an irksome and time-consuming chore and permit him to give his full attention to the job for which he has been hired in the first place—the job of conducting. He would, of course, have a full vote as a member of such a committee and, in addition to that, the power of veto. A meritorious work, deemed worthy of a performance by the committee, may not be the conductor's "meat," and he would reserve the right to reject it summarily, or hand it over to the assistant or associate conductor for a possible inclusion in the latter's programs. By the same token, the committee should feel free to prevent the conductor from exercising tender care on a particularly repellent piece of musical foolishness he may have happened to select for a performance.

One of America's most capable native-born conductors, Alfred Wallenstein, "composed into a few words an attitude developed over a lifetime" (Hope Stoddard. *Symphony Conductors of the U.S.A.,* 1957): "The conductor is not a star, is not Beethoven, is not the orchestra expressed in one man. He is only a tool. Humility before a great work of art—that is the first thing in conducting. If the orchestra men must arbitrarily follow a conductor sometimes, it is because deadlines must be met. Really the men and the conductor have the same task—to get at the composer's intentions." How wonderful, I thought. Would that all conductors would develop such an attitude; if this would only happen, the composer would really have a future in this country. And then I turned to another lady's findings—this time it was a copy of Mildred Norton's snappy piece printed on April 6, 1954, in the now defunct Los Angeles *Daily News*. She chanced to check the results of the poll instigated by *Musical America* (February, 1954) and was particularly struck by two questions and the replies supplied by Messrs. Ormandy, Munch, Szell, Golschmann, Leinsdorf, Thor Johnson, and the self-confessed tool, Alfred Wallenstein. To the first question: "What percentage of your program is made up of contemporary music?" Golschmann replied, "A great part"; Johnson claimed an average of 33⅓ per cent, while Munch and Ormandy approximated 25 per cent; Szell between 25 and 33 per cent, while Wallenstein admitted to only 13 to 14 per cent being allotted to his contemporaries. To the second question: "Do you consider this percentage adequate representation, or would you personally like to have more?" Leinsdorf replied that "In our case, I consider it sufficient"; Munch also thought his representation adequate; Szell wanted "the largest number of new works to be heard by the largest number of persons," which he deemed of primary importance; Ormandy's answer radiated Brotherly Love: "The presentation of new music is one of our primary responsibilities"; generous Golschmann wished he "could give entire programs devoted exclusively to contemporary music"; and Wallenstein blurted out: *"Would like none."* Miss Norton became indignant at this: "In three short words, Wallenstein appears to sum up his own personal opinion of the music written by our distinguished colony of the world-famous composers, no less than that of our many talented younger ones, and, in fact, puts under the blight of his sovereign disapproval the music of all contemporary composers everywhere. How do you feel about this, all you young composers whose only chance to be heard depends upon the whims and personal quirks of symphony conductors?"

The next day (April 7), Miss Norton went after Wallenstein's hide with renewed energy. She picked out yet another of the *Musical America* poll's questions, which read: "Do members of your orchestra undertake the study of new works with enthusiasm, apathy, or hostility?" Five out of the seven conductors hastened to assure their interrogator that the orchestra musicians responded with interest and enthusiasm, the sixth, Thor Johnson, even stating that "most players consider it their privilege to launch new works." Wallenstein's findings were "curiously at variance with those of his colleagues." Asked in his turn how the orchestra musicians reacted to the study of new works, Wallenstein tersely answered: "With apathy, as all orchestra players generally feel the same about new music." Aghast, Miss Norton countered with: "Leadership means, very simply, the ability to inspire an orchestra with a sense of purpose and joy in its work . . . They can do their own counting. What they cannot do is stand up against the year-in, year-out routine of deadening, stultifying readings, entered into without love and brought forth without life." This was written during Wallenstein's reign at the Los Angeles Philharmonic— and it must be said, in all fairness, that the stern conductor may have been short on imagination, but he was certainly long on discipline. It was thanks to his efforts that the hitherto unremarkable symphonic body was turned into one of the best orchestras in the country. Discipline was not good enough for idealistic Miss Norton: "Even though in recent winter seasons we have been carefully protected from practically all eligible conductors, a qualified one has only to step on the podium for the orchestra suddenly to come alive. No visiting conductor has found them apathetic, either for new music, or for old."

Knee-deep in all these polls—domestic and foreign—I decided to run yet another for the purposes of this book; and not one, but three of them. Two were directed at composers and critics, and the reader will find the questions and the answers in the Appendix; the third, addressed to some thirty conductors, resulted in only seven replies. True, I sent off my questionnaires at an inopportune time—in the summer (1962), when the hardworking batoneers are known to rest from their labors; obviously, composers and critics do not rest so soundly as their performing colleagues, because their answers to my questions were far more numerous. The conductors who did reply in time (to satisfy my publishers) were an interesting and articulate septet: Victor Alessandro (conductor of the San Antonio Symphony), Frank Brieff (New Haven Symphony), George Barati (Honolulu), Siegfried Landau (Brooklyn Philharmonia), Edwin McArthur (Harrisburg Symphony and St. Louis Municipal Opera), Stanislaw Skrowaczewski (Minneapolis), and Theodore Bloomfield (Rochester Philharmonic). Herewith are my questions and the conductors' replies:

1. *Do you like your job or do you think it could be improved upon; if so, how?*

ALESSANDRO:

Yes; improved by: larger orchestra personnel, better auditorium to play in, and higher salaries for the musicians in the orchestra.

BARATI:

Yes. It could be improved: larger budget, better orchestra, better (not larger) audiences, better hall, possibility of long-range planning.

BLOOMFIELD:

I like the responsibilities of conductor of a fine symphony orchestra, making programs to stimulate its audiences, and, above all, building it from year to year in both proficiency and importance to its community. I knew this satisfaction as conductor of the Portland Symphony Orchestra from 1955 to 1959. The Rochester position, however, is surrounded by many local conditions which render it undesirable to me.

BRIEFF:

Of course I like my job; otherwise I would do something else. As far as improving it is concerned, there is nothing like having some extra cash to extend the activities of the orchestra in the form of more concerts which will benefit not only the community but the musicians as well.

LANDAU:

. . . . [could be improved by] long-range budgetary planning, which would make it possible to make long-range program plans.

McARTHUR:

I do very much like my "job." It could be greatly improved upon, specifically if the community where I conduct were able economically to increase the number of concerts. My orchestra is a typical "community" orchestra made up of several professional players, but largely consisting of semi-professionals and amateurs. The work is much harder than when conducting entirely professionals, but the results are rewarding.

SKROWACZEWSKI:

Didn't answer first question.

2. *Do you have absolute power over (a) the hiring and firing of the members of your orchestra; (b) the choice of programs; (c) engaging soloists, choral groups, etc; (d) orchestra trustees and other influential patrons?*

ALESSANDRO:

Yes, with the understanding that you do not exceed the approved budget.

BARATI:

I propose; board approves or not; union ditto regarding (a).

BLOOMFIELD:

(a) No. (b) Yes. (c) Yes, within limits of budget and policy. (d) I have no influence in policies of the Association and no voice in the decisions of its directors.

BRIEFF:

(a) I do and I don't. We have, I think, a most equitable plan in dealing with the release of players. I hire anyone I choose after the routine audition, and then suggest to my orchestra committee that we ought to re-audition some players, who are duly notified to appear. More often than not they pass their audition; however, should they not succeed, they are given one year's notice.

(b) I do have to consult with my music committee, to whom I submit my programs. I have been very fortunate in having knowledgeable people to work with and, but for a few suggestions, I have had no problems in having my programs accepted.

(c) Here too there has been very little disagreement. Our soloists, the famous ones and the newcomers, have always been of the highest caliber.

(d) As long as we can maintain the same mutual respect and admiration we have for one another, my trustees, patrons and myself will continue to work harmoniously. Power in this sense is the confidence they place in me, which gives me the freedom (power?) to make decisions they are more likely than not willing to accept.

LANDAU:

Not over (d).

McARTHUR:

(a) Being a non-professional "community" orchestra, there

is not much choice in players; we need almost everyone who can play. (b) I make the programs for our concerts, but they are submitted to a music committee for sanction. In my twelve years in Harrisburg, I have been asked only two or three times to make changes. (c) Almost without exception my choice of soloists and recommendations have been accepted without question by the Music Committee and Board of Directors of the Orchestra. (d) I have no power whatsoever over trustees or influential patrons, but as I would presume to be the case in every city, as Musical Director and Conductor, I do have a very definite "influence."

SKROWACZEWSKI:

(a) I have the privilege of hiring whom I wish, but firing is an extremely difficult problem nowadays because of the union regulations. I would say that I can only propose to dismiss a man and the real decision is made by a kind of committee in which (stupidly) the music director is not included.

3. *Do you like contemporary music and, if so, what kind?*

ALESSANDRO:

Yes, that which expresses creativity and superb craftsmanship.

BARATI:

All that is well constructed, has a point to make, and is playable.

BLOOMFIELD:

I like *good* contemporary music, regardless of length, nationality, idiom, or date of composition.

BRIEFF:

It is not only a question of liking modern music, it is more than that—it is having a belief in it—and that I have; you have only to see my programming of contemporary music over the last ten years. I try to include the different schools from Schoenberg to the electronic, this last school to be represented by a commissioned work not yet completed.

LANDAU:

All, when it is not complex for the sole purpose of being complex.

McARTHUR:

I am very interested in contemporary music, but must use considerable care in the amount presented to our public and also tend to avoid the "ultra-extreme." In my opinion, many conductors today do a disservice to contemporary music by trying to force too large a dose down the musical throat of our listening public.

SKROWACZEWSKI:

Yes, very much; the good ones.

4. *Are your audiences receptive to new music? What kind of music do they prefer? Is there any real, healthy interest in the unexplored and the unfamiliar?*

ALESSANDRO:

A certain percentage—yes, to the opposite pole of actual hostility. They are not too interested in the unexplored and unfamiliar.

BARATI:

Yes, to a limited extent; prefer what "they know," (b) Not among the majority, or only to some extent; mostly if music stays close to the line of the past.

BLOOMFIELD:

Our audiences are reasonably receptive to new music, though often cool to a work of over 20 minutes' duration whose idiom and "thread" they find difficult to grasp. They expect a concert to appeal more to emotion than to intellect; consequently they prefer a work of melodic interest or of rhythmic excitement. There is healthy interest in the unfamiliar, including that of the classic and romantic periods as well as the contemporary.

BRIEFF:

Living in a college community (Yale), I find a small hard

core of an audience that is most receptive to new music, and, if this receptivity does not extend to the majority of my audience, at least there is a willingness to listen, albeit reluctantly. It is encouraging, however, to receive letters, not many, from lay people who say they liked the Webern, Bartók, Ives, Dallapiccola, Stravinsky, etc.

LANDAU:

Audiences can be *taught* to be receptive to new music; they do not really like the unfamiliar—except young audiences.

McARTHUR:

Our audience is only passively interested in the new music of today. If a new piece is introduced, it must be coupled with one of the popular and accepted standards. If not, its success is doomed. And as stated in answer No. 3, there must not be an overdose.

SKROWACZEWSKI:

Our audiences are very receptive to new music (any kind) if the proportion between unknown modern music and familiar music is not more than one to four.

5. *What is the approximate number of first performances you give in the course of a season?*

ALESSANDRO:

Very few, if any.

BARATI:

With my own orchestra, about eight firsts "at home," one or two world premières.

BLOOMFIELD:

Average per season: one world première, five first local performances of classic or romantic works (e.g. Mahler's 2nd, Schubert's 3rd Symphony).

BRIEFF:

One première, a commission, each year.

LANDAU:

Two to four (in five adult and three youth concerts).

McArthur:

As we in Harrisburg give five concerts a season, we would not be a fair yardstick of first performances. However, during my twelve years there, we have given about ten premières, including four pieces especially commissioned for the orchestra.

Skrowaczewski:

We do two to four world premières yearly and sometimes up to ten first performances in this city.

6. *Do you insist on premières? Do you prefer not to program works premièred elsewhere?*

Alessandro:

No; do not consider this important so long as the music is good.

Barati:

No preference so long as the work is as stated in No. 8.

Bloomfield:

No. No.

Brieff:

No. I do not insist on premières and do works premièred elsewhere.

Landau:

I don't mind doing local first performances at all. That way the parts are often cleared of many errors.

McArthur:

I most certainly do not insist on premières. I have always felt this to be a silly idiosyncrasy even in the days when I was accompanying some of the world's greatest singers. For instance, the late John Charles Thomas often let a fine song go by because it had been sung one or twice by a competitive artist. And the mere fact that he sang a new song once in the Town Hall in New York did by no means assure its success.

SKROWACZEWSKI:

I don't insist on premières and I even prefer to play the works already performed which have evoked some discussions or critiques.

7. *Did you ever score a resounding popular success with atonal or dodecaphonic music?*

ALESSANDRO:

No.

BARATI:

It's a question of evaluation—probably not.

BLOOMFIELD:

No.

BRIEFF:

Once—Op. 10 Webern, if you choose to call it atonal.

LANDAU:

No.

MCARTHUR:

No!

SKROWACZEWSKI:

Yes, many times and in many cities of the world.

8. *Do you commission works from native composers and, if so, what is the basis of your choice of a composer?*

ALESSANDRO:

A few; whenever possible, preference is given to composers of the area.

BARATI:

(1) Fitting the purpose; (2) Availability.

BLOOMFIELD:

Yes. We commissioned Bernard Rogers to write "Variations on a Song of Moussorgsky" in 1960 and Ron Nelson to write "Overture for Latecomers" in 1961. In the former instance we chose an esteemed local figure deserving greater recognition; in the latter, a gifted young composer whose student years here had marked him as a "comer."

BRIEFF:

From native as well as foreign composers, although emphasis is on the former. We have commissioned John LaMontaine, Quincy Porter, Alexei Haieff (already performed) in the future, Dallapiccola (this year), Brant (award) next year and also Billy Jim Layton; in succeeding years, Mel Powell, Robert Helps and Don Martino. Some are well known, others relatively little known. Five of the composers are local, I know their music and like to encourage them, although this is not the criterion by which they are chosen.

LANDAU:

I strongly advise it to my boards. The choice is mainly made to encourage local composers.

McARTHUR:

Partly covered in Answer No. 5. Two of the works commissioned by the orchestra were by local Harrisburgers. Others were by Ned Rorem and John LaMontaine, who are both personal friends of mine and whose talents I greatly admire.

SKROWACZEWSKI:

I try to create the habit in the Minneapolis Association to commission native and foreign composers every year. This year, for instance, which is the sixtieth season of the Minneapolis Symphony Orchestra, I have been able to commission two American composers.

9. *What is the procedure you employ in dealing with unrequested scores sent you with a view to performance?*

ALESSANDRO:

Screened by our staff.

BARATI:

I read them *when* I have time.   Perform them—some of them—when fitting program needs.

BLOOMFIELD:

I study them with the same impartiality received by those requested, although they generally wait longer for perusal. Most scores receive two or three perusals. A work interesting me to the point of a fourth perusal is likely to be performed, either in the following season or at an appropriate future time.

BRIEFF:

I attempt to read every score sent me, generally after my season is over.

LANDAU:

I look at them and return after study. Often you do not have to see the whole score, as you do not need to eat the whole egg to know that it is rotten!

McARTHUR:

Without fail, I carefully examine every score sent to me. But I cannot guarantee how quickly this can be done, and being a busy man, it is sometimes several weeks before I can get to a score. I believe it is important for the composer to exercise patience in the direction of the conductor. But I believe it is a responsibility of the conductor to give the composer every possible attention and consideration.

SKROWACZEWSKI:

The problem arises with the quantity. In a year I have about 300 scores, mostly unrequested, sent to me for perusal. Fortunately, it is possible to judge 95% of these in a few minutes. In the two years I have spent in my present post, I believe that not more than 3% of these scores could be considered for performance.

10. *Do you encourage composers to see you personally whenever possible or do you prefer to receive their music through the mails?*

ALESSANDRO:

Personally, when time permits.

BARATI:

No preference. I like to judge the music on its own merit. If composer helps, fine.

BLOOMFIELD:

I prefer to receive music through the mail. A personal interview adds nothing and may distract attention from the music. Once a work has been accepted for performance, however, a personal interview is welcome.

BRIEFF:

I like to meet with composers personally rather than receive their music through the mails.

LANDAU:

I prefer to study scores in my study. Too many composers "talk" better than they write.

McARTHUR:

I would prefer to have scores sent to me through the mail and I would not like to be personally influenced by the presence of the composer; and also there are times when it might be embarrassing as well.

SKROWACZEWSKI:

Only the scores.

11. *Do you or does your secretary answer composers' letters and requests for meetings or auditions?*

ALESSANDRO:

I answer personally whenever possible.

BARATI:

I answer all unless away for longer time.

BLOOMFIELD:

I answer all such letters personally.

BRIEFF:

Whenever possible, yes.

LANDAU:

I try to do most of this work myself.

McArthur:

I answer all of my mail directly, assisted of course by my wife.

Skrowaczewski:

I reply myself, dictating the letters to my secretary.

12. *When accepting a work for performance in the course of your regular season are you guided by (a) the composer's promise or reputation; (b) previous acquaintance with his music; (c) opinions of musicians and critics in whose judgment you have faith?*

Alessandro:

By all three, but primarily the value of the music itself.

Barati:

(1) Fitting our needs; (2) I must perform some famous contemporaries to be able to play the others.

Bloomfield:

(a) Rarely. (b) Greatly. (c) Occasionally. But these three "guides" only encourage me to request a score, and not until I have perused it and found it appropriate for performance will I schedule it.

Brieff:

In some cases by previous acquaintance with their music, in others by their promise, and to a small degree by opinions of musicians and critics.

Landau:

Only (a) and (b).

McArthur:

The reputation of a composer whose new work we are playing is of absolutely no interest to me; previous acquaintance with his music is of little or no importance; I make my own decisions as regards musical value, and am not influenced by the opinions of other musicians or critics. If I did not have the confidence in my own ability to judge and the strength of my conviction, I would not believe I had even the elemental requirements to fill the post of a musical director and conductor.

SKROWACZEWSKI:

The score is the only guide, with the exception of more popular works that sometimes will fill the hall. See No. 2 (b) and (c).

13. *How many new scores do you receive in the course of a regular orchestral season?*

ALESSANDRO:

Well over 100.

BARATI:

Last 12 months I received over 200. Read them all.

BLOOMFIELD:

An average of six.

BRIEFF:

About a dozen.

LANDAU:

At least 20.

McARTHUR:

This varies and I cannot give an answer.

SKROWACZEWSKI:

See No. 9.

14. *Do you get much mail from your subscribers condemning this or that piece you programmed, or clamoring for their favorites you may have neglected? If so, name the neglected favorites and the condemned pieces.*

ALESSANDRO:

Not enough.

BARATI:

Mail, phone, social occasions; whatever one plays gets its share of wrongs (and rights to some extent). Condemned mostly the new.

BLOOMFIELD:

No. I used to receive more in Portland. Generally subscribers want a greater proportion of romantic music. Saint-Saëns's Third Symphony has been requested (and given) in both cities.

BRIEFF:

No, I do not get much mail; I would welcome a lot more of any kind of opinion, pro or con.

LANDAU:

Yes, Berlioz is often mentioned as receiving too little attention.

McARTHUR:

I often receive letters of criticism and seldom letters of commendation. I believe this is general most everywhere. A few seasons ago, as in many cities, we asked for program suggestions from our subscribers and promised to perform the symphony which received the most requests. The previous season we had played Beethoven's Fifth Symphony. Despite its recent hearing, this symphony received by far the most requests and we had to program it again, although it is our policy, with so few concerts, not to repeat any composition within five or six seasons.

SKROWACZEWSKI:

Yes I do, and I find it extremely interesting and try always to answer these letters and to discuss this with my public. The favorites and also the condemned go from Bach via Bruckner to "My Heart Belongs to Daddy."

15. *Are you tired of box-office-proven symphonic standards, or are you happiest when interpreting them in your own, highly personal way?*

ALESSANDRO:

I do not tire of conducting good music. I do not think a good work should be penalized just because it appears to be box-office.

BARATI:

    I try to play as little of the proven as the balance of good programming permits.

BLOOMFIELD:

    To be "tired" of box-office-proven standard symphonic works is, in my opinion, to abjure one of the conductor's duties to his art, which is to infuse new life into works thrice-familiar to his audiences and to him. A conductor who loves music, be it Beethoven, Tchaikovsky, or Prokofiev, will give it his best each time, constantly seeking something further in it, and will not lose his incentive with repetition. He need not interpret it in a "highly personal way" merely to keep up his interest. His interpretation should be his own, however, in the sense that he is convinced of it.

BRIEFF:

    No, I am not tired of the proven box-office standards. They are and always will remain for me great works of art whose many unfathomable mysteries reveal themselves only after many repetitions. This will also be true of some of our contemporary composers whose music will eventually gain wide acceptance.

LANDAU:

    I do not think of repertory in this manner.

McARTHUR:

    I am *not* tired of "box-office-proven symphonic standards." It is of the greatest importance to have full houses at our concerts, and if the proven favorites are the ones to fill the house, we must continue to play them and with discretion expose our faithful public to the "new." I believe the late Dr. Koussevitzky had the right formula. I followed his programs here in New York for many seasons. He introduced new work after new work—but at his closing concert of the season he almost invariably played Tchaikovsky's Fifth or Sixth Symphony and sent his old faithful subscribers home with a familiar and palatable memory of the season.

SKROWACZEWSKI:

There are no box-office-proven symphony standards, but good and bad music. There are also no standards of interpretation, and everything the conductor does—if he is not a copyer—is always his "highly personal way."

16. *Do you believe in the state support of the Arts in the United States and, if so, what shape do you think it should take?*

ALESSANDRO:

Would prefer support of the arts to be maintained by the people of San Antonio, but if this becomes an economical impossibility, would like the trend developed towards an incentive and rewarding plan—that is, the amount of local money raised to be matched either by foundations or government.

BARATI:

Yes, without "State control," however, Tax benefits, preferential endowment fund treatment, hall construction, and free use, free office space, increased recording income possibilities, through better radio system, educational opportunities, etc.

BLOOMFIELD:

I believe in support of the arts in the U.S. first on a municipal, then on a state, and only thereafter on the federal level, with standards of qualification and without interference in artistic autonomy.

BRIEFF:

There should be some help from the state toward the support of the arts, more in partnership with our existing organizations than complete support. It should be a joint enterprise between government and the citizenry, each contributing a share, with control left in the hands of the musicians and able administrators.

LANDAU:

Yes, it should help organizations do what "they can not do

for themselves," i.e. pay for maintenance of halls and personnel. This was the original concept of Federal aid as envisioned by our founding fathers.

McArthur:

I have very definite ideas on this subject, but frankly I would not choose to even touch upon this matter in such a questionnaire.

Skrowaczewski:

Yes, I do. There are many ways of such Federal support. The best seems to me to be the one which does not replace personal contributions but encourages them.

VII

Critics on the Carpet

—•—•—•—•—•—•—•—•—•—•—•—•—•—•—•—•—•—•—•—

Please don't expect a blast at the virtuosi of the pan, or
the dead pan—the dreaded members of the critical brother-
hood. By and large, I have no quarrel with them. The present
crop is more than satisfactory—not a bloomin' prima donna in
the lot. In the music field, the day of the autocratic judge, whose
verdict alone could bring sudden glory or inglorious oblivion
to a composer, the day of Cui, Serov, H. F. Chorley, Hanslick,
Cecil Gray, and Ernest Newman is no more; in the States,
Huneker, H. T. Parker, Carl Van Vechten and, perhaps, Paul
Rosenfeld, exercised similar authority, but they were writers
on music rather than everyday critics (with the exception of
Parker, whose style was, in its way, as singular as Rosenfeld's
but whose judgments were more accurate).

Of U. S. music critics, those regularly employed by metropolitan newspapers, Boston's hard to please Philip Hale and
New York's W. J. Henderson, Lawrence Gilman, Richard
Aldrich—conservatives all—and Oscar Thompson, more receptive to modern tendencies, were able chroniclers who threw
their weight around in the first half of the present century.
Competent though they were—each in his own, often erratic
way—their over-all influence was nowhere as far-reaching as

that exercised by Olin Downes of the New York *Times* or Virgil Thomson, who held forth on the pages of the New York *Herald Tribune.*

Olin Downes (1886-1955), dutifully read but barely tolerated and often mocked by the "progressives," was, in reality, an extremely honest and conscientious appraiser, whose tastes were broadly eclectic and who was given to spurts of contagious enthusiasm; he was also easily bored and never afraid to voice his boredom, even when it meant challenging Fashion. Downes had the rare faculty of treating a failure as though it were a success, if he happened to be genuinely taken with the music, and denouncing a puffed-up victory, the condemnation of which was dangerous from the musico-political angle.

Virgil Thomson (b. 1896), the Kansas City Satie, has been called "the finest musical intelligence writing in the U.S. today" by Clifford Odets. In the *New Yorker,* Edmund Wilson stated that "with the exception of Virgil Thomson, not one first-rate critical journalist has appeared since Woollcott's time." The notes on the jacket of *The Art of Judging Music,* one of Thomson's books, assert: "It was New York's gain when, in 1940, Thomson became music critic of the *Herald Tribune* and began illuminating the sometimes miasmic field of daily and weekly musical comment with flashes that seemed pyrotechnical but have come to look like the *steady light of truth.*" (Italics mine. V.D.)

Let's examine this assertion. Whether his "musical intelligence" is "finest" or otherwise, whether he is really witty or merely coy, whether his qualities have "endeared Virgil Thomson to countless readers" (his publishers' claim) or only succeeded in titillating them, is of no real importance. As for the "steady light of truth," I don't think there has ever been a less reliable, less accurate reporter on our musical scene. Thomson, while covering Paris music in 1947, made this comment on one of Balanchine's new ballets: "*Serenade,* a ballet to the music of Tchaikovsky's Trio, orchestrated anonymously, is a light fantasy rather long for its substance . . ." I pointed out in a letter to the Paris *Tribune* that *Serenade* was Tchaikovsky's well-known *Serenade for Strings,* and that the orchestration, far from being anonymous, was by Peter Ilyich himself! In retrospect, this amuses me the more upon reading the pundit's comment in his Sunday article of February 21, 1954, in which he sententiously pointed out: "Another common fault of the reviewer, and one which causes the greatest bitterness among artists, is carelessness in statement." Just a small matter of whose ox is gored, one deduces (*Passport,* p. 447). In a *Musical America* (January, 1961) article, Thomson was guilty of eighteen factual errors duly pointed out by Everett Helm, then the magazine's chief European correspondent. While they were not in themselves of earth-shaking proportions, the extreme carelessness of our fearless torchbearer of truth was again startlingly manifested. Among other things, Thomson declared Baden-Baden a capital city (which it is not); placed Schott, the publishing house, in Cologne instead of Mainz; omitted Breitkopf and Hartel from the list of West Germany's active publishing firms; claimed that Heidelberg was in the Rhineland (false again); attributed (wrongly) the post of director of the Heidelberg Conservatory to Wolfgang Fortner; held forth on Eric Satie's "major" influence in Germany (which he never had); and so on. Thomson's rebuttals to these charges—in the June, 1961, issue of *Musical America*—consisted of petulant persiflage in the spoiled-but-oh-so-precious-brat manner he continually affects. Paraphrasing his gibes at Gershwin, we might say that what might have been thought "precious" in a lad in his twenties is downright tiresome in a sexagenarian.

Accuracy may be considered unimportant, provided the "steady light of truth" is directed at broader issues—such as

judging new music, certainly. An extremely typical sample
of Thomson's fine musical intelligence at work is his 1935
job on Gershwin's *Porgy and Bess*. Herewith, a few excerpts
from the *Modern Music* article: "One can see through *Porgy*
that Gershwin has not and never did have any power of sustained musical development ... [The] material is straight
from the melting-pot. At best it is a piquant but highly un-
savory stirring-up-together of Israel, Africa and the Gaelic
Isles [?] . . . his lack of understanding of all the major problems of form, of continuity, and of serious or direct musical
expression is not surprising in view of the impurity of his
musical sources and his frank acceptance of the same. Such
frankness is admirable. At twenty-five it was also charming.
Gaminerie of any kind at 35 is more difficult to stomach.
So that quite often *Porgy and Bess*, instead of being pretty,
is a little hoydenish, like a sort of *musique de la pas tres
bonne société* ... it is clear, by now, that Gershwin hasn't
learned his business. At least he hasn't learned the business
of being a serious composer, which one has always gathered
to be the business he wanted to learn . . . The most authentic
thing about it all, about a work that is otherwise the purist
Tecla [!] is Gershwin's sincere desire to write an opera, a real
opera that somebody might remember. I rather fancy he has
succeeded in that, which is pretty incredible of him, too,
seeing how little he knew of how to go about it . . . But his
prose declamation is all exaggerated leaps and unimportant
accents. It is vocally uneasy and dramatically cumbersome.
Whenever he has to get on with the play he uses spoken
dialogue. *It would have been better if he had stuck to that
all the time.*" (Italics mine. V.D.).

So much for the technical aspects of Gershwin's *Porgy;*
Thomson's comments on the opera's *musical* substance are
shot through with capricious ambiguity of the cattiest sort:
"Nothing of much interest, little exercises in the jazzo-mod-

ernistic style, quite cute for the most part, but leading nowhere. The scoring is heavy, over-rich and vulgar. It is nervous,
too, like the whole musical texture. Throughout the opera
there is, however, a constant stream of lyrical invention and a
wealth of harmonic ingenuity." That would, doubtless, lead
"somewhere," one concludes. But wait: another about-face
is in the offing: "*Porgy* is falsely conceived and rather clumsily
executed, *but* it is an important work because it is abundantly
conceived and entirely executed by hand." It would appear
that, having "entirely executed" *Porgy* by his own hand, the
"courageous" and "fearlessly sincere" critic was in a hurry to
pour a few drops of healing balsam on poor *Porgy's* corpse.
"I do, however, like being able to listen to a work for three
hours and to be fascinated at every moment," Thomson offered
condescendingly, again retracing his steps for the summing-up:
"*Green Pastures*, the last act of *Run, Little Chillun, Four
Saints in Three Acts* [!] and *Porgy* are all little eminences on
the flat horizon of American opera . . . Two of these are straight
folklore. The third is straight opera [Thomson's very own.
V.D.]. *Porgy and Bess* is the least interesting of the four, because it is not straight anything. [Straight flush, perhaps?
V.D.] It is crooked folklore and halfway opera, a strong but
crippled work."

Some of the pundit's capsule criticisms will show that be-
heading contemporaries need not take as much time as the
above thorough performance. "Three Piano Moods by Roger
Sessions, though harmonically sophisticated, were as dead as
the day of their birth." "Prokofiev's Fifth Symphony's more
picturesque sections present no novelty of any kind . . . The
first of these being a sort of Soviet-style blues, or [!] Muscovite
one-step.* Slow movements have never been Prokofiev's forte,

---

* Just how Prokofiev achieved the miracle of writing a blues — a slow dirge
— which happened also to be a 2/4 "allegro molto" one-step is not explained.

and of late years he has taken more and more to concealing this lack of expressivity . . with an overlay of cinema sentiment." Thomson is especially good at praising with faint damns, of which procedure I'll give you a telling specimen: "We have . . . a national glory in the form of Aaron Copland, who so skillfully combines, in the Bartók manner, folk feeling with neoclassic techniques that foreigners often *fail to recognize his music as American at all.*" (Italics mine. V.D.) When Thomson praises "on the level," his compliments have a tired triteness about them, as though the composer-critic considered handing such fading bouquets to fellow creators a boring business. Of Alban Berg's wonderful Violin Concerto he said: "It is a work of art, not a madman's dream, though its gloom is almost too consistent to be real [?]. Nevertheless, it would not be fair to suspect a piece clearly so inspired in musical detail of essential second-rateness. One must, I think, take it or leave it as a whole. Your reviewer has long been willing to take it," while your reader, Mr. T., has long, too long, been willing to mistake such stuff for criticism. Bohuslav Martinu's Fifth Symphony "shows this living master [the year was 1948. V.D.] at his highest point, for the present, of originality and freedom. Martinu is clearly, as of today [?], a symphonist. He moves in the form with ease, makes it speak for him. This symphony speaks in double-talk, says always two things at once." So does Thomson—always. On Stravinsky's neoclassical productions: "This is a compound of grace and of brusqueness, thoroughly Russian [?] in its charm and its rudeness and so utterly sophisticated intellectually that few musicians of intellectual bent can resist it . . . I don't think musical ticket buyers are overfond of indirectness, and certainly most of anybody's neoclassic works are indirect." On Messiaen's *Trois Petites Liturgies*: "This work is the product of a delicate ear and an ingenious musical mind . . . [The] author is a case not unlike that of Scriabin. That is to say that he is a skilled harmonist and orchestrator,* full of theories and animated by no over-all afflatus, *but* that there is a sticky syrup in his product which hinders its flow at concert temperatures." Our reviewer got so carried away by his favorite game of sticking pins into musical flesh that he forgot that Messiaen was a Frenchman! Thomson reduced his liturgies to the level of the late Aimee Semple McPherson. In yet another about-face he magnanimously granted that Messiaen's novelty was "for all its silliness, musically highly original." Ruggles's *Angels* he thought an "extraordinary and secretly [?] powerful work"; Roy Harris's Concerto for String Quartet, Clarinet and Piano was "real chamber music, with no more faults than are to be found in Brahms [!], and with all the virtues." For all its silliness, this statement is, indeed, highly original. The witty critic thought the "color and tunes" of Moeran's *In the Mountain Country* "not ugly," and Gershwin's Concerto "not an ugly piece, either—but a pretty empty one." A moment later, we read of "all the sweet rapture and ease of the Gershwin style." The two composers he admired unreservedly were Manuel Rosenthal, French conductor, and John Cage.

As you see from these quotes, chosen at random, "your reporter" wrote "around" music, very seldom *about* it. His opinions were never stated with the rugged simplicity and directness of an Olin Downes, who was not preoccupied with style (Thomson's stylistic virtues elude me) but gave the reader an honest evaluation of what he heard—which is, after all, the critic's true function. The height of pretentious nonsense was reached in Thomson's pronouncements on American Music. After listing nearly every twentieth-century U.S. composer of renown, which list included Walter Piston, "a strictly Parisian [?] neoclassicist," and Roger Sessions, "the Germano-eclectic modernist" [!!], Thomson smugly announced that "we have everything." He lessened the effect of so optimistic a

* Scriabin's orchestration was notoriously thick and unimaginative. V.D.

statement by insisting that "there is no such thing as an American style," while, "all this music is American, nevertheless, because it is made by Americans." "Two devices typical of American practice are the *nonaccelerating crescendo* [Italics mine. V.D.] and a steady ground rhythm of equalized eighth notes (expressed or not)." Not knowing what equalized eighth notes—expressed or not—may possibly be, I can assure the reader that the "nonaccelerating crescendo" was Gioacchino Rossini's favorite device, which used to bring the audience to its feet in the Italian composer's opera finales.

We haven't had many critics who were also composers (which was often the case in France with Debussy, Dukas, Bruneau, and others), although the trend appears to be on the upswing today. Virgil Thomson's activities in both realms are so closely interwoven that I think it fitting to discuss him both as creator and commentator concurrently. Thomson would, I'm sure, like to be put down as the local leader of the already legendary "tongue-in-cheek" school, of which gifted folk like Chabrier, Satie, and Lord Berners were the best-known protagonists. After one or two hearings of Thomson's music, the truth emerges—our Kansas City Satie is tongue-tied and not half cheeky enough. Is there anything duller than a musical joke that does not come off? Listen, if you can, to any of Thomson's "portraits," his Third Piano Sonata, or the mockingly grandiloquent songs, and try to get a laugh—it will not be easy. There was a measure of fun in the deliberate incongruity of wedding Gertrude Stein's word-juggling to the homophonically plain, nakedly diatonic musical accompaniment—and the notion sat well with the black-and-white motive of Florence Stettheimer's décor and costumes. The meagerness of Thomson's musical substance caused Prokofiev to refer to the *Four Saints* as the "Four *Notes* in Three Acts"; this kind of fun palled all too rapidly, and the "repeat" attempt (*Mother of Us All*) proved entirely unconvincing.

Having studiously labored on a facsimile of the airs and graces of a Paris dilettante, Thomson succeeded in one sense only; he *was* and *is* a dilettante. As to the Parisian pretentions, his music is about as Parisian as shoofly pie; he never had the slightest vogue in his beloved France, and the *Four Saints* fell flat in Paris, where the opera was presented as a feature of the "L'Oeuvre du XXe Siècle" 1952 Festival. Of Thomson's other theatrical attempts, the score for *Filling Station,* a ballet, is moderately cute. An indifferent craftsman, of which his cyclic efforts are ample proof, Thomson is so bereft of musical ideas that his reluctance—or inability—to develop them is understandable. Following the *Four Saints,* his magnum opus, Thomson has written a mess of notes, none of them especially memorable; thus, we could put him down as a composer of note—well, *notes,* to be precise. We already appraised his claims to the status of a noted critic.

Music critics functioning today may not be as colorful as the Hunekers, Van Vechtens, or Rosenfelds of yore, but they are resourceful and thorough. Outside of Downes's and Thomson's successors—Harold C. Schonberg and Paul Henry Lang, Howard Taubman having taken over Brooks Atkinson's berth as drama critic—there are the always readable and substantial Irving Kolodin of the *Saturday Review,* optimistic Alfred Frankenstein (San Francisco) and competent Albert Goldberg (Los Angeles). Winthrop Sargeant of the *New Yorker* (Stravinsky's Mr. Deaf) has his admirers and does write a lively piece now and again, however you may regard his predilections and somewhat anachronistic affinities. The younger men on the metropolitan newspapers and a few employed by magazines devoted to gramophonic equipment and the reviewing of phonograph records write with considerable zest and savvy but are a little too anxious to keep in step with the dodecaphonic, or just plain cacophonic, army and to dismiss all other music, especially the kind that does not shun tonal centers, as a shameful malady, hopelessly dated, in fact, antediluvian, since some of it managed to sneak in *before* Stravinsky's *Flood*. Several of the young critics also compose —which is, of course, all to the good.

The New York *Times* man, Harold C. Schonberg, really started something with a Sunday article (January 14, 1962) titled, "Where Are They?"—"they" being new composers of stature. "U.S. has much compositional activity, but the young generation lacks power," said he. "Over the holidays we were talking at different times to two American composers, both of them highly respected, both of them middle generation, both active as teachers. After the knives were sheathed, we got into the problem of the young composer. Gloom settled down. 'There are a lot of them,' said Composer A. 'But where are they?' said Composer B. 'If I had to name an outstanding compositional talent in America among the younger generation, I would be stopped cold. I know there's a lot of writing going on, but nothing seems to be happening.' These were not idle remarks carelessly thrown off. Both of these men are propagandists for American music and are desperately looking for talent. So are the music publishers." Schonberg then touched upon an "imposing set of reasons. One might be the presence of so many major European composers permanently in America after the late 1930's. Instead of pollinating, they tend to dilute. Instead of opening up new vistas, they tend to form schools around themselves." After describing the onslaught of twelve-tonism, Schonberg correctly reported that "any kind of romantic writing was hooted down, and academic figures like Howard Hanson or Douglas Moore were accepted only on sufferance and never by intellectuals." Whether he is equally correct in assuming that "right now there are indications that romanticism is on its way back" is open to question. In support of his conjecture, Schonberg lists such operas as Moore's *Wings of The Dove*, Ward's *The Crucible*, and

Giannini's *The Harvest,* all heard for the first time in 1961, and insists that they "would not have had a chance of being staged ten years ago." That, I think, is a factual error; what about *The Ballad of Baby Doe* (1956), by the self-same Douglas Moore, or the thoroughly successful *Susannah,* by Carlisle Floyd (1955), or a flock of Menotti's operas (1948-1954), all of these romantic and diatonic, and all done to the King Public's taste?

Schonberg's insistence on the over-all sterility of the U-boys' output brought a positively deafening chorus of protests in its wake. Two wives wrote in to say that, since the critic was obviously unfamiliar with their husbands' music, he didn't know what he was talking about and hadn't lived. A saxophonist named Sigmund Roscher wanted to know whether Schonberg had ever heard of one Carl Anton Wirth; Charles Frink, Ph.D., of New London, Connecticut, dared the critic to put his, Frink's, arrogance to the test. "My Symphony No. 8 [!!] will be performed in November by the Eastern Connecticut Symphony," Mr. Frink wrote to the New York *Times.* "I hope that he [Schonberg] will attend. I also hope that he will review the work in the *Times* as ruthlessly as he wishes. It is my sincere belief that he will be the first major critic to discover an American composer of the mid-20th-Century whose work will endure." That's tellin' 'em, dear Mr. Frink, Ph.D.; the sad part of it is that no composer unconvinced about the durability of his product, exists. The entire struggling mass of composers with the technique to express themselves but without the genius to make their message memorable would stop writing music the moment an authentic clairvoyant assured them that their work would not survive. I've never met an "authentic" clairvoyant—and neither, obviously, have my struggling brethren.

In a riposte to the indignant letter writers, titled "Mediocrity Prevalent," Schonberg said, "Most of the correspondents, who were angry about the conclusions I drew, seemed to think that it is the duty of a critic to pat everybody on the back. This is known as 'encouraging talent' and is supposed to be 'constructive.' I call it coddling."

The country's drama critics—particularly those who labor in the cities where new shows start (and, only too often, end) their careers and thus hold the fate of such costly enterprises in their hands—are on sure ground where drama or a theatrical vehicle employing the spoken word exclusively is concerned. That, of course, includes comedy, but *not* musical comedy. "There is only one absolutely indispensable element that a musical play must have—it must have music," Oscar Hammerstein II once wrote. "And there is only one thing that it has to be—it has to be good." There is another equally indispensable element that a critic employed in reviewing a "musical" (note that the current word for such vehicles is not musical play or comedy, just plain "musical") must have: he must know his music in order to qualify as an appraiser of it. On perusing the book reviews in any of the glossier (and bossier) magazines, you may take exception to the reviewer's remarks, but you can be sure that a man so employed knows his grammar. Do critics who cover musical plays (and their bosses do not hire two kinds—one for the musical, the other for the unmusical theater) know their *musical* grammar? I'll lay you the most outrageous odds they do not.

Having pointed out in another chapter that American musicals are seldom written by musicians nowadays, we really shouldn't insist on a critic adding music to his academic equipment. Would it be too much to entertain the slender hope that, if and when the composing of a musical play is again entrusted to those skilled in a composer's craft, newspaper coverage of such men's labors be turned over to judges who can provide even the most rudimentary proof of being conversant with music?

I have no way of knowing whether prewar critics were at all musically inclined, but at least they made a show of singling out sundry numbers that especially pleased them, described a given score's suitability to the book, extolled or deplored the tunesmith's style, and so on. This healthy approach was present in the critical work of a Brooks Atkinson, the late Percy Hammond, and even, on occasion, in the often merciless pieces by the late George Jean Nathan. Mighty little of it is found in the accounts signed by the otherwise competent critics now in power; to sweat over the elaborate mechanics of a dramatico-musical setting, to rewrite page after page of one's score, to throw out one's favorite songs when they do not happen to "make it" on the road and replace them with last-minute brainstorms—and then to get *one line* in a New York critic's estimate of the show to some ninety lines devoted to its other ingredients, is, assuredly, vexing and unfair—even if this one line is a laudatory one. Since it is the score that (forgive me, O librettists) makes or breaks the show, isn't it worthy of a more detailed dissection? Such a dissection is seldom, very seldom offered; can it be because the critic made uncomfortable by a lack of familiarity with a composer's (or even an *ersatz* songwriter's) problems shuns his responsibility and dismisses the pesky chore with one pithy sentence?

American critics were always noted for their extremely free and easy treatment of the creative man in the theater. Playwrights, lyricists and composers alike were only as good as their last entry; an illustrious signature seldom swayed an unprejudiced critic, which, in a sense, was rather refreshing. Thus every new score of Cole Porter was always condemned as "not as good as the one before that," a statement that became a standard joke between the composer-lyricist and his adoring friends.

In my own experience, will I ever forget the ecstatic report on my 1940 *Cabin in the Sky* from (You'll never guess it!)

George Jean Nathan, who went all-out to proclaim the show
the best musical of the year, and "Taking a Chance on Love"
the best song? Smugly, I said to myself, "Boy, with George
Jean in my corner I can do no wrong!" No wrong, eh? Upon
enlisting in the Coast Guard shortly after Pearl Harbor, I was
hired to musicalize an opus called *Jackpot*, by Vinton Freedley
—a show employing the services of the scintillating Nanette
Fabray, among others. Being in basic training, technically
speaking, I could not pay too much attention either to writing
the score or rehearsing it, and was not even permitted by my
commanding officer to attend the opening out of town. I then
started pulling strings, and was told by the ever-amiable
Vinton: "Don't worry about a thing, my boy, the show is a
smash and a sell-out. I don't have a seat to give you, and if
you want to see it in Washington you'll have to share the piano
stool with the orchestra pit pianist"—which is exactly what
I did.

The lyrics were by Howard Dietz, and the "word around
town" was anything but a four-letter one. Proud as a peacock
in achieving a hit with practically no effort, I invited three of
the most elegant first-nighters to the opening, and made quite
a splash with my entrance, attired in the full dress of a petty
officer, third class. After the initial ten minutes, *Jackpot*, which
had seemed to strike the provincial public's fancy, fell apart
with such astonishing rapidity that I was suddenly seized with
a violent desire to be shipped overseas posthaste. George Jean
Nathan's article, which occupied his entire Saturday column
in the New York *Journal*, was to the effect that Vinton, Howard
and I had got stinking drunk at the Harvard Club (of all
places!) and decided to put together a musical show—for want
of something better to do, obviously. According to Nathan,
none of the three knew what the other two were doing, with
the result that the sets and costumes were spoken for at Kane's
warehouse *before* the opening. There was not one grain of

truth in any of this; but since the other critics hadn't liked the show either, we decided to let the thing go, and better luck next time.

I notice that the new crop of critics, full- or part-time, are more deferential these days, so that when Tennessee Williams lays an egg, the egg is minutely examined only because it is Tennessee's. Richard Rodgers has been called everything from "magician" to "sorcerer" to "emperor," and goodness knows what else, so that if he writes a set of lyrics for his own show they must be carefully inspected, if not necessarily respected.

I, for one, think that both the *No Strings* and the newest *State Fair* lyrical investitures by the erstwhile melody man are not lacking in occasional sparkle—*State Fair* especially so; but when Douglas Watt of the *New Yorker* devotes three columns to Rodgers's lyrical efforts and winds up by saying very little that's tangible, either for or against, I cannot help but fret, and also wonder whether Mr. Watt really listens to lyrics or merely lets them slide by effortlessly. The score of *No Strings* contains the following lines: "A lady's life must be dreary/ Without a lady to call dearie," which appear and reappear in a song entitled "How Sad to be a Woman" and which made me violently uncomfortable. I'm still not old enough to recall the days when the typical Victorian male, as depicted by George Moore or Arnold Bennett, addressed females as "dearie" *only* if they were members of the *demimonde.**

I suspect that Mr. Watt is even younger than I, because he displays sweet wonderment at a song entitled "The Sweetest Sounds," somehow gypsyish in flavor, but which, to Mr. Watt, is "a dreamy thing with a melody that slips back and forth between major and minor and that is not quite like any other

---

* In another lyric ("Nobody Told Me"), Mr. Rodgers wistfully inquires: 'Should they have told me/ Love was made of hunger/ Crimson, surrounded by blue?" If "they" did, I wouldn't have believed him. ("Nobody Told Me" © 1962 by Richard Rodgers. Williamson Music, Inc., owner of publication and allied rights.)

of Rodgers's that I can bring to mind." May I be of assistance, Mr. Watt? Mr. Rodgers did the very same thing with more telling effect in his justly immortal "My Funny Valentine" many, many years ago—a song that starts in a minor key and ends up in parallel major. Other distinguished and well-worn samples of the same bittersweet procedure would be "By Myself," by Arthur Schwartz and Howard Dietz, "It's All Right With Me," by Cole Porter, and, of course, the daddy of them all—Emmerich Kalman's title song from *Die Bajadere*, which drove Russian teen-agers plumb crazy in the golden days preceding the 1917 October Revolution and which went something like this: "Oh, Bajadere, ta ta toom; ta ta tum." Any Russian who is still alive and has dreamy recollections of skating-rink flirtations will sing it for you at the drop of a hat.

I must acknowledge, however, that Mr. Watt did (and, I believe, still does) mention the *music* of a musical, which is a welcome and novel departure in itself.

VIII

The American Musical Here and Abroad

▸•••••••••••••••••••••••◂

Our government's global public relations have often been severely criticized both here and overseas. If the vague term "public relations" is understood to mean "cultural propaganda," there is, palpably, room for improvement, although there has been some laudable progress in that direction of late. That some of the efforts boomeranged is hardly this country's fault: taking our newly acquired culture to culture-saturated Europe and Asia is, in a sense, but another "carrying coals to New-castle" enterprise. If, on the other hand, our Madison Avenue-styled public-relations system were to continue extolling the American Way of Life, or, rather the American Way of Making Life Bearable, I would be all for curtailing such activities; our technical achievements no longer need selling. Trans-Atlantic or trans-Pacific neighbors may sniff at our culture, but they always admired our plumbing. The "physical" Americanization of the world outside has not been altogether of our doing—non-Americans are more than eager to Ameri-canize themselves, loath though they are to admit it. I'll wager that the French communists who swooned at the sight of Khrushchev did so while chewing capitalistic gum and revived themselves with swigs of warmongering Coca-Cola;

that "spontaneous" demonstrators in South America or Japan wore U.S.-made blue jeans and carried baseball bats while vociferously suggesting that "Yankee Go Home."

Our jazz and films do not need further selling either. The Cannes Festival, influential left-wing critics, and the New Wave boys may strive to disqualify our product, but entertainment-hungry masses do patronize the American "action" picture over the homemade variety two to one. Jazz commentators and plain cats are more numerous abroad than here; opinions may vary about the quality of "progressive jazz" and our *un*progressive cinema, but there exists a healthy respect for yet another U.S.A.-perfected semi-cultural product—Musical Comedy. From *No, No, Nanette* through *Show Boat, Oklahoma!* and *Guys and Dolls* to *My Fair Lady* and *West Side Story*, America climbs to the top with no indications of any impending change, unless . . . but we'll get to that later.

"A menace lies heavy over France, we are Americanized!" asserted Marcel Aymé, brilliant novelist (*The Wine of Paris*) and playwright (*Clérambard*), in a title-page editorial in *Les Arts*, the Paris weekly. This was in April, 1957—and it touched off an explosive "special" issue devoted exclusively to the burning question of Americanization. Why be concerned about the French and their understandable resentment of *Les Yanquis* in a chapter dealing with the American Musical, you may well ask? Simple. Adam de la Hale, a Frenchman who dwelt in the thirteenth century, was responsible for the first known musical comedy, *Le Jeu de Robin et Marion* (1275 or 1285). Sterling Mackinlay, the English author of books on Light Opera, asserts that it contained "26 songs, all of them delightful"; the song hit, too, was born in France, circa 1707. Light musical entertainment (in France) was confined to "theatrical booths"—a feature of the Fairs; the song was first played by the orchestra, after which "Friends of the Management" [?] were secretly scattered among the audience "to make the vocal running," Mackinlay reported. A practice not unknown here, and which might be revived with profit.

Skipping lightly over one Deshayes, who tried to soothe the Terror's victims in 1792 with his *Le Petit Orphée,* we come to the real inventor of Operetta—Florimond Hervé, another intrepid Frenchman. Born in 1825 near Arras, de la Hale's birthplace, he was nicknamed "The Crazy Composer"; he was not that crazy, having beaten Offenbach to the punch in the Operetta sweepstakes. In 1847, the celebrated actor Désiré asked Hervé (also an actor) to compose a musical "sketch" for his benefit; Désiré was small and fat, Hervé tall and thin. Understandably, a musico-farcial version of "Don Quixote and Sancho Panza" emerged. That, Paul Souday assures us, *was* the First Operetta.

The French, having thus laid claim to inventing the genre, can hardly be blamed for frowning on the present-day usurpation of it by the Americans. French operetta flourished to the end of the past century, amiably guided by Offenbach, his adroit rival Lecocq, and lesser men like Audran and Planquette. I cannot share the enthusiasm of some for Claude Terrasse, whose musicianship was shaky and whose humor was crude, but composers like André Messager and Reynaldo Hahn brought new distinction to the idiom. Hahn's *Ciboulette* (1923) is a shining masterpiece and I deplore our producers' ignorance of the work; *No, No, Nanette,* produced two years later, became an international favorite almost instantly, while the equally fresh *Ciboulette* remains a perennial success for home consumption alone.

The only serious rivals of the French in the operetta field were the Viennese, the English brand never having caught on in France. The evergreen *Beggar's Opera* did not begin to sprout on the French shore until Kurt Weill wrote his own version. Those Viennese invaders—the Strausses (two Johanns, Josef and Eduard), Oskar Straus, Lehár and Kalman—

proved to the world that the waltz could be sung as well as danced. The Carnival of 1826 marked the triumphant debut of Johann Strauss—to be eclipsed by his eldest son, of "Blue Danube" and "Wiener Blut" renown—who eventually caused the waltz to become the mainstay of Viennese Operetta, while the sturdy English (and, later, the frantic Americans) preferred the steadier 4/4. The capricious French paid obeisance to both schools, adding their own *galop* (Musard), which shortly graduated to the diabolical *cancan*—both dances in a fast and furious 2/4. Offenbach, German-born, practiced both the waltz and the *galop-cancan* with equal éclat.

What the French, the Viennese, and the English could not foresee was that they would soon make room for another competitor, pooh-poohed for his vulgarity and sundry provincial failings by Marryat, Mrs. Trollope, Dickens and, a bit more gently, by urbane Offenbach himself. With the passing of Offenbach and Lecocq, followed by only partial acceptance of Messager and Hahn, came the reign of luscious Lehár (from the *Merry Widow* of 1905 to the 1910 *Gypsy Love*) and his rivals, Emmerich Kalman, Oskar Straus, and Leo Fall; but, in the admission of Bernard Grun, Straus's biographer, "in 1914 the Viennese operetta, like the society which it mirrored, has achieved its climax: The twenty-four more years which it still had to live constituted only a more or less splendid fadeout." A blood transfusion was urgently needed, the fine "Wiener Blut" having run ominously thin by the time World War I exploded.

The English, even the more gifted ones like Ivan Caryll, Lionel Monckton, or Leslie Stuart, of *Florodora* fame, were past their prime and—pleasant writers all—failed to break any really fresh ground. No, the new blood was supplied by the Broadway boys. Not by florid, sweetly sentimental, Vienna-influenced Victor Herbert, not by young Jerome Kern, still swayed by the polite and placid muses of a Messager and a

Victor Jacobi, that unjustly neglected forerunner of "smart" musical comedy, beloved also by George Gershwin; the job of releasing the world from Viennese and French inhibitions fell to a Tin Pan Alley newcomer "who set the world's shoulders a-swaying with the syncopated jubilance of 'Alexander's Ragtime Band'" (Alexander Woollcott), Irving Berlin, né Israel Baline, by name. This was in 1911. Berlin, incidentally, was the second songwriter to invade the theater without bothering to study a composer's craft—George M. Cohan having been the first.

The first registered complaint about America's infiltration into the Paris musical-comedy market dates back to 1913, at which time Messager, Hahn, and Terrasse were still firmly entrenched in the Boulevards. The American ragtime influence outraged Mr. Adolphe Brisson, a widely read journalist (*Annales*, 1913), who declared that "the operetta of 1913 in France did not resemble the 1880 genre in the least. She is, let's admit it, less *French*, being permeated by unwelcome exoticism. There is an unmistakable odor of the music-hall about her; she has become multi-colored, steeped in absurdity, a bit on the vulgar side; *American* in her brusque, suddenly broken rhythms, Viennese in the undulation of her waltzes, English by virtue of her clowns and her girls."

Came World War I and, before long, Americans got into the act: the arm-pumping one- and two-steps, the sinuous tango gave way to the fox trot (referred to by the French as *un fox*), the blues (*un blue*)—musical equivalents of a transAtlantic dry martini (*un dry*). "The cakewalk wasn't sufficiently wanton, the tango was rather lewd—they've had their day. Now the fox trot is taking their place. It no longer has anything to do with choreography, alas! Nor even with the obscene pantomime of the tango. Fates preserve us from offending America, from laying the blame on France's allies, but, each one of us owes our efficient and loyal friends an indication to what risks they expose the respect and the tenderness that our hearts have vowed to the compatriots of Washington and Wilson. The indecency of the fox trot is such, that . . . it would be better to see one's wife take off her clothes in public and appear in Phryne's costume, rather than satisfy the appetites of the curious with her writhings." (Laurent Tailhade, *Les Reflets de Paris*, 1918) The Fitzgeraldian flapper then took over and, while she did not wear Phryne's costume, she displayed her knees and, on occasion, her thighs, when dancing—thanks to the cunningly rolled stockings. *No, No, Nanette* embodied these tantalizing American imports; it boasted an enchanting score ("Tea for Two" fooled no one; outside of the first two bars, no tea drinking went on in the bars that followed), an innocuously idiotic book, some slam-bang comedy and plenty of blondes, the kind preferred by gentlemen the world over. The invasion was on —and no Brissons or British Hannen Swaffers (who fumed impotently for thirty years about American crassness) could do a thing to stop or counteract it.

Rocked by the *Nanette* explosion, producers everywhere hastened to get on the American jazz-bandwagon. In England, whose Ungrand Opera high spots were the *Beggar's Opera* (1728) and the productions of Gilbert and Sullivan, a *marasmus,* caused by an overdose of Viennese operetta, had set in, when the lighthearted hussy *Nanette* set up shop at the Palace Theater.

Those were the days of *Vortex, The Green Hat,* Charlie Cochran-imported Spinelli and Delysia, Diaghilev's last gasp and, of course, the inimitable *Blackbirds*—another Cochran importation. *Nanette* was the final *coup de grâce*—or disgrace —if you believed Swaffer. Russians reigned at the ballet, the French in Cochran's revues, but when it came to your musical comedy and radio, America was in the driver's seat. "The shock did but swell the thrill," as Max Beerbohm said. English producers, alarmed by poor box-office receipts at such Mittel-Europa strongholds as Daly's, began importing American stars, songwriters, and dance directors—the "choreographer" being confined to the ballet in those days. The Gershwins and the Astaires soon had London at their feet; *Rose-Marie* and *The Desert Song*, canny conglomerates of Viennese schmaltz and Yankee streamlining, appealed to young and old alike; even British stalwarts like Jack Buchanan and the husband-and-wife team of Hulbert and Courtneidge commissioned musicals from promising New Yorkers named Rodgers and Hart (*Lido Lady*) and the relatively unknown Charig and Myers (*That's a Good Girl*). Out of self-protection, English tunesmiths like Vivian Ellis and Noel Gay hastily adopted the chic American style, and even Noel Coward, when not deploring the "Poor Little Rich Girl's" plight in her delectable cocktail-laden Hell, danced a painstakingly professional Charleston at Mayfair soirées.

The transition was not all that painless on the Paris front. The time seemed ripe: venerable Messager was still doing distinguished operetta work, but he was seventy-three when his subtly modernized *Passionément* clicked modestly (1926), while Hahn's production, Yvonne Printemps's vehicle *Mozart* excepted, went steadily downhill in public favor. Both composers tried their hand at *un fox;* in *Le Temps d'Aimer* (also 1926) Hahn and his lyricists conspired to make fun of that Yankee abomination—the cocktail. Suzette, played by the redoubtable Marie Dubas, instructs her eager friends in the poison's preparation thus: "One mixes the juice of an orange with a pimiento," *Chorus:* "A pimiento!" *Suzette:* "One adds, drop by drop, some *crème de menthe,* gin, a little *good* whisky," *Chorus:* "Astonishing!" *Armand* (the lover boy): "It is both refreshing and nourishing; to these, pray, add—mirabella, citronella, Anisette, Framboisette, a soupçon of Koka, a bit of Vodka—et *Voila!*" The title of the "fox" was

"This mixture is really exquisite." Messager, not to be out-done, penned a dignified "fox" for *Passionément*, the point of which, freely translated, was: "What a nice guy one gets to be after one drink." Others resisted the American invasion by having their jazz made in France, by way of a series of home-grown musicals: *La Haut, Ta Bouche* and *Pas sur la Bouche* (Maurice Yvain), *Trois Jeunes Filles Nues* (Raoul Moretti). The songsmiths shrewdly dressed up their *caf' conc'* ditties with trumpet and saxophone frills. They even flirted with *le Charleston*—although no one, to my knowledge, called it *"un Charlie."*

Further international tension thus averted, the French in-vented their own, peculiarly Gallic cocktail—the "grand spec-tacle" operetta, which combined the *Nanette* and *Rose-Marie* precision stunts with nude ballets and virile sex appeal, sup-plied by midinettes' idols — Tino Rossi, Mariano, Guètary. Gargantuan *olla podridas* with music, obsolescent elsewhere (although the English readily bought similar fare, dished out by Ivor Novello), still reign supreme in state-supported Paris theaters such as the Châtelet and the Gaîté Lyrique.

These sagacious moves could not altogether arrest the Yankee infiltration—with the years *le Jazz Hot* reached a boiling point, as did jitterbugging; demure French matrons and their existentialist daughters grimly applied their danc-ing zeal to *Le Swing*—a dance unknown to its would-be origi-nators. After World War II pinball machines, styled *Le Tilt*, clinked and clanged to the raucous rock 'n' roll of the juke boxes; Balanchine and Robbins triumphed at the Opéra and elsewhere, *Porgy and Bess* brought huzzas to the Théâtre des Champs Elysées, and, for the lower in the brow, there was the art of the strip tease, which conquered the French—ever the gallant *voyeurs.*

The afore-cited *Les Arts* quiz touched on every aspect of postwar France, so cruelly bedeviled by things American. It condemned the calamitous Coca-Cola, the tantalizing "tilt," the sterile swing; it deplored the fact that those Narcissuses of Imbecility, the departed G.I.'s, brushed their teeth four times a day; it lamented over the French girl, who got into the habit of saying: *"J'ai les blues ce soir."*

The system used by the instigators of the inquiry was to take every modern commodity, every art, science, and sport and to prove by "irrefutable documentation" that the American influence, outside of superficialities, was, happily, nonexistent. Among the sensational findings, headlined in the Paris sheet, were those pertaining to (1) *Painting:* The Americans buy paintings, but do not paint. (2) *The Dance:* "There is no American influence. It's the French ballet that influenced America. They don't respect beauty in the U.S.A.—what they have is hysteria in plastics" (Serge Lifar). "There is no American Ballet" (Jean Babilée). This in 1957; (3) *The Cinema:* "Before 1939 the American films exercised a beneficial influence; now we can do without them" (Autant-Lara). "Hollywood is the seat of Royalty, laid to waste by intermarriage. The American film has had no serious influence on important work, because such work thrives on contrast" (Jean Cocteau). (4) *The Theater Named Desire* (so ran the headline): "The record of the American theater in France is a record of failure. Paris believes that Broadway writing for the theater is vulgar, based as it is on prefabricated themes and childish psychology." (5) *American music:* "[It] does not exist," affirmed Bernard Gavoty, one of France's leading music critics. "Copland, Piston, Barber, Thomson and that musician whose only claim to genius lies in his name, which is Schumann [!]—all confess—with hundreds of other American musicians: 'It is *we* who are Europeanized.'" "There remains Gershwin," chime in the editors, "who is [!] successful—but he does not exercise any influence." Among the composers interviewed, André Jolivet claimed that the only influential American com-

poser may be Edgard Varèse . . . who happens to be French.
Olivier Messiaen, who did a bit of teaching at Tanglewood,
felt that America, musically speaking, is "more of a recep-
tacle."

We now come to the lively art under discussion here—the art
of the Musical Play—which was never considered worthy of
being classified as part of "serious" theatrical endeavor by the
French; it is, therefore, dumped, on the pages of *Les Arts*,
with the . . . music hall. "The American Music Hall [in other
words, vaudeville. V.D.] is a myth," proclaims the headline;
for once the statement is correct. American vaudeville died
a painful death a good many years ago; but neither vaudeville
nor burlesque was ever linked with the legitimate theater in
the States. Musical comedy, on the other hand, was always
so honored, both here and in England, where the dividing line
between the Music Hall and the Music Theater is clearly
drawn. Bruno Coquatrix, one of France's "big three" Music
Hall men, states: "The American influence is—zero; at Rio,
New York or Stockholm, I always heard French songs being
hummed." His confrère, P. L. Guèrin, the boss of the Paris
Lido, goes even further: "Every time I produce a new revue,
the French newspapermen, in their desire to make me happy,
say that it's as good as a Broadway show. Well, I am ready
to pay for their trip, so they could see how negligible these
famous Broadway shows really are."

Chauvinistic rodomantades of this type need not have occupied us here, were it not for their authorship: Cocteau,
Messiaen, Aymé are big names and carry weight. Guèrin's
foolish statement is interesting because it echoes fairly accurately his countrymen's views (although Guèrin's own Lido
is frequented largely by Americans). Since the advent of the
thirty-eight-year-old *Nanette* and *Rose-Marie*—they are constantly revived in France—no American musical has made any
sizable impact, financially speaking, on the French. *Annie Get*

Your Gun was, certainly, no triumph in Paris; the Arlen & Mercer *Blues Opera,* well enough received by the press, was a commercial disaster; *West Side Story,* greatly admired by the cognoscenti, didn't show great box-office strength.

It is not in the nature of the French to want to elevate what is to them frivolous escapist entertainment to the state of an honorable art form. Not for them the literate libretto, the "integrated" music and lyrics, stemming, as does the dance, from the story. The old formula, complete with romantic goo, a moon-faced comic and the spicing of pectoral splendor, works; the customers are happy—why experiment? *Irma La Douce* had a fresh look about it and, at least, a modicum of literacy, but the sound was far from revolutionary; *Le Patron,* put on some years ago by Roland Petit, was, from available reports, a try for a French *Guys and Dolls.* The critics slaughtered it, and the adventurous Petit lost his savings and returned to ballet. There remains *La Plume de Ma Tante,* a brilliant piece of nonsense; similar nonsense was known as a Crazy Show in London, as *Hellzapoppin'* in New York.

III

In pre-Hitler days, Germans and Austrians made several heavy-handed attempts to lift Old Lady Operetta's face by jazzing it up. Kalman's 1928 *Duchess of Chicago* will serve as a sample: in it, King Pankraz XXVII of Slavoria is confronted with the "*Milliardärstochter*" from America's "Young Lady Club" (sic). The adorable moneybags answered to the names of Daisy Vanderbilt, Dolly Astor, Maud Carnegie, Edith Rockefeller, and so on. An elephantine "Charleston" opens the show, wherein the chorus submits: "*Charleston, du bist der clou, es schlagt das herz den takt dazu!*" Next come the *Rakoczymarsch Blues* and a mysterious *Beethoven Foxtrot von Nussbaum,* which the renegade crown prince, Sandor Boris, finds "*Ausgezeichnet.*" The chorus, duly patriotic, reaffirms its faith in "Wiener Music," but to no avail. Mary Lloyd, the heroine, is ushered in and thanks the "Ladies and Gentlemans" for the wonderful reception (eight bars of our national anthem plus eight bars of "Yankee Doodle"), then plunges into "Ladies aus Amerika," a surefire *Schlager.* In Act II another colossal *Schlager* appears, titled *"Ein Kleiner Slow-fox mit Mary,"* wherein "der Husband" is made to rhyme with *"Yazzband."*

There were others who profited from their lessons in Tin Pan Alley Americana; Krenek, of whom we already spoke, had a flash-in-the-pan hit with the supposedly jazzy *Jonny Spielt Auf* (1927). The weird and wonderful Kurt Weill, Dessau-born, starting out as an Alban Berg and Busoni pupil, wrote dry and dissonant stuff when a young man. Came the un-cannily powerful *Threepenny Opera* (1928) and Weill found himself—while the world found itself yelling for more. He never returned to the grim tenets of atonality: *Mahagonny,* his next, proved less potent—because less straightforward—but the touching *Der Jasager* (1930) was another minor mir-acle. After a few intermittently successful years in Paris (*Marie Galante, The Seven Deadly Sins*), Weill settled in the United States to embark on a richly productive career in our musical theater.

Touching but briefly on Spain, where a local brand of op-eretta named *Zarzuela* flourished in the nineteenth century, and on Italy, the home of Opera-Buffa, now partial to folksy revues in the Neapolitan manner, we come to mighty Russia.

Gaiety was never Russia's strong point: Its popular songs were—and are—predominantly in a minor key, often derived from the catchpenny jeremiads of *ersatz* Gypsies. Imported operetta was extremely popular with the bourgeoisie and the Czarist upper classes; upper-class communists replaced *The Merry Widow* with the unmerry Kolhoz, the *Gypsy Baron* with the Downfall of Dastardly Baron Wrangel, the Geisha with a Komsomol girl-athlete and *The Chimes of Normandy* with "The Chimes of Kremlin." The only pre-revolutionary native musical that attained popularity was a moronic pastiche entitled *On the Waves of Passion,* its airs pilfered by one Valentinov from *Aida, Traviata, Faust,* etc., said airs equipped with crudely salacious lyrics, in no way suited to the music, by then in public domain. Lehár, Offenbach, and Valentinov were succeeded by the fashioners of "patriotic" Soviet operetta; the less said about its nondescript composers, the better. A strutting march (the late, much decorated Dunaievsky was a specialist on those) in praise of Stalin, or the always safe Lenin, was an officially imposed feature. I have yet to hear a Serenade to Khrushchev, but I suspect that his name is not euphonious enough for such an undertaking. Earlier Russian "jazz," frowned upon but popular, has no bearing on that sorely abused term; if you haven't listened to Shostakovich's version of "Tea for Two," do try to dig up a record. It has to be heard to be believed. Of American imports, *My Fair Lady* appears to have been an unqualified success, *Porgy and Bess* (not a musical comedy, but still Gershwin at his melodious best) a qualified one.

James Agate, who could ramble on for pages on his favorite German classics, had, unlike the younger Russians, no ear for American light music. He panned *Show Boat* and managed to review that superb musical (produced in London in 1928) without once mentioning Jerome Kern. He welcomed the absence of "jazz" in a "purely English" musical comedy (*Merely Molly,* an abject flop), one of whose two composers was the purely American Joe Meyer. Agate made short work of a lyricist, a Mr. Lorenz Hart, who committed his leading lady to such English as "Here in my arms it's adora*bull,* it's deplora*bull,* etc.," the melodic accent falling on the last syllable. Granting that Gershwin's *Oh, Kay!* was well orchestrated ("One saw, and occasionally heard, a harp"), Agate stated that the score was "largely made up of two tunes." *Oh, Kay?* He must have been thinking of *Nanette,* which established the custom of plugging two "big" songs throughout the evening. That is precisely what Gershwin avoided. He saw no reason why an entire score should be built around two strains, repeated *ad nauseam,* and took good care to make every number stand on its own feet—which it did, by George.

Increasingly irritated by American innovations in the musical-comedy field and healthier profits at the Drury Lane when U.S. imports hold the stage, the English critics refuse to give in. The shows get panned, which does not affect the box office—wish it were so in the States. One Gervase Hughes, M.A., B. Mus. (Oxon.), published a volume entitled *Composers of Operetta* (1962), and what a volume! Of 255 pages of text, *two* are devoted to contemporary Americans; Vincent Youmans, De Sylva, Brown and Henderson, Cole Porter (whose *Kiss Me, Kate* is the best *modern* operetta, in my book), Schwartz and Dietz, Adler and Ross, Harold Arlen, Burton Lane, E.Y. Harburg, etc., etc., are omitted—their names being absent even from the general index. The style is arch and airy, some of the dissertations on the music examined show a modicum of erudition, as befits an M.A., B. Mus. (Oxon.)—but consider these pearls: *On Jerome Kern*—"He admitted a few stylistic incongruities like 'Only Make Believe' "; "One may tire quickly of 'Old Man River' . . . but not so soon of such invigorating expositions as 'Niggers All Work on de Mississippi' (which, as the whole world knows, is part of "Old Man River's" verse). "One is sorry to have to debit Kern with that last desperate resort of the dismal crooner—'Smoke Gets in Your Eyes.' " That "last desperate resort" saved the life of *Roberta,* the show it graced. All Mr. Hughes has to say about Gershwin is that "everything that Kern did, Gershwin did just a little bit better." There is no mention of Lorenz Hart; but—"outstanding collaborators have been Oscar Hammerstein II, the librettist [I thought he also wrote some lyrics. V.D.], Richard

Rodgers, who provides the tunes, *and the less well publicized Albert Sirmay, who 'edits' them."* Dr. Sirmay, a many-sided but modest musician, and Rodgers, King Richard of Musical Broadway, must have had a fit when they read those lines.

IV

Back in the States, the song-and-dance format firmly established, two other genres also found public favor. These were the modernized Viennese-type operetta, mostly by Romberg and Friml—the old lady took a long time dying—and the intimate revue, borrowed from the English. The "book" show may have been on a steady decline in London (although the Anglo-Austrian nostalgia of Novello and Coward did pour its bittersweet elixir down eager throats for a spell), but Charlot's Revues and the *Co-Optimists* were models, on which our *Garrick Gaieties* and the three *Little Shows* were based. The Cochran revue, a glittering blend of opulence and sophistication, doubtless influenced Schwartz and Dietz corkers such as *The Band Wagon.*

The top stylists of the song-and-dance "book" musical, in addition to Gershwin and Youmans, were Cole Porter, Irving Berlin—more at home in Revue before turning out *Louisiana Purchase* (1940) and *Annie Get Your Gun* (1946)—and the prolific trio of De Sylva, Brown & Henderson. Rodgers and Kern had their own separate niches, dance rhythms never having been their forte; Berlin's ready, steady beat, Youmans's exuberant verve, Porter's cocky swagger or Gershwin's variegated metric invention did not figure in their musical vocabulary. They required charm, rather than animal high spirits, poetry rather than snappily rhymed slang, in their lyricists and librettists; thus *Dearest Enemy, Peggy Ann,* and *A Connecticut Yankee* were tailored to order for Rodgers & Hart, while Kern, who introduced cozy informality in the 1915-18 Princess Theater shows, was at his best in such idyllic entries as *Sally, Sweet Adeline,* later *The Cat and the Fiddle* and *Music in the*

Air. None of these were in the ribald and rowdy song-and-dance tradition; the tradition upheld by such electrifying humdingers as *Good News, Hold Everything,* and *Follow Through* by the irrepressible De Sylva, Brown & Henderson, or the more pungent *Tip-Toes, Funny Face,* and *Girl Crazy* by the brothers Gershwin.

The birth pains accompanying the emergence of a new musical were less acute in the thirties than they are in the sixties. Messrs. Schwab and Mandel, or Aarons & Freedley, would telephone George and Ira, or Dick and Larry, or Buddy, Lew and Ray or Cole and say: "Boys, we have Gaxton and Moore, or Ethel, or Bert, or Fred or Gertie, and we plan to go in rehearsal in September. Guy [Bolton], or Jack [McGowan] or Herb [Fields] has a swell idea for the book and Bobby [Connolly] or Georgie [Hale]—will do the dances. O.K.?" "O.K.!" the "boys" would chorus, except Porter, who would solo, being his own lyricist. The backers of the impending "smash" presented no problem; they had backed the previous smash and were ready to sign on the dotted line. Backers' auditions, the curse of the forties, with "token" casts often earning their living by "presenting" three or four hopeful entries a week, hoarse lyricists, perspiring composers, overly eager producers hawking their wares to bored "financiers," who came chiefly because the entertainment was free, were unknown then.

The song-and-dance show was, in reality, a vehicle for the star: all that the star required, other than the right salary and billing, was faultless musical tailoring. The tailors seldom disappointed the star or the producer, and the formula prospered; but even the best formulae and the most durable stars have a habit of fading, little by little. The two leading producers' teams were teams no longer, Astaire and the Gershwins left Broadway for Hollywood, Larry Hart, De Sylva, and Brown died—and the remaining stars were left queasy and tailorless. The opulent revues written around a Fanny Brice or a Beatrice Lillie were, too, dealt a mortal blow by Vincente Minnelli's removal to the West Coast.

The three Gershwin excursions into musico-political satire— *Strike Up the Band, Of Thee I Sing* and *Let 'Em Eat Cake*— the second of which was a near-masterpiece—were a courageous attempt to get away from the Broadway-canonized song-and-dance yoke. Modeled, technically speaking, on Gilbert and Sullivan, foreign to our national temperament (fun, *not wit*, is our idea of comedy) these shows did not start any recognizable trend here; *I'd Rather Be Right* was hardly among Rodgers & Hart's best efforts, and I would hesitate to place the "socially significant" revues by Rome, Blitzstein and Moross in this category.

It became evident that what our musical play needed was not politics but plain old "human interest." The characters depicted in the scatterbrained "song-and-dancers" of yore were not characters, but caricatures. You could fall out of your seat laughing at a Bobby Clark, but swallowing the syrupy "love interest" in the shape of a Bolton-Wodehouse L. I. couple (*Oh, Kay!*, recently revived, would prove my point) was as difficult as emoting over friend Mary, the Millionairess, who enslaved Pankraz of Slavoria. Rodgers and Hart came close to "integrating" a show with *Pal Joey* (1940): The O'Hara characters appeared almost uncomfortably realistic, and Vivienne Segal's immortal "Bewitched" was also *believable*, coming from the mouth of the sex-seeking hedonist she portrayed; *but*—and a big "but" it is—when Joey, an illiterate cad with charm, attempted to pick up his "mouse" by singing "I Could Write a Book," the illusion of realism vanished. Joey never did read a book and couldn't care less about writing one.

Integrated or not, *Joey* was thought by Louis Kronenberger to be "the most unhackneyed musical he had ever seen"; but Brooks Atkinson, who endorsed another attempt at "integration" in the same year—*Cabin in the Sky* by Lynn Root, the late John Latouche and this writer—was repelled by *Joey.* "Although it is expertly done, can you draw sweet water from a foul well?" he queried. Apparently you could—*Joey* was successfully revived in 1952 and did all right as a motion picture.

It would be unfair to disregard Kurt Weill's pioneer work in the realm of "adult" musical comedy. Max Reinhardt (as quoted by David Ewen) sought to make *The Eternal Road* a perfect fusion of speech and music, but it emerged as little more than a "Bible with Tangos," as one Broadway wag had it. *Johnny Johnson* (1936) was overladen with propaganda, but the 1938 *Knickerbocker Holiday* caused you to think and feel, not merely smirk and snap your fingers. Weill's contribution was significant: The songs did continue the dialogue and they fitted the play's characters. The unforgettable "September Song" was more than a fine piece of music: It intensified the human side of peg-legged Peter Stuyvesant. Great, and possibly greater, songs were written before by Kern and Gershwin and Rodgers and Youmans—but (Paul Robeson's "Ol' Man River" excepted) they lost something of their greatness when performed by pleasant musical-comedy folk, whose function was scarcely more than that assigned to beguiling marionettes.

V

By 1942, with Larry Hart ill and unable to work (he died a year later), Rodgers teamed with Hammerstein, and a collaboration that began with *Oklahoma!* brought about "the most profound change in forty years of musical comedy" (Cole Porter).

The late Olin Downes had this to say regarding the change: "*Oklahoma!* shows one of the ways to an integrated and indigenous form of American lyric theater." Of the ensuing long series, I think *The King and I* the team's all-time high; while admiring *Carousel's* music and lyrics unreservedly, I prefer to take my *Liliom* straight. These three entries, plus *South Pacific, Flower Drum Song,* and *Sound of Music,* make up the powerful sextet of R. & H. triumphs. *Allegro, Me and Juliet* (both containing some good things), and *Pipe Dream* were the mistakes.

R. & H. were at the peak of their powers when Hammerstein died (1960) and a summing up may seem premature. The team is already eponymous insofar as the American musical scene is concerned, and certain deductions may be allowed. Let us give them full marks for teaching us that a musical play can be adult entertainment; yet they did not appear to be writing for the adults in the audience. The emphasis on "fun for the entire family" was becoming too strong for comfort; not a thing wrong with a children's spectacle, except that we are children no longer. Having become accustomed to doing without old operetta trappings, startlingly revived in *The Sound of Music,* are we being unreasonable when we expect adventurous, creative thinking, imaginative writing, the enchantments of the unpredictable? Yet, Hammerstein did pontify forever and ever on a point he made eminently clear in each of his and Mr. Rodgers's shows: Life is something wonderful, keep it gay, marriage-type love is bustin' out all over, so let's all become cockeyed optimists and whistle a happy tune.

Granted that it pays to be good, that the "finer things in life" are very fine indeed, that the advantages of marriage far outweigh the pitfalls, we cannot fall into the oh, so comfy Pollyanna trap sprung for us again and again. There is an X number of songs in *Carousel* devoted to the splendid state of matrimony; splendid though it certainly is, we suspect that there may be other things to sing about. I am not advocating setting *Sweet Smell of Success* or *Waiting for Godot* to music, but I did get a little bleary-eyed from seeing so many starry-eyed people on the stage. Even the bums in *Pipe Dream* seemed to be awful sweet guys and so nicely laundered, too; but Hammerstein was an astute and dedicated showman and his incurable faith in the intrinsic goodness of this world was as touching as it was rare. Fighting aberrations and deviations of every imaginable kind, that were fast becoming the modish mood of our theater, required steely courage; and Hammerstein's sticking to his ideals was worthy of the greatest respect. His recent death was a grievous and irreparable loss; heroically industrious in the last two years of his life, although stricken by a grave malady, Hammerstein must have left a rich lyrical heritage which should be brought to light and result in another "enchanted evening" or two.

Other sedulous students of the new musical techniques are Frank Loesser and Leonard Bernstein. The first-named, brilliant lyricist and intuitive musician with no scholastic training (This, as we shall soon see, became the alarming trademark of the New Wave scorers), debuted with *Where's Charley?* which had a long run but was shortish on quality, although the lyrics were neatly turned. Nothing in *Charley* presaged the really novel *Guys and Dolls* (1950), one of the most impressive achievements in the annals of our musical theater. A seething soundfest of New York streets, it contributed the ideal musical counterpart to the hard-boiled world of Damon Runyon; the crackling music intensifying the Manhattanese high-voltage lyrics with bull's-eye accuracy.

The restlessly ambitious Loesser then essayed a semi-operatic version of Sidney Howard's *They Knew What They Wanted*, which became *The Most Happy Fella*. In this overblown attempt at Italian-American *verismo*, the opera models were not Britten or Berg or, even, Menotti—but Puccini and Mascagni: An artless striving for *Grrrand* Opera effects in the *Tosca* or *Pagliacci* manner was perversely manifested. A huge orchestra was called upon to accentuate the simple tale of humble folk and, to add to the confusion, Tin Pan Alley type of "up tempo" numbers were added. The result was distinctly up-and-down tempo, although "Standin' on the Corner" and "Happy to Make Your Acquaintance" were fine songs that would have made their mark in another *Guys and Dolls*.

Loesser was an even less happy fella with *Greenwillow*, an excursion into the land of Barrie-and-Water. This sort of thing worked in Lerner and Loewe's *Brigadoon*, overly lachrymose, perhaps, but neatly put together; in *Greenwillow* the tortured music was a poor fit for the oddly disjointed book. Worst of all, the lyrics, always Loesser's strong point, lacked bite and were—in two instances—downright objectionable, without being funny: "Could've Been a Ring" and "What a Blessing." I don't know whether Loesser really tries, but he *is* a hugely successful businessman—and *How to Succeed in Business Without Really Trying* is a howling success. It would be difficult to single out any one number as a musical high spot, for they all fit in beautifully, all are right as rain: there are no interchangeable parts—every bar belongs exactly where the lyricist-composer placed it with such infallible showmanship that the play's intricate mechanics appear to be of childish simplicity. This is American musical theater at its best—and at its most theatrical; listening to the show album is rather like lapping up the sauce of a steak *au poivre*, and not touching the steak.

The omnific Leonard Bernstein is a four-way whopping winner; on Broadway he has three hits and a *flop d'estime* to his credit. From the moment *Fancy Free* intoxicated ballet audiences, it became evident that such dazzling, rhythmically ebullient music was destined for the musical stage. Bernstein took off with *On the Town*, wherein his fancy was even freer than in the gay dancing romp with the three swaggering sailors, one of which was the now eminent Jerome Robbins. The book and lyrics by the Comden-Green team, one of Broadway's busiest, helped their collaborator's brash, yet tender music at every turn. *Wonderful Town* (1953) was not nearly so wonderful as the other town outing, but it, too, had its moments. *Candide,* produced three years later, belongs with semi-operatic vehicles, in the Blitzstein *Regina* and the Latouche-Moross *Golden Apple* class; both were better shows than the Hellman-Wilbur-Bernstein "musical comedy," which was in no way comical and, though stuffed with every type of vocal and unvocal music from a gavotte to a tango, resulted in an only occasionally diverting potpourri.

The next year's *West Side Story* removed all doubts about Bernstein's place in the musical theater. *Story* and *Guys and Dolls* can be regarded as the awesome twin peaks of stage realism, expressed in fused song and dance. Bernstein's dance music of supercharged pathos, of desperate, last-resort abandon, permitted Jerome Robbins to depict choreographically his Romeo and Juliet of the slums as no lovers were ever depicted before in dance terms. The only thing missing was a hormone-packed ballad of the type Tchaikovsky wrote for *his Romeo and Juliet.* But then, Piotr Ilyich was a born tunesmith, which is the very thing Lenny is not; on the other hand, the Russian's (also his compatriot, Prokofiev's, in *his Romeo*) depiction of the warring Capulets and Montagues was not a patch on Bernstein's wildly rhythmical hysteria of their slum-dwelling counterparts. Young Stephen Sondheim's lyrics—"Gee, Officer Krupke," fully as good as Loesser at his best—were just right, too.

Other distinguished landmarks in the "adult musical" category were Burton Lane's and E. Y. Harburg's *Finian's Rainbow* (1947), replete with first-rate tunes and lyrics, and Cole Porter's best achievement away from the strictly commercial market—the delectable *Kiss Me, Kate* (1948); here, the deftly literate book by the Spewacks was adorned by Porter's wittiest lines and choicest lilts. The undeservedly overlooked *A Tree Grows in Brooklyn* (1951) contained Arthur Schwartz's best score for a "book" show, a well-fashioned libretto and a neat set of lyrics by Dorothy Fields.

In the last nine years of his life, Kurt Weill turned out score
after score, full of personal and imaginative music; only two
of them really rang the bell. These were *Lady in the Dark* (Ira
Gershwin-Moss Hart) and *One Touch of Venus* (Ogden Nash-
S. J. Perelman). One could hardly call the first-named (produced in 1941) a truly "integrated" show; Hart's book, evolving
around fashion and psychoanalysis, was a peg for a multi-
colored myriorama of dream sequences, the designer's sequins
and show-stopping "specialties" by Gertie Lawrence ("Saga
of Jenny") and Danny Kaye with his tongue-twisting Saga
of Russian Composers. The lines were light, the lyrics bright,
the music Weill at his best: lives there a soul that hasn't been
haunted by "My Ship"? The 1943 *One Touch of Venus* had a
longer run than *Lady in the Dark,* but some shows go down
in history as triumphs, others as also-rans, without any justification; *Venus* is unfairly regarded as an also-ran. True, it
wasn't everybody's meat: Perelman, hilarious between covers,
does not fare equally well in the theater—perhaps because his
brand of humor does not communicate itself readily across
the footlights. The same is true of Thurber; it also applies,
to some extent, to Nash, the first really *original* lyricist to succeed Larry Hart, with Loesser a close contender. Nash's
words are difficult to set to music: they lose something of their
spontaneity in the process. A line that makes you bellow
when read or recited elicits a raising of eyebrows and a
whispered: "Huh? What was *that* again?" when sung. It was
to Weill's credit that he, a foreigner, managed to overcome the
difficulty and never get in the way of the words; "Speak
Low," where the music predominates, is now an "evergreen"
(in the trade's parlance), while "That's Him" and "The
Trouble With Women Is Men" "worked" in the theater because the self-effacing music permitted the words to shine.
Venus was an elegant freak, a stylish harlequinade—and isolated *jeux d'esprit* of this sort do not make for wholesale
Broadway acceptance. Neither did *Street Scene* (1947); a

"Symphony of the City" (Rosamond Gilder) it may have been, but a *Guys and Dolls* it wasn't.

VI

To say that the influx of successful "adult" musicals sounded the knell of the song-and-dance tradition would be erroneous. The "song-and-dancers" are as American as a hot dog and will be with us, in one shape or another, as long as the musical theater stays alive. Why shouldn't they? An expertly made "song-and-dancer" is better entertainment by far than overly arty experiments, with or without a message. Musical comedy and significance — political and otherwise — are not readily miscible.

We must grant honorable mention to some better samples of the fun-for-fun's-sake musical, even at the risk of an occasional parachronism. The very early *Fine and Dandy* (1930) had dandy music by Kay Swift, also taste and quality seldom associated with a "song-and-dancer." Neither Miss Swift, nor the gifted Martin & Blane, whose *Best Foot Forward* was one of the joys of 1941, are often heard from nowadays. Why? Harold Rome, veteran purveyor of topical lyrics, seemed very much at home in revues like *Pins and Needles* (1937); here the "progressive" attitude was introduced with such skill that one swallowed it gladly. *Call Me Mister* (1946), an effective posy to the returning G.I., was better yet; the title song, along with "Sunday in the Park" from the earlier offering, are among Rome's better melodic finds. In the out-and-out song-and-dance tradition were such free-for-all festivals as Cahn & Styne's *High Button Shoes* (1947); the spotty, though gutsy *Gentlemen Prefer Blondes* (1949) by Jule Styne again, this time teamed with Leo Robin; the even less worthy, but equally remunerative *Follow the Girls* (1944), tunes by Phil Charig (of "Sunny Disposish" fame); and the two slick and spiffy George Abbott-directed "smashes"—*The Pajama Game*

(1954) and *Damn Yankees* (1955) with hot-as-a-pistol music and lyrics by the brand-new duo—Adler and Ross; the latter died before reaching the age of thirty.

Fine though these were, none could compare with *Nanette's* gun-toting daughter—Annie. In *Annie Get Your Gun* (1946), Irving Berlin again demonstrated his perfervid gift for melody and was ably seconded by his collaborators. The next Merman-Berlin showpiece, *Call Me Madam,* had less sparkle.

The fifties were responsible for the spectacular emergence of Lerner and Loewe and the one-man team of Meredith Willson. Frederick (Fritz) Loewe, Vienna-born, had a difficult start, as did his soon-to-be partner, Alan Jay Lerner, of New York and Harvard. Loewe first came a cropper with a doddering *Great Lady* (1938), a termagant in no way related to the fair female who made him rich twenty years later; matters didn't improve noticeably when he and Lerner met and joined forces on something called *What's Up?* It contained, however, an amusing "Ill-tempered Clavichord," and some of the theater folk in the audience pricked up their ears. *The Day Before Spring* (1945) had a certain pallid amiability, vaguely reminiscent of early Kern, and was almost, but not quite, a success. Their luck turned in 1947 with the rapturously reviewed *Brigadoon;* Lerner then collaborated with Weill on a lackluster *Love Life,* for which Weill wrote his poorest score. Back together again by 1951, Lerner and Loewe essayed an "adult" Western with *Paint Your Wagon,* which, in spite of a rewarding number or two ("They Call the Wind Maria"), failed to thrill the adult easterners. With so spotty a beginning, there was little to presage the great heights to which the two soared with *My Fair Lady* (1956), generally regarded as the best twentieth-century musical, with few, if any, dissenters.

There is little to be added to the lavish and well-merited

praise already heaped upon Lerner and Loewe's masterwork. Much was said about the authors' daring in tackling Shaw as musical source material: That, of course, is piffle—Oskar Straus did all right, too, by turning *Arms and the Man* into a disarming *Chocolate Soldier*. Nor was *Pygmalion* the loser by Lerner and Loewe's rejuvenating legerdemain—and were Shaw alive today, he (no mean musician himself) would certainly have succumbed to the ingenious direction, the skillful lyrics, and the deceptively simple, always smartly turned music.

Meredith Willson's achievement is on another level entirely —*The Music Man* could hardly be called distinguished *per se*, although it does boast the rare distinction of having been wrought by a true man of music. Willson learned his trade under men like Hadley and Wagenaar, played the flute with the New York Philharmonic and wrote symphonies as well as popular songs. He invaded the theater late in life by writing book, lyrics, and music for a show he had a tough time peddling. *Music Man* is a generous helping of extroverted Ameriicana, spanking-fresh wordage married to infectious melodies and deliberately lopsided rhythms like "Gary, Indiana" which would have delighted a George Gershwin.

It is difficult enough to live up to one's promise—in the theater, especially; living up to the fulfillment of such a promise is not given to many. Rodgers and Hammerstein managed to follow up *Oklahoma!* with a long series of box-office successes, but, generally speaking, a bad letdown after a solid click is the rule, rather than the exception. Consider the record of those responsible for the two biggest musical hits in recent years—*My Fair Lady* and *Music Man*. The followups—*Camelot* and *The Unsinkable Molly Brown*—are not, even remotely, in the same class.

Skipping the inevitable comparison with the toothsome delights of a *Fair Lady* and the equally fair *Gigi*, we can only wonder at the weakness of *Camelot's* tunes. By contrast with the rest of the score, even the moderately alluring "If Ever I Would Leave You" appears hummable at first; perish the thought—you won't find yourself humming it while battling your way to the exit. Another eyebrow-raiser is Loewe's stylistic insecurity, hard to understand in a man who displayed a fine feeling for stylization in earlier entries. Too many of the jauntier burthens of *Camelot* seem to spring from Emmerich Kalman, rather than Purcell or the Lutenists; with the ill-considered "Guinevere" chorus commentary on the heroine's woes, we get a wholly unwelcome whiff of a tired *chinoiserie* in the manner of a Hollywood "specialist," hired to tune up a lurid Shanghai melodrama. I suspect that Loewe tried for another "Mack the Knife"—if so, why the Oriental overtones? The striving for supersmartness in Lerner's lyrics is so relentless that they often unmake their point; an exception must be made for "C'est Moi" and "What Do Simple Folk Do?", both excellent in their special way.

The Unsinkable (Should it be unsingable?) *Molly Brown* suffered from a paradoxically uneven score by amiable and nimble Meredith Willson. Blessed as he was by a golden-voiced singer named Harve Presnell, why didn't Willson give the man something to sink his teeth—or, rather, his vocal chords—into? By that I don't mean sustained high notes, which are fine when deftly organized *lower* notes precede them; the greatest climaxes seem hollow without meaningful beginnings. The shape of Willson's ballads in *Molly* is patterned after Reginald de Koven, or (for *schmaltz* purposes) Charles Wakefield Cadman—not what I would call fresher founts of inspiration. The good cheer and good sass of square-dance type of romps is all there again and downright engaging it is—"Belly Up to the Bar, Boys" and "Are You Sure?" are full of meat—but, not even the most determined square dancing can make up for square songwriting.

Harold Arlen's 1944 *Bloomer Girl* with tangy Harburg lyrics

was his most rewarding Broadway exhibit; Arlen, at first
Gershwin-influenced, has a voice and a style all his own. The
producers and librettists seldom "do right" by this fascinating
musician. Jule Styne, with a long record of experience, may
be no Arlen when it comes to originality, but he is a consistently dependable melody man. The *Bells Are Ringing* tunes
were certainly superior to everything else in that production
and, in the excellent *Gypsy*, fully the equal of Styne's co-
workers' contributions.

Two top-notch lyricists made their bows in the late fifties—
the already noted Stephen Sondheim (two hits in two tries and
a third, for which he wrote the music as well) and razor-sharp-
witted Sheldon Harnick, who achieved hitdom (the Pulitzer
Prize-winning *Fiorello!*) after a long apprenticeship in night
clubs and off- and on-Broadway revues.

VII

So far, so good. What's wrong with the picture then? Isn't
our musical theater in the best possible shape? The libretti are
occasionally intelligent as well as entertaining; the sets good
enough to grace the walls of a National Gallery; civilized
humor is crowding out raw gags and half-baked blackouts; the
dancing is of so high a caliber that fanatical balletomanes who
wouldn't be caught dead outside the City Center now do
their slumming quite openly on Broadway. Haven't we forgotten something? Yes, we have; and that forgotten something
is . . . *Music*, which is gradually being relegated to the role
of a necessary but unimportant ornament. For we are entering
the Era of the Musicless Musical. Most show composers no
longer compose—they collaborate with three or four "specialists," whose names can be found on the program, if you
can read the small print. Show composing today is, actually,
a *communal* effort, the head man, who is listed under "Music
by . . ." getting the credit *and* the box-office royalties.

How did it all start? From Offenbach to Meredith Willson,

musical comedy was composed by skilled craftsmen with impressive academic records, men who could toss off a double
canon as easily as a song hit destined for an LP "single."
Messager and Hahn in France, England's Sullivan, the
Strausses, Straus, Lehár, and Kalman in Mittel-Europa, Weill
of Dessau and New York orchestrated their own music; Americans, De Koven, Herbert, and Kern were trained musicians,
while Gershwin was "in training" all his life. The run-of-the-
mill (1963) Broadway "composer" may barely be able to
struggle through a "lead sheet," yet will discourse eloquently
on his (?) next "score."

The process of composing such a "score" is, roughly, as
follows: The composer plays, or whistles, his song to a musical
secretary, who "takes it down," note by note. The secretary's
job is then handed to the publisher's Editor, entrusted with
making a full "piano copy"—in publishable form, to be used
by the cast and the production pianist. The producers have
already hired (1) the best available orchestrator, usually a
pretty good composer himself (the top man used to be Robert
Russell Bennett, an expert in both departments),* (2) a vocal
arranger and (3) a dance-music ditto, generally supplied by
the all-powerful choreographer (the mightiest of these get
billing equal to that of the star and their names in a "box" in
the ads—something never accorded a mere composer). What
the dance-music man supplies is the so-called "extensions" of
the original tune for ballet and specialty purposes, habitually
getting as far away from the theme as possible. Such work is
listed as "dance arangements" in the program! The vocal
arranger twists and turns the thirty-two-bar chorus at will,
adding his own "extensions" to obtain choral sound effects.

These competent men are paid "scale" or "over scale," as
per union rules, for creating music subsequently used in the

---

* An outstanding new trio of superlative orchestrators appeared in the
fifties—Irwin Kostal, Sid Ramin and the late Robert Ginzler.

play and credited to the man who "wrote" the songs. Thus, our tunesmith's ignorance is expertly camouflaged; all he is requested to do is whistle, hum, or pick out the tune with one finger—if the remaining nine are not up to it. The "experts" attend to the rest. There is but one catch: If the show flops, and the score gets panned, the "composer" *alone* gets the blame.

The communal effort described would be justified were the producer to engage a hit-writer from the "pop" field; the Brill Building habitués may not know what a cancrizans is, but they do bring home the bacon. Some producers may hire such people on occasion, and a strange thing happens: Our Brill Building boy begins to drop his aitches in the manner of Liza Doolittle and feels as though he'd just donned his first dinner jacket. That garment—alas!—proves more of a strait jacket when "legitimate" songwriting is attempted: Striving to master the "production type" of number, the man avoids "low" idioms, long his very own—such as country 'n' western or rock 'n' roll. What he produces is an oddly crossbred article, not "pop" enough, yet not "smart" enough either. Sleep soundly, Mr. Producer—the "experts" will smarten it up, and no one will know the difference.

John Mason Brown, ex-drama critic, fine writer, and raconteur, was once taken to task by me; this was before the war, in Harrisburg, Pennsylvania, safely away from the Broadway scene. "Mr. Brown," I asked brazenly, "why is it that, when covering a musical show, you devote ninety-nine per cent of your notice to the plot, the cast, the sets, and sum up the score in one brief line? What you are reviewing *is a musical,* after all." Brown smiled affably. "That's easy, Mr. Duke," said he, "I don't happen to like music."

I have a gnawing fear that our producers, critics, and ticket-buyers no longer care for music, either. Otherwise, how to explain the critical hosannas and the long runs accorded so many songless musicals? *Sounds* abound in these—nice, lush, piercing or brassy *frissons* galore; the "experts" always come through, and I admire them unreservedly. But—where are the tunes? A really good song, the kind I call "inevitable," the kind that obsesses and haunts you for months to come, is easy to recognize. Nothing can kill such a song; wretched performance, bad spotting, the reluctance of jockeys unknown to Runyon—the "disk" kind—to give it a "spin," may delay its progress, but it will "happen" some day and make the listener happy and the writer rich. On the other hand, you can dress up a "dog" in the fanciest togs, make him roar like a lion or yodel like a demented Tyrolean—and a "dog" he'll stay.

To get back to the new producers and a very old joke, they'll let you whistle the scenery, for all they care; their motto seems to be, "No song hits, no errors, long runs." Rodgers's excepted, the fare offered on Broadway these days is incomprehensibly devoid of big, fat, hummable tunes. It must be said in the producer's defense, that the numbers in his show are theatrically grateful and that they "come across"; the integrated musical needs the closest interweaving of the elements that go into its making, to click—and it's just possible that a really roof-raising song might knock the stuffing out of the fabric. "A ballad slows up a show," the producer will tell you. "Remember 'The Man I Love'? Well, it was kicked out of three of 'em."

Let's consider *Fiorello!, Bye Bye Birdie* and *Take Me Along*—two huge hits and a hitlet; also their aftermaths by the same writers. Their music was industrious, easy to take and "up tempo" enough to be tagged uptemporary. All three scores are well (in *Birdie's* case, magnificently) orchestrated. *Fiorello's!* lyrics shine like a new dime, but the two ballads—a "period" type of waltz and a dark-hued girl's lament, peculiarly harmonized—are not memorable. *Tenderloin,* Bock and Harnick's second entry, was hardly more melodious than *Fiorello!*, although "Artificial Flowers," a clever take-off on an old-fashioned tear-jerker, attained a measure of popularity. The songwriters, by continuing to imitate the voices of another era, seem to be in danger of losing their own. Hopefully, Bock's music—in two instances—indicated possibilities not manifest in *Fiorello!*: the somber and fanciful "My Gentle Young Johnny" and the innocently pretty "Tommy, Tommy," the sort of thing formerly turned out by *Little Show* contributors. Harnick's lyrics in *Tenderloin* lacked their habitual zest. *Bye Bye Birdie*, with book by one of Broadway's most promising talents, Michael Stewart, and flawlessly directed and choreographed by Gower Champion, had a gay set of songs that left you as soon as you left the theater. The last scene of the play with its sweet pastoral feeling, more than welcome after the scary noises made by the teen-age elves of the Elvis cult, provided Adams & Strouse, the songwriters, with a grand opportunity to create another "There's a Small Hotel." What they created was an (intentionally?) corny "Rosie" which is made to rhyme with "chose me." The same team then went to work on *All American*, which boasted at least one really charming song entitled (in 1962!) "Once Upon a Time"; another, not half so good, suggested that "If I Were You, I'd Marry Me," which idea has been around for some time, too. These were topped by a solo for Ray Bolger—"I'm Fascinating." Bobby Howes, the English comedian, sang Desmond Carter's "I'm Wonderful" with a smarter treatment of the same subject in *The Yellow Mask* (my first London show) in 1928. Why do the young rely on relics?

Bob Merrill, who embraced the theater after successfully exploring both flora and fauna in a series of "pops," was responsible for lyrics and music of *Take Me Along;* Merrill has a sure touch with lyrics, but his musical equipment (here and in the earlier *New Girl in Town*) is of the direst poverty. There was a song in the Jackie Gleason starrer, which was a reworking of "Three Blind Mice" ("We're Home") and another that was "Three Blind Mice" backwards, entitled "I Could Cry." So could I. When the curtain went up on *Carnival,* I was ready to eat my words—the note struck by Gower Champion, the director, was a happy one and the notes produced on Mr. Merrill's xylophone underlined the traveling-circus atmosphere with telling effect. That the effect was used far more tellingly in Henri Sauguet's poetic *Les Forains* (1946) —adored all over Europe, unappreciated here—to which the late Christian Bérard contributed his best theatrical work and Roland Petit his best choreography, didn't dampen my spirits one whit; the model was only a short ballet, after all, and building a musical play on it seemed a sound notion. The first four numbers provided some solid theatrical music, thanks (probably) to Philip Lang's sure hand with the orchestrations; then came the oh, so wide-eyed and whimsy-stuffed "Mira," and I found myself squirming uncomfortably. The show soon became self-consciously tricky, then increasingly treacly, then unashamedly trite—and, toward the middle of Act II, downright tiresome.

Carnival represents the triumph of matter over mind—the mind is well aware that "acrobatics" and "theatrics" do *not* rhyme, and that "Love Makes the World Go 'Round" emerged many years ago in the guise of a 4/4 "Dance, Ballerina"—but the *matter,* the stuff of which theatrical dreams are made, is there to spare—and, consequently, all is well at the box office. And who's to cavil with that?

It must be emphasized that Mr. Merrill possesses the knack for a stageworthy lyric to a very high degree. The spontaneous laughter that greeted some of his smartly timed sallies (*Timing* is everything in making a funny line come across, especially when sung) must be the envy of his wittier competitors; I sat through shows studded with brilliant lyrical sleight of hand, with nary a cackle from the audience. It is Merrill's musical inadequacy that betrays him and lets him down—with an unmusical thud. Just at the time when Michael Stewart's story (based on Helen Deutsch's "material," whatever that may mean—the lady received equal billing) begins gaining momentum, Mr. Merrill's resourcefulness deserts him utterly: the *last* four numbers in his score display lamentable bathos, when Pucciniesque pathos is clearly in order.

Even the usually dependable Arlen followed the trend, *Jamaica* and *Saratoga* having been unnotable, melodically. Ditto for Rome's *Fanny* and *Destry*, although the latter had no end of high spirits. Ditto for the tuneless *Redhead* by promising Albert Hague, who did better with *Plain and Fancy*, his first success.

As for prolific and musically well-rounded Jule Styne, in the recent *Do Re Mi*, jovial Jule does tackle a few "fa, sol, la, ti's," as well, but not nearly often enough. *Subways are For Sleeping*, which followed, did not sound as if it were composed by Styne. The tunes don't start promisingly and are developed in so ungainly a fashion as to make one wonder whether the composer's heart was in his job—his imagination clearly was not. Ungrateful skips and jumps abound, the melodies fail to flow; two "specialties"—"Shoo-In" and "A Strange Duet"—are the only bright spots in the whole pedestrian evening, unrelieved by the contributions of the chronically cute Comden and Green. Both Noel Coward (*Sail Away*) and Schwartz and Dietz (*Gay Life*) did better in the tune department and displayed a greater stylistic consistency than did Styne: Schwartz's "Magic Moment" was one luscious morsel of a love song, especially as served up by Barbara Cook, and Coward's "Something Strange" is a warmer ballad than most of his earlier efforts, which were often tinged with a rather gauche mawkishness. Both shows failed to register; they were just a bit too pat, too predictable. The songs rolled on, rolled off; the proceedings were never stopped by excessive applause —they jes' kept rollin'—but not for long.

The sleeper of the year, 1962, was, to my profound amaze-
ment, the unheralded and unappreciated A *Family Affair*. The
notices were anything but encouraging, and the usually reliable *Variety* thought the score "ordinary." In this one
musician's testimony, the music of *Family Affair* bristles with
delightful surprises, new departures in song construction, and
a sort of unrestrained lust for tonal adventure exceedingly
hard to come by these days. The venture was a failure—and
such is the Broadway order of things, that all the ingredients
of a show that fails to make the grade are blamed for the
"bomb" once the producers give up the struggle. Flops of the
past are a happy hunting ground for adventurous balladeers
(like Bobby Short) and sheet-music collectors; a flop's songs
often fool the overly hasty critics and become indestructible
standards many years after the show's demise. Do you recall
Rainbow, Great Day, and *Through the Years,* the three Vincent
Youmans turkeys? Of course not. How about "More Than
You Know," "Without a Song," "I Want a Man"? Sure thing.
Well, they were the turkeys' stuffing. Let's hope that "Harmony," "Anything for You," and "Revenge," by James Goldman, John Kander, and William Goldman, the *Family Affair*
team, and "Love Will Find Out a Way," "Agreeable," and
"The Heart Has Won the Game" (from *First Impressions* of
1959), another fiasco (by Robert Goldman, Glenn Paxton and
George Weiss), will be resurrected before long and prove as
many gold mines for the three Goldmans (unrelated) and their
collaborators. A healthy predilection for broad, flowing, rhythmically energetic show-music writing, so typical of the late
Vincent Youmans, characterizes the score of the otherwise
undistinguished, though remunerative *Milk and Honey*; young
Jerry Herman's job may not be strong on individuality, but
his ballads do sing and his brighter numbers show plenty of
muscle.

Off-Broadway musicals flourish these days; some graduate

to Broadway and make good there. *Once Upon a Mattress,* a sunny frolic with inventive lyrics by Marshall Barer and acceptable music by Richard Rodgers's gifted daughter, Mary, is intermittently lively. Rick Besoyan's *Little Mary Sunshine* is modest fun in *The Boy Friend* tradition.

The Fantasticks, an exercise in throat-catching whimsy, boasts the best love song (by Harvey Schmidt and Tom Jones) I've heard in years—the title of it, oh, Jockeys of the Disk, is "Soon It's Gonna Rain"—and it needs no payola to get a playola.

One swallow, however, does not a summer make, and the new style Musicless Musical is upon us. "Anyone may turn up with a hit song," says Ira Gershwin in *Lyrics on Several Occasions.* Lend an ear, Mr. Producer, and latch on to this elusive "anyone," who is not among those turning up lately.

The musicals fared especially badly in the disastrous 1962-63 New York season. Their quality was mediocre, on the whole, but some entries were unreservedly blessed by the critics, others by supposedly critic-proof box-office names on the marquee. Neither the names nor the notices helped. The readers, on scanning their papers at breakfast, would be astonished to read that such-and-such world-beater was about to beat it to the warehouse. One of these, which boasted a two-million advance sale and was to "make a million people happy" (as a drama reviewer, quoted in the ads by the management, prophesied) called a halt to the million's happiness with chilling abruptness.

Tickets for the choicest locations were to be had at the box office on the morning of the performance (an alarming state of affairs in itself), although the two musicals I inspected in the first week of June, 1963, were, presumably, of hit-standing. *Little Me,* pointless nonsense, not nearly hilarious enough, had Bob Fosse's inventive choreography and Cy Coleman's brash and brisk music on the credit side. Mr. Coleman, none too ably seconded by Carolyn Leigh, his lyricist, who tried mighty hard in achieving mighty little, shows—upon occasion—a lusty, Gershwinesque vitality ("I've Got Your Number," "Be a Performer") and a flair for solving cross-rhythm puzzles, another Gershwin trait. *She Loves Me* (with a Bock-Harnick score), beloved by the critics, is an all-round charmer, also the best musicless musical to date. Not that the fresh and witty Harnick sallies in rhyme are not properly underlined by musical sounds: the coupling is near perfect here—perfect, that is, insofar as lyric-projection is concerned. You do hear the lyrics in this one, the considerate Mr. Bock having taken inhuman pains to drain the musical juices out of his accompaniments, elegantly turned though they are. Barbara Cook could sing "chopsticks" in a minor key and make you choke with emotion; I choked a little on listening to her two "ballads" in *She Loves Me*, but whether emotion or annoyance (not at angelic Barbara!) were responsible, I wouldn't know. *She Loves Me* is the most insistently "integrated" musical play known—vocal intrusions are woven in and out of the spoken dialogue with rare and enviable smoothness. Ironically, the only song with an attractive melodic curve to it ("Ilona") is entrusted to the brilliantly nasty villain, Jack Cassidy.

Yes, I know that Irving Berlin can play only in the key of F sharp, yet manages to be one of ASCAP's top money-earners. So what? There is only one Berlin, which is probably just as well. Signing illiterate songwriters is about as logical as engaging nonsinging actors merely because Rex Harrison got away with it in *My Fair Lady*. The procedure is also wrought with danger for another reason—talented and thoroughly professional musical-comedy composers are beginning to throw their weight around in England, of all places! If we want to retain our supremacy in the field, let's bring music back to the musical.

IX

Opera and Ballet U. S. Style

┝•━•━•━•━•━•━•━•━•━•━•━•━•━•━•━•━•━•━•━┥

The height of cultural refinement to the average American is what he naïvely persists in calling Grand Opera; should said American speak with a strong southern accent, it will come out as *Grind* Opera. And that's precisely what it is; the same old grind. No sooner does a newly born Hicksville Opera Co. pitch its hopeful tents than the community is bedazzled by huge signs announcing *Carmen, Rigoletto, Lah Traviata, Lah Beau Aim,* and *Eye-ee-dah.* Nothing could be grander than the above quintet, nothing safer at the box office.

We all know that quite a few people are opera-thirsty in this land of ours, because even Hicksville-type ventures have been known to show a profit; whether they would continue to thrive away from the tried-and-true repertory, with the grind quintet and two or three additional favorites as a basis, is highly problematical. "In Europe every opera house operates by virtue of government or municipal subsidy, and always has since princes and dukes ceased to be the chief patrons of the arts," stated Cecil Smith (*Worlds of Music*). Our Presidents in the pre-Kennedy era were not opera-oriented and, since no government or state subsidy has been forthcoming thus far, U.S. opera houses are still at the mercy of private guarantors. "Instead of the fifty or so opera houses of Western Germany, or the forty-odd in Italy and Soviet Russia, America has only two or three repertory houses." (Ernst Bacon, in *Words on Music*). "The operas like San Francisco or St. Louis, splendid as their productions are, are as yet little more than temporary tent-platforms, so long as they supply a local orchestra and chorus only, and do not harbor under their roof a staff of their own conductors, stage directors, and principal singers." There is additional and promising opera activity in Chicago, Cincinnati, Dallas, Santa Fe, Philadelphia (irate city fathers are invited to write and help swell this list), but to the best of my knowledge none of them can be considered repertory opera houses with full season's schedules, salaried performers and employees.

With so unsatisfactory a state of affairs, is it any wonder that "the singer is in a bad way today . . . [with] virtually no profession to turn to, after his schooling?" (Bacon) I would not hesitate to emphasize that the vocal resources of this country are richer by far than those available anywhere else in the world. Every vocal teacher—and there are myriads of them all over the place—has a pupil or two, and some have a round dozen of them who, with proper training and the right opportunities, could become valued members of an opera repertory house. Since, with the exception of church work and some oratorio engagements (there is no steady public for this type of music here, as there is in England), a nonoperatic singer has virtually no chance of employment —where is he to turn? *Lieder* singing in the form of cozy recitals in smaller halls used to be an accepted, if limited, form of professional music-making; it is, in this country especially, a thing of the past. "The solo recital singer has nearly disappeared, being accepted, and then rarely, only by virtue of his operatic, or television fame," wrote Ernst Bacon. And so—since no concert chicken can emerge without an operatic egg—our singers flock to home-base incubators, where they get excellent professional training for an operatic career. That such a career is hardly more than a heady pipe dream bothers them not one whit at first; a young singer of promise becomes used to the fascinating paraphernalia of the theater, to the smell of grease paint, to backstage jitters and the coveted possibility of "stopping the show cold." All of these copies of the real article are present in the opera workshops in schools and colleges throughout the country. As long ago as 1952, *Opera News* listed over a hundred such workshops in thirty-four states; their number has increased considerably since.

This may well be "the most arresting indication of the interest the American public is beginning to take in opera," which was Cecil Smith's optimistic 1952 contention. Philip L. Miller, in his "Opera, the Story of an Immigrant" article in Paul Henry Lang-edited *One Hundred Years of Music in America* (1961), went even further. "With companies blossoming in many cities, notably Chicago, Dallas, Washington and Santa Fe," said he, "with opera long established as a part of the program at the Berkshire Festival, the Empire State Music Festival, and New York City's Stadium Concerts; with small 'off-Broadway' companies like the Amato Opera running continuously in New York and with opera workshops in many of our universities and conservatories, unprecedented opportunities are offered today for the native singer, without the necessity of going abroad to gain experience." I suspect that Mr. Miller is *not* speaking from experience, else he couldn't make so foolhardy a statement—a statement that can be disproved by the majority of our young aspirants to operatic honors. Said aspirants, having lulled themselves into a state of false confident security, brought about by their school successes and the enthusiasm of their fellow pupils and teachers, begin auditioning for managers and impresarios

—only to learn that no amount of talent and outstanding vocal equipment will serve to gain admission into a going operatic enterprise; a solid academic background or workshop training is of no practical use without what's known as "professional experience."

Admirable though our workshops are, there exists "a sometimes sorry confusion about the respective functions of music school, workshop, and professional company," Herbert Graf (who should know) stated in his *Opera for the People* (1951). "The schools, which ought to devote themselves to basic training in techniques and to inculcating the best standards of performance achieved by great practitioners of the art, are instead often busy experimenting with new works and production methods. Professional companies, which ought to be modernizing their productions and repertoires, are instead holding fast to the models of past ages. And workshops, which ought to be laboratories for analysis and experimentation, are instead trying to assume the functions of both the schools and the professional companies without performing either satisfactorily. We may hope that if we get enough community opera companies . . . this tangle will gradually sort itself out into some sort of ordered division of labors." These lines were written twelve years ago; I am not aware of any systematic "untangling," even gradual, of this ever-present problem. The young hopefuls of our opera, rightly impatient to get started in their chosen field while still in their twenties (in opera all hope is usually abandoned after the aspirant reaches the age of thirty), having mastered all aspects of their difficult profession, are faced with the necessity of finding employment; and, unable to get a paying job, forget their operatic ambitions or take the European plunge—the latter still being the only realistic solution. A young artist who manages to finance himself and get to

Europe "is bound to be pleasantly surprised at first at the esteem in which the artist is held in many circles abroad, and is equally shocked on returning home to discover that he is judged not by his art, but by the degree of success it has yielded him" (Ernst Bacon).

To illustrate this point, let us take the Music Academy of the West in Santa Barbara—a typically efficient and results-producing institution, dedicated to developing and nurturing young vocalists and instrumentalists of promise; the accent is on singers here, the Academy's leading spirit and chief magnet having been, since its inception, the incomparable Lotte Lehmann, now succeeded by universally admired Martial Singher. These two, having had long and distinguished careers as opera stars of the first order, do not train voices; they teach vocally well-equipped and intelligent young men and women the art of *using* their voices effectively, of using their faces and bodies competently and persuasively—in other words, they turn promising beginners into professionally acceptable performers. The results obtained have been little short of miraculous. The Academy's pupils, under the able guidance of Maurice Abravanel, musical director, give three performances of one opera, specially selected to suit their abilities, in the course of the Academy's Summer Session. The staging was attended to by Mme. Lehmann and, beginning with 1962 (Massenet's *Manon*), by Mr. Singher. The performances were, on almost all occasions, of an exceptionally high caliber; the casts usually included one or two "leads" of such sparkling quality that a great future was predicted for them by those in the know. With the exception of a hugely gifted actor-singer named Ron Holgate, a baritone who, after bringing the house down in Strauss's *Arabella* (1960), found employment on Broadway, not on the corner of Thirty-ninth Street, where the old Met is situated, but farther uptown—in *A Funny Thing Happened on the Way* *to the Forum,* at the Alvin*—nearly all of Mme. Lehmann's alumni had to repair to Europe to "break the ice." And break the ice they did, resoundingly: Grace Bumbry, the young Negro contralto, was the toast of the European continent after graduating from the Academy. Hailed as Carmen in Paris and as Venus (*in Tannhäuser*) in Bayreuth, she also gave several successful recitals.

Miss Bumbry was Lotte Lehmann's star student, the great prima donna having taught her all she knew—and she knew *everything*—about projecting her voice and personality on the opera stage. Grace Bumbry is now, I understand, under a long-term contract to one of our noisiest concert managers with a $50,000 yearly guarantee—and her "debut" New York recital, eagerly awaited, was a sellout. Miss Bumbry would have been forced to "paper" the hall, had she not had her European triumphs behind her. Other greatly gifted alumnae of the Santa Barbara Academy now pursuing their careers in Germany are: Jean Cook, Zurich's favorite soprano; Benita Valente, who holds forth in Freiburg, and Judith Beckman, employed at the Braunshweig Opera House. Among the male graduates, only Norman Mittleman "made" the Met, but he has singing engagements in Germany concurrently.

In the summer of 1962, my wife, Kay, née McCracken (herself a graduate of the Santa Barbara Academy and a classmate of the Misses Bumbry, Cook, and Valente), and I were invited to an Evening of Opera in the Rendezvous Room of the Beverly Hilton Hotel (in Beverly Hills) by Fred Hayman, the hotel's energetic managing director, who, with some spirited help from Johnny Green, was responsible for the venture. The Evening of Opera consisted of excerpts from standard operas (the grind quintet featured, of course—and why not?) admirably sung and partially acted by a round

---

* Wherein Stephen Sondheim, the author of both lyrics and music, proved as engaging and skillful a composer as he is a lyricist.

dozen of talented "hopefuls" with USC and UCLA academic records, mainly, but little "professional" experience. Their audience consisted of well-dressed couples and convivial groups, imbibing their favorite libations while soothed by the young people's beautifully trained voices; this was quite a change from the customary ballad-belters and raucous rock 'n' rollers or "sick" comedians with healthy bank accounts. Though the singing of solos, duets, trios, and quartets was of uniformly high quality, though the eager faces of the performers had the refreshingly healthy look of American collegians, I thought their gyrations between cabaret tables oddly pathetic. Natalie Limonick, a skilled pianist and coach with a long list of UCLA and Santa Barbara Academy credits, presided at the piano and guided her young operatic charges with tact and precision—but her introductory remarks combined references to the music about to be sung with invitations to merry drinking conviviality.

Lauritz Melchior, the veteran *"helden* tenor," was in our party and obviously shared my uneasiness, while applauding with genuine enthusiasm. During a short break, he was introduced by Miss Limonick, then asked her permission to deliver an "impromptu" speech, which was graciously granted. He praised the young singers' efforts but chastised those responsible for their plight—their fellow citizens. Mr. Melchior pointed out indignantly that, owing to the lack of opportunity at home, over six hundred Americans were working in German opera houses alone—thirteen of them employed at a small theater in Gelsenkirchen. He made a stirring appeal to the Opera Rendezvous patrons for a concerted drive to help their talented young further their careers at home—while deploring the fact that a proper home has been denied their talents. Mr. Melchior later intimated to me that he had been asked to head a music department of one of California's larger universities and had declined, stating that he would not "deceive young people of talent by training them for careers they will be unable to pursue in their native land." *

The Beverly Hilton experiment may be a good enough show window—as are, on a bigger scale, the operatic workshops at USC, UCLA, and other seats of learning. I attended first-rate productions of such fare as Janácek's *Jenufa*, Britten's *The Turning of the Screw*, several Menotti operas, as well as ably performed classics at both USC and UCLA, and can vouch for the astonishingly high standard of staging, singing, and orchestra playing, for which Jan Popper and Walter Ducloux, the music directors, were responsible. Similarly high standards are the rule in the East, the Middle West, and the South; lack of space prevents me from giving a full listing of schools noted for the excellence of their operatic work. Notwithstanding these pioneers' heroic and woefully ill-rewarded efforts, efforts that deserve the greatest encouragement and stepped-up help, Virgil Thomson dismissed them with this sneering tirade: "The college workshops are a last resort, full of a mighty good will and little else, with immature singing and amateur acting—sometimes, however, with quite a good orchestra." ("The Rocky Road of American Opera" in *Hi Fi/ Stereo Review*, February, 1962.)

I don't know whether the college opera workshop did right by our "finest musical intelligence," but where would our composers be without them—and the New York City Center? A new opera, lovingly prepared and properly cast by a college opera group, has its tryout in attractive surroundings, is listened to and watched by an eager, bright audience—and, if it clicks, becomes a strong candidate for the City Center's masterminds. Chief of them is the discerning and energetic

---

* Even the somewhat austere and unapproachable Rudolf Bing, general manager of the Metropolitan Opera, got into the act. Speaking as honored guest of the Concert Artists Guild on March 8, 1963, Mr. Bing expressed sorrow over the limited opportunities this country offered "[to] its richly endowed young artists." Any suggestions, Mr. Bing?

Julius Rudel, whose American operatic victories with music by Douglas Moore, Carlisle Floyd, Robert Ward, and several others we have already listed. As for our Number One Operatic Citadel—New York's Metropolitan Opera House—it did well by Berg's *Wozzeck* a few seasons back, but its record of Walter Damrosch's three operas, *The Scarlet Letter* (1896), *Cyrano de Bergerac* (1913), and *The Man Without a Country* (1937)—three abject failures; Parker's *Mona* (1912), already discussed, and two insignificant entries by Converse and Hadley, is pretty dismal. Howard Hanson's *Merry Mount* (1934) and Bernard Rogers's *The Warrior* (1947) didn't make the grade, either. "Many American operas have been condemned for not being good theater." Gilbert Chase wrote, "On the other hand, when a particularly effective dramatic work has been set to music, the complaint is sometimes made that the music is more or less superfluous. Something of the sort occurred with Louis Gruenberg's operatic version of Eugene O'Neill's drama *Emperor Jones* (produced at the Met in 1933) . . . As Olin Downes remarked, Gruenberg showed dramatic instinct and intuition for the theater, and it is this which makes his work a landmark among American operas produced at the Metropolitan." The *only* landmark among Metropolitan-presented Americans, we might add; for the initially successful Deems Taylor essays *The King's Henchman* (1927) and *Peter Ibbetson* (1931) displayed "neither originality nor any special aptitude for the theater" (Olin Downes), being "at times conventional and noisily effective." Nor did remarkably consistent Gian Carlo Menotti "deliver" when he came to grips with the Met's venerable mechanics: his *The Island God* (1942) failed there, as did his friend Samuel Barber's *Vanessa* (1956), for which Menotti wrote the stilted and pretentiously tepid libretto.

Menotti's other operatic ventures—almost without exception —were markedly successful with the audience and at the box office, and had a good, though not unanimously good, press. Menotti was praised for his theatrical deftness and criticized for "approximating the successful formulas developed by Verdi and Puccini" (Slonimsky in *Baker's*), without possessing these composers' melodic gift. These reservations did not detract in the slightest from Menotti's operatic prowess: from the 1937 *Amelia Goes to the Ball,* through *The Old Maid and the Thief, The Medium, The Telephone, The Consul* (1950 —perhaps Menotti's strongest achievement to date), the enchanting *Amahl and the Night Visitors* (1951), the only successful television-created opera extant, to the Pulitzer Prize-winning *The Saint of Bleecker Street* (1954), the still young composer exhibited an amazing and enviable consistency in striking the public fancy. Just as *Porgy and Bess's* success irritated Virgil Thomson and resulted in one of his nastiest articles (already quoted), so did Menotti's several hits rub our distinguished critic the wrong way. "The operas of Gian Carlo Menotti, through their propinquity to veristic, turn-of-the-century melodrama, bear a strong perfume of Leoncavallo and Mascagni. This smell of the past has not prevented their world-wide success, but it has tended to remove them from serious musical consideration." (V.T. in "The Rocky Road of American Opera.") More *musique de la pas tres bonne société,* eh, Virgil?

II

Next to our supremacy in the musical-comedy sphere, still fairly secure in spite of the inroads made by the English and just beginning to be felt, I would place America's all-important role in the field of ballet. I know that I will immediately be sat upon by the Russians, the English, and the French for such chauvinistic heresy—but, while all three nations give government support to choreographic, as well as other arts, it is in the U.S. that, bereft of such aid, the most gifted choreographers and dancers are to be found. There is a static, uniform "grandness" about a Bolshoi and a Maryinsky ballet show; a curiously stilted academicism pervades too many of the English Royal Ballet productions, even some of their more "radical" departures; while the French, who boast a really brilliant, though uneven, choreographer in the person of Roland Petit, and a "comer" named Marcel Bejart, have made and continue to make an infernal fuss over Serge Lifar, whose choreographic stature is great in France alone.

This book being about music, let us concentrate on the present role of the ballet composer in this country and elsewhere; thanks to the firmness of Serge Diaghilev's convictions, music—after being scarcely more than a balletically grateful accompaniment to the dancers' gyrations—became, and remained for a spell, the axis of every newly created ballet. Diaghilev had a perhaps paradoxical aversion to balletomanes: after music, sets and costumes came next in order of importance, then choreography, and lastly a good or at least an adequate performance by the dancers, who, to him, were choreographers' tools, no more. "A balletomane—I was one myself in the Maryinsky Theater days—has a fixation: a dancer's legs and feet. To him a ballet is a jewel box, with his idol—be it a he or a she—the jewel. They have no ears for the music, no eyes for the décor—they are nothing but fetishists," Diaghilev told me. "God help us if they ever become critics!" "Alas, most ballet critics today are balletomanes; one has only to read a typical account of a ballet première in a London or New York newspaper or magazine and see the music dismissed with 'poor' or 'brilliant,' the décor barely touched upon, the choreographer given plenty of space, but most of the space devoted to the interpreters. That was not so in my Diaghilev days because music critics (and sometimes composers), both in Paris and London, wrote ballet criticism. It is still possible to get a non-amateurish notice for one's ballet score—in Paris—but not in London or New York" (*Passport to Paris*). Although

Alain Vigot opened his article on dance criticism (in *La Musique et le Ballet*, Paris, 1953) with: "A dance critic must have a sharp eye and a fine ear," I fear that the domestic brand use their organs of hearing to catch ballet gossip instead of ballet music.

Among American ballet pioneers, both Catherine Littlefield, who died in 1951, and still active Ruth Page turned to native folklore and music willingly, Littlefield ballet repertoire having included such entries as *Barn Dance, Terminal, Cafe Society,* and *H.P.,* while Miss Page was responsible for *Frankie and Johnnie, The Bells,* and *Billy Sunday.* Even Adolph Bolm, former Diaghilev star, achieved some success with J. A. Carpenter's *Krazy Kat.* Made-in-America music was used extensively in Martha Graham's repertory, but, with the exception of Barber's *Medea* (originally *The Serpent Heart,* 1946, which became *Cave of the Heart* in 1947), all of it was created for the dance stage exclusively and had little significance as music *per se.*

It was with the advent of George Balanchine (1934) that the golden era of our ballet began in earnest. A sensitive musician himself (he plays the piano, composes nostalgic waltzes and tangos, and even conducts the orchestra occasionally), Balanchine has always been noted for his rare ability to fuse music and dance into a harmonious whole. "All those who followed the New York City Ballet presentation *saw* music danced," said Dinah Maggie in a *La Musique et le Ballet* article. "They could *see* not only the rhythm of the music, but also melodic line and contrapuntal architecture. They could almost, by stuffing their ears, *guess* to what music were certain ballets danced." "If he is deeply moved by his music, Balanchine visualizes amazing cross-currents and short-circuits of representational emotion," added Lincoln Kirstein in *Blast at Ballet* (1938). Due to Kirstein's enthusiasm and dogged efforts, Balanchine was brought to these shores and put in

charge of the School of American Ballet, and in December,
1934, of the American Ballet Company—the forerunner of
the New York City Ballet. "From the moment I saw *Les Ballets 1933* [in Paris], I knew *he should be used by Americans
in America,*" Kirstein further tells us.

One would think that American composers' talents would
have been used by the new all-American (in personnel) company; they were—but only intermittently so. Balanchine never
showed any real interest in the American composer; he choreographed *Alma Mater* in 1935, a John Held Jr. cartoon-like
spoof on the flappers-football-and-hip-flasks era, which, according to Kirstein, was the early American Ballet Company's
"most popular ballet." This had infectious music by Kay (*Fine
and Dandy*) Swift, "arranged" by Morton Gould; but Kirstein
had little to say about it in his *Blast*, admitting a "personal"
preference for *Transcendence* with music by Liszt, orchestrated by George Antheil, who also contributed a new score
for *Les Songes*, a carry-over from *Les Ballets 1933*. These
American entries were never revived, while the durable *Serenade* (Tchaikovsky) was, to Kirstein, "one of Balanchine's
most beautiful lyric works, in the uniquely human manner
that only he can realize." From 1935 until the late fifties,
Balanchine employed but a single American score (with the
exception of the 1947 *Divertimento* to music by the Russian-
American Alexis Haieff); and the American so honored—together with Kay Swift twenty-four years earlier—was another
Kay from the musical-comedy field—Hershy Kay—previously
known as a clever arranger. Kay composed the music for
Western Symphony, wherein Balanchine "deliberately invoked
the genre *Americana* in a formal ballet" (Olga Maynard, *The
American Ballet*, 1959). For accuracy's sake, I may add *Stars
and Stripes*, danced to Sousa's marches ("The debate has not
yet been settled as to whether Balanchine intends that as a
compliment to the United States or a joke on its natives, who
love a brass band and a parade"), and a complete fiasco

named *Bayou* to Virgil Thomson's strains (1952). There is a good reason for Balanchine's reluctance to commission ballet music from native Americans, other than those who employed a lighter vernacular The Russian choreographer had a long and distinguished career in the musical-comedy and film fields with such credits as Rodgers and Hart's *On Your Toes, I Married an Angel,* and *Babes in Arms,* as well as the 1936 *Ziegfeld Follies,* the *Goldwyn Follies* (film) ballet, and *Cabin in the Sky* by this writer. He had a liking for and a fresh approach to the "popular" idiom and felt more at home with musical-comedy recruits' dance music than with those higher in the brow who essayed the ballet genre. Above all, "Balanchine had always had an admiration for Stravinsky bordering on filial idolatry" (Kirstein), and staged eight Stravinsky ballets for the Kirstein-directed companies. (A ninth, *The Cage,* was entrusted to Jerome Robbins.) American works such as *Juke Box* (Alec Wilder), *Pastorela* (Paul Bowles), *Pocahontas* (Elliott Carter), *Filling Station* (Virgil Thomson), *Capricorn Concerto* (Barber), *Age of Anxiety* (Bernstein), and *The Seasons* (John Cage) were invariably turned over to native choreographers, men like Jerome Robbins, Eugene Loring, William Dollar, Lew Christensen, Todd Bolender, John Taras, and Merce Cunningham. While these artists acquitted themselves well, and some of them brilliantly, none of the works listed came anywhere near the dazzling classical displays and the earlier Stravinskyana, authored (or as Lifar would have it, "chore authored") by the master himself George Balanchine.

"All sorts of collaborations are open to American ballets of the future," wrote Lincoln Kirstein in *Blast at Ballet.* "These collaborations will not be a mere haphazard juxtaposition of a convenient composer, a fashionable designer with any given balletmaster." Good. Why is it then that the Kirstein-guided New York City Ballet is known chiefly, from the musical point of view, as a Stravinsky-Balanchine Russian duet? Why is it that the really significant American ballets were created by

other companies? Does Mr. Kirstein really imagine that his
splendid organization can be truly representative of the U.S.
simply because most of its dancers and some of the scenic
designers are native Americans—or because Stravinsky and
Balanchine are naturalized citizens? In Part III of his *Blast,*
Kirstein said that he "should welcome a working arrangement
with young English and American poets" for the purposes of
ballet scenarios; he discusses such poets at some length, but,
outside of a jejune statement on "our American [musical]
repertory being as distinguished as the Russian" (in 1938!),
and a vague proposal to "local sponsors" to commission American ballet scores, he didn't manifest any burning desire to
"buy American," musically speaking. When the New York
City Ballet made its debut in Paris, as a feature of the 1953
L'Oeuvre du XXe Siècle, financed by Americans, its programs
listed *seven* scores by foreigners (Ravel, Stravinsky, Richard
Strauss, Hindemith, and Prokofiev) to *one* composed by a
U.S. native—Aaron Copland. Stravinsky, of course, had three
entries, other Europeans but one apiece. That's like Diaghilev's
taking his Ballets Russes to Paris before World War I and
omitting Russian music. On September 26, 1962, *Variety*
reported: "NY City Ballet failed to sell out in Zurich owing
to the staggeringly high scale of $11.80 top . . . latest pricing
decision pushed popularity beyond its local tolerance point."
The outrageous sums charged for tickets were hard to understand "since the company is under support subsidy from the
U.S. State Department's Cultural Program." In truth, there
was precious little U.S. Culture in the company's overpriced
offerings: the "three different programs included 11 items (received with 'unanimous approval'), with music by Glazunov,
Tchaikovsky, Stravinsky, Ravel, Rieti, Bizet, Milhaud, Prokofiev, Anton Webern and Hershy Kay. . . . If business was below
expectations, the five-day Zurich stint must be termed an un-
questionable hit for the American arts in general." *American*

arts? The American Ballet Theater, which Olga Maynard claims "is our best known company internationally," may not have the City Ballet's uniform excellence and is constantly beset by financial difficulties, but it certainly earned a right to its patriotic title by featuring American fare, written, composed, and danced by natives.

At the beginning, the American element (in the Ballet Theater), was not much in evidence: Agnes de Mille's *Obeah* and Eugene Loring's *Great American Goof* were indifferently received. Then came the Freudian ballets of Antony Tudor (Maynard) and "some regretted the passing of Ballet Theater's vigorous American element from the company . . . A large part of the audience had hoped, and expected, that Ballet Theater would develop compositions to rank with other national ballets, in which the Classic Dance would join with American choreography, libretto, music, and design to form a native ballet like that in England." Obviously, Kirstein and Balanchine succeeded in training *their* audience not to expect any such thing and be content with the breathless anticipation of yet another Stravinsky-Balanchine masterpiece. Some of the ballets Jerome Robbins created for the New York City Ballet (*The Guests, Age of Anxiety, The Pied Piper*) employed American scores and depicted American neurasthenia, fears, quirks, and prejudices fascinatingly, but, as I have already said, such material was never the mainstay of the Kirstein-Balanchine company; nor were nostalgically tender and subtly amusing American keepsakes like Todd Bolender's *Souvenirs*, with charming Sam Barber music. The New York City Ballet conquered Russia, which is all to the good, but it was hardly an American victory. *Time* magazine told us (October 19, 1962) that "it remained for the third number on the program—the Balanchine-Stravinsky *Agon*—to electrify the audience" that attended the New York City Ballet's opening night in Moscow. That is in no way surprising; saturated with the red boots-

cum-samovar type of Stalin-and-Zhdanov-endorsed music for
over thirty years, the novelty-thirsty theatergoers would have
welcomed any non-Volga-Boatman-inspired sounds. But it's a
safe bet that a steady dodecaphonic diet would bring Khatchaturian back with a vengeance within a week.

Beginning with the 1944 *Fancy Free* (Bernstein-Robbins),
the American Ballet Theater really went American on a big
scale, without having to resort to Sousa marches. Catherine
Littlefield revised her *Barn Dance* for the company (1944),
Michael Kidd contributed *On Stage!* (1945) to Dello Joio's
music; then came the *Billy the Kid* (Loring) revival and Agnes
de Mille's regionally evocative works (following her apparently
immortal *Rodeo*) such as the 1948 *Fall River Legend* (Morton
Gould) and the 1952 *The Harvest According* (to a Virgil Thomson potpourri). The San Francisco Ballet, guided by Lew
Christensen (Balanchine-trained and influenced), did some
experimenting with "progressive jazz," using a John Lewis
score, but Christensen's best works are *Con Amore* (Rossini)
and grand spectacle classical displays such as *The Beauty
and the Beast* (Tchaikovsky); for more modern entries, Christensen has been known to engage Ernst Krenek and Sir Arthur
Bliss, who composed the nondescript *Lady of Shalott* (1958)
score, attributed by Olga Maynard to Sir (sic) Benjamin Britten, who has not been knighted to date.

I would like to end this short survey with the hope that the
New York City Ballet and other solvent organizations will see
fit to commission music from people like Walter Piston (whose
Incredible Flutist, a "standard," was a ballet suite, incidentally),
the ever-engaging and rhythmically infectious Leonard Bernstein, provocative Elliott Carter, who did not disdain the Ballet
in his salad days, and other gifted younger Americans—in order
to help emphasize that native music is essential to every dance
effort made in the United States; also to restore all good music
to its rightful place in the ballet world—the *first* place.

X

Euterpe Mechanized

╟─•─•─•─•─•─•─•─•─•─•─•─•─•─•─•─•─•─•─╢

With advancing years I've become subject to fits of romantic nostalgia and I am not ashamed to say that I rather welcome them—a sure sign of what polite folk are good enough to call middle-aged mellowness. I never did think that the universally regretted good old days were really all that good, but I do miss the company of musical simpletons—people who made music for their own amusement and solace and cared little about the quality or global significance of their innocent pastimes. Music-making at home in my early Russian years consisted of piano duet-playing (or two-piano-playing, if your parents owned an extra instrument): accompanying a cousin or an aunt who possessed a voice of sorts and was not above trotting out her meager repertoire of Glinka and Tchaikovsky; mastering the domra or the balalaika, neither of which had the slightest professional future; or (in a pinch) listening to the piercing, cackling tones emanating from a huge, shiny horn that looked exactly like the upper part of a tuba. The extra-large horn we owned reposed on a fancily carved soundbox that bore the likeness of a music-minded dog and the legend "His Master's Voice." The sounds produced by the bulky contraption could hardly be called masterful and they caused our own dogs to whine and even howl as though in acute pain. My par-

ents were, of course, impressed by the record labels' assurances
to the effect that Anselmi's, Battistini's, Titta Ruffo's and
Caruso's voices were exclusively and faithfully reproduced
thereon, which neither my brother nor myself could bring ourselves to believe. Turning off the gramophone and plunging
into a piano duet version of Mozart's G minor Symphony
brought immediate relief—you were back in your own funny
little world, after a scary trip to a mechanically reproduced
unfunny big one.

Practically no one wastes time on piano duets any more—and
I seriously doubt that music publishers would spend money on
"*quatre mains*" versions of the symphonic repertory today.
Every orchestral piece used to be issued in two versions in the
fairly recent past: the full orchestral score and the piano-duet
arrangement—some publishers even adding a two-piano version
for the richer and more ambitious customers. Who wants to
bother with such childish games in the nineteen-sixties when
"Heath offers a seventy-watt, transformerless, semiconductor
amplifier with bimetral circuit breakers replacing fuses and
the less-often-used controls behind a foldaway panel?" (Ivan
Berger in "Audio '63," *Saturday Review,* September 29, 1962).
And my feeling is that if a "semiconductor" is not good enough
for you, a few extra dollars may provide the other conducting
half, not merely amplified, but preamplified "with a virtually
flat response," which is Harman-Kardon's claim. These, according to Mr. Berger, are "the areas in which man retires to
replenish himself by home listening," such replenishment made
imperative by "apartment living and the duple demands of
stereo." Now, I have nothing against stereo and its duple demands, having but a single demand—not even a demand, but
actually a request; could I *please* make music once in a while,
instead of having it made for me at all times? After all, I do
own a house and am not a sucker for apartment living with
or without semiconductors. On careful consideration, I can see

that my request is unrealistic and, therefore, presumptuous: didn't Barbara Anne, the smart heroine of Al Hine's savagely amusing *Lord Love a Duck* (1961), revel in the realization that she owned "truly her own house and life, [that] she could put a Bach record on the hi-fi phonograph . . . and be wafted away to another world of perfect peace"? The trouble with me is, I suppose, that I don't wish to be "wafted away"—not yet, at any rate.

Indifferent though I am to mechanically *reproduced* music (although just as keen to get my own music recorded as the next man), I would rather have *that*, than the mechanically *produced* brand; there is always the realization that the music thus reproduced was originally performed by living humans— and that helps. Also, one cannot get away from it—it's all around you; the four better-established varieties being re- corded music (stereo or monaural), radio, television, and the films. The last three use music only intermittently, the radio depending almost entirely on the canned product in this coun- try. The NBC and CBS Symphonies are no more, the WOR (New York) station never used a full-size orchestra regularly and the so-called Symphony of the Air (Alfred Wallenstein conducting) is more of a trademark for an independent sym- phonic group than a radio stand-by. Some symphony concerts are broadcast, as are music festivals of the type sponsored by WNYC (another New York station)—grab bags of contem- porary music, by and large, without any great stress on quality of either material or performance. One could also mention the excellent WQXR Quartet and duo-pianists as well as the SFM (Society for Forgotten Music) broadcasts over KPFK-FM in Los Angeles; these had to be a mixture of recorded and live music, for economy reasons.

The recording companies continue turning out LP's of excel- lent quality, with an accent on proven favorites, re-recorded *ad nauseam*, for a valid reason: there is a steady market for the stuff. They also continue deleting fresher entries, the reason being equally valid; no market for the untested and the unfamiliar exists. Thus, with the change of management, nearly the entire MGM classical catalog was scrapped a few years ago to make room, I suppose, for potential best sellers. The "majors"—Columbia, for one—permit themselves relatively frequent excursions into dangerously unknown spheres, such as von Webern's complete works, anything signed by Stravinsky, and even Boulez-Stockhausen-Cage gasps and whimpers; but small companies, attempting to cash in on the unexplored, go bankrupt with maddening monotony. The two American music stalwarts, Composers Recordings, Inc., and the Louisville Orchestra, have to rely on a subscription plan and various endowments and sponsorships, such as BMI, ASCAP's rival and, presumably, a collecting agency.

Bob Rolontz in a piece titled "Record-Makers Search for Magic Classic Angle," in *Billboard* (August 11, 1962), stated that "classical sales are not increasing in proportion to the increase in LP sales. That is one concern. Another is over what is happening to catalog items, now that a goodly percentage of LP's are sold by racks and chains that handle only cream and current sellers. Still another is that the number of key classical dealers is smaller than it used to be . . . Victor, still the leader in classical sales in the U.S., had a poor Red Seal year in 1961. Capitol, unhappy with its classical sales, is reportedly going to put all of its classical artists on the Angel label starting in 1963." The only company whose "classical business has shown a dramatic upsurge this year" (1962) was Columbia. "Growing acceptance of many of Columbia's artists (Leonard Bernstein, Isaac Stern), and the steady sales of Eugene Ormandy and others have helped Columbia move its Masterworks sales upward." A combination of a proven Masterwork and the proven Ormandy sound is, indeed, unbeatable.

Although Hollywood film production is admittedly in the

doldrums, having been going downhill since 1953—some majors filming most of their product abroad, others, like 20th-Century Fox, even shutting up shop temporarily—California film-music mores have not undergone any radical change. The "big-wheel" composers are still handsomely paid for de luxe scores used in Class A epics, while the rank and file and the new aspirants, undeterred by scarcity of jobs, do the best they can picking up the crumbs—"independents," "low-budget quickies," "nudies," documentaries, travelogues and what have you. A curious feature of the Hollywood scene used to be the "musical packager"—a combination sound-track cutter, recording engineer, P.D. (public domain) sleuth, ever on the alert for "standard" material on which the copyright has expired, orchestra conductor, contractor, and general fixer-upper. Such men have been known to "turn out" a picture score without composing a single note of music; they were not composers in the first place, not even arrangers, but deft manipulators of musical leftovers, which they pieced together exactly like pieces in an elaborate jigsaw puzzle. When a composer was needed for an extra-fancy job requiring more than this kind of expert juggling, the packager has been known to approach an ambitious, but still "creditless" youngster and bluntly propose the "you compose, I collect" scheme, which was simplicity itself. There was nothing dishonest about it either; the "new boy" was offered a "separate card" on the screen, meaning that his name would appear in full—in large letters—for which coveted credit he would write the score (and often arrange it as well) for free. The "packager" having eliminated his rivals by offering to deliver the entire musical job for, say, $5,000, to the low-budget "independent" producer, had to pay the orchestra, the copyist and, occasionally, the orchestrator out of the $5,000, and would pocket the small balance, as well he should, having contributed his knowledge and experience to the "creation" of the score; his conducting fee, too, had to come out of the small total mutually agreed upon, no other money being available. The "real" composer got his name on the screen and a good chance of a repeat performance—paid for, this time. There have been cases—and I know of one especially striking one—where an ambitious newcomer actually (and gladly) *paid* a shoe-string producer for the privilege of supplying him with music —yards and yards of it. The producer happily accepted the cash; the composer just as happily applied himself to the task— the picture was an unexpectedly happy hit; everybody was supremely happy about the venture, the composer particularly so—his score having been universally admired, he collected $35,000 for his next job!

Such freakish success stories are not common; for the most part, film composers are employed for single specific scores by the studio or the producer. I have it on the authority of George Bassman, excellent musician and top-notch arranger (*Guys and Dolls*, the Decca Gershwin triple-decker), that a Hollywood composer gets up to $50,000 for a nonorchestrating job—a job, that is, where composing *alone* is involved. Alex North, one of the better men in this category, earned over $100,000 with his *Spartacus* assignment; his guarantee was $25,000, but he was paid an additional weekly stipend until the score was completed. On the whole, the established craftsman is still doing well and still supplying the kind of "big sound" music, which has been Hollywood's trademark since the advent of the "talkies." The producers of Hollywood extravaganzas have always been convinced that they had to be extravagant in order to achieve greatness; this meant big orchestras, big sound, big money. The two most unpopular words in Holly-wood are "gentleman" and "vulgarity"—the first is unpopular because there are so few gentlemen in the place (a business agent I had in my Warner Bros. days told me quite earnestly that I had better earn plenty of money *before* learning how to be a gentleman), the second because vulgarity has always been rampant in the film industry and the "big" boys don't like to be reminded of it. The rule is, to this day, the bigger the picture the bigger the orchestra, and the rule has been enforced by the musicians' union: the Class AA film producer has to employ a certain (large) number of men, whether he uses them or not; a slightly less grandiose spectacle can employ a slightly smaller orchestra, and so on. Naturally, when a full-size orchestral army is mobilized, the big boys are unwilling to use fewer men (if the composer and arranger show a preference for clarity and "clean lines," rather than wholesale padding) and let the additional musicians, helping to fill the prescribed quota, remain idle while being paid. I remember (this was back in 1938) how startled I was by the effect used by Shostakovich in an early Russian film to depict the frightening vastness of an Asian desert—*one* flute was employed to depict the loneliness and the utter helplessness of man in such a place. I also recall the astonishing sound obtained by the late Karol Rathaus (a Czech) in his pre-America days in the score he wrote for *Brothers Karamazov*, an earlier, Mittel-Europa version; Rathaus, I was told, used only seven men.

The contract for my first musical assignment securely pocketed, I approached the celebrated and omnipotent producer in his sanctum and glibly requested that I be permitted to orchestrate my own music, (the picture was an outsize music carnival of the "expenses be blowed" variety), using *nine* men only; it has always been my contention—and it hasn't changed, even with the advent of stereo—that the smaller the orchestra or chamber combination, the better it reproduces, mechanically speaking. The producer, not thinking much of my revolutionary notion, frowned and sent me to his musical director (a titan in his sphere, owing to a positively titanic salary he was getting) for a "conference." The conference resulted in a near catastrophe. "What's the big idea, little man?" the titan thundered. "Do you want me to lose the job, the arrangers go hungry, the union throw the boss out of business? Aren't you getting your weekly check? Do you realize that the Warners are using *seventy* men for *their* next musical? So why don't you go back to your room and compose some nice music, like a good little boy, and let me worry about orchestrations, eh?" My private revolution, unlike the bigger Russian one, was thus checked (in 1938!) and the sound has gotten bigger, if not better, ever since. The style in which most American film music is written went out of fashion elsewhere circa 1914, but what do movie moguls know about music fashions? They are accustomed to a thick brew consisting of one part Tchaikovsky, one part Wagner, one part early Richard Strauss, mix well and add a dash of Debussy or Ravel bitters and a few drops of Gershwin, if the picture uses a twentieth-century story. The orchestration is nearly always of the bombastic, also pre-World War I type, complete with "safe" padding, brass outbursts, harp glissandi for erotic innuendo, thunderous percussion for battle scenes and domestic misunderstandings, crisp xylophone clucking to depict urban hustle and bustle, and—of course—the molasses-laden violin solo, underlining heartfelt or soulful passages. The turgid musical mass (a mess, really) is held together with Wagnerian leitmotifs of doubtful origin, but always comfortingly reminiscent of the classics, whose purpose is to characterize musically the screenplay's characters, comedy relief, such as an unusually astute canine, or the menacing approach of "trouble." Then there is the all-important musical "peg" known as the theme song before War II, which then became the "title song"—and is really the very same thing, firmly in the "Woman Disputed, I Love You" category. Such a song is necessary for exploitation purposes and, equipped with appropriate lyrics— appropriate to the music, that is, seldom to the picture (*Separate Tables* was a typical example)—often becomes commercially successful outside of the screen and helps at the box office.

Television adopts this practice wholesale-fashion—no established series can survive (to the producers' way of thinking) without a bloodcurdling, sense-lifting or mind-numbing "theme" which creeps in, under, over and against the dialogue at short intervals, driving a music-conscious TV-set owner to ever-mounting despair. Thus, the Wagner leitmotif principle, mercifully dispensed with in the Opera House a half-century ago, has become the curse of music—or of what passes for music—in the film and television industries. It is considered good form —on the viewer-listener's part—to become exasperated by the inane commercials and the equally inane leitmotif-type jingles that appear and reappear, either between programs, or—which is infinitely worse——just at the point when the mystery or the Western is about to reach its impatiently awaited climax and provide the audience with a first-rate thrill; a gimmick has been invented for turning off such ill-timed intrusions. The pity of it is that the commercial leitmotifs are instantly replaced by equally irritating "themes," which "identify" a given program—the established "series" kind; the higher the program's rating, the more strident and obvious the leitmotif.

Not content with saturating the listener with the relentless drone of insistent musical mottoes, TV composers and arrangers found a ready market for their overworked material in the recording field. It all began with Henry Mancini's "progressive jazz" (and very good of its kind, too) recorded backgrounds for *Peter Gunn*, which catapulted into a Number One best seller and gave the rock 'n' roll-jostled industry the possibility of another moneymaking concept. "Now that the new television season has opened, the Nelson Riddle *Route 66 Theme* (Capitol) is a timely, sharp entry featuring the themes of a dozen top TV series in striking arrangements by Riddle," *Variety* reported (September 26, 1962). "From the cha-cha beat of 'The Alvin Show' theme to the pounding motif of 'The Untouchables,' these tunes all pack highly commercial impact.

Included are the identifying themes for such shows as 'Ben Casey,' 'Dr. Kildare,' 'Sam Benedict,' 'Naked City,' 'The Andy Griffith' and 'Steve Allen' stanzas, and 'Sing Along with Mitch,' the latter without voices." Singing along without voices was the only welcome item on the list.

I have no knowledge of musicians union regulations in France and Italy, but it would appear that any kind or amount of instruments is permitted to be used to suit the composer's and the picture's needs—from the lowly ocarina to the majestic sarrusophone. The sound of French and Italian film scores is seldom "big" in the Hollywood sense, but it is refreshingly clear and transparent—somewhat like a musical water color, which is a tremendous relief after the heavy oils of the domestic palette. Our Latin competitors are able to reproduce the smells and the squalor of the city street without resorting to a xylophone's clatter, but by confining the realistically non-fancy music to a guitar or an accordion. Love is not necessarily depicted by a Vaseline-oozing fiddle, and gangsters have been known to gang up on the audience without the hoary *Dragnet* type musical signature. Such modest but refreshing innovations leave the Hollywood dollaristocrats unmoved and unconvinced—they want their music deafening (twelve brass, count 'em, twelve) or aphrodisiacally cloying (get that string section—Stradivariuses only used); there is no in-between. The purveyors of our musical film fare can be divided into three categories: (a) the old masters such as Max Steiner, Al Newman, or the late Victor Young; (b) the conservatively modern conformists—Miklos Rosza, Franz Waxman, Ernest Gold, and Elmer Bernstein (who attracted deserved attention with a sparkling *Toccata for Trains* short subject, but has been "conforming" since); and (c) the individualists who are more adventurous and can be counted upon to turn out a really fresh score now and again—Bernard Herrmann, Alex North, David Raksin and, especially, the always interesting Leonard Rosenman. Then there is the spectacular Dimitri Tiomkin, who is in a class—or rather, Klass—by himself. His favorite procedure is to concoct a luscious ballad, aimed at Academy Oscar honors, and plug it to death through the entire length of the picture; the strain, which has often been familiar to the film patron in previous non-Tiomkin versions, becomes inescapable and is aimed straight at the patron's heart, while apocalyptic fanfares and percussive pyramids subdue the man's ears and actually make him long for the already memorized ballad's balm. I once sat through a moronic saga called *Friendly Persuasion*, wherein the Oscar-slanted leitmotif reappeared some two hundred times; such excessive friendliness finally persuaded me to beat a hasty retreat. I understand that Mr. Tiomkin is the highest-paid film composer hereabouts, that he constantly lectures on The Art of Film Music and that worshipping producers stand in line waiting for a chance to show their scripts to the Magnificent Maestro. What chance does poor old Boris Godunov have while the False Dimitri rules Hollywood's music?

And so it goes. Music, mechanically produced and reproduced, is all around us; it's attractively packaged, sensibly priced, and as far removed from everyday life as inhumanly possible. "If there is any form of musical reproduction that is able to touch the collective feelings of large groups of people, it can only be choral singing. I am convinced that such singing, on a scale completely unknown thus far, will be one of the important forms of musical life in the future" (Paul Hindemith in *A Composer's World*). I fervently hope so; as for the present, a family that prays together may stay together, but it does not sing together; how can it with all these handily packed sounds around it, shrieking, squeaking, cooing and booming from radios, phonographs, and television sets? When I lived in Westwood, California, both my television set and hi fi equipment were stolen by some enterprising college men who made a practice of raiding neighborhood fraternities and sororities for such articles. Two young policemen paid me a visit after I reported the theft to the local police station, and diligently looked for fingerprints. These they didn't find, naturally—but it was *I* who made a find; one of the two cops turned out to be an amateur songwriter. He came to see me the next day and asked timidly: "Say, would you give a listen to a song I wrote?" With that he whipped out a recorder and tootled a pretty good "pop" chorus. There was something touching about the young man's earnestness and modesty—and I took his song to a publisher; the lyrics weren't bad either. The weary publisher didn't buy. This was some six years ago— but, every once in a while, I'm seized with a sudden desire to turn off the phonograph, junk the radio, shut out the television and invite the humble Pan of the Police Force to dust off his artless old flute and regale me with a few poor, but *living* notes of music.

My stay in Florence (October, 1962) was marred by the especially deadly—because awkward and forced—American-style television commercials to which I was subjected in the hotel's "salon"; the flowing melodiousness of the Italian language sadistically mutilated in jazzy jingles glorifying American, as well as local, produce seemed an unforgivable sacrilege. "Le Tveest" and "Rockarolla" replaced the native *barcarolla* in Venice—just as the gondola is muscled out of the Venetian canals by the motorboat and the equally speedy *aliscafo*. The idol of the French teen-agers, a term that rapidly found its way into *le parler Parisien,* is a nineteen-year-old Frenchman who calls himself Johnny Halliday, and who sounds, acts, and looks like a blond Elvis Presley; like Presley, he is a millionaire. Gilbert Becaud, the French Sinatra, in addition to respectable vocal equipment and considerable charm, writes pleasantly atmospheric popular songs. He did an unusual and brave thing; skipping the musical-comedy idiom, still considered *peu de chose* in France, Becaud, with some conservatoire training behind him, plunged straight into opera and caused his *Opéra d'Aran* (pronounced "Aranne") to be produced in Paris, which event attracted the most chic audience in ten years. The reviewers were not "chic" at all—they lambasted the ambitious songster, his grammatically defective Leonca-vallo-Massenet vinaigrette, as well as the tedious librettists. Most of the critics confessed that they hoped for a French Gershwin (or, at least, a Menotti)—but our George wrote a dozen successful musicals before tackling *Porgy*; Becaud's small-scale talent should have been employed on an operetta or two, before attempting opera—but, as I have already said, the genre is in such disrepute in France these days that ambitious (and already rich) songsmiths couldn't be bothered.

XI

States, Not State, to the Rescue

Now there's an awkward title for a chapter intended as a constructive summing-up of what went on before and what we are saddled with now in our troubled music world. It is awkward because the word "state" has two meanings in our country; it may denote the federation as a whole (as in "State Department") or it may refer to any of the fifty states, united officially, but basically independent of one another. Thus, while "state support" means only one thing—government sponsorship and financial subsidy to the rest of the world—we Americans may construe the term as either a federal enterprise or as backing provided by a given state's administration.

A statement handed this writer by Al Manuti, then president of Local 802 of the Musicians Union, in 1955, was about as terse and direct as anything ever said on the subject, and is herewith reproduced in full: "Governments, like individuals, cannot live on bread alone. The growth of a country's culture and art is as important as the growth of its material resources. Both should receive the material encouragement and support they require to flourish. This principle is recognized by every large country in the world with one exception—the United States. Because of government neglect in this country, arts like music are confronted with such serious conditions that legitimate fears are widely expressed for their very survival. It is ironical to observe that our own government, through the Marshall Plan, has helped a number of countries to continue their long-standing policies of government aid for music, and at the same time has turned a deaf ear to the same arguments in favor of aid to music here. I feel that the time has come for a combined effort by all who have the interest of music in America at heart to secure the implementation of this policy of government aid for music here. Speaking for Local 802 of the American Federation of Musicians and its 30,000 members, we will be glad to join in the initiation of such an effort, and to participate in the development of practical proposals for its implementation."

This statement was made eight years ago—and our music did receive generous support from various foundations and private individuals, but very little of it came from Washington, while both the Wainwright (1955) and the Thompson (1956) bills, proposed in Congress and referred to the Committee on Education and Labor, followed the sad fate of other such tentatives. The wording of the Wainwright and other similar bills was intentionally overcareful; even so, Mr. Eisenhower said, "This is *not* the American way of doing things," to Mr. Petrillo when the latter began selling him the state-support gimmick. What, pray, *is* the American way, in our ex-President's opinion (in which he is certainly not alone), all attempts to inaugurate a state subsidy for the arts having been methodically railroaded in Congress? Dorothy Gillam Baker, college teacher of drama and former actress, has made an extensive study of the historical movement for a national theater—and allied arts—in America. "Any critic who says that government support of the arts is un-American and contrary to our national tradition is not aware of the facts," she wrote me. "Government responsibility for the arts was expressed in constitutions and other documents of the Colonies, prior to the Declaration of Independence. Before the close of the 18th century, government leaders of individual states recognized this responsibility and attempted to establish a government [supported] theater. It failed to pass only because of other more urgent needs of the youthful country. The movement for government support has been almost continuous since that time, parallel with our awareness of the inadequacy of our commercial theater by comparison with the state-supported artistic activity abroad."

Since the other Americas have achieved state support for their arts and theater, what's the matter with this one? Why should *our* American way be so different from theirs? Representative Thompson (in his statement in support of H.R. 4215 made on February 3, 1955), after mincing no words and effectively flaying the deplorable and shameful situation resulting from the federal government's failure to supply funds for cultural projects, admitted defeat; his efforts simmered down to "plans for the construction of a civic auditorium in the District of Columbia." "In 1958 Congress enacted a law providing for the creation of the National Cultural Center in Washington, D.C. The bill enjoyed bipartisan support and it passed with considerable majorities in both houses. But one of the reasons the proposal passed so handily was that under the bill, construction of the Center had to be funded *solely by voluntary private contributions*. [Italics mine. V.D.] ... To prove my point about the reasons for the success of the Cultural Center Bill, I need only point to a recent vote on a bill to create a Federal Advisory Council on the Arts. This bill involved money —it authorized expenditures of $100,000 annually ... [this] must have weighed heavily in the minds of many legislators. More than seventy-five of the 261 who had voted in *favor* of the Cultural Center voted *against* the Advisory Council." (Representative Frank Thompson, Jr., of New Jersey in "The Musical State of the Union," *Music Journal*, April, 1962.)

Turning Washington—or New York, for that matter—into one of the cultural centers of the world is a perfectly sound idea, but I don't see how that would be a convincing way of answering "foreign lies" about our inartistic inadequacy. V. Konen, in his interesting and not overly biased *Paths of American Music* (Moscow, 1961), states emphatically that "the Chicago Opera accepted a monetary subsidy from the *Italian* government, without which its further activities would have been unthinkable." This curious piece of intelligence was reprinted from a publication (magazine?) named "Sing Out" for 1959, Volume 8, 14th issue; the publication is unknown to me and the "fact," as reported, has not been checked—but stories of this sort are widely circulated abroad and gleefully commented upon. The United States will continue being the target of perhaps slanderous but, on the whole, justifiable attacks by Russia or any other country, so long as all arts and the theater remain unsupported by the state on a full-scale national basis. Erecting an auditorium in the capital of the United States, or a Lincoln Center (splendid though it may be), is hardly synonymous with a regular state subsidy; besides, it is a matter of plain fact—see the "Lincoln Center" September, 1962 issue of *Musical America*—that not the federal government, but business firms, industry-sponsored foundations, and private individuals picked up the tab. The budget for Lincoln Center, originally estimated at $142,000,000, is now $160,700,000, compared with the cost of constructing U.N. Headquarters, which was $67,000,000, or erecting the Golden Gate Bridge, which involved the expenditure of only $24,000,000. Among the Lincoln Center contributors are the American Tobacco Co., R. J. Reynolds, Philip Morris, Eastman Kodak, Con Edison, A. T. and T., General Motors, I.B.M., U.S. Steel, American Airlines, Borden Dairy Products, Steuben and Corning Glass, and countless other business "biggies." "One large grant, designated for the new Metropolitan Opera House, was received from a foreign government, that of the Federal Republic of Germany" (I hope they don't insist on a Karlheinz von Stockhausen opera as our token of gratitude). Note that the United States Government is not on the list of contributors.

"Even JFK finds D.C. Cultural Center a tough VIP sell at $1,000 a table," *Variety* front-paged on November 21, 1962. Although "The New Frontier is pulling out the stops in a last-ditch effort to bolster sagging ticket sales for Natural Cultural Center fund-raising dinner," Washington's big wheels remain unwashed, culturally speaking. Of "170 upper-echelon types" invited by the President, only 120 "showed." Increasingly uncomfortable was the intelligence concerning French Ambassador Hervé Alphand and his wife, who gave a party "to boost participation." One can be sure, however, that wise and conservative General de Gaulle will *not* commission Mr. Boulez to compose a musical bone-crusher for the grand opening.

"Unlike Gaul, musical America is divided into two parts: Manhattan Island and whatever remains. Yet through it all runs a unifying idea: Manhattan believes it possesses everything of consequence, and in this the provinces appear to concur" (Ernst Bacon, *Words on Music*). Well, it now possesses the Lincoln Center, but I seriously doubt that even that magnificent edifice is the equivalent of "everything of consequence." "Philharmonic Hall's Historic Preem: Glam, Traffic Jam and Copland Capers," trumpeted *Variety* on September 26, 1962. Using *Variety's* own terminology, the article was not a "rave," only a "yes—but" notice, the "but" heavily underscored. "Part of the trouble with Leonard Bernstein's inaugural program was that it was overcrowded, overproduced, too aware of television," *Variety* charged. The real trouble lay elsewhere: "Even the avant-garde and the musicologists conceded that the night's commissioned work, *Connotations for Orchestra* by Aaron Copland, was 'difficult' music." But for the majority of the audience it was totally evident that Copland represented an assault on their nervous systems which they resented. Seldom has this reviewer heard such outspoken comment in the lobbies after such dull response in the auditorium. It is strictly accurate to declare that an audience paying $100 a seat, and in a mood for self-congratulation and schmaltz, hated Copland's reminder of the ugly realities of industrialization, inflation and cold war—which his music seemed to be talking about. Consider, too, the incongruity of a concert that curtails Beethoven (Missa Solemnis) and Mahler (8th Symphony) but gives Copland full text." Nothing incongruous in that to the ever-zealous U-boys, who were, obviously, at work as "gray eminences" (éminences grises), and whose advice had to be heeded respectfully. "The festive mood, after intermission, and the departure of Jacqueline Kennedy, never recovered from the pummeling given it by Copland's cacophonous and percussive brutalities," Variety noted. Regardless of the cost of the tickets, the "historic opening" of a "great new music shrine" was a public, not a private function; just who was responsible for foisting on the public yet another tired exercise by yet another convert to doddering dodecaphony, we'll never learn. People are only too anxious to take credit for "hits"; they are equally anxious to disavow any association with a "bomb."

William Schuman, the able president of the Lincoln Center for the Performing Arts, and Leonard Bernstein redeemed themselves with laudable speed by presenting two worth-while American premières immediately following the Copland disaster. The two works were Samuel Barber's Piano Concerto and Mr. Schuman's own Eighth Symphony—both favorably and, as an antidote to Copland, gratefully received by the audience and the press. I have no doubt of the bright future of Lincoln Center, or of such smaller centers as the beautifully designed Santa Monica Auditorium or the Winston-Salem Community Center, sponsored by the Community Arts Councils, Inc. (CACI) and inaugurated in 1958, at which time Lincoln Center "had just completed purchase of its site" (Musical America), but I fail to see how these happy beginnings can be construed as part of our government's plan to support the arts. Speaking at the dedication ceremony in Winston-Salem five years ago, John D. Rockefeller III called the Community Center a "happy symbol of the growing role of business in the philanthropic support of the arts." Did our federal government —does it still—consider its hoped-for participation in such philanthropy un-American?

I am indebted to Mrs. Dorothy Gillam Baker for valuable data on the countless "un-American" attempts to get government support for the theater and the arts. In the Colonial period "interest in government subsidy of the arts was already manifest *before* the actual existence of the American government itself." In 1785 an unsuccessful proposal was made for a government-supported theater. In the debate, General Wayne not only asserted that "a well regulated theater was universally acknowledged to be an efficient engine for the improvement of morals," but declared that "a theater in the hands of a republican government, regulated and directed as such, would be, instead of a dangerous instrument, a happy and efficient one." Robert Morris was among those who also upheld this view, warning his colleagues that "people will find out amusements for themselves unless government do it." In pre-Civil War times (1859), the first Commission of Fine Arts was appointed by President Buchanan, a petition signed by 127 artists having led to the creation of this body; the "Commission" was abolished a year later because Congress regarded its request for appropriations to carry out its plans exorbitant. "Mild, perennial agitations in Congress for a National Conservatory of Music, which should make our country musically independent of the rest of the world" began about 1879. In some instances, legislative bills for a National Department of Fine Arts accompanied the Conservatory bills. By 1891 "the Conservatory lobbyists succeeded in putting through Congress an act providing for the incorporation (as a National Conservatory) of a music

STATES, NOT STATE, TO THE RESCUE **319**

school, founded a few years earlier in N.Y., by Mrs. Jeanette
Thurber . . . the bill became law with the approval of President
Harrison." Anton Dvořák was imported as director of the Conservatory. No appropriation is mentioned, however, in the
Congressional Records of that period; lacking funds, the school
met with no success, Dvořák returning in disappointment to
his native land. In 1897, the Public Art League of the U.S.,
with some 500 members, was formed for the express purpose
of sponsoring a bill for the creation of a national office of the
arts. Presented that year, the bill did not come to a vote in
Congress; neither did McKinley's 1896 campaign promise to
back the establishment of a national theater have any realistic
repercussions.

At the turn of the century (1901-1902) there was much controversy as to whether Andrew Carnegie would subsidize a
national theater. He finally gave his answer: "On the continent
of Europe many theaters are subsidized by the government,
but none by English-speaking peoples in any part of the world.
It would be an experiment here, and, if to be made, should be
by the government, as in Europe. It does not seem a proper
field for private gift." William Dean Howells, the novelist,
also expressed himself against private subsidy, to the effect
that those who donated would be in charge, would not permit any satire of their world, and thus a free theater would
be an impossibility. In 1901 a new bill was introduced into
Congress, *again* for the creation of a national office of the arts.
It did not pass, but the movement helped to lead eventually
toward the 1909 establishment of the National Commission
of Fine Arts—the first official connection between the government and the arts. The limitation of its functions caused President Theodore Roosevelt to set up (additionally) a Fine Arts
Council. President Taft was obliged to abolish the Council
shortly after his inauguration *because Congress refused to appropriate funds for its maintenance.*

In post-World War I days, shortly after the Armistice, the creation of a Fine Arts Department was proposed as a "reconstruction measure" and endorsed by Joseph Pennell, the National Federation of Art, and the College Art Association. In 1925 *three* Fine Arts bills were introduced into the 68th Congress—*three* more bills went to the 74th Congress ten years later. These included the first Sirovich bill and the Connery bill to establish a "Commission for the Advancement of Music and Art." The latter "originated with the American Federation of Musicians and had the endorsement of the A. F. of L. This, so far as we know, was the first legislative measure concerning the Arts to claim the attention of organized labor."

Then there was Representative Emanuel Celler's bill granting a charter to the American National Theater and Academy, which was passed by both houses of Congress in July, 1935. According to the preamble: "A people's project organized and conducted in their interests, free from commercialism, but with the firm intent of being—as far as possible—self-supporting. A national theater should bring to the people throughout the country their heritage of the great drama of the past and the best of the present, which has been too frequently unavailable to them under existing conditions." No funds were included with the philosophy.

The instigation for this charter began with a movement in Philadelphia in 1931, led by Leopold Stokowski. Some fifty civic and social leaders of that city met in an attempt to further the arts and, specifically, to establish a Civic Repertory Theater. Thirty years later Mr. Stokowski was "just one of many performing artists who had gathered at the bedside of culture during a Congressional investigation into the plight of the American artist." He warned: "The future of the fine arts in the U.S. is in great danger," (see Russell Lynes: "The Case Against Government Aid to the Arts," New York *Times*, March 25, 1962.) The dilettante efforts of the committee met with indignation from one of its members, Mrs. Amory Hare Hutchinson, the author, who raised the question of a National Theater. The committee adopted the suggestion, and Mrs. Hutchinson set up an office. In 1932, Otto Kahn joined the project and influenced other prominent citizens to do the same. It was Mr. Kahn, in fact, who chose the name of ANTA from the list of suggestions. For months in Washington the influential supporters of a national theater, led by Mrs. Hutchinson, met with congressmen, discussed plans, and brought pressure to bear. The energetic conspirators appeared before the House Judiciary Committee on July 5, 1935, and shortly thereafter the bill was passed. The problem of federal financing was not even broached.

Not long after ANTA's inception, the Four Arts Projects were established under the WPA, the board of ANTA deciding against soliciting private funds. The Music Project included in its achievements an Index of American Composers which, after two years of work, listed 5,500 works by about 1,500 native or resident Americans—including nearly seventy symphonies and thirty-five concerti. In a total of 110 cities, 122 symphony and chamber-size orchestras, made up of players of high professional competence, were established by the Project; sixty-seven bands and fifty-five dance orchestras, choral groups, opera units, and chamber ensembles. Composers' Forum Laboratories were held in New York, Boston, Chicago, Detroit, Milwaukee, Los Angeles, and Indianapolis. There were more than 250 music-teaching centers employing 1,400 former private music teachers. The Federal Theater Project produced fifty-one musicals and plays with music in many cities.

In the three-session 75th Congress (1937-38), at least *eight* measures concerning the arts were introduced. All but one of these urged the creation of a division, bureau, or department of the arts. Three of them constituted the Coffee-Pepper bill (H.R. 3239, H.R. 9102, and S.3296). The bill did not come to a vote, but it achieved national fame and stirred up a heated controversy. It proposed a bureau for artists, rather than a bureau of the arts; it demanded that working conditions and wages should be similar to those established by labor unions for comparable work in private industry, etc. Seventy organizations of artists were behind the bill, as well as a score of labor unions having no connection with the arts.

Two of the eight measures were the Sirovich resolutions (H.J. Res. 671). His "Federal Arts Act" proposed a fine arts bureau in the Department of the Interior, and "had the distinction of being one of the very few arts bureau bills ever to come to a vote in Congress ... With a lack of dignity unworthy of a legislative body (on a torrid day in June), the proposal was dismissed without due regard for its merits or its faults." The Sirovich resolutions had many aspects similar to the Coffee-Pepper bills.

The three remaining of the eight proposed measures were the Gasque bill (H.R. 1521), the Moser bill (H.R. 5705), and the McGranery bill (H.R. 8132). In 1939, Walter Damrosch prepared a bill to introduce to the 76th Congress, for a National Bureau of Fine Arts; neither Mrs. Baker nor myself has any further information on this. "1945 saw the end of World War II and the beginning of ANTA's emergence as a functioning and effective organization. 1946 was ANTA's real 'year of decision.' Under Presidents Vinton Freedley and Helen Hayes, ANTA began to grow and flourish. Membership increased and the services expanded. Now—on the eve of its twentieth anniversary—ANTA and President Clarence Derwent are proud to announce that membership stands at almost 2,000 individuals and theaters in 48 states, Hawaii and the Canal Zone." (Louisette Roser, Associate Director, National Theater Service, in *The ANTA Story,* 1954.) Among ANTA's greatest achievements in the musical-theater field was the triumphal tour of *Porgy and Bess* (1954-1955), a work generally dismissed by local cognoscenti as a Broadway-tinged, non-operatic opera. *Porgy* brought down the house not only in Paris but also in Zagreb ("Magnificent performance, fourteen curtain calls and twenty minutes thunder and bravos, stopped only by descent of steel curtain," read the cable received by Robert Breen and Blevins Davis, *Porgy's* producers), the Near East and—most surprising of all—at La Scala in Milan, which marked the first occasion that an American company had been invited to appear there. According to an ANTA "immediate" release: *"Porgy and Bess* has proven itself one of the finest ambassadors of good will ever to leave the shores of this country." Under the management of Robert C. Schnitzer (formerly General Manager for Gilbert Miller), ANTA's International Exchange Program was responsible for *Oklahoma!, Medea,* New York City Ballet, Ballet Theater, Hall Johnson Choir, Juilliard String Quartet and other groups and attractions enhancing the prestige of American Arts abroad, in addition to *Porgy and Bess.*

But to go on with Mrs. Baker's recital of frustrated efforts to get federal support for the arts on a *national* scale (we seem to be anxious to put our best foot forward abroad, while turning a deaf ear to the unceasing cries for help at home base): Representative Jacob K. Javits (1949) introduced H.J.R. 104, a joint resolution which was referred to the Committee on House Administration, calling for the establishment of a National Theater and a National Opera and Ballet.

In February, 1954, Representative Charles R. Howell sponsored a bill (H.R. 452) for the establishment of a national theater, with branches throughout the country, devoted to the drama, opera, ballet, instrumental music, motion pictures and other art forms. His bill would establish nine separate divisions all told, including, besides those mentioned above, literature and poetry, architecture, radio and television, painting and sculpture as well as "fine arts personnel [?] and education." Representative Howell's request was for a $20,000,000 federal yearly grant. This bill, referred to the House Committee on Education and Labor, failed, as did innumerable other such bills. Mrs. Baker adds wryly: "Representative Howell was not re-elected." For the record, the Multer bill (H.R. 7953), similar to Howell's, has been similarly "referred." The Wainwright (1955) and Thompson (1956) bills we already know about; whatever has happened since was certainly inconclusive because at hearings instituted in the United States Court House in New York (1961), the burden of the three days of testimony was that "if the Federal Government did not subsidize the performing arts, an important part of our culture would soon become an item of Americana—as quaint and out-of-date as the butter tub and the cracker barrel" (Russell Lynes). Mr. Lynes, however, is *against* government aid to the arts and presents several pretty valid arguments in support of his stand. While reporting on concerted pleas for federal aid, he observed: "It is increasingly apparent that . . . the tide seems to be running in favor of direct government subsidies for the arts. Governor Nelson Rockefeller has already instituted a program of traveling exhibitions and theatrical performances in New York State. Secretary of Labor Arthur J. Goldberg has come out strongly in favor of Federal aid for opera (and not only opera, since he recommended that the arts be represented by a 'Federal Advisory Council, composed largely of artists themselves' in the New York *Times* of March 11, 1962). And August Heckscher has recently been appointed a cultural adviser to the White House. These are signs and portents of an eventual marriage between the fine arts in the government. The flirtation has, of course, been going on for years." You can say that again, Mr. Lynes.

Dr. Everett Helm, who helped build a dodecaphonic fortress in Germany with government dollars at the end of the war, published an editorial titled "Is Culture a Luxury?" in the March, 1962, issue of *Musical America*. It started thus: "On

January 25th, the U. S. Army newspaper 'The Stars and Stripes,' carried the announcement that the Seventh Army Symphony is to be disbanded as of March 31st to increase USAREUR combat capabilities" and to divert the half-million dollars a year "more directly to the combat readiness effort." General Bruce C. Clarke, USAREUR Commander-in-Chief, stated that "the orchestra is now a military luxury rather than a necessity." Since its founding in 1952, the Seventh Army Symphony has done more for American prestige abroad than a whole flock of diplomats, several columns of tanks, and a large covey of jet fighters put together. One of the most frequent European criticisms leveled at the United States is that we are a nation of materialists, living from bread, refrigerators, two-car garages, and Elvis Presley alone—that we have no interest in or feeling for the higher things of life, such as art, literature, and what for want of a better word we have to call "serious music." Dr. Helm then suggests that "every taxpayer in America rear up on his hind legs and snort fire at the idea of stopping the orchestra. For the amount it costs to keep this operation going is too insignificant. The official figure of $500,000 a year is the cost of a single tank. A recent letter of the orchestra to the White House, however, insists that the amount spent in 1961 was not even $100,000." I have no way of learning the contents of the White House's answer to the Army spokesman's letter—but I fervently hope it was a favorable and encouraging one. For Mr. Kennedy and our First Lady have repeatedly demonstrated their genuine interest in and concern for the arts—one need only recall the program of the National Symphony's Inaugural Concert, which was, according to reports, selected by the President himself; the Pablo Casals soirée; Mrs. Kennedy's praiseworthy efforts to beautify the White House, and so on.

"In the early and artistically optimistic days of the Kennedy administration, there was a good deal of enthusiastic talk about a cabinet post for a Minister of Culture," Russell Lynes wrote. "Such talk now seems to have died to a whisper. But if there is going to be a direct government subsidy of the arts, there has to be someone to administer it, and there is now a proposal before Congress to establish a Federal Arts Council. [What, again? V.D.] The bill is a modest one. It does not ask for subsidies; it merely asks that the President be authorized to appoint a council of twenty-one men and women [This bill must have been modeled on the 1956 Thompson bill, H.R. 7973. V.D.] 'widely recognized for their knowledge of or experience in the arts.' It sounds as innocuous as a literary tea party and about as likely to come to any useful conclusions." It was also about as likely to be passed as were its many unsuccessful though equally innocuous forerunners. Sure enough— "last year [1961], when the Arts Council bill was proposed to the 87th Congress (its sponsors were Representatives John V. Lindsay of New York and Frank [Never-say-die. V.D.] Thompson Jr. of New Jersey), it came a cropper. *173 Congressmen voted against it."* Herman Kenin, president of the American Federation of Musicians, remarked with some bitterness: "A handful of willful men on Capitol Hill laughed the proposal off the floor of the House of Representatives while speculating aloud if poker playing might not also be considered a performing art. Is this the kind of statesmanship to which we must entrust our national culture?"

In all fairness, it must be admitted that a good many intelligent and cultured citizens have also declared themselves against government support for the arts by writing letters to music editors all over the country. Together with Mr. Russell Lynes they believe (with some justification) that "art and politics make nervous and scratchy bedfellows" and that "the less the arts have to do without our political processes, the healthier they will be." This, of course, is guesswork; nobody, and I'm sure not even Mr. Lynes himself, believes that arts in America are enjoying good health at this point. In a foreword to the 1962 *Music Journal Anthology* Robert Cumming sounded this warning: "Let's explode the rumor that the United States is experiencing a cultural boom. We are doing so in only two respects—directionally and statistically. But the direction is still superficial and the statistics are sorrowfully misleading . . ."

"The U.S. Department of Labor, in its occupational outlook handbook on the performing arts (BLS bulletin No. 1300), stated: 'Don't raise your child to be a singer, dancer, musician, actor or actress. A government survey reveals that the field of performing arts is overcrowded, that candidates for these occupations have little hope of making a decent living.' " Mr. Cumming added: ". . . with many politicians who have been working against token assistance to the performing arts, the idea is held that poverty and adversity are positive advantages to the musician—that if he lives comfortably and in health he will not give his best. Little wonder is it that parents and government alike are discouraging their children from entering the hazardous profession of music!" I know several top-notch instrumentalists in Los Angeles whose chief source of income is making rock 'n' roll records, stuff abhorred by every self-respecting musician. Can you blame such people for not investing in a costly musical education for their young, only to have them graduate as unholy rock 'n' rollers?

Ex-Secretary of Labor Arthur Goldberg's oft-quoted statement ran: "America has a long way to go before our musicians, performers and creative artists are accorded the dignity and honor to which their contribution to American life entitles them." Mr. Cumming rightly added: "A long way to go before they are assured a modest living wage." If the electronic "wizards" have their way, it won't be long before even a *modest* living wage will be denied to a living and breathing human foolish enough to choose music as his profession.

The "dehumanizing" of music, overoptimistically reported by some as being on the wane, continues unabashed, and it will

take more than a few pinpricks to arrest its progress. While our
practicing musicians (*and* composers—those who do not live
from grant to grant) are often compelled to pick another profession in order to provide a living wage for their families,
U-boys continue with seminars, learned discussions, and get-
togethers such as the one held at the Stratford Festival, Stratford, Ontario (Canada), in August, 1960. This was grandly
styled "The International Conference of Composers" and gave
birth to a 170-page book titled *Modern Composer and His
World* (University of Toronto Press, 1961). Although ever-
present Ernst Krenek "got it two years ago in Darmstadt
straight from the horse's mouth [I'd give anything to learn
the horse's name. V.D.] that the era of serialism was over,"
no such miracle is apparent to even a casual reader of the volume. Krenek himself started his monologue with: "Two years
ago I caused some raised eyebrows when, in a lecture, I stated
that in turning to serialism the composer has liberated himself
from the dictatorship of inspiration." "Here we go again," I
sighed. "The phony liberators must be here—or even in Canada
—to stay." Aurelio de la Vega, a Cuban, after complimenting
France for having been "a relatively fertile ground for the development of the first rhythmically oriented serial ideas," went
on to say that, "in the meantime in America, the cult of Hindemith, the belated discovery of Bartók after his death, the typical Eastman [Rochester, N.Y.] style, and the nationalistic
fever carried to extreme nonsense were innocuous achievements
in our [Cuban?] musical life. Everyone in this part of the
world spoke glowingly about Prokofiev's lyricism and praised
Shostakovich's *Leningrad Symphony* as a masterpiece, obviously with the curiously political overtones of that memorable
era when Russia was still for the Western powers our white
dove.' " Then the white dove, suspected (rightly) of a basic
redness, flew out the window and—lo and behold!—the dodecaphonic Don Quixote appeared on an emaciated, but resplen-

dently white stallion, surrounded by assorted international Sancho Panzas—a good many of whom could be called Sancho Pansies, for accuracy's sake. Their dedicated boss promptly engaged in a bloody battle with the windmills of "lush romanticism," with the sheep of chauvinistic regionalism. The battle is still going on, but all—or nearly all—was sweetness and light in Stratford, Ontario; somehow Otar Taktakishvili, a gifted, yet distinctly conservative Georgian, was smuggled in from the USSR along with a fellow Soviet citizen, Vassily Kukharski, a critic. The two, taken aback by the endless rhetoric of the atonalist, dodecaphonic, and syntheticist forces, had little to say—and what they said was, of course, dismissed instantly as anachronistic bilge. How could it be taken seriously when Roger Sessions decreed that "harmonic effect as such has clearly ceased to be a major interest of composers," or when Aurelio de la Vega gloated over "a definite desire finally to bridge the eternal cleavage that has separated the Americas from Europe"? Commenting on the Princeton Seminar for Advanced Musical Studies (1959), de la Vega triumphantly concluded that this "desire to bridge the eternal cleavage" was one of the seminar's "most important and touching [!] consequences which might well stand as a kind of incipient Darmstadt in our Western Hemisphere." All we need now is to send for René Leibowitz.

Iain Hamilton (Great Britain) chimed in ecstatically: "Why then do I feel that we are in the process of restoring to music some of the great power at least that it had as music before the dreadful inclusiveness [??] of the Romantic era?" Why, indeed, Mr. Hamilton; I'm sure that your feeling is not shared by those not in your serial entourage, who may look askance at your own far more "dreadful" exclusiveness. ". . . I have never heard more nonsense talked about anything, by men who ought to know better, than when ill-informed and arrogant musicians talk about serial technique," Mr. Hamilton raced on. I am equally sure that, when it comes to arrogance, no one can hold a candle to Messrs. Boulez, Craft, and Stravinsky. Fascinated by the sound of his own words, Mr. Hamilton became positively orgiastic: "Once aware of the infinite possibilities open to him in the new world of sound, the composer may often feel intoxicated," he exclaimed; perversely, "entertainment music," which is usually sought as an accompaniment to one's drinking, is not our learned English confrère's concern. Regretfully he admits that such music "will . . . for a long time retain its tonal basis" and, intoxicated though he may be, Mr. Hamilton finds "no pleasure in the confusion of attitudes which might impel one to waltz or samba to serial dance music." Such attitudes may, indeed, prove confusing even to a body of inebriated dodecaphonists, bent on a serial spree; stick to the tonal twist, gentlemen.

It was refreshing to find Gunther Schuller, composer and performer both, striking a sour note in the otherwise harmonious (Sorry, I didn't really mean it, harmony haters) meeting. "I would like to make a plea," said Schuller, "a plea to the serial composer to take into consideration the innate, intrinsic characteristics of the instruments for which he is writing." Reduced to a nutshell, this plea would sound like this: "If you are writing for instruments to be played by human beings, then take those into consideration and make those a part of your compositional material . . . If you feel that the human being, the human instrumentalist, is limiting you—well then, write for other means, possibly electronic means. *It is just not within the means of human beings to do some of the things which composers have been asking performers to do.*" (Italics mine. V.D.) Now, that was a fine and bold move on Mr. Schuller's part; his own so-called "Third Stream" music is certainly performable, although it was never clear to me just what this "Third Stream" business stood for. If, boiled down to its essentials, it merely represents another attempt to wed jazz and "classical" music—see here, Mr. Schuller, *on en à soupé*—but whatever it is, the stuff is listenable. Mr. Schuller "happens to feel that Luigi Nono is one of the finest composers of his generation, or of our time . . . and yet the curious fact is that his music is great *despite* the way he actually writes for the instruments. By that I mean that he writes virtual impossibilities; and I've argued this with him personally for years." And a fat lot of good it did either Nono or Schuller or a Venezuelan composer quoted by Guillermo Espinosa, conductor and music director for the Pan American Union in Washington; this enterprising gent boasted to Mr. Espinosa "apropos a violin sonata he'd just completed, that it was so difficult even Heifetz couldn't play it." A piece heard recently in Cologne composed by Boulez (another "great" composer to Schuller, who is especially fond of that adjective) also showed Pierre in "this trap of writing things which are literally impossible." Apparently performers who came to grips with the Nono-and-Boulez type of musical greatness were "the finest available." Mr. Schuller concluded his plea thus: "If these men say to a composer, 'It's not possible'—then the composer, I think, must listen." Victor Feldbrill (Canada) made an additional plea, which, I am convinced, was the one *truly great* contribution to the Stratford International Conference of Composers: "I had a very unusual experience this week for the first time, and if it indicates a growing tendency, then I'm a little [!] afraid of the future of music *as far as the human performer is concerned.* [Italics mine. V.D.] I was asked specifically by one of the composers *not to become emotionally involved with the music that we were performing.* I would answer: if we, as performers, cannot become emotionally involved in what we are playing—and I don't mean emotions in a saccharine sense, but just emotions, any kind you want— then your audience will never become emotionally involved. I make this plea: if you want music that has no emotional involvement, I beg you to write for the electronic instruments; I'll be in the audience listening, but rather glad I won't have to perform."

The picture is clear. We have, on one hand, a vast body of gifted performers—instrumentalists and vocalists both—pleading for a chance to be heard, to be employed and adequately remunerated. We also have a great number of composers whose gifts cannot always be correctly evaluated because of the obscure and, to most ears, unmusical idiom many employ (I have it on excellent authority that two of Europe's best-advertised dodecaphonists — not Boulez — flunked their conservatory tests and were expelled *for lack of musical talent*); composers, who *boast* of dehumanizing music, either by vetoing "emotional involvement" on the performer's part, or by deliberately turning out unplayable material, or, lastly, by dispensing with human services altogether and confining their "musical" brain children to mechanically operated gadgets. Somewhere in between is the huge, faceless mass of people, known as "laymen," "auditors," "listeners," etc. — the button-pushers and the ticket-buyers, most of them potential music lovers, all of them taxpayers. They know what they like, but they are willing to learn to like and even support music they have not been previously exposed to—provided such music has communicative power, the power to *engage* the listener, to involve him emotionally or to touch his human sensibilities. We already know the serial fraternity's stand on these obsolete inanities. What is the average listener's stand when exposed to "liberated" music—liberated, that is, from all connection with humanity? He will not heed the false prophets, like Luciano Berio (another "great" dodecaphonist), who hasten to assure fellow composers that "basically music has a real, a concrete function in the human community — always — *even John Cage* [Italics mine. V.D.]—as well as Verdi." The unbiased, but sensitive, auditor's attitude was most tellingly expressed in the agonized yell: "Stop it, damn it!" with which one of their number attempted to arrest the "progress" of Copland's *Connotations* at Lincoln Center's opening concert. Alas, such demonstrations are too feeble, too sporadic to stop our musical avant-gardists, although their increasingly unpalatable productions may come in for wholesale condemnation by the uninitiated. 1962 saw two grandiose fiascos—*Noah and the Flood* by Stravinsky and *Connotations* by Copland, acknowledged leaders both. Will they learn their lesson and try to extricate themselves from the dodecaphonic morass? Why should they? Both can comfortably fall back on their proven "standards," give the audience a breather, then produce more monstrosities which will be even more extravagantly pre-sold. While these lines are being written, Stravinsky is "wowing 'em" in Mother Russia with his earlier thrillers, while Copland consoles himself (and the audience) with his *A Lincoln Portrait* eloquently recited by Adlai Stevenson.

The hope for a radical, healthy change in our younger composers' outlook and for a desire on their part for a closer alliance with the people is very slender indeed. The hope for the people's readiness to support an art whose deliberate inaccessibility and remoteness repulse them is even more slender. "But there is a vitality and faith in America that cannot be matched in the older corners of Europe, and it is bound to lead to some kind of musical outpouring greater than any we have yet experienced. It will cause, or be caused by, some larger, indigenous artistic freedoms. [Being liberated from dodecaphonic and aleatory "liberators" would be a healthy start. V.D.] There will doubtless be a patriotic note in it, maybe even some strategy. But in the end, the only proper strategy for art, as well as politics, today is humanity" (Ernst Bacon: *Words on Music*). That, then, is where art and politics must—and will—finally effect the long-awaited merger; *human needs*—not vote-getting considerations—will, in one shape or another, bring about a government subsidy for the arts.

What shape will it take? Judging from all those well-inten-

tioned bills brushed aside so relentlessly by Congress, judging
from the people's misgivings, from the understandable skepticism of so many commentators, taking into consideration
the perpetual state of global unrest in which we live, a full-
scale federal subsidy may be put down as an unrealistic dream
for the present. On perusing the Paris edition of the N. Y.
Herald Tribune (October 18, 1962), I read of the "startlingly
enthusiastic" reception accorded the Robert Shaw Chorale on
its first appearance in Moscow. "We might note . . . that the
United States Cultural Exchange Program is productive of results whose importance in terms of understanding and respect
may run deeper than we know. Also, American cultural prestige abroad is by no means limited to the field of jazz—more
and more, Europeans are coming to know us as a people with
an original contribution to make in ballet, serious music, the
theater, and similar fields," the editorial reported glowingly.
Now all we need is a little "understanding and respect" from
fellow Americans, too—yes, even congressmen, who, in spite
of their lamentable record, are Americans after all. But we
cannot wait for the leopard—especially of the "Southern
Block" variety*—to change his spots; we've waited long
enough. Let's not worry about more ill-timed and ill-considered
bills; let's get as many dollar bills, from art-minded fellow
citizens, as possible, instead.

*Arthur Gelb, in the New York *Times,* announced (on April 1, 1963) President Kennedy's plan "to create this country's first Federal Advisory Council
on the Arts within the next two or three weeks. He will do so by executive
order because he has been persuaded that there is no hope this session of gaining the Congressional legislation he has long sought." Having (jointly with
Frank Thompson Jr.) "lost an intensive battle with the Rules Committee,
which refused to let the bill reach the floor for a vote," Representative John
V. Lindsay, Republican of New York, "felt at the time that an executive order
was desirable only as a last resort," as reported by Mr. Gelb. On making an
"informal survey of the 15 members of the committtee," Messrs. Thompson
and Lindsay discovered that they "had only five, or at the most six, votes" and
that the others apparently felt "that their constituents were not interested in
the arts. So I threw in the towel," Mr. Lindsay concluded. Good luck, Mr.
President.

Some communities are actually hostile to the possibility of federal subsidy, even *before* it is offered. A typical instance was the recent tragic-comic dispute in Indianapolis. "Subsidy Not Offered, Indianapolis Sez Nix," ran *Variety's* headline (March 14, 1962): "No Federal aid to the Indianapolis Symphony is offered, none presumably would be available without a special act of Congress, but the symphony's board and its musicians are divided in a dispute over 'subsidy.' The pile of money, which isn't there, would not be accepted, say the directors. And why not, ask the tooters, if that's the only way musicians in America can make a living? . . . Board apparently feels the business community will respond best if assured that only private enterprise will be called upon to give. The idea of subsidy is nasty, per president Herbert E. Wilson. It would separate the symphony from its volunteer workers and fund-raisers and alienate donors." Union musicians responded with a statement of their own, declaring: "Those of us who have been waging a losing battle to bring musicians' wages up to at least the level of unskilled labor hold a glimmer of hope for a future in which an enlightened government will lend some support to the performing arts. To summarily reject all such support before it is even offered, and without knowing under what conditions it might be offered, seems to us a very premature and negative action." Maybe so. But introducing bills, however attractively and realistically worded, to unenlightened Congress, only to see them voted down by a whopping majority, is equally negative. "It is not realistic to assume that the 87th—or the 88th or 89th—Congress will look with favor on a new Department of Culture," Harold Weston, Chairman of the National Council on the Arts and Government, wrote in a letter to *Musical America* published in March, 1962. "Congress has traditionally shown strong aversion to adding new tentacles to the Executive Branch. We started in 1789 with four Departments. After 173 years only ten have Cabinet rank . . . the majority in Congress is well aware of the entrenched, almost fanatic, feeling in many parts of the country against concentration of power in Washington. This majority will be far more inclined to favor legislation for the arts that is geared to state and community needs, administered by states with a minimum of Federal supervision, and so devised as to increase support of cultural ventures from private sources, including industry and labor. Furthermore, the danger of political influences is far more acute if the over-all administrator is a 'political' appointment, such as a Cabinet member with his entirely political tenure of office. This evaluation does not preclude at some future time sympathetic consideration of a Department of Culture—but not for many years."

Since we can no longer be concerned with "some future time" but only with the glaringly realistic exigencies of today, let us become practical and act in concert. Justice Arthur J. Goldberg, who talked and wrote freely of federal assistance, indicated that "community support must come first" (as interpreted by the other Goldberg, Albert, in the Los Angeles *Times*, June 24, 1962). "Had the Secretary cared to give specific examples, he could have done no better than to cite our own community [Los Angeles], where private and county resources are erecting the fabulous new Music Center, and where the county and municipal governments contribute to the L. A. Philharmonic Orchestra, Hollywood Bowl, the Los Angeles Music Festival and other enterprises." August Heckscher, the White House arts consultant, too, believes that "industry as well as foundations should be encouraged to support the arts in their own areas." One idea he came up with is that a firm employing 5,000 people would be asked to make "a contribution of $5,000 toward cultural enterprises." *

---

*According to the Los Angeles *Times* (May 24, 1963), Mr. Heckscher "will resign his post within a month. . . . Appointed 15 months ago to the first office related to cultural affairs ever established in the White House, Heckscher was 'happy to say that our experiment seems to have been a success.'" He "spoke

Lauritz Melchior, whom I went to see in his Coldwater Canyon home following his impassioned speech at the Beverly-Hilton "Opera Rendezvous," proposed that every state print its own "Art" stamps (of twenty-five cents value, say), total income from the sale of which would go toward Arts support; such stamps could be placed on radio and television sets, also stereo or monaural equipment, as a species of sales tax. "Billions of dollars will be spent on experimental trips to the moon," Mr. Melchior opined. "Music, an indispensable vitamin in an ordinary human's life here on earth, will remain unsupported in our country unless something drastic is done *now*. In times of war, artists are called upon to sing and play for soldiers and sailors, for the wounded in hospitals, for the war effort generally; in peacetime they are not urgently needed. To help them, draw upon your own state's resources. Let us have schools run by old pros, natives, or residents of a given state; unless good music is restored to its rightful place in the community, unless those practicing our art are again enabled to make a living, we artists will continue going down hill." Mr. Melchior, now seventy-three, has just made two tape recordings to help insure the Austin Symphony's next season; Ezra Rachlin, the orchestra's conductor, was formerly the singer's accompanist. "The German saying goes: 'Where they sing, you can sit down safely; bad people have no song," Mr. Melchior said. "Let's hope that the good people of Texas will be the first to underwrite both opera and symphony in the United States."

All this boils down to a plan, as simple as it is workmanlike: each of the fifty states of the Union should set itself a goal of underwriting a State Opera House, a State Symphony Orchestra, a State Ballet Company, and a State Repertory Theater;

appreciatively of the White House interest," the *Times* continued, but "indicated the real reasons for this imminent resignation when he said 'the majority in political life at all levels still tend to talk of culture as if they were telling an off-color story.' "

choral and chamber music groups to be similarly endowed. There could also be a state-supported laboratory where "new sound" experiments would be conducted, the results tested *privately* and discussed in composers' seminars, conferences, and forums—instead of being foisted on an uncomprehending public. A committee of twelve (not twenty-one, as per the Thompson bill) selected from the leading musicians—composers, musicologists, critics—of a given state would be appointed to establish the repertory of each of the four organizations, the conductor to have *one* vote, also the right of veto; all new scores, operas, ballets, and plays to be submitted to said committee. Preference, in all instances, would be given to native or resident composers and authors; to native or resident singers, instrumentalists, conductors, actors, and dancers.

This seems to be the only thoroughly American, thoroughly democratic way of getting our performing arts on the official map at long last; of enlarging and broadening our musical horizons through friendly competition with other states; of challenging the Philistines and status-seekers bent on decomposing music; of returning music to humanity by reinstating humanity in music; of teaching our children that they, too, can produce music without the necessity of having it *reproduced* for them by buck-grabbing opportunists, "quickie" single-record manufacturers, and jukebox tycoons. Now let's roll up our sleeves, clean house, and go to work.

APPENDIX

Herewith the answers to the composers' and the critics' questionnaires. The conductors' answers were included in the "Conductors' Conduct" chapter. Approximately twenty composers—in the under-fifty bracket—were sent questionnaires; nine replies were received. Of the twenty-five critics approached, eleven favored me with answers. Of the composers, Milton Babbitt was the most discursive; of the critics, Peregrine White of the Durham, North Carolina, *Sun.* For lack of space, their replies (as well as Alexander Fried's, San Francisco *Examiner*) had to be somewhat abridged, for which I apologize. I don't know whether any deductions are to be drawn from the fact, but no replies were received from New York critics and only one from a New York composer (California-trained)—Alex Horak.

Besides the Messrs. Horak and Babbitt (New Jersey), the other seven composers who responded were Robert Gross (California), Andrew Imbrie (California), Ellis B. Kohs (California), Benjamin Lees (Maryland), Leonard Rosenman (California-Rome), George Rochberg (University of Pennsylvania), and Halsey Stevens (California).

1. *Do you adhere to any specific group or school of musical composition?*

BABBITT:
> Certainly not . . . I do not regard the obvious fact that my works are instances of twelve-tone composition as descriptively significant enough to serve to assign them to a "group" or "school."

GROSS:
> No.

339

HORAK:
> I adhere to no school of musical thinking; my musical godfathers are more probably Moussorgsky and Prokofiev than anyone else I can think of.

IMBRIE:
> Your first question is loaded with booby traps. My teacher was Roger Sessions, and I admire him immensely; in fact I think he is America's Number One composer. Does this mean that I adhere to a school? Does my music sound like his? I frankly don't know, but I rather think not. I admire Stravinsky, Bartók, and Schoenberg, too (not necessarily in that order).

KOHS:
> No.

LEES:
> No, none at all.

ROSENMAN:
> No, but most of my works are organized in some phase of serial technique.

ROCHBERG:
> Serial; although I do not carry out serial procedures on duration, dynamics, register, etc., at least not in an obvious arithmetically or mathematically determined way.

STEVENS:
> No.

2. *Have your views on writing music changed, and what was the determining factor that caused the change? Do you employ the serial row technique and, if so, when did you adopt it?*

BABBITT:
> ... my views have not changed basically since the age of 17 ... I have written twelve-tone music almost exclusively since 1939.

GROSS:
>   (a) Continual growth has produced continual change.
>   (b) Yes, I do, but not exclusively. Frequent use over last 20 years.

HORAK:
>   There has been no conscious change in my musical thinking . . . I do not use the serial technique except as an occasional "effect." I consider devotees of it as any combination of the following: fraudulent, limited, disgusting.

IMBRIE:
>   . . . Yes and no. Yes, because I have changed. No, because I believe that the impulse to write music is the impulse to sing and to dance; . . . I have occasionally employed a row, and find it an interesting technical resource. I have not adopted it as a first principle.

KOHS:
>   No basic change in esthetics—modified (simplified) serial techniques used in *some,* but not all works (since 1946).

LEES:
>   I never held any preconceived views on this to begin with. Creativity is an obsession, and I have always felt that the writing of music should be left to composers who are obsessed with the creative drive, not to those who write because they possess larger egos than talents.

ROSENMAN:
>   Basically I do not think my view of music changes. I do, however, hope that my musical knowledge, esthetic interests, and awareness of compositional challenges constantly change and grow. I have always been interested in some aspect of serial composition.

ROCHBERG:

They are always changing to an extent because I am always searching for the most direct way to say what I want to. The first major change occurred around 1948-51, a period in which I discovered Schoenberg. My first twelve-tone piece was composed in '52 . . .

STEVENS:

Around 1945-48 I underwent a *crise de style*, finding my music static . . . I do not employ the twelve-tone technique, though, of course, I have experimented with it and feel that it has contributed in certain ways to my musical language.

3. Do you believe in absolute freedom in your musical utterance?

BABBITT:

Surely, I insist upon my freedom to choose those systematic compositional assumptions which seem to me to yield the most interesting and fruitful compositional possibilities; otherwise, I would not be interested in composing.

GROSS:

Absolutely.

HORAK:

. . . The form grows out of the nature of the thing to be expressed . . . All questions of the freedom of musical utterance are questions of the leeway one has in determining that nature. I believe artistic expression is possible no matter what limitation is placed on the means of expression. The only real limitation is the imagination of the artist.

IMBRIE:

There is no such thing as absolute freedom. Thank God. The artist must be responsible, not irresponsible.

Freedom to exploit sound comes through discipline,
like freedom to walk tightropes. But the tightrope-
walker must look as if he is enjoying himself. If he's
really good, he *is* enjoying himself.

KOHS:
Don't know what this means.

LEES:
Yes, pre-supposing that "absolute freedom" is supported by, and based upon, logic and discipline.

ROSENMAN:
... In my estimation, no composer is totally free,
since he ramifies his ideas by exploring relationships
to his original idea; hence, form.

ROCHBERG:
I don't know what you mean by "absolute freedom."
I don't believe it exists in any case. Every piece I've
ever written tries to express itself in a highly organized
fashion, even though the *surface* of the music sometimes seems "free"... For me there is nothing arbitrary in musical expression; it must be guided, chan-
nelled, shaped, and formed.

STEVENS:
Of course.

**4. *Do you have difficulty getting performances? How do
you go about getting your music recorded?***

BABBITT:
I have never sought a performance, therefore I cannot claim to have encountered difficulties in obtaining
performances.... I have never sought a recording.
The recordings have been arranged by the performers, or as a result of the representative of the recording
company coming to me directly, or as the result of a
recording grant.

GROSS:

(a) Yes. (b) Haven't been very successful in this regard.

HORAK:

No comment.

IMBRIE:

Not for music written for small combinations. Large orchestral works are hard . . . The hardest thing is to get third or ninth performances . . . I have had a very modest number of works recorded. In no case did I initiate the project . . .

KOHS:

Yes, especially in Los Angeles. There is no special method to secure recordings.

LEES:

It was never an easy task, but is relatively easier now than it was five years ago.

ROSENMAN:

Yes. I don't go about getting my work recorded, since it takes away precious compositional time, already made precious little by the task of making a living. If someone is interested in performing or recording my work, I cooperate to the fullest extent. Otherwise, I do not knock on doors for this purpose. This is not to say that I object to having my works recorded. Quite the contrary.

ROCHBERG:

I waited ten years to hear my first symphony, four to hear my second. I've a few large works I've not heard at all yet. On the whole, however, my music is becoming more frequently performed. I have made no effort to have my music recorded.

STEVENS:

Naturally I have difficulty getting performances; but

I do not "work" at it ... Such recordings as I have, have come about through no effort of my own.

5. *Do you attach real importance to the way the audience reacts to your work? Do you want to (a) move the audience; (b) interest it; (c) startle it? Are you indifferent to the possibility of universal acceptance?*

BABBITT:

I attach significance to those statements on the part of members of the audience which reveal internally the auditor's capacity to hear accurately, and formulate his descriptive and evaluative statements rigorously and responsibly. Above all, I wish to remove my music from that audience which regards physical presence in the concert hall or before a loud-speaker as a sufficient condition for justifying assertions about music. I would be extremely suspicious of any music which achieved universal acceptance, but I am not aware of any that has.

GROSS:

Yes. (a) and (b) Yes.

HORAK:

No comment.

IMBRIE:

I do not attach importance to audience reaction. I want my music to be moving and interesting. Startling, too, if necessary in order to accomplish one of the two other goals. The greatest sin a composer can commit is to be boring.

KOHS:

To (a) and (b) yes, definitely. To (c) the answer is *No*. *Every* composer has a limited audience—the size is only a matter of degree.

LEES:

> I am certainly interested in an audience's reactions, but am in no way influenced by this. The primary objective is to communicate to *myself* in the clearest terms possible.... No, I do not have the slightest desire to move, startle, or shock an audience *per se.*

ROSENMAN:

> In the case of the functional music, my livelihood depends upon this acceptance; therefore, it behooves me to write with this strictly in mind.... With regard to my concert works, while I most assuredly am of that human frail stuff which would love universal acclaim and acceptance, I prefer to please myself first.

ROCHBERG:

> Yes, I do. It's the degree to which what my music expresses gets across, makes its impact. I prefer to move my audience rather than merely to interest it. They have sometimes been startled, but this was not my intention. I do not play games with either my music or my audience.

STEVENS:

> I should hope that my music might interest a part of the audience; I have no desire to startle it. Occasionally a few people profess to have been moved. I have never considered the possibility of "universal" acceptance, since I know of nothing acceptable to everybody.

6. *Do you find better conditions, better chances of a performance, more interest in your output abroad than in your native land?*

BABBITT:

> Certainly not.

GROSS:

> Yes indeed.

HORAK:
No comment.

IMBRIE:
I have had performances both abroad and in the U.S. I think the chances are best if the composer is on the spot. . . . I do feel that abroad there is a tendency not to take American music seriously.

KOHS:
No.

LEES:
Without hesitation or qualification, I would say that conditions, opportunities for performance and interest are far greater here than abroad. At least in the area of new music, and I presume we are speaking of this exclusively for the moment.

ROSENMAN:
I cannot answer this question at present, never having been abroad. [Since answering the questionnaire Mr. Rosenman has become a resident of Rome.]

ROCHBERG:
My experience with performances abroad is very small. Occasionally performances have taken place through no effort of mine.

STEVENS:
Doubtful; my performances abroad have come about mainly through proximity and friendship.

7. *Are you a good performer of your own music or do you prefer others to interpret it?*

BABBITT:
I prefer specialists to perform my music. Naturally, in my electronically produced music, there is no separable act of performance, and I am responsible completely for every aspect of the final work.

GROSS:
> I am—but I still prefer to have others do it.

HORAK:
> I believe I am a capable performer when I work at it. My favorite performance has been that by another.

IMBRIE:
> I am, or was, a pianist, and have performed and recorded my only work for piano solo (a sonata). There are better pianists.

KOHS:
> Others.

LEES:
> As a rule I prefer others to interpret it simply because I do not have sufficient time for practice. Given such time I could perform my own music in certain instances.

ROSENMAN:
> I prefer to perform my own work first and thus set some kind of tradition for its execution.

ROCHBERG:
> I have performed piano works, but largely prefer others to play my music. I have no time to practice.

STEVENS:
> I perform very little, at least in recent years, though I occasionally appear as a conductor of my own music, and more rarely as pianist.

8. *How do you go about making contacts with conductors and/or performers with established reputations?*

BABBITT:
> I never have and do not. I do not admit that performing ability implies necessarily the ability to comprehend and judge music. Therefore, I do not submit music for the approval or disapproval of performers.

GROSS:
> Personal contacts entirely. By now I know most of them, and most of the others know me.

HORAK:
> Hit and miss—and to date, all miss.

IMBRIE:
> I very seldom attempt to make unsolicited contacts with conductors or performers in order to persuade them to perform my music. I don't object to others doing so; I simply find it embarrassing and painful to do it myself.

KOHS:
> Social contacts, letters.

LEES:
> Throughout the year one meets many conductors and performing artists. Some of them are genuinely interested in performing new works and will ask the composer for a score.

ROSENMAN:
> Thus far, I haven't.

ROCHBERG:
> This is too difficult to answer, except to say for the most part I leave them alone. Where I have made an effort, I've had some success.

STEVENS:
> See answer to Question 4.

9. *Do you, did you have difficulty getting your music published?*

BABBITT:
> Very little of my music has been published, and that, long after its composition. That works have been recorded without having been published indicates how

little the needs and wishes of professionals determine such matters.

GROSS:
Yes.

HORAK:
Yes.

IMBRIE:
Publication I find to be the most baffling thing of all, and admit the greatest difficulty in this area.

KOHS:
Have had reasonable success in publication, less success in recordings.

LEES:
In the beginning there was a great deal of difficulty.

ROSENMAN:
Yes.

ROCHBERG:
Not while I was working for a publishing firm. Now I do experience some difficulty, but this will be resolved shortly, I hope.

STEVENS:
The great majority of my music is still unpublished.

10. *Do you, did you experiment with commercial music such as radio, TV, musical comedy, popular songs, etc.; with what success?*

BABBITT:
Only perfunctorily, since I found the milieu repellent in its presumption, pretension, and ignorance.

GROSS:
Film scores only, to date (documentaries); they have all turned out well, I'm happy to say.

HORAK:
Yes, but not very thoroughly, and with no success to date.

IMBRIE:

I have written music in the popular style for informal army shows, campus productions, etc., but have never attempted to sell such music in a big commercial way. The music achieved its purpose, and was well received.

KOHS:

None at all—not interested.

LEES:

No.

ROSENMAN:

I write music for films and television.

ROCHBERG:

As a very young man (17-21) I earned money as a jazz pianist, arranger, etc. I would not now engage in such commercial activities since they have nothing to do with real music.

STEVENS:

No.

11. *What do you do for a living other than compose music?*

BABBITT:

University teaching.

GROSS:

I'm a professional violinist (concerts, recording, etc.) and I teach both composition and violin in a college.

HORAK:

Operate a studio, teach and sell accordions.

IMBRIE:

I am a professor of music at the University of California, Berkeley.

KOHS:

College teaching.

LEES:

A little teaching.

ROSENMAN:
> See answer to Question 10.

ROCHBERG:
> I am presently chairman of the music department of the University of Pennsylvania and teach composition there.

STEVENS:
> ... Member of the faculty of the University of Southern California (since 1946) ....

12. *Do you rely on commissions, grants, prizes to help you meet expenses?*

BABBITT:
> Fortunately, no.

GROSS:
> No, only as "bonuses."

HORAK:
> No.

IMBRIE:
> I have received commissions, grants, and prizes, but I can't say that income from such sources is so reliable as to be counted upon. I have received a stipend from BMI over a period of a few years, which does help.

KOHS:
> Not much. Some help from royalties, however.

LEES:
> The best approach to this is to welcome with open arms all commissions, grants and prizes when they fall from heaven, but not for one moment rely upon such manna to fall regularly.

ROSENMAN:
> No.

ROCHBERG:
> Not at all; it would be impossible. But it does help

when from time to time a lump sum of money comes my way.

STEVENS:

I do not rely on them, but it's nice when they turn up. Most of the time I use the proceeds of grants and commissions for publication. (See answer to Question 9.)

13. *Do you believe jazz to be a significant factor in America's musical development? In your own development?*

BABBITT:

Obviously no American can avoid the informal force of popular music as a factor in his conditioning. However, I regard it largely as a different form and field of activity from serious composition: I believe it to the advantage of popular music to be so considered.

GROSS:

(a) Yes. (b) No.

HORAK:

I believe jazz to be potentially a tremendous influence that has never yet been successfully interpreted in known serious music. Many of the surface devices have been used without conveying the particular emotions special to jazz—dissolute, promiscuous, abandoned. . . .

IMBRIE:

I consider jazz to be of great importance, both in America and in my own music. However, the influence on my music is indirect rather than direct: that is to say, I don't write jazz as such, but rather I have developed a style in which certain jazz elements, procedures, or turns of phrase can occasionally be detected—in some pieces more than in others.

KOHS:

Yes, for the country. Only peripherally for myself, largely in the matter of rhythmic liveness.

ROSENMAN:

Yes to both questions.

ROCHBERG:

Yes, because it represents the spontaneous side of our musical nature. . . .

STEVENS:

I believe jazz is a significant factor in a certain segment of America's musical development. I believe also that so far it has proved of very little importance in relation to "serious" or "concert" music; and I find attempts to marry the two, with or without shotgun, irksome if not embarrassing.

14. *Are you pleased with the present-day conditions in American music-making here and abroad? If not, state your reasons.*

BABBITT:

I'm pleased with the conditions that have made it necessary and possible for the universities to assume the role of patrons of and havens for serious musical activity in all its manifestations. I am displeased with the publication situation (which should be remedied by university presses), the presumption of journalism in the field of music, and the confusion of compositional categories.

GROSS:

Far too little dependence on new creations; too much of the "star system"; not enough public contact or involvement.

HORAK:

I have no comments on music abroad. I am infuriated with conditions here—the age-old complaint that far

too much money and effort are spent on thoroughly
incompetent music.

IMBRIE:

I am not pleased about present-day conditions in
American music-making. I suppose what I really want
is an audience that really goes to concerts, or listens
to broadcasts, in order to hear new music. . . . What
I really hate is official art: this is worse by far than
merely commercial art. I think you know what I mean,
so I'll quit while I'm ahead.

KOHS:

No. Too much attention is given sensational works.
Novelty seems more important than quality, perhaps
because it is easier to identify.

LEES:

I have found American music-making to be of a very
high order. The artists are dedicated and open-minded,
anxious to bring new music before the public in this
country. There is an adventurous approach here which
is healthy and exciting.

ROSENMAN:

No. I can't speak for conditions abroad (see answer
to Question 6), but conditions in the U.S. for composers are deplorable. . . .

ROCHBERG:

No. Impossible to answer briefly here. . . .

STEVENS:

No; reasons self-evident.

15. *How does the native product stack up again the imported kind, in your opinion?*

BABBITT:

The music of the younger American composer reflects,
above all, that he is university trained, while that of
the young European composer that he is not. . . . In

intellectual responsibility, fundamental sophistication, and informed originality, the best of American music and writings on music are far ahead of the rest of the world . . .

GROSS:

Far superior, in every respect—with one exception. Our conductors don't get the chance for enough apprenticeship, and their training is too restricted.

HORAK:

Foundationmusik is foundationmusik. With the death of Prokofiev we have not seen the emergence of anyone else, although Lord knows I am trying.

IMBRIE:

I have never given much thought to the comparison between American and non-American music, since I think these categories are artificial. There are a few American composers whom I think are the equal of any composers outside the country. There is a great deal of bad music all over the world.

KOHS:

Every bit as good. We hold our own or better. But there is far too much emphasis on technique, as if it were the end-all and be-all (twelve-tone, dodecaphonic, *musique concrète*, serial, etc.) of music. . . .

LEES:

. . . the European product is generally more daring and experimental than that of the U.S. In most cases it is also better. The reasons for this and why it was also true before World War II are exactly the same.

ROSENMAN:

The atmosphere in which the composer thrives is evidently traditionally different in both countries.

ROCHBERG:

... [Europe] is still adventurous while we in America are conservative to the point of regressing. If it weren't for a few centers of activity, largely in the universities, serious composition in America would go under. ...

STEVENS:

In recent years, much better than what I heard of new European music. Unfortunately, our younger composers are finding it expedient (profitable) to join the bandwagon, and they are beginning to turn out music as faceless and anonymous as most of their European confrères.

16. *Do you believe in state support of the Arts in the United States and, if so, what shape do you think it should take?*

BABBITT:

No, because of the shape I am obliged to fear it would take if the precedents of the New York State Arts Council, of the presumption of Congress, and the influence of Presidential wives and press secretaries are to be regarded as significant. If it could take the form of the National Science Foundation, I would favor it.

GROSS:

Definitely! Hopefully, it should start with something like British Arts Council support, and eventually develop into a civilized system of full sponsorship as in Italy, Austria, etc.

HORAK:

I believe in state support if one of two conditions is met. Either (a) I am generously supported by this aid, or (b) I am named director of the agency dispensing this aid ... The dedicated composer has an impossible bargaining position *vis-à-vis* the foundation or state agency. The incompetent says, "Support me or I have to stop composing," and he is supported. The dedicated composer will compose in spite of all obstacles. Why help him? . . .

IMBRIE:

My remarks about official art should give the clue to my opinion about state support. I'm very suspicious about mixing art with politics, though such a step may eventually prove necessary, particularly in the event of a depression . . .

KOHS:

I *do* believe it should exist, but in such a way as to avoid the abuses of the pork barrel and political interference. Probably *matching* grants and subsidies, in cooperation with support from individual *states* and *municipalities*. The directors should be chosen from recognized professionals, with advice and counsel from such bodies as the National Musical Council, e.g.

LEES:

I believe that state support of the Arts in this country is but a matter of time. When it arrives, I hope it will take the form of direct aid to the organizations and individuals involved, without any government control or restrictions as exists in Europe.

ROSENMAN:

I believe in government support of the arts. I believe that *all* artists should be supported and that their works should be performed for as wide a public as possible . . .

ROCHBERG:

I firmly believe in government support of the arts. What form it shall take is more difficult to state . . .

STEVENS:

With no experience of state-supported art, I do not feel qualified to comment.

The names of the eleven critics whose answers to my questionnaire appear below are: Robert E. Cumming (*Music Journal*), Robert Dettmer (Chicago's *American*), Alfred V. Frankenstein (San Francisco *Chronicle*), Alexander Fried (San Francisco *Examiner*), Joseph Gale (*New Jersey Music and Arts*), Albert Goldberg (Los Angeles *Times*), Hilmar Grondahl (Portland *Oregonian*), Nell Lawson (Buffalo *Evening Express*), Jack Loughner (San Francisco *News-Call Bulletin*), Peregrine White (Durham *Sun*), and Les Zacheis (Cedar Rapids *Gazette*).

1. *What is your opinion of the present state of American music?*

CUMMING:
> The cultural explosion theory is a myth; American Music Conference statistics are questionable. The greatest glimmer of hope for improvement rests with the music foundations, of which there are approximately thirty.

DETTMER:
> (a) Solemnly derivative, in the most stultifying academic tradition, or just as solemnly experimental, in the most stultifying non-academic tradition. (b) Busy.

FRANKENSTEIN:
> Extremely good.

FRIED:
> State of American music is immensely, amazingly active, and if you isolate the best (by any reasonable standard of cultured taste) the situation is immensely wholesome—except that we do not have enough truly important composers.

GALE:
> The present state of American music is resurgent in commission and even slightly so in performance. Composers true to themselves always will be moved by

compulsion to write, even in the depths of non-performing despair.

GOLDBERG:

The quantity of music by American composers is more than sufficient. The quality in the sense of music that can stand frequent repetition and hold the interest is not all it should be.

GRONDAHL:

I feel hopeful because of the increased opportunities for outstanding talent to be noticed, because there are more sources commissioning new music, and because a better attitude is developing toward subsidy for worthy organizations.

LAWSON:

The present state of American music is fair but a bit laggard, with not enough vitality.

LOUGHNER:

Interesting and promising.

WHITE:

If one interprets liberally American music to include composers born abroad who have come to live here, plus native-born composers, there are certainly a large number who are writing extremely interesting music, plus a far larger group whose efforts are commendable but not destined to be included in the "ultimate" list of lasting works of art . . . I do not agree with one of my New York critic friends who feels that none of the contemporary music is any good whatever . . .

ZACHEIS:

American music is in the midst of a transitional period. A new music is being formulated from the influence of jazz, traditional, modern and hybrid. Right now it has growing pains—but it is coming along . . .

2. *Do you think that the American composer by and large is heading in the (a) right; (b) wrong direction?*

CUMMING:

Neither. It takes a genius to recognize genius. How can I know what is right?

DETTMER:

No evident direction, right or wrong. The composer of any nationality can only head inward, into himself, and from himself bring out what is the best, most characteristic, and most personal expression. I do think the trend toward non-programmatic neoclassicism is approaching death by self-asphyxiation, thank God, at last.

FRANKENSTEIN:

Right direction.

FRIED:

The direction of composers, in a sense, makes little difference. What counts is talent, genius, creativity, "inspiration." Given such quality, a composer will produce significant work in almost any idiom. As it is, composers of talent that is less than great are using up an awful lot of time and paper writing peculiarly academic or imitative or dryly intellectual music.

GALE:

There is no wrong direction. All music set to paper is a step in the right direction ... Whether the American composer has discovered, or is developing, a homogeneous musical form is another question.

GOLDBERG:

I do not know that there is any right or wrong direction for a composer to head. He simply has to write good music.

GRONDAHL:

The "right" direction for a composer of artistic integrity would be the one toward which he feels impelled by an inner conviction as to his ability and worth. If he isn't up to that, he may be able to do clever hack writing, which has a value of its own, and generally much better pay.

LAWSON:

The American composer is heading in the right direction, but not passionately enough; he doesn't devote enough time to it.

LOUGHNER:

Right direction.

WHITE:

Are there several directions in evidence? To my taste the revival of interest in serial music seems puzzling, but this may be a way station on the road to better things ... I believe our 1962 era is more sane, by far, than the 1920's ... We have many composers today who are not trying to pull the wool over the eyes of an ignorant public with extremist hi-jinks.

ZACHEIS:

Regarding legitimate American composition . . . yes, *most* of the writers are heading in the right direction. However, one word of caution—American composers should not conclude that harmonization must necessarily be dissonant to be "good." Observe that Robert Ward's score to the opera *The Crucible* is a highly acceptable piece of writing, devastatingly effective, yet is extremely modest in harmonic structure.

3. *Do you think that there is (a) not enough new music played in concerts; (b) too much; (c) the wrong kind?*

CUMMING:

Not enough new music played in concerts.

DETTMER:
>
> Both not enough and the wrong kind. And I might add, for the wrong motives.

FRANKENSTEIN:
>
> Not enough new music played in concerts.

FRIED:
>
> I think there is a surprisingly wholesome proportion of new music performed—least of all by celebrity recitalists (who in fact do almost nothing in this direction) but considerably more in symphony, even more so in chamber music and professional university music.

GALE:
>
> I think not. There is a universality in American music today that is neither romantic nor classical but, rather, absolute. Composers of all nations are headed in the right direction, but we must not forget that something like a revolution in music is in progress. The "new music" began to appear in World War II and today reaches upward toward full bloom. It is too soon to chart its direction, but as in prior periods of music history, the direction cannot but terminate at the summit.

GOLDBERG:
>
> I do not think there is enough new music played in concerts, and that which is played is not generally representative.

GRONDAHL:
>
> Any critic, I think, would say that there is not an adequate proportion of new music played, but he doesn't control the proportioning. I would say that there is altogether too much music played which has too little reason for being. Many rate themselves as composers who, in some conservatory or school of music, have

learned the tools of composition without having the
capacity to dredge up musical ideas worth expressing.

LAWSON:

Here, in Buffalo, for the last few years one modern
work has been played at every Philharmonic program.
It seems to satisfy everybody here.

LOUGHNER:

Not enough new music played in concerts.

WHITE:

This is the old refrain, of course . . . The pros who
could play the new music stick to the old. The amateurs who might do well with some of the venerable
scores too frequently fence with stuff they cannot
cope with. Needless to say, this does not particularly aid the cause of contemporary music.

ZACHEIS:

I do feel that there is not enough new music played
in formal American concerts. It's awfully rough for a
contemporary composer to get his work properly
presented. Here in the Midwest, a special nod of approval to the Sioux City (Iowa) Symphony, which
has a policy of playing one work by a contemporary
American composer at each concert.

4. *Do you have an assistant? By what are you guided in
distributing concert coverage between yourselves?*

CUMMING:

Yes.

DETTMER:

I have a part-time assistant. He is marshalled when
there is a head-on collision between major events, in
which case I make the more personally appealing one
my own province; or when I am ill; or when I am
away on a reviewing trip elsewhere.

FRANKENSTEIN:
    Yes.
FRIED:
    No. I cover what I can—mostly in the city, sometimes out of town, often on campuses. Sometimes I pick events which are important or big-scale in public appeal (I'm speaking of "real music," not "popular"). Sometimes I go to specialized concerts at which there are only a few dozen listeners, and write up the event in a circulation of 300,000—simply because I consider the event artistically valid. I usually don't divide myself into two pieces to run from one event to another on a single evening. Instead, I make the hard choice and go to one event, leaving the other out (and trying to catch its equivalent at some other time).
GALE:
    As recordings editor of *New Jersey Music and Arts,* a monthly magazine, I work alone. As a staff member of the Newark *News,* a daily newspaper, I cover particular items which incur my interest.
GOLDBERG:
    I have a first assistant and several others who help out on occasion. Since I am the head of the department, I usually cover the most important or newsworthy events, although, sometimes personal taste enters into the choice if other things are equal.
GRONDAHL:
    Only rarely.
LAWSON:
    No.
LOUGHNER:
    No.
WHITE:
    No.

ZACHEIS:
> No, no assistant.

5. *If a celebrated virtuoso were performing a well-known concerto in Carnegie Hall while a new quartet or sonata by an unknown but promising young composer were given in Town Hall, which of the two would you tend to cover?*

CUMMING:
> The new work, whether I wanted to or not. It is my duty.

DETTMER:
> That would depend entirely upon the virtuoso and what well-known concerto vs. the "promising but unknown" composer's music and its purveyors . . . There is, in other words, no rule of thumb but rather a sixth sense at work here; and also the matter, which is not inconsiderable, of what the average reader cares to have covered. The critic does not, I repeat, *not*, abide in an Ivory Tower, except possibly in New York City.

FRANKENSTEIN:
> I always prefer the new work to the celebrated virtuoso; in fact, I seldom attend the recitals of celebrated virtuosi, even when there is no competition, but send my assistant and stay home. When a virtuoso and a new work come together on a single program, as they often do at symphony concerts, I play the new work over the soloist if it is good.

FRIED:
> As a music critic and reporter I'd feel bound to go first to the celebrated performer in a big-series concert; but I'd go so far as to try to listen in on a rehearsal of the young composer's concert, and write a review from that.

GALE:

Unless the celebrated virtuoso is an Oistrakh on his first visit to the United States, or unless the scheduled work has transcendent personal importance, I tend to cover the promising young composer—where there is a conflict in time. I seldom subscribe to the practice of sending second- and third-line reviewers to eat the chaff while I confine myself to the wheat. Part of the task of a responsible critic, it seems to me, is to know where and when to reap.

GOLDBERG:

I can't answer this precisely. It would depend on who was playing, what concerto, and what kind of piece, by which composer, was competing.

GRONDAHL:

Who is the virtuoso, who the composer? If it were the last time around by a Casals against another effort of a Gilels or a Gould, I would take the virtuoso now and catch the other on a repeat. But as between another round of Gould the pianist and Haieff the composer, I would probably settle for the latter.

LAWSON:

It would depend on the mood I was in. If I felt gay and full of good spirits I'd go to the performance of the young composer's work. If I were dispirited and not up to snuff, I'd go to the classical concert because it would be easier to understand and to enjoy and to write about.

LOUGHNER:

No problem: I live in San Francisco. Silly question, I might add.

WHITE:

Get me a job on the N.Y. *Times,* where I really belong (Clifford Curzon once told me as much) and I will be glad to answer this. If the critic had been covering a great deal of contemporary music at the time, he might reasonably elect to hear the well-known concerto.... He has purposes other than appraising new music, certainly. Many readers are interested in the virtuoso's current state of artistry... I submit that your question is trying to set up a sense of sin if one finesses contemporary music. Granted that there may be a continuing struggle for the new composer—and I suspect there is—I suggest that it is a sure disservice to stress the either-or dilemma, which carries with it the nuance that to elect contemporary is to reject the established.

ZACHEIS:

It isn't that I would "tend" to cover—there is no question but that the newspaper would order me to cover the well-known artist because he would be the most newsworthy.

6. *How many times do you listen to a new recording before reviewing it?*

CUMMING:

Sometimes twice; sometimes fifty.

DETTMER:

That depends, once more, entirely on the music and its purveyor. As a general rule, with many exceptions, once.

FRANKENSTEIN:

Once. How much time do you think there is?

FRIED:

Usually I listen to a record twice when reviewing it, sometimes more. Rarely only once. I should add my sour opinion that more inaccurate buncombe is written by reviewers about records than about any other type of musical performance. The records are doctored. Hi-fi apparatuses are so different that no one who reads a review can feel for certain that the record will sound to him the way the reviewer says it sounded to *him*. The most useful record reviewing, artistically speaking, is that of new music—for while the performance may or may not be cockeyed and the average reviewer (not having a score) may or may not be aware of how cockeyed it is, at least something of the character of the piece creates a new vision for him (and hence for the reviewer's interested readers). I find repeatedly that performing artists who sound one way on records sound very differently (usually not as well) in person.

GALE:

A single listening is sufficient to indicate whether the recording is ordinary. If so, an attentive run-through will produce an appropriate and honest review. All other reasons lead to second and third hearings, possibly with research into prose and certainly with research into past recordings.

GOLDBERG:

Unless I am utterly fascinated with a new recording, I find that one hearing is sufficient.

GRONDAHL:

Do you mean a new release of the recording of a new composition? Familiar scores in new performances may not even get a single run through, and a new piece of music may get two to four.

LAWSON:

Once, if it's a familiar work—unless something "unusual" is done to the music. The modern works as many times as necessary to be sure I understand and appreciate what is in the music.

LOUGHNER:
Depends on my degree of familiarity with the music. For Handel's *Water Music*, once is enough, etc.

WHITE:
With new music that is unfamiliar to me I listen to it a number of times, at intervals, read whatever commentaries I can lay hands on and try, inescapably on the fly, to scrape up some kind of acquaintance with it. The established repertoire requires less effort of this sort.

ZACHEIS:
If at all possible, three times. Exceptions are the quite impossible stereotyped pop releases.

7. Is your job as critic a vocation, avocation or both?

CUMMING:
Avocation.

DETTMER:
My job as critic is a vocation.

FRANKENSTEIN:
Vocation.

FRIED:
My job is my vocation (my daily, nightly joy and torment—the torment coming mainly from the difficult task of getting into words a decent, just image of what I am reviewing). Incidentally, I am also reviewer of the pictorial arts, and I think the two vocations refresh each other. They keep a critic from narrowing down his thoughts to a single track. They throw valuable and enjoyable light from one art to another. . . . But the double job is hard and continuous.

GALE:
Both; vocation on the *News*, paid avocation on *New Jersey Music and Arts*.

GOLDBERG:
>I do not know whether my job as a critic is a vocation or an avocation. It is just a full-time job that I consider calls for professional services.

GRONDAHL:
>An enforced avocation, since the musical situation here will not support a full-time critic. (How many cities do?)

LAWSON:
>Yes. [I assume Miss Lawson means that her job is both a vocation and an avocation. V.D.]

LOUGHNER:
>Vocation.

WHITE:
>It is not a full-time job. I put in a 40-hour week in other employment. I am, however, paid for my reviews.

ZACHEIS:
>A subordinate occupation, with remuneration.

8. *Do you have to contend with outside pressures, abusive letters, intimidations of any kind, and how do you deal with such intrusions in your professional activites?*

CUMMING:
>Outside pressures, occasionally.

DETTMER:
>Outside pressures, if you mean directives from the front office to "like" something *ipso facto*, emphatically no ... I have not been bothered from within, which may be supposed to count most, and cannot therefore speak from bitter, or pleasant, experience.

FRANKENSTEIN:
>Outside pressures, abusive letters, and intimidation are three quite separate things, and a single answer is, therefore, impossible. In 29 years on the San Fran-

cisco *Chronicle* I have never once experienced any pressure or intimidation from the paper's management, but have had an absolutely free hand. I receive countless abusive letters, all of which I answer as politely as possible and immediately forget.

FRIED:

As life goes, I have been fortunate in having a negligible experience with pressures. I write what I like, within limits of what I believe is justice, good sense, an educational purpose for my readers. I get a few abusive letters—not enough to entertain or guide me as much as I'd like. I get a few complimentary letters ... A painful lot of mail every day takes the form of everybody's and anybody's trying with all his heart to get his name and activity into the papers.

GALE:

Time is the only incessant pressure. Argumentative letters arrive, but abusive letters—almost never. The former excite me, since they prove there is an audience way out there, and that its members are as firm about ther convictions as I am about mine. It is a good thing.

GOLDBERG:

Outside pressures and intimidation of a critic are usually more imaginary than real. I print the abusive letters, which makes the writers happy and doesn't seem to do me any harm.

GRONDAHL:

Inevitable. Try to deal with as much understanding and sympathy as possible. Even the Liberace fans are entitled to their moment in music, and may, with tact, be shown how one such is not what his publicity purports him to be.

LAWSON:

No comment.

LOUGHNER:

(b) With equal abusiveness. Seriously, my editor backs me up all the way. No problem.

WHITE:

. . . To a considerable extent one cannot criticize adversely local talent with impunity, nor is one likely to escape censure where a well-known artist or orchestra plays falsely and below standard—for it—and this comment is made and shocks those who have been ballyhooed into a state of daze and apply no solid standards. . . . Normally there is no reply to an adverse letter, which is simply published. This being a Southern city, it is interesting to note that as a single, continuing subject of letters to the editor, the music reviews generate a larger volume than any other subject with the exception of integration. I am told the N.Y. *Times* receives many letters also, but does not publish them, although I suppose if Samuel Barber or Stravinsky sent in a communication it would appear. I would hope so . . . generally speaking, the letters to the editor are in the interest of the trade, rather than an intrusion on my activity.

ZACHEIS:

Hell, yes! An unfavorable review of a local symphony concert even brings informal women's auxiliary committees calling on friend wife to see if she can't bring pressure to bear on friend husband to write more tolerant reviews. How do I deal with it? Ignore it—but if pressed for rebuttal—"Play better!"

9. *What kind of music do you really like?*

CUMMING:

The universal "kind"—all good music—heavy, light, and in-between.

DETTMER:

Wow! Let me say I like music that is good music . . .

Easier, perhaps, to say that I do not like, generally
speaking, the centuries before Monteverdi, or after,
until Bach; that is not sewing machine music; nor the
musique-concrète kids, nor the hack-contemporary.
Too big, really, for a questionnaire. Or better, what
Herbert set to music: "I want what I want when I
want it."

FRANKENSTEIN:
All kinds.

FRIED:
I like many kinds of music—from ancient to electronic
—so long as it fascinates me intellectually, touches and
excites me physically and emotionally. It must have
"the spark," but don't ask me what that is.

GALE:
Tastes and preferences both are broad. I lean, however, toward the heavy romanticists, the brilliant
orchestrators, the technicians, and yet, the lean, the
spare, the functional. I admire impressionism, but am
not moved.

GOLDBERG:
I like any kind of good music.

GRONDAHL:
Fortunately, all kinds worth doing well, and this includes jazz. My special favorite is chamber music,
including string quartets from Haydn to Bartók and
Bloch. I am sorry Duke Ellington hasn't lived up to
the promise of bringing jazz and "serious" composition together that was evident in *Black, Brown and
Beige.*

LAWSON:
Piano concertos, solo piano, all symphonies that are
full-bodied and dynamic, classical and modern and
ballet music.

LOUGHNER:
All.

WHITE:
Self-analysis can be folly. A critic should have catholic taste, and I believe that I do ... Your question suggests that the critic really likes some music and hates other music. I don't think he is well assigned if he has too narrow a span of likes.

ZACHEIS:
Music I *don't* like makes a much shorter list: rock 'n' roll, barbershop, polka bands, and syrupy sweet dance bands.

10. *Have you done any composing, performing or conducting?*

CUMMING:
Yes, all three.

DETTMER:
I have composed, and destroyed it. I have performed for myself, and perhaps eavesdroppers, but not publicly since school days. Conducting? Only phonograph records for exercise, or concert performances surreptitiously (and quite unconsciously) out of empathy or indignation, depending.

FRANKENSTEIN:
Performing.

FRIED:
No, I've never been a practicing or aspiring music-composer, although I did begin studying the piano at the age of eight.

GALE:
I've lost my notes and your question.

GOLDBERG:
I have never done anything except student composing,

but I once conducted and still play the piano for myself.

GRONDAHL:
No composing or conducting, and performing mostly in private.

LAWSON:
No.

LOUGHNER:
Yes.

WHITE:
No, save that at one point I used to conduct a small group of amateur singers during the war, primarily as a means of aiding them to begin and end together.

ZACHEIS:
Some arranging and dance and pit or reed work.

11. *How do you visualize the future of music in this country and elsewhere?*

CUMMING:
See answer to Question 1.

DETTMER:
I don't visualize music. I think there will go on being music for always more and more persons, who will become more and more discriminating, and, we can hope, demanding.

FRANKENSTEIN:
Very bright.

FRIED:
Music in the future? It will go on as it does, and the most important thing that will happen to it (and it periodically will happen) is that now and then truly important composers and performers will emerge among the mass... Sometimes we won't know how important the composers are until later. Much more often we'll throw our hats in the air about composers

and performers who in the long run won't live up to our praise. That's not too harmful—because in the life of art, you have to climb ladders to the stars all the time, even when there really aren't steps in the ladders and your imagination artificially provides them.

GALE:

American music, despite signs of a relaxing in performance requirements, still needs that lucky break, that beneficial angel, that willingness to listen.

GOLDBERG:

I suppose there will always be music. But if the supply is not reduced, the public is going to become satiated with it and the minority who support it will be smaller than ever.

GRONDAHL:

Included in answers to Questions 1 and 12.

LAWSON:

Perhaps for the next two or three generations classical music of the past will be listened to, with more and more "modern" music being played. But, as the earth turns and years pass, possibly by the year 2000, our classical music will be as unintelligible to those living then as "old English" is to us now. I think that if we who live now could hear the music that will be composed and played then, it would be a fright and shock to us. Music then will have new "rules," or perhaps, none at all. I hope that each composer will be free to write as the spirit moves him and that he will have an incentive to create from his deepest resources.

LOUGHNER:

Nowhere to go but up.

WHITE:

Music has always had to depend upon audiences, when one regards music in the large sense ... Due to efficiency of modern life, and increased leisure time, and such things as a growing number of older people kept vigorous by modern medicine and supported by annuities, music has a tremendous future ... No graybeard, I look back 30 years to my own college years and feel certain that the accessibility of music to everyone has been tremendously enlarged.

ZACHEIS:

See answer to Question 1.

12. *Do you believe in the state support of the Arts in the United States and, if so, what shape to you think it should take?*

CUMMING:

See answer to Question 1.

DETTMER:

I believe in government support of music in theory and tend to reject it in practice. It should, in any case, be as free as possible of politics in their vulgar, cretinous, regional, featherbedding natural state ...

FRANKENSTEIN:

We already have enormous quantities of state support for the arts in all manner of ways. I should be happier about the state support of concerts and opera in the U.S.A. if the direction thereof were in the hands of trained personnel, like the curators and directors of our museums. Unfortunately, we have no such trained personnel, and all projects or plans or proposals for state support of music in our country visualize a directorship made up of politicians, New York concert managers, press agents, and their hangers-on. For this reason, I am against all these projects but not necessarily against the idea behind them.

FRIED:

I think high costs will eventually draw more and more government subsidy into the arts. Lack of it may cause much of our big-scaled music to collapse and disappear. Government subsidy will be both good and bad; solving present problems and creating new ones. *C'est la vie* . . . Subsidy in this country won't be comprehensive and orderly as in Germany, but, rather, mixed and accidental—that's the way we do things.

GALE:

State support of the arts would appear to be the only present solution. Federal concern with the arts should merit cabinet rank . . . It should become possible in this country to earn one's living through composition, and to this end pensions and subsidies should be considered in those cases where there is indication of intent and fulfillment.

GOLDBERG:

I think the best solution for government subsidy in the United States is the principle of matching contributions.

GRONDAHL:

I am heartily in favor of state support for the arts. I would like to see the National Cultural Center in Washington, D. C. built with public funds rather than by private solicitation. Furthermore, I would wish that we might establish a national orchestra, national ballet, national opera, etc.—all our selected best performers to show in the National Cultural Center, to tour the U.S. and tour abroad. Only in this way will we give the Americans themselves a healthy view of our cultural image, and expose our vast cultural potential to the rest of the world.

LAWSON:

There are adequate supports for the arts now. Wouldn't a highly bureaucratic set-up be a drag on initiative?

LOUGHNER:

Should be on a matching-fund basis, like unemployment insurance, to assure local control of the expenditures, subject, of course, to reasonable federal or state standards.

WHITE:

As in many other areas of federal aid, it is possible to keep control decentralized via a system of grants-and-aid, administered locally, the state or region providing part of the funds and the Federal Government the rest. It may be that the local people are the ones to fear, not Washington bureaucrats . . . In other countries there are ministries of art, and I see no reason why we should not be able to have one, productively, also.

ZACHEIS:

Definitely yes. I would like to see federal subsidy for symphony and opera projects based on a formula of a matching lesser sum from the state government and a still lesser sum put up by the local city government.

(An index of musical compositions will be found on page 398)

Index of Compositions, Ballets, Motion Picture Scores and Musical Shows

70
71
72

75
77
79
81
83
89